D0089993

Tonight she was no lighthearted, frivolous Parisienne. Tonight she was Italian, dangerous, possessed. A ring sounded at the door. The taxi was waiting. She was ready.

Standing in a pool of light was the strange, oddly dramatic figure of a woman in a black evening cloak. Guy felt his senses prickle. Slowly, almost as if she were enjoying her audience, the woman loosed her hood and let the cloak slip from her shoulders.

A muffled gasp rose from the assembled guests. It was as if the sun had suddenly come out from behind a cloud, as if before their very eyes, from a dusty black chrysalis, an enameled butterfly had emerged. She was dazzling, her dress of gold cloth starred and studded with a riot of jewels, ringing the hem of her skirt, edging the deep neckline of her close-fitting bodice, out of which rose her golden neck and shoulders, glowing with a pagan radiance. She was summer incarnate, an icon, an Aztec queen, a Medici princess.

Guy advanced. The woman spun in front of him, her crazy panoply of jewels striking fire.

"Corrie." He was torn between anger and a curious, ridiculous uplifting of the heart. He maintained his composure with an effort. "What on earth are you doing here?"

She dimpled at him outrageously. "I've come to ruin your engagement party, of course . . ."

Chase The Moon

Catherine Nicolson

BANTAM BOOKS
TORONTO • NEW YORK • LONDON • SYDNEY • AUCKLAND

CHASE THE MOON
A Bantam Book

PRINTING HISTORY
First published in Great Britain by Sphere Books Ltd. 1984
Bantam edition / December 1984

ISBN 0-553-24427-2

Published simultaneously in the United States and Canada

Bantam Books are published by Bantam Books, Inc. Its trademark, consisting of the words "Bantam Books" and the portrayal of a rooster, is Registered in U.S. Patent and Trademark Office and in other countries. Marca Registrada. Bantam Books, Inc., 666 Fifth Avenue, New York, New York 10103.

PRINTED IN THE UNITED STATES OF AMERICA

H 0 9 8 7 6 5 4 3 2 1

PROLOGUE

Sure as a shadow in the warm summer darkness, a young man descended the steps that led from the esplanade to the beach below. Not a light from the sleeping township behind broke the blackness. A moon, if there had been a moon, would have shown the pallor and determination on his face.

Beneath the stone wall of the esplanade, he methodically removed his clothes. Naked, the soft Atlantic wind lifting his short dark hair, he shivered once, then squared his powerful shoulders. The sea ahead was calm, glistening with a phosphorescent light. How cool and soothing the water would feel against his burning skin.

He lifted his head defiantly. Ahead was darkness, oblivion, anonymity. The endless rocking embrace of the sea, a silence beyond tears or laughter or caring. He walked with a light, measured stride that left only a fleeting imprint in the wet sand. Like a matador with a tired bull, he wanted it to be over. The conclusion was foregone. His lifeblood had already drained away.

"You are a romantic," she had said to him, playful, half amused, half concerned, altogether satisfied by the passion she had aroused in this clumsy, ignorant boy, this unsophisticated savage.

"Not anymore," he'd answered, hardly knowing what he was saying. Now, too late, he knew that it was true. He had lost everything. There was no escape.

Except one. His heart lifted suddenly as he stepped into the crystalline water. It was like plunging into stone, it sheared away the breath from his body. He smiled. So it was to be a battle. He welcomed it. He might have signed away his life, his future, his soul itself, but his body and will were still his.

He moved forward. The undertow tugged at his body. He willed himself on. There was no going back. Nothing and no one would touch him, ever again.

Something glanced against his hand and he flinched. What was it? Among the reflections on the water he made out a strange shape, soft light dancing on its many facets. A glassy shell, a sea jewel. Astonished, he reached out, touched it gently. It bobbed away, swung back, nudged his hand like something alive. He lifted it, grimaced. After all, no melodrama, no mystery. It was merely a bottle, an empty absinthe bottle, designed, like women's charm, to disguise the lethal effects of what lay inside.

He raised his arm, ready to hurl it away, let it shatter on the rocks behind. But then he felt something inside the bottle move with a tiny birdlike flutter.

Curiosity, like pain returning to a numbed limb, stirred in him, bringing with it an unwanted awareness of the coldness of the water and the air on his bare shoulders. He hesitated. There would be nothing inside the bottle, he knew that. A fragment of debris, seaweed, sand . . .

The bottle had been recorked. With a sudden feverishness he wrenched the stopper out. Attached to it by a thread of cotton was a small roll of paper, still dry. Something was written on it, but it was too dark to make out what it was. He became aware that his hands were trembling. He was getting colder, uncomfortably cold. He'd steeled himself against any imaginable pain, but discomfort, the trivial, demeaning irritation of it, was somehow harder to bear. And there, in his hands, yet another irritation, was the note. It was nothing, it could have no meaning for him. He of all people knew that miracles were not possible, that the world was full of strangers.

He looked down, looked up at the sky.

"*Merde.*" His curse was brief but nonetheless heartfelt. Miracles are not possible, the world is full of strangers, but he could not leave the note unread. He began to laugh, a deep laugh that welled up from his diaphragm, making him gasp for breath, making his ribs ache. So. Fate had chosen to make one last attempt to mock him.

But this time he would not be denied. He would go back to the beach, read what was written on this damnably intrusive piece of paper, then return to his task. No words, in any language on earth, could dissuade him now.

Resolutely he waded back to the beach, ignoring the siren pull of the undertow. He sat down on the sand, his legs suddenly weak. The line of writing was just visible in the lamp glow from the esplanade.

He looked at it for a long time. Then he looked out to sea, to the dim pale line of the horizon. Stiff now with the cold, he bent and slowly, methodically, began to put on his clothes.

CHAPTER ONE

Mr. Whitaker looked at his watch and frowned. It wasn't yet time, and he'd never known a woman to arrive early for an appointment in all his forty years at Harby, Jarndyce and Harby. But today he found himself unaccountably nervous, unable to settle to his normal routine. Against his will his eyes strayed to the long flat cardboard box with its yellowed label. He was prey to a most unprofessional curiosity, not just about the bequest, unusual enough in itself, but about its recipient. What would she be like? If what she claimed was true, she had the most extraordinary heritage . . .

But speculation was inappropriate for a man in his position. Irritated with himself he pushed away the book he'd been consulting and crossed to the window. The quiet courtyards below, through which Lord Chancellors and Prime Ministers had passed, had remained unchanged for centuries. The elegant Georgian terraces enclosing the central garden with its ancient chestnut trees had looked the same to Charles Dickens when he worked in the square as a lawyer's clerk. Beyond the Chapel where John Donne once preached was the satisfying Victorian bulk of the Great Hall and Library, and beyond that the tall bastions of Elizabethan stone and brick that separated the Inn from bustling Holborn and Chancery Lane. All was calm, quiet, ordered, from the smooth sweep of lawn to the discreetly numberless black and gold clockface above the belfry. Now, as he looked down, the only stir of movement in the cold March air was a young porter hurrying silently by, his trolley piled high with legal documents, red tape fluttering.

Still restless, Mr. Whitaker turned away. Summer was far away still but sunlight seemed to linger in the wood-paneled walls, awaking uncomfortable memories. Had he, as the family's agent, been partly responsible for mismanagement of the affair? It had been something quite outside his experience, but perhaps there was more he could have done, should have done . . . The intercom on his desk leaped into life, startling him.

"Mr. Whitaker?"

"Yes?"

"Miss Traverne to see you, sir."

He glanced automatically at his watch. She was early, a full quarter of an hour too early. He hesitated, thrown off balance.

"Could you ask her to wait a few moments—no, send her up." He found his heart beating too fast for comfort. Perhaps this interview might not be quite as simple as he'd thought. The confident use of the Traverne name . . . it wasn't a good sign.

Perhaps that was partly his fault. It had seemed advisable, eight years ago, to keep the exact circumstances of the girl's birth from her prospective school. It was only because of the Traverne name that she'd been accepted at all on such short notice. In the intervening years she'd presumably come to think of the name as hers by right. He had to disabuse her of that notion.

For it was too much to hope that she might have inherited her father's gentleness and breeding, if indeed Anthony was her father. Reports from Mayfields', the exclusive and conveniently remote boarding school he'd found for her in the north of England, had hardly been encouraging. The girl lived up to her outlandish first name and doubtful heritage. She was a troublemaker, an unsettling influence. There was bad blood in her, and her ragamuffin upbringing in the seaports of the Mediterranean had done nothing to counteract it. She was fluent in three languages and educated in none.

Her written English was atrocious. By comparison with her classmates she was an unschooled savage.

For a time the situation had seemed hopeless. No one, least of all Mr. Whitaker, knew quite what to do with her. That first year she ran away persistently, once even as far as Liverpool, where she was found attempting to board a cargo boat. From then on she had to be watched night and day. The school authorities threatened to have her expelled, despite the cachet of the Traverne connection.

Then suddenly, that autumn, she changed. She didn't settle down exactly, she simply retired to a world of her own. No one queried the cease-fire, it came as too much of a relief. There were no more troubling reports of disruption in the classroom, even brawling with the other girls. Her English began to improve, though she still refused to apply herself to her other studies. But by that time no one cared. It was a qualified victory.

And today was the girl's eighteenth birthday. She would soon be beginning her last term at school. It now fell to Mr. Whitaker to resolve the problem of her future once and for all. Fortunately her mother's bequest supplied him with the ideal excuse for summoning her to London. Now, with all his experience, he shouldn't find it too difficult to steer a callow eighteen-year-old in the right direction, out of harm's way. And he still had a few moments' grace to marshal his thoughts, reassure himself that what he was planning, though it had questionable elements, was perfectly legal and above board. He pushed the package a few inches forward on his desk. It wouldn't hurt to have her curiosity about its contents distract her from his purpose. Sooner than he'd expected he heard a knock on the door. She must have run up the stairs instead of taking the elevator.

"Come in."

The door swung open and he rose to his feet. But the words of welcome he'd been preparing died on his lips. This, surely, was no callow schoolgirl. The sullen, stocky child of the official photograph had turned into a young woman of the most extraordinary self-possession. Dark eyes under strangely smoky lids met his with a level, intent gaze, probing, assessing. Her hair too was very dark, a smooth shining mass drawn severely back from her face and tied at the nape of her neck. The effect was rigorously simple, but somehow sophisticated, striking, accentuating the challenging planes of her face and the pure creamy pallor of her skin. Surely it was illegal, or at least unnatural, to have skin so pale and hair so dark? The contrast was startling, electric. Her face was oddly definite for so young a girl. Pride showed in the tilt of her chin, the pronounced modeling of cheekbone and her slightly aquiline nose. Her level black brows, the exact tilt and angle of a seabird's wings gave her an intense look of concentration. She wasn't tall, but looked taller because of the erectness of her carriage, her shoulders squared beneath the proud column of her neck. The simple gray and white uniform she was wearing seemed very far from girlish, for she had discarded her gray wool coat and flung a vivid scarlet shawl across her shoulders.

Was she pretty? No, the contrast between the luminous pallor of her skin and the darkness of her hair was too dramatic for that. But she had something, a sort of vibrancy, which made mere prettiness seem irrelevant. For some reason—perhaps the scarlet shawl—she made him think of the first Picasso he'd ever seen. He'd felt the same sense of shock and recognition. The colors had seemed unnaturally strong, too full of southern light, the lines too simple—and yet the image had stayed with him for months, making every other painting he saw seem foolish and mannered.

Yes, that was it. Despite the severity of her expression and the institutional simplicity of her clothes, she was somehow exotic, with those smoky heavy eyelids and that wide, surprisingly full mouth, with its curious deep cleft in the lower lip, unsmiling now but looking as if it would be capable of passion and laughter.

"Miss . . . er . . . Corrie. What a pleasure to meet you at last." He thought it best for the moment to dodge the issue of her surname. She didn't smile or answer. After a long moment in the doorway, scanning the room, she entered, leaving the door ajar behind her. Something in the way she moved, a mixture of caution and alertness, a sort of controlled energy, made it impossible for him to take his eyes off her. He had the sense of something finely tuned, rebellious even, a precision which might at any time explode into action.

Abruptly, she held out her hand. A continental habit. He took it awkwardly, still off-balance, uncomfortably aware that she still hadn't said a word.

"Mr. Whitaker. How do you do?"

Her voice was unusually low, with a strange carrying quality despite its softness, a suggestion of power held in reserve. A woodnote voice. For some reason it sent a shiver down his spine. Her handclasp was cool and firm. It came to him suddenly—she's as suspicious of me as I am of her. Then a second thought—only she has more reason to be.

"Thank you for my birthday present."

He was surprised again. He felt an unaccustomed heat rising to his face under that level, penetrating gaze. There was something faintly familiar about that look, if he could only place it.

"It was you, wasn't it . . . not the family?" She must have seen his surprise.

"Well, I . . ." Better not answer that question, it was full of pitfalls. It had in fact been his idea. It was only fitting, he had felt, to send a small sum of money for her birthday and at Christmas. Nothing excessive, but a token, on the family's behalf. How had she guessed? He cleared his throat, ready to fabricate a story, but she had lost interest already. Instead of sitting in the chair he'd indicated she threw her coat negligently over the back and crossed to the window. He felt a moment's ridiculous panic. He wished she would sit down. He didn't want her roaming about his beloved sanctum any more than he'd want a tiger doing so. For a mad moment he had the uneasy feeling she was going to jump, leaving him to make all the explanations. Looking at her averted profile he saw that her eyes were strangely long in shape, like those of a wild animal, a jungle cat, or a Greek statue. This was certainly no sweet, gauche English girl.

"Of course, congratulations are in order." He had to say something. She turned toward him, her face still inscrutable, with that look of inner concentration. "You have attained your majority."

"Yes." In the light from the window he saw for the first time that her eyes weren't brown, as he'd first thought, but a deep violet blue, a blue of a warmth and darkness he'd never seen before. Or had he?

"You have your father's eyes." He blurted it out without thinking. Suddenly her face was transformed. Her eyes lit up, her mouth curved in a dazzling three-cornered smile, the smile of a buccaneer. All at once she looked what she was, a mere eighteen.

"Antonio? Did you know him well? My mother told me so much about him. She always said, 'Antonio could make stones sing.' " For the first time Mr. Whitaker heard the lilt of Italian in her voice, reproducing uncannily the intonation and timbre of an older woman's speech. "I didn't understand then, I was too young. But you knew him. What was he like?"

Mr. Whitaker hesitated. "Antonio" indeed . . . It made him wonder how well in fact he had known Anthony Traverne. Maybe inside that quiet inarticulate exterior there'd been another man, not Anthony but Antonio, dashing, capable of passion—and tragedy.

"He was . . . an unusual man. I'm not sure I knew him that well. Maybe no one did."

Against his will his mind went back to that golden May afternoon twenty years ago. The last time he was to see Anthony Traverne, if he'd only known it. Surely he should have suspected something of what was to come? After all, he'd known Anthony since boyhood. He'd always had a soft spot for him, he wasn't sure why. Perhaps because he was so obviously unfitted for the exalted station in life to which he'd been born. A quiet, undemonstrative boy, grown into a reserved young man, with that very particular Englishness, unremarkable in every way except for his passion for what he himself, self-deprecating as always, called "old bones and stones." The family hid its disappointment well, though it was obvious to everyone that his younger brother Frederick, a success in everything he undertook, would have made a better heir to the earldom and the estate.

But for once, on that summer afternoon, Anthony Traverne had seemed set on the right track. He'd done well, most unexpectedly well for himself. Somehow he'd managed to snare as his bride-to-be the catch of the season; a lovely girl, well-born and most appropriately wealthy. And the young couple looked well together. He, with his immaculate manners and that preoccupied, almost absentminded air that lent a touch of distinction to his otherwise unremarkable exterior, was an excellent foil for her exquisite English fairness. Everyone agreed it was the perfect match.

It was strange, now, to remember that he'd envied Anthony Traverne that day. The young couple were driving that same afternoon to Oxford to Anthony's old college for the annual May Ball. The wedding at St. Paul's was only a week away. How could he have known that what was intended as the wedding of the year would turn out to be the scandal of the decade, with repercussions that were to haunt the Travernes to this very day?

That night, while the Ball was in full swing, Anthony Traverne disappeared. It was a full week before it was discovered that one Maria Modena, an Italian nightclub singer hired to entertain the guests, had gone with him. He left behind a stunned family, an estate in chaos, and, in Mr. Whitaker's mind at least, a great many unanswered questions.

Two years later, one bleak November Sunday, a taxi driver nearing the end of his shift attempted to overtake a heavily laden truck on the Eastbound highway leading from Heathrow, and collided with a guard rail. Both driver and passenger were killed outright. Anthony Traverne had been back in England for just under an hour.

It was a tragedy, of course, but also a blessing. The scandal was laid to rest at last, his younger brother took over the estate, and barring a certain ineradicable bitterness, the case was considered closed.

Ten years went by. Then—the bombshell. A telegram, addressed to Mr. Whitaker personally, from a hospital in Marseilles, informing him that Maria Modena was dead—and that wasn't all. There was a child, a ten-year-old girl. Corrie.

Of course the old scandal enjoyed a new lease on life. Was the girl Anthony Traverne's daughter? Her mother stated in her will that the child was his. But it didn't take long to discover that there had been no marriage. It seemed that Anthony Traverne had remained absent-minded to the last. But there was still the question of her claim upon the estate.

Corrie herself was penniless, of course. All Maria Modena's belongings had been sold to pay her hospital bills—except for one package, forwarded to his firm's office just before she died. That package now rested beside him on his desk. "For Corrie, on her eighteenth birthday." The graceful Italianate script had faded over the years, but the impression of a formidable woman lingered on.

"I am like him . . . a little?"

Corrie's voice jerked Mr. Whitaker back to the present. He looked up to confront that level dark blue gaze.

"Yes. You have his eyes . . . and something of his expression." This wasn't the sort of conversation he'd intended to have at all. But now he knew why there was something familiar about her. Her father's look of absent-minded preoccupation, his air of listening to some distant music no one else could hear, was hers too.

With an effort he returned to his purpose.

"Now you are eighteen, of course, there is your future to consider." He paused weightily. "Have you given any thought to what you will do after your final examinations this summer?"

Reluctantly she sat down. Her eyes met his warily. "What had you in mind?"

"Well . . ." He was on home ground now, well-prepared territory. He steepled his fingers and leaned back in his chair. "There are quite a few possibilities."

"Some more possible than others." Was there a trace of irony in her tone?

"Of course, some are more suitable for a girl in your . . . er . . . unusual position. But the final choice is up to you." Now was the time to play his trump card. "The family has very generously offered to provide you with an allowance until you are twenty-one, and to finance a suitable course of training." She was still looking at him with that searching gaze. He hurried on. "As I say, there are several alternatives available. A secretarial course, perhaps. There is always a demand for office skills."

"I see." Again she cut him short. "That's very generous." That uncomfortable hint of irony again. "What are the conditions?"

He blinked. Surely she didn't suspect . . . no, she couldn't have known. "Well . . ." He slid open a drawer, drew out the sheet of paper with its short paragraph of typescript. "There's just one thing. A formality." He slid the paper across the desk, watching her carefully. She picked it up, scanned it.

"You want me to sign this?"

He coughed delicately.

"If you would." His tone was deliberately casual. "As a matter of routine." There was a long pause. He glanced down, pretending to sort through the other papers on his desk.

"Could I have a pen?"

"Of course." He uncapped his own fountain pen and handed it to her. Without a moment's hesitation she scrawled her signature. He expelled his long-held breath in a small, silent sigh.

"Thank you." As he took the paper from her a pang of conscience seized him. After all, it had been too easy. Her face was calm, almost indifferent. She didn't look like a girl who had just signed away all future claim to one of the richest estates in England. Discreetly he checked the signature. Corrie Modena. Excellent. He looked up to find her eyes watching him with a trace of amusement.

"I signed my mother's last name." Her voice was satin smooth, but her eyes danced. "I thought, in these circumstances, you would prefer it."

"I see." His mind racing, he leaned back in his chair and eyed the young woman opposite. She returned his gaze with composure, more composure than he'd seen on many a hardened conman in the dock. Where had she got it from, this calm confidence? He'd been prepared to feel sorry for her, a girl alone in the world, a victim of circumstances. But she didn't need his pity. He'd never seen anyone so blatantly uncowed.

Deliberately he let the silence lengthen, but she didn't weaken. Eventually curiosity got the better of him.

"If you knew all along what I wanted, why did you sign the paper?" She shrugged with the first sign of impatience he'd seen.

"Because it doesn't matter. It's irrelevant."

He hid a smile. She must be more naïve than she seemed. Then another more sinister possibility struck him.

"Have you taken advice on this?"

"Oh yes." She smiled brilliantly. "The best there is."

His anxiety deepened. An advisor . . . how on earth had she had time and opportunity to find one? But it was ominous news. Quickly he ran over the legal phrasing in his mind. It was a standard formulation, surely she couldn't have found a loophole? No, it was cast-iron.

Suddenly she was on her feet and reaching for her coat.

"Wait." He struggled from his chair. He felt out of his depth. He wouldn't have been surprised if she'd reached into her coat pocket and pulled out a pistol. "We haven't discussed the arrangements . . . your future . . . we must make some decision."

She shook her head.

"I'm not going back." The glimmer of a smile. "There's no point. You know that as well as I do."

"But Corrie . . ." To his annoyance he heard himself begin to bluster. "You must . . . you have to." It's in the terms of the contract, he almost said. A simple enough bargain—financial support in exchange for good behavior.

"I'm eighteen. As of today I don't have to do anything I don't want to do."

Seeing the tilt of her chin a pang of foreboding struck him.

"Corrie, my dear, I don't think you understand. Eighteenth birthday or not, I'm afraid the family won't look at all kindly on your failure to complete your education. To put it bluntly, your going back isn't a matter of choice."

"They can't make me." There wasn't a trace of doubt in her voice. He sighed at her naïveté.

"I'm afraid you underestimate the Travernes. You must realize that you are dependent on them financially, and will be for some time to come. If you refuse to go back to school they quite simply will stop your allowance. And then what will you do?" She said nothing. He noticed again the obstinate cleft in her lower lip. He felt a pang of sympathy. She was hardly more than a child, ignorant of the ways of the world. She didn't understand that if the Travernes of this world wanted something, they would get it.

"My dear, you've led a sheltered life. I know it must seem irksome to you now, but you need the Travernes and their money. Alone, without money, without qualifications, you would find it impossible to survive."

"Mr. Whitaker, nothing is impossible." He stared at her. Those deep violet blue eyes with their fringe of black lashes met his squarely. "And I am not alone." Silenced, he watched her as she dug deep into the pocket of her overcoat.

"You see, I've had a long time to think about this." She drew out something, just what he couldn't see. "I knew the family would stop my allowance. I'd probably do the same in their position. There's no reason why they should go on supporting me, especially as I've no intention of doing what they want."

"But Corrie . . . you don't realize . . . you can't just walk into the wide world and expect to be taken care of."

"Mr. Whitaker, I think you've forgotten something. I've had a lot of training. I can take care of myself. Here." Before his astonished gaze she held up a sizable wad of five-pound notes, counted them carefully, and slapped them down on his desk.

"What's this?"

"A retainer." Her voice was matter-of-fact. "I don't know any lawyers, but you seem like a good one. I want you to work for me."

Numbly he stared at the proffered money. At last he recovered his powers of speech.

"Corrie, I can't work for you. It's out of the question. Apart from anything else, I'm advisor to the Travernes. The conflict of interest—"

"Don't worry." Her tone was soothing. "It's nothing to do with the Travernes. From their point of view I don't exist anymore, remember?"

She was right. She'd signed the form. He shook his head.

"But what can you possibly want with a lawyer?"

For the first time since she'd entered his office she looked off-balance and unsure. A faint flush stained her cheeks.

"I need . . . someone I can trust." She hesitated. "You see, I'll be getting letters, very important letters. I want you to keep them for me, and send them on when I know where I'm going to be. I may be traveling a lot."

"That's all?" He smiled. "In that case, if you only want me to act as a glorified *poste restante*, there's no need to pay me at all. I'd do it as a favor to the family." He held out the notes. But she shook her head fiercely.

"Please don't patronize me, Mr. Whitaker. I've had

enough favors to last me a lifetime. From now on I don't want to owe anybody anything. Especially the Travernes. Do you understand? From today I am Corrie Modena. The Travernes never heard of me, and I never heard of them."

"But—"

"You need more?" She reached for her overcoat.

"No, no!" He gave a gesture of mock despair as he gathered up the notes. He knew when he was beaten. "This is ample."

"There'll be more. When I'm famous I'll need a good lawyer." He smiled at her youthful confidence.

"Famous? And just how do you intend to become famous?"

"I'm afraid I can't tell you that. It's a secret."

"Like the letters?"

"Yes." She frowned. "Mr. Whitaker, are you taking me seriously?"

Hurriedly, he suppressed the smile. "Yes indeed, Corrie. Yes indeed."

"Good." With a businesslike air she scooped up her overcoat then held out her hand. He was surprised at his own reluctance to let her go. He hadn't had such an entertaining afternoon in years.

"Goodbye . . . no, wait!" He'd almost forgotten the pretext for this meeting. "I have a little surprise for you." The long light package rustled slightly as he slid it toward her.

A small smile played over her lips as she saw the handwriting on the package, but she made no move to pick it up, not even to give it an exploratory shake. His eyes widened. What kind of girl was she? She must be made of stone. Her calmness was now driving his own curiosity to fever pitch.

"Aren't you going to open it?" He pushed a pair of scissors toward her encouragingly.

"No." She didn't even hesitate.

"Why on earth not?" Frustration lent an aggrieved tone to his voice which he immediately regretted. She looked up reprovingly.

"Because I know what's inside."

She picked up the package gently and tucked it under her arm, smiling as if at some secret joke.

"The family jewels."

In that moment he knew for certain that she was Anthony Traverne's daughter. Instantly, as if a floodgate had opened, he remembered all the questions he'd wanted to ask Anthony Traverne and never had. Why had he disappeared without warning all those years ago? Why, if he loved her, had he never married Corrie's mother? Now, instead of satisfying his curiosity, his daughter had provided more mysteries to plague him. Who was her advisor? What was this correspondence in which she was engaged, so important that she needed his services? What was the source of her extraordinary composure? Where was she going, what was she going to do, what was her plan?

"Goodbye, Mr. Whitaker." She was leaving, he might never see her again. One thing he would know. He picked up the notes, brandished them at her retreating figure.

"The money . . . I have to know . . . where did you get it?"

She turned in the doorway, a small smile touched her lips.

"You should know, Mr. Whitaker. Christmas and birthday, remember?"

Speechless he watched her leave the room. In a few moments, from his window, he saw her emerge down the steps at a half run, her breath a small plume behind her in the chilly air.

Corrie laughed out loud, ignoring the startled glances of two passing barristers, sober in their dark gray suits and with their rolled umbrellas, as she swept through the ancient Elizabethan gateway into Chancery Lane. The narrow medieval lane was crowded with people like her, busy people, with places to go, things to do. Traffic packed the road from curb to curb. She glanced at her watch. It was late, later than she'd thought.

Boldly she stepped out into the roadway and hailed a taxi with an imperious wave. Like an obedient black seal it swung in to the pavement.

"Where to, miss?"

"The Savoy." Her voice was calm and clear, she was pleased with it. As the taxi slipped smoothly away up Chancery Lane and doubled back into the mêlée where Fleet Street joined the Strand she knew she'd been right to take a cab. Beginnings were important. She took a deep breath, trying to still the excited beating of her heart. She must seem calm, matter-of-fact, or everything would go wrong. She glanced at herself in the driver's mirror, smoothed back her hair, straightened her collar. Did she look the part? Not quite. Regretfully she removed the scarlet shawl and tucked it under the package. Her gray pleated skirt, simple white blouse and gray pullover would do, now that she had abandoned the betraying schoolgirl coat.

The taxi wheeled sharply left in to Savoy Court and careened to a halt with a squeal of brakes. She waited. She was another person now, reserved, conscious of protocol. The cabby reached behind and opened the door.

"Thank you." She said goodbye to her last pound note with a pang. "Keep the change." A grand gesture, but it had been a day of grand gestures. She smiled. Her offer of more money to Mr. Whitaker had been the purest bluff—but it had worked, that was all that mattered. As Harlequin said, empty pockets leave room for inspiration . . .

A doorman in a dark green gold-buttoned frock coat, white gloves and peaked cap was waiting in the shadow of the entrance arcade. The dimness was lit by rectangular lanterns, even though it was still daylight outside. Above, the huge, dramatically simple silver steel sign, in a miracle of understatement, read "Savoy," as stark and elegant as the grille on a Rolls-Royce.

Under the arcade, despite the lanterns, the light was dim. There was marble everywhere, forest green, cream and inky black. Head high but eyes demurely cast down she swept past the doorman and through the tall mahogany revolving doors. Once inside she was instantly conscious of having entered a different world. The first thing she noticed was the quiet, a calm, discreet, ultimately expensive hush. It was almost as if she had inadvertently wandered into someone's home, or stepped back a hundred years, before the invention of steam and speed. The light was restfully dim, lamps glowing islands in the vast space, crystal chandeliers outlining the white friezes beneath the paneled ceiling. The air was filled with a subtle fragrance, light and peppery, from the banks of golden and white hothouse narcissi on every low table. Everywhere there was the pale sheen of marble, the gleam of brass inlay, the deeper glow of mahogany. To her left, deep and infinitely comfortable, black leather chesterfields waited to welcome tired guests, while from a tall archway beneath an exquisite chandelier came the discreet chink of cutlery and glassware, the civilized hum that is the aftermath of leisurely dining.

Corrie took a deep breath. She felt like an intruder, yet curiously at home. A stir of movement caught her eye, drawing her attention to the long mahogany counter sited unobtrusively on her right. Now that she looked more closely into the enchanted gloom, she realized the hall was full of uniformed staff, gliding quietly about their business, so smoothly they were almost invisible.

"May I help you?"

The dark-suited young man behind the counter was exquisitely courteous. His expression showed no surprise at her lack of luggage, she might have been a princess of the blood. She warmed to him at once. His performance was faultless.

"I am Corrie Modena." Her new name felt good. "I have an appointment with Mrs. Andrews."

"Of course." There was no change in the young man's deferential tone. Her admiration deepened. With a discreet gesture he summoned from nowhere a tailcoated pageboy. "Please take Miss Modena to the Lady Superintendent's office."

Regretfully she followed the pageboy's tails out of the great Front Hall and along an eternity of noiseless carpeted corridors, past an infinity of golden walnut doors framed in silver steel. The Lady Superintendent was stern and imposing in her severe black uniform with its spotless white collar and cuffs and the big bunch of keys fixed to a brass chain at her waist.

"Good morning, ma'am." The Lady Superintendent scanned her from head to toe, evidently taking in the immaculate neatness of her black hair, the perfect suitability of her gray and white. Corrie kept her hands demurely clasped in front of her. The Lady Superintendent's face softened slightly with what might have been approval. She picked up two pieces of paper from her desk. Corrie caught sight of the two letterheads bearing the names of well-established French hotels that Harlequin had sent her, and held her breath.

"Good, good. Everything seems in order." Corrie kept her eyes suitably downcast. "I see you have worked mostly abroad?"

"Yes ma'am. I speak French, Italian, and a little Greek." The Lady Superintendent nodded approvingly. Corrie felt a surge of exhilaration. It was working, it was working. She was on her way.

"Excellent." The Lady Superintendent rose briskly to her feet and extended her hand. "In that case, Miss Modena, welcome to the staff." She paused. "With your experience I expect you will understand that there are very strict rules governing your work here. The Savoy has a reputation for service of which it is justifiably proud, and it is up to you to help maintain that reputation. Our motto is 'For Excellence We Strive,' and that is what our guests expect from us as a matter of course. Our clientele is exclusive, and they come to us because they require comfort and above all privacy. The watchword is discretion, discretion above all. Is that understood?"

"Yes ma'am."

"Good. Now the Floor Supervisor will fit you with your uniform and have you shown to your room. One of the other chambermaids will show you your duties tomorrow. I take it that you can start at once?"

"Yes ma'am. I have taken the liberty of having my luggage forwarded."

"Excellent. I hope you will be very happy working here, Miss Modena."

Inside five minutes she was ushered into a tiny boxroom in the staff wing. It was cramped but spotlessly clean; moreover, as the Floor Housekeeper had explained to her, in keeping with the Savoy's tradition of service, it would be cleaned for her. A single bed stood against the cream-painted walls, there were flowered print curtains at the small window and a narrow strip of carpet on the floor, a basin nestled in one corner and her case was waiting by the bed.

She laid the two chambermaid's uniforms over the back of the chair and eyed them appraisingly. For day there was a short-sleeved cotton blouse in a purple and white narrow pinstripe, with crisp white Peter Pan collar and cuffs, and a voluminous white linen apron which covered the plain skirt. For evening duty the blouse and skirt were dove gray and the apron smaller. Both uniforms were clearly designed to match the subtle pastel shades of the hotel décor. Last of all came her own brass chain, which she would wear looped round her waist to carry the keys to the rooms on her floor.

She sat down, suddenly exhausted. She'd passed the audition and now she had the costume—but could she play the part? From her own childhood experience she knew roughly how a chambermaid looked and behaved, but what one actually did was another matter. Until she could learn the ropes she would simply have to bluff her way through. It would all be good practice. Now she'd got the job she was determined to hold on to it. It was her gateway, the first step in the master plan.

And there, proof positive that she was on her way at last, was her case. As she picked up the familiar handle a rush of memories assailed her. It was an old leather one of her father's, too heavy to be practical, but his initials in faded gold gave it a battered distinction of its own. It had seen so much, that case. It had been her constant companion as she and her mother progressed through the hotels and boarding houses of the Riviera. They had started out in the four star palaces of Nice and Cannes, in the early days when Maria was still sought after as an entertainer, and mobbed by admirers in the chic clubs and casinos of the Côte d'Azur and the Côte d'Or. As the years passed and money grew scarce they had drifted down the scale, to seedier resting places farther and farther from the sea and the center of town, ending up with the bleak, windswept new resorts of the Côte Vermeille.

But that hadn't mattered to Corrie. One hotel room was the same as another, for her mother's mere presence could turn disaster into diversion, loneliness into laughter. Together, they were a cavalcade. They were friends and allies and fellow conspirators, with their own impenetrable language, a secret code of peasant Greek and Provençal and Neapolitan slang, and wherever they went there was sunshine and music. And when they had to be apart, during the long summer evenings when Maria was performing, Corrie would be busy setting the stage for the next day's adventures, adapting costumes, sorting music, plotting itineraries.

"My little manager," her mother would say with enormous pride when she returned. "My sorcerer's apprentice. What would I do without you?" Then, no matter how late it was, they would slip outside, for her mother couldn't bear to stay indoors a moment longer, and sit in the sweet-smelling darkness under an apricot moon, swapping choruses from *Pagliacci* and feasting on slabs of bitter chocolate and Montelimar nougat on rounds of bread, which Corrie had smuggled in readiness from the hotel dining room . . .

Corrie smiled. Looking back, she could see that it had been a strange existence for a young girl. She'd been brought up on a diet of legends and love songs and midnight picnics under the cypresses, so how could she settle for anything less? She didn't regret a moment of it. They were magical days, brimful of southern light and the sound of her mother's singing. Forever after sunshine and the sound of the human voice would be inseparable in her mind.

Occasionally, though, her mother would worry about her lack of education.

"Whatever have I done to you, my darling?" she would cry, throwing her arms about her daughter with a despair that was only half feigned. "I have taught you nothing a woman should know. Why, you cannot even cook!"

"But I can do so many other things . . ." It was true. She could swear like a sailor in three languages, haggle like a Marseilles fishwife, sing on an empty stomach and find a friend in a desert.

"No, no, it doesn't count." Her mother would shake her head, her long mobile mouth, which she could turn into a tragic mask or a clown's grimace at will, drooping at the corners. So then Corrie would play her trump card.

"And I have perfect pitch." Her mother would pause, and consider, and then a gleam would come into her smoky-lidded eyes, so like Corrie's own, and she would begin to laugh, and reach over to tousle her daughter's hair.

"In that case, my darling, there is nothing more you need to know." For they both knew, with a secret, unshakable conviction, that music was the answer to everything.

Or almost everything.

Toward the end it was the sunlight that Maria craved most of all. During the last months Corrie managed each time to find them a room with a balcony facing west, so that her mother, now with a gray tinge behind her entertainer's pallor, could sit there in the late afternoon when she woke from sleep and soak up the last warmth before the evening's performance. One day, she would say to her daughter, we will find a place where the sun never sets, where there are no nights at all. Corrie, if she could have managed it, would have trapped the sun itself and hung it in their room. But she was only a child, and her magic wasn't strong enough. The best she could do was bring her mother a glass of absinthe, curl up at her feet and ask her to tell her about Antonio.

At the mention of his name a warm flush would come to her mother's cheeks and her eyes would regain their sparkle. "Oh, what a man he was, that one. He knew everything. He was truly a magician. The stories he could tell, they would spirit the heart out of your body." Then she would tell Corrie about Perseus, who slew the snake-headed Medusa, and rescued maidens from monsters, and Jason, who sailed the world in search of the Golden Fleece, and Orpheus, the singer who lost his wife to the Underworld.

Then she would tell her how she first met Antonio, on the first day of summer, and fell in love.

At midnight that same day they escaped together, she from her immigrant's isolation, he from his dull English responsibilities, to make her dreams and his books come true. Happiness was there waiting for them, in a small white room on a Greek island hillside. There, the following spring, when the hillside was a blue haze of hyacinths, Corrie was born. Antonio held the tiny baby in his arms, stiff but proud, "proud as a general, my darling," and without hesitation, from the depths of his classical knowledge, named her after the long ago princess who was captured by the King of the Underworld and forced to spend three months of every year in his cold, dark palace underground, because she'd eaten six of his pomegranate seeds. Not Persephone—for that, he said, was too ponderous a name for such a tiny scrap of humanity—but Kore, as she came to be known, summer's daughter and the spirit of spring itself.

"I wouldn't have eaten those seeds," Corrie would insist. "Not even if I was starving to death."

"No, my darling?" Her mother would smile at the conviction in her voice. "How can you be so sure?" Her face would cloud again. "You see, there are so many different kinds of hunger."

Corrie knew she was thinking of the years without Antonio.

"Why did he go, mama?" It was the one element of the story she didn't understand. How could Antonio ever have wanted to leave her mother, who was so beautiful, with her golden skin and her blue-black hair? Maria would smile at her daughter's earnestness and take her hand. "You forget, *cara*. He was an Englishman, a gentleman. He wanted us to marry, but I refused. I knew his family would never accept me. But I didn't care. The two years we had together were the happiest of my life. We lived simply, we loved each other. It was enough.

"But when you were born . . . he wanted so much for you. He was worried about the future. We had very little money left, my health was not good . . . he wanted to provide for us both. So he went back, to make his peace with his father, to come to an arrangement." Then she would sigh. "I tried to make him stay. It was foolish of me. I could not cure him of his Englishness, his sense of duty. I would not have wanted to. I loved him."

Silent, watching her mother's face, Corrie made another, private resolution. She would never fall in love with a rich man, it was too dangerous. If she could not love as an equal, she would not love at all.

"I worry about you, my darling." Her mother, sensing her preoccupation, would ruffle her hair. "You are so serious, so intense—like your father. You live too much for tomorrow."

The question hung in the air: What will become of you when I am gone?

During the terrible days after her mother's death she began to understand what Maria had meant by the many different kinds of hunger. There was an awful aching emptiness inside her which she would have filled with anything if she could. Even her name, of which she was so proud, was taken from her. Her English classmates found it outlandish and foreign and, despite its simplicity, impossible to pronounce. They amended it to Corrie, and Kore accepted the compromise, saving her real name and her real self for that far-off day when she could escape back into the sunlight.

She told the other girls nothing about her birth, knowing instinctively that there was nothing about her mother's relationship with Antonio that they would have understood. But she made a vow. The gods and goddesses on Mount Olympus never confused love and marriage and neither would she. Live as if you are going to live forever, her mother had told her. Live as if summer begins today.

Oh, but it was difficult. She wanted to die. There was no one she could turn to. No one spoke her language. There was no music. Humming or even whistling in the corridors was strictly forbidden. There was only silence and grayness, flat English voices and stiff English faces, chilly English weather and colder English ways. She wanted to die, but some steely inner instinct wouldn't let her. Instead she retreated to her own private Mount Olympus. Slowly, in that first year, she learned endurance and secrecy, but she hated every minute of it, feeling herself suffocating, as if she'd been buried underground. It was truly the Underworld.

What would have happened to her if nothing had changed she didn't know. Perhaps she would never have come down from her secret mountain, perhaps she would have stayed locked up in the safety of her memories. But then, by what seemed a miracle, the smallest chink of light entered her prison. Secretly, passionately, she widened that small chink of invisible radiance until it was a flood that filled her imagination.

Slowly, reverently, Corrie lifted a small fabric-wrapped bundle out of the case. Casting aside the layers of institutional white she uncovered a small cassette tape recorder. She placed it gently on the dresser and lined up her precious collection of cassettes beside it. Cassettes . . . in French that meant little boxes, and that's what they were, little boxes of distilled sunlight. Now they were here the room was full.

Then, with a hesitancy she only half understood, she

turned to her mother's bequest. She held the long flat package gingerly in her hands, as if it was an unexploded bomb. At last she made up her mind. The time wasn't yet ripe, she wasn't ready. She wasn't quite out of the Underworld yet. Gently, half-relieved, half-disappointed, she placed the package on top of the wardrobe. For the moment she must store it away, just as she used to pack away her mother's glittering jet-beaded costumes before a journey, seeding them with lavender from the Provençal hillsides, to keep them fresh for the time when the adventures would begin again.

Pen and paper in hand, she dragged a chair to the window. Outside it was already dark. A flurry of rain beaded the glass. The roofs were slick with moisture, a sparrow hopped and pecked in the gutter. In the small patch of cold, black sky there was no moon.

But Corrie didn't care. She was impervious now to the worst that winter could do. Soon she would be out of the Underworld forever, and then . . . she would make it come true again, her Riviera dream. She leaned forward, breathed on the glass, transforming the raindrops into luminous pearls.

Dear Harlequin,

I have a new address for you. Care of Mr. Whitaker, Harby, Jarndyce and Harby, New Square, Lincoln's Inn, London WC1. Surprised? And that's not all—I've also got a job, a hotel and a lawyer!

Yes, I know I should have waited, but I couldn't bear another wasted summer. I would have killed to get out of that place. Je n'exagère pas. *Even you can't possibly imagine what it means to me to be able to walk about the streets, go where I want, do what I please. And London . . . I still can't believe it. From my window, if I concentrate very hard, I can almost see the Opera House. All those years, I never dared to hope that one day I'd really be here, with the maps coming to life under my feet. My blood is fizzing like champagne! I have made a resolution. When I'm famous I shall drink nothing but champagne, and leave lights burning all night in every room. No more darkness, ever . . .*

As for my job . . . I'm not sure you'd approve. I aimed high, as you told me, but I did have to tell a few lies. So I won't tell you about it, until I'm sure it works out. But don't worry—it will be good practice for the soubrette parts, and it gives me lots of time off (afternoons one week, evenings the next) for the only thing that matters.

I wish you could have seen Mr. Whitaker's face when I signed away my prospects! He obviously thought I'd lost my mind, heading off into the big wide world with no money, no family, no home . . . But you and I know better, n'est-ce pas? *There are worse kinds of poverty, worse kinds of exile. Now, looking out of my window, I feel very close to all the people in their houses, curtains drawn, fires lit. Maybe they too are dreaming of other lives, faraway countries. But my dream is different. I am going to make it come true.*

And for that, how can I ever thank you? If it hadn't been for you, I'd have given up long ago. I might have been trapped in the dark forever, beating my wings against the glass.

But now . . . no more money, no more rules, no more writing to you by flashlight under the covers. I'm light as air, free as a bird!

In flight at last,

Your Columbine

CHAPTER TWO

"There's a letter for you, Corrie."

Shevaun, one of the many Irish maids at the Savoy and Corrie's next-door neighbor in the staff wing, eyed the envelope with interest as she passed it over.

"Good news?" Shevaun asked hopefully as Corrie glanced at the solicitor's imprint. But her curiosity was thwarted when Corrie merely smiled, slipped the letter into the cavernous pocket of her starched apron and calmly continued her breakfast.

Corrie buttered her toast methodically and spread it thick with bitter marmalade to hide the excited beating of her heart. If she showed an ounce of what she was feeling, she'd never hear the last of it. All the chambermaids were romantically inclined, she knew. It had something to do with the luxury and elegance of the Savoy itself, its long history of glamour. Diaghilev, Picasso, Marlene Dietrich, Marilyn Monroe, Noel Coward—they'd all fallen under its spell. Maharajahs, ministers and crowned kings had luxuriated in its old-world service, actresses and opera singers in its famous hip-deep cast-iron baths. But she herself was too busy for romance and all its implications. She had work to do, work to fill every waking minute, and no time to waste.

"I'm going shopping in Oxford Street this afternoon," Shevaun announced. "Anyone want to come? How about you, Corrie?"

"I haven't been paid yet."

"You could always look. If you see something you

like, I'll lend you some money." Shevaun's round blue eyes were persuasive.

"Maybe another day." Corrie smiled. "I'm busy this afternoon." Shevaun nudged her next-door neighbor, exchanging a conspiratorial glance. Corrie smiled to herself. She knew what the other maids thought. They were sure she had a lover. And in a way she had—a demanding, all-consuming lover, who would be satisfied with nothing but her whole devotion. She had a rendezvous with him each day in the Pinafore Room, whenever there was no function scheduled. It made the perfect rehearsal space. The wood paneling deadened the sound of her voice, swallowed up every bit of resonance and intonation, no matter how cleverly she sang. And Kaspar, the tall cat made of ebony which occupied the fourteenth chair when thirteen sat down to dinner, was the ideal audience. Silent, unmoved, he urged her to new heights with his baleful, critical stare.

As soon as she could she excused herself from the table. She wanted to start work as soon as possible. When she'd finished, then, only then would she allow herself the luxury of reading her letter. Filled with anticipation she whisked round her rooms. Now, in her second week at the Savoy, the routine was familiar to her, each room like an old friend. They were all different in décor and furnishings, but throughout there was the mellow, subtly distinctive atmosphere particular to the Savoy. Everything was of the best, from the antique sporting prints on the paneled walls to the old-fashioned spaciousness of the suites, with their huge closets fit for the age of steamer trunks and personal valets, and their priceless Chippendale furniture. The accent was on simplicity, from the snow-white Castile soap in the bathrooms to the fluffy white bathrobes with the tiny Savoy insignia in black.

In two short weeks she'd learned a lot. She'd acquired the knack of fading out of sight whenever she spotted a guest, either by disappearing into a vacant room or behind a staff door, discreetly provided with a porthole window so that she could see when the coast was clear. She'd learned the difference between a *sous-chef* and a *maître chef*, a foyer waiter and a floor waiter, a wet tea and a dry tea. She'd learned about the long-running rivalry between the Grill Room and the River Restaurant (the Restaurant boasted a better view, the Grill Room a larger quota of celebrities). She'd visited the frenzied chaos of the kitchens, where the French, Viennese and Italian cooks made themselves understood in a frantic multilingual babble, and where Escoffier had invented Pêche Melba for Nellie Melba, the famous opera singer. She knew that every single article of furniture in the rooms, right down to the carpet, had a duplicate in the furnishing department, so that it could be replaced immediately if required. She knew that the barman in the American Bar could compose by heart a hundred and thirteen different cocktails. She knew that the Savoy would obtain for a guest, at any hour of the day or night, whatever he desired—even, once for the Aga Khan, a special kind of fish found only in Africa's Lake Victoria. The Savoy pumped its own water, did its own laundry, made its own sausages, bread and ice cream, blended its own coffee, cellared its own wine in what were once the dungeons of the original Savoy Palace, way under the Thames. And, most miraculous of all in a labor-saving age, its staff outnumbered its guests by three to one.

To Corrie, as she darted in and out of her allotted rooms, it was as if the Savoy was a huge liner, moored out of space and time. Guests came and went, but the Savoy remained the same, humming quietly in readiness as its crew worked away at their tasks.

At last her work was done. She placed the last tray of breakfast crockery, Worcester bone china with the distinctive little gold and scarlet gondolier and thin gold line, outside the door for the floor waiter to collect, and returned her trolley to the service room, where the staff kept all the tools of their trade—from the double dumbwaiter with its hot and cold shelves to the special machine for shaving ice to put around oysters. Shevaun was there, refilling the locker on her tray with fresh handtowels.

"My, you were quick today. It's only twelve o'clock."

"I was lucky. All the rooms were empty." Often guests stayed in their rooms till late in the morning, which meant the maids couldn't get in to clean. It even had been known for a maid to make a bed with a guest still in it, if he'd forgotten to put out the Do Not Disturb sign and the curtains weren't drawn.

"Have you got time for a quick cup of tea?"

Mineral waters, fruit, bread, biscuits and iced water were all kept in the service room, as well as tea and coffee.

"No, I've got to fly." Shevaun watched her go with an envious look.

Corrie sped noiselessly along the corridor, the letter, her first since she'd arrived at the Savoy, seeming to burn a hole in her apron pocket.

Outside the stairs leading to the staff wing she hesitated. For some reason she didn't feel like going back to her tiny room just yet. It was unlikely that the maid would have finished cleaning . . . and in any case Harlequin's letter deserved something better. She debated. Where could she read it in peace and privacy? The canteen was hopeless, and she mustn't be seen in the corridors if a guest came by. She thought long and hard, then made up her mind. Keeping a weather eye out for the Floor Supervisor, she took the lift to the fourth floor. That was where the suites were, high above the trees of Embankment Gardens, with their lovely views over the Thames.

Her heart beating hard, she slipped her key into the lock of the Maria Callas suite, whisked in through the door and locked it behind her.

She leaned against it, breathing deeply. The faint scent of beeswax polish on old wood came to her nostrils. The Callas suite was decorated in soft green, its paneled walls inlaid with delicately beveled mirrors. The silence was broken only by the faint chug of pleasure boats from the river below. The room was full of light streaming through the scalloped curtains, gleaming off satinwood and mahogany, etching the classical relief on the gray marble fireplace. As her heartbeat slowed she had to fight back an impulse to kick off her shoes and sink into one of the awesomely comfortable club chairs drawn invitingly near. On a low table a bowl of white narcissi looked as if they too were made of marble and would never fade.

She ignored the pull of the club chairs and sat down instead at the leather-topped writing desk. She drew up the chair primly behind her and reached for her letter. Inside the lawyer's readdressed envelope was the familiar, distinctive French paper, with its delectable foreign crackle. She savored the texture, remembering all the other letters, a whole paper chain of them, a fragile drawbridge leading her slowly back to the real world. Then she could wait no longer. She picked up the ivory paperknife laid ready on the desk and opened it.

Ma chère petite Columbine,

A job, a hotel, a lawyer . . . what next? You are a constant source of surprises. Lies apart, how could I disapprove? I have only one caution—this job you've found, I hope it doesn't involve singing? Remember, this is the most dangerous point in your career. You're very young, and voices can be made or broken in less than a year. Please, if you can, wait for M. Beyer.

As for the rest, I'm glad you're finally "cured" of the money. Expectations can paralyze, and you need to be free just now, to find your voice, to test your limits to the utmost. But poor Mr. Whitaker . . . I have the greatest sympathy for him. I hope you dealt with him kindly, though I have my doubts. I know my Columbine. Patience is hardly your strong suit. But believe me, I would not change you for the world.

Yes, I am impressed, I admit it. Surprised and impressed and even a little sad. It feels strange, after so long, not to know exactly where you are and what you are doing. And I enjoyed them very much, those letters scrawled under the covers. We've been a family so long. Now you're free, a grown woman, with a job, a hotel and a lawyer of your own . . . it's almost as if you've left home. I ask myself, supposing you fell ill or were in danger, how could I reach you? I know I am ridiculous to think like this, but the fact is, you matter to me very much, my Columbine.

And there is no need to thank me. I would like to help you more, but I understand and respect your need for independence. We are alike in this as in everything else. Believe me, over the years you have given me as much if not more than I have ever given you. You owe me nothing. We are equals. My life would be very dull without you, my little impatient friend.

It was full moon last night. I thought of you, at your window.

Harlequin

P.S. Don't forget—Scarlatti's "Care e dolce" and Caccini's "Amarilli mia belli." Pure vowels and a Tuscan accent. I insist.

Corrie smiled. Then, without a moment's hesitation, she placed the letter in an ashtray and held a lighted match to it. A spiral of smoke, one orange flame and nothing was left but pale curling ash. It was what he'd asked her to do, right from the beginning. "*What I say is for you alone. Think of my letters as a friend's voice talking to you. It is the only way.*" She understood. Their friendship could only be kept alive inside her, not on some piece of paper. It was like a live performance, it couldn't be replayed. This way she remembered every word he'd ever written as if it was her own.

She opened the window wide. Beneath the dark outline of Cleopatra's Needle, framed by its twin sphinxes, Embankment Gardens with its bandstand and periwigged statue was shrouded in mist. The sky was pewter. She cupped the ashes in the palm of her hand and leaned out of the window, letting them drift down like snow.

You are safe with me, my Harlequin. My brother, my secret, my friend.

Still smiling she sat down again at the desk. On impulse she reached for pen and paper. She would surprise him with the Savoy crest. She would sit here, like a millionairess, in perfect peace, and write her answer. "*Dear Harlequin . . .*" She frowned. The pen was dry, someone had slipped up. She opened the desk drawer where a replacement was always kept. It was then, to her horror, that she heard the faintest sound of footsteps outside and the murmur of voices. She froze, praying for them to go by. But they didn't. Her heart leaped into her mouth as she heard the scrape of a key in the lock. Panicking, her eyes darted around the room. She could have sworn it was unoccupied. She should have checked, only she'd been too eager for her letter. Now, too late, she saw a book resting on one of the low tables beside a chair—and those narcissi, they were all white, not white and gold like the other displays . . . She should have known.

Desperately she looked for a hiding place. Perhaps the guests had only come back to freshen up before lunch . . . but she knew as well as anyone that those who could afford the suites could certainly afford the luxury of dining in their rooms.

Then there was no time left. The inner door swung open. She barely had time to crumple the piece of paper with Harlequin's name on it, stuff it into her apron pocket and leap to her feet.

"Just exactly what do you think you're doing?" It was the coldest voice she'd ever heard, with a slight accent which she couldn't identify. Framed in the curved doorway, frozen in the act of ushering his companion, stood a tall, dark man with the palest ice-gray eyes she'd ever seen.

"I've . . . I've just finished cleaning the room, sir." She knew the excuse was lame. If she'd been cleaning, the door should have been left ajar, with the maid's green loop over the handles.

"I see." The man scanned the room expressionlessly,

his gaze finally coming to rest on the half-open drawer. His eyes narrowed. The silence developed an icy edge.

Hurriedly Corrie reached forward and closed the drawer. She could feel a scalding blush rising in her cheeks. It was obvious that the man assumed she'd been prying, or worse, attempting to steal something of value.

"I—"

"That's enough." He cut her short with appalling abruptness. His face set, he advanced into the room. Corrie fell back a step, inadvertently. She noticed the beautiful cut of his suit, pale gray to match those falcon eyes with their predatory dark ring around the iris, the grace with which he moved. She also noticed that his eyes didn't really see her at all.

With a movement that totally excluded her, dismissed her as beneath contempt, he ushered in his companion, a sweet-faced blonde with soft blue eyes. She was beautifully dressed in honey-toned cashmere that matched her hair. Corrie told herself she looked expensive but dull, though she herself felt instantly small, shabby and in the wrong, even though she knew she'd done nothing.

"You."

Corrie jumped. It was the man's voice again, cold as a knife. He pointed to the door. "Out."

Stung, Corrie hesitated. "But you haven't given me a chance. I can explain . . ."

The man raised one dark eyebrow.

"I'm sure you can." Now his voice was chillingly soft. "But it so happens I do not care to listen to any explanations you might offer. I understand only too well what it is you were doing."

"Darling . . ." It was the woman's voice, with a pleading note in it. Seeing her expression, Corrie felt another shock. Only too obvious in those gentle cornflower blue eyes was pure, naked adoration. She felt an instant's pity. How could any woman be so foolish? What a man to choose to love—a cold, insensitive, autocratic icicle of a man. And it was clear, from the careless politeness with which he treated her, that he didn't love her in return. He will never make you happy, Corrie thought pityingly. Your affair is coming to an end. And it's the best thing that could happen to you.

The man, as she'd expected, ignored his companion's interruption. "I shall of course report you to your supervisor."

Corrie felt a jolt of alarm.

"That's not fair. I haven't done anything." She was getting angry now, his coldness was infuriating.

"Yet." The single syllable was as wounding as an insult. He turned away, began to check the drawers of the desk. It was as if she didn't exist. Furious with herself and him Corrie burst out: "I'm not a thief!"

The man answered without looking up.

"I suggest you leave it to your supervisor to decide the issue." His tone was indifferent.

"I shall lose my job."

"You should have thought of that before."

Corrie felt tears of outrage start at the back of her eyes, but fought them away. She wouldn't cry, wouldn't show how much it mattered to her.

The man reached toward the panel of buttons inlaid into the table.

"Do you want me to summon your superior?"

"No. I'm going." She struggled to keep her voice calm. "But I'd just like to say one thing." Impassive, the man pressed the button, but she refused to be deterred. If she was going to lose her job, it might as well be for a good reason. Just once, she was determined to break his composure.

"Even if I were a thief . . ." She turned at the door. "You wouldn't have anything to worry about." She drew a breath, anger filling her voice with a deep vibration. "You haven't anything left worth stealing!" She turned on her heel and closed the door behind her with a slam, catching as she did so one last glimpse of the man's face behind her, those cold dead eyes with a spark of something—anger, maybe, curiosity, certainly dislike—in their depths at last.

Her wave of righteous indignation carried her back to

her room, but once there the full impact of what had happened struck her. She had not only invaded a guest's privacy, the hotel's cardinal sin, but she had been rude as well, no matter how richly he deserved it. Once the Head Housekeeper heard of it, she would be sacked for certain. With a pang she realized how much that would mean to her. It wasn't just that being here fitted in so perfectly with her requirements. She'd come to love the grace and elegance of the hotel itself. It was going to be hard to adjust to ordinary life.

Of course the monster in the Callas suite couldn't have known how much losing her job would mean to her, but he hadn't bothered to find out, either. She knew the type. If she'd begged and pleaded, she might have persuaded him to be magnanimous, but no power on earth could have brought her to give him that satisfaction.

She sat on her bed and thought furiously. There was no denying it was her own fault. She'd broken the first rule; silence, exile, cunning. If you wanted your own kind of freedom you had to be as circumspect as a guerilla. Now, her master plan was collapsing like an accordion.

But she wouldn't give in so easily. One thing at least was in her favor. It was Sunday, the supervisor's afternoon off, something the devil in the Callas suite couldn't have known, so she had a few hours' grace. She'd put those few hours to the best possible use. When you feel like retreating, Harlequin always said, take two steps forward instead. Logically, that meant this was just the right moment for the biggest bluff of her life so far . . .

Before she could change her mind she reached up for the long flat package on top of the closet. The lid lifted off easily, releasing a hint of her mother's favorite scent, *Fuite des Heures*. Elusive, bittersweet, sophisticated, a scent for dry Mediterranean nights. As a child she remembered standing beside her mother as she dressed for the evening, accepting little dabs of this and that, a drop of cologne here, a touch of rouge there, with a connoisseur's relish. Now she parted the layers of yellowed tissue paper as if they were the pages of an old diary. Iridescent, the fabric swam up to meet her. She'd forgotten how it caught the light, like a black pearl. Scarcely breathing she lifted it out, letting the marvelous metallic luster spill through her fingers with a life of its own, and laid it on the bed.

There it was, in all its arrogant, faintly sinister glory. The talisman, the family jewel. The Balenciaga. Glowing with the secret luster of a midnight sky, or a fish in the deep dark sea. There was green and silver and purple hidden in the folds of the black shot silk, like lightning in a thundercloud.

Reverently Corrie lifted it by the shoulders and held it against herself. The color eddied and shimmered, at once dark and bright. The Balenciaga. It was always the first thing to be unpacked, the first to be packed away again. Even once when she and her mother had to flit at midnight from their unpaid and unpayable bill, leaving most of their belongings behind to clear the debt, the Balenciaga was not abandoned. It was their secret, their shared vice, a symbol of the glorious past, a hope for the future. And now here it was, lying in her hands inert and innocent as a poisoned chalice.

"This one," her mother used to say, touching the stiff lustrous silk with a mixture of pride and caution, as if it might turn and bite her, "this one is for serious business only." She would suck in her breath and shake her head, thinking partly of the dangerously nipped-in waistline, partly of its extraordinary, earth-shattering expensiveness, but mostly of Antonio, who would insist on buying it for her on their one day in Paris, because it was ebony for her gold . . .

Corrie laid the dress back on the bed, suddenly doubtful. Could she, should she wear it? It was a dress for a grown woman, a woman sure of herself and her powers. Even her mother had been in awe of it. She'd only worn it once, but she said once worn it was the sort of dress that entered your dreams and refused to leave.

Well, there was only one way to find out. Corrie

slipped out of her chambermaid's uniform. As she slid the glossy fabric over her head and felt it fall with a delicate chill over her bare shoulders, she had the strange feeling she was crossing some sort of barrier and that life would never be quite the same on the other side. She felt almost giddy as she reached behind to do up the many hidden hooks which closed the back. She reached into the box and lifted out the narrow-strapped lizard-skin shoes. The heels were high, far higher than anything she'd worn before. "One is not a woman," her mother would say didactically, "until one has crossed the Champs Élysées, in the rush hour, in stiletto heels."

So this was what it felt like to be a woman. Precarious. Corrie concentrated hard, drawing herself up to a new balance, feeling the line of elastic tension from her calves to her spine. She took a step and turned to the mirror.

Her eyes opened wide. She stared at herself with a sort of fascination, riveted to the spot. In front of her was a tall, elegant stranger, white shoulders cupped in a dramatic flare of bodice, and narrowing to a waist so tiny it looked impossible. She looked older, slimmer, immeasurably sophisticated. She'd never noticed before how white her skin was, with that warm creamy tinge, the blue-black highlights in the darkness of her hair. She took a step closer. She was the center of a storm, color shimmering off her every movement, intensifying the blue of her eyes with brilliant shadows, now green, now violet, filling them with a catlike glow. She looked fascinating, dangerous, vulnerable yet infinitely poised, a snake secure in her shining skin.

She took a tentative step back, watching the intricate structure of the bodice dip and swell, threatening to reveal but never revealing. She felt the rustle of silk like tiny voices. She turned, experimentally. She could hardly breathe, but she knew that in this dress she was above such mundane considerations. She walked, feeling herself sway from the hips, forced by the dress to walk on air. She glanced back, amazed at the long lovely line of her neck, the dazzling V where the dress plunged to her waist. The back said "I am yours," the front said, "If you can catch me." A treacherous, deceiving dress, a dress that would steal all the light in the room and make it its own. In it she was a matador, a dark angel, a vampire. A chill went down her naked spine. Suddenly she felt renewed doubt. It was there, the authentic, seductive temptation . . . to draw eyes, break hearts, steal souls . . . But what would it lead to? "Serious business," her mother had said.

With an effort Corrie abandoned her reflection. She must concentrate on the job in hand. What she was wearing was just another uniform, a vehicle to get her where she wanted to go, a key to open certain doors. Frowning, she twisted up her hair into a chignon and pinned it securely.

Outside it was already dark. She glanced at her watch, then unfastened it and left it on the dresser. It was time to go. Walking slowly on the unaccustomed heels she slipped down the staff stairs and into the great Front Hall. There was a slight hush as she entered. She looked straight ahead, feeling her heart beat faster. She didn't care if any of the staff recognized her, she had nothing left to lose. As she passed the front desk there was a sigh, a collective outbreathing of envy and appreciation. Her skin prickled with awareness, the unaccustomed weight of her hair slowed the movement of her neck as she inclined her head gracefully. She began to glow, to walk taller. As she approached the revolving doors the doorman hurried to usher her through. She smiled to herself. If he only knew . . .

"Guy."

Guy de Chardonnet looked up warily. They had ordered dinner—Craigellachie smoked salmon and Ogen melon, spring lamb from the salt marshes of the Cotentin, Lauris asparagus, to be accompanied by the best bread in London and fine unsalted Isigny butter—but the note in his companion's voice made him lose his appetite. It was only too familiar.

"It's over, isn't it?"

He looked at her without expression for a long moment. She was a beautiful woman, charming, soignée, exquisitely dressed, the perfect companion. He gave an inward sigh.

"That is for you to say, *chérie*."

His narrowed gray eyes gave nothing away.

"You are impossible!"

Her voice was husky, there were tears in her eyes as she turned her head away. "I don't understand. What's wrong with me?"

He took her hand. "There's nothing wrong with you."

She wrenched her hand away. "Don't you love me?"

"Oh, Victoria . . ."

She bit her lip. "I know. I sound like a lovesick girl. But that is how you make me feel. I hate it, I hate myself, but I can't help it. I'm in love with you, I want you to be in love with me."

He looked away across the immaculate ranks of tables with their delicate pink-tinged napery, the sparkle of crystal and silver. In such perfect surroundings the raw note of her voice was like an assault. He looked longingly out to the river, a network of reflections in the darkness. If only he could disappear, lose himself, drift with the river out to sea . . .

"Guy, please . . ."

"You know what I am." His voice was calm, factual. "I told you in the beginning you should not fall in love with me. I did not want you to fall in love with me."

"Words." She made a helpless gesture. There was a short pause. She played nervously with a silver salt cellar, then looked up, her eyes suspiciously bright. "I would be willing to leave Richard, you know. Just one word—"

"No." His voice was suddenly harsh. "I told you before. Marriage is out of the question."

She flinched. Tears began to trace slowly down her cheeks. He watched her silently.

"You are cruel."

He shrugged.

"I do not mean to be. I simply tell the truth." Suddenly he was tired, with an infinite weariness which made it difficult to speak. It was happening again. How many times would he have to live through this charade, the inevitable third act in an indifferent drama? He heard the hum of conversation around him recede, felt the room darken.

"You don't care about anyone."

"That is true." Abruptly he rose to his feet, signaled to a waiter to bring her coat and settled the light vicuña wool over her shoulders. Automatically Victoria found herself rising to her feet, the touch of his hand under her elbow impersonal as a blow. "You are an observant woman, Victoria. I do not care for anyone. Not even myself."

The emptiness in his ice-gray eyes was chilling. Victoria had a sudden disconcerting memory of his voice in her ear at other moments, murmuring French words full of passion, the touch of those strong slender fingers on her body, the smell of his skin.

"I have hurt you," she whispered. He paused consideringly, unfailingly polite.

"No." His tone was mildly regretful. "You could not hurt me, Victoria."

Looking at him she saw, with a strange easing of the tight band around her heart, that in his way he was trying to be kind. She hadn't lost him after all. He had never been hers to lose.

"I shall miss you, Guy."

He lifted her hand gracefully to his lips. "And I you."

As he escorted her from the River Restaurant to the Front Hall Guy found himself hoping against hope that the platitude would come true. He helped her into the taxi, waiting for the numbness to pass, to feel—what? Pain, regret, loneliness—whatever he was meant to feel.

He watched her taxi draw away into the darkness. She did not look back or wave. After it had disappeared into the Strand he tried to fix her face in his memory, searching for something that would remain. Her eyes were blue, quite lovely in their way. He stood looking out into the darkness, barely conscious of the Head Doorman hovering discreetly at his elbow. In the light he saw without surprise that it had begun to snow. No one can hurt me, he thought with a bleak satisfaction. It is always winter where I am.

He hesitated a moment longer, debating whether to return to his suite. Then he made up his mind. He wanted to forget her pain and his own indifference. Tonight he wanted warmth and light and people around him . . . to remind him he was alive.

CHAPTER THREE

Slowly the house lights dimmed. The murmur of conversation died away instantly to a breathless hush. Darkness and stillness settled over the huge scarlet and gold auditorium, broken only by the glitter of diamonds and the last nervous clearing of throats. The house was packed, from pit to stalls. It was gala night.

High up in her red plush box in the Grand Tier Corrie let out a silent sigh of complete satisfaction. She spared a moment's pity for the box's rightful tenant, who was so wasteful of his assets as to miss a gala first night, and a double bill at that. But she would make good use of them on his behalf. She had no ticket, of course. All the seats in the auditorium had been booked up months in advance. But an air of arrogance tinged with a little boredom, some strategic mingling with the mêlée of patrons returning from the Crush Bar after the intermission and, of course, the Balenciaga, had convinced the usher that it was advisable to let this haughty young lady into the box she claimed was hers rather than risk offending her.

And now . . . the orchestra struck up the first faint strains of the overture, the wide velvet curtains topped with the gold and white royal cypher trembled once then parted with a noiseless swish. What had seemed like hours of waiting out of sight in the corridors and the ladies' cloakroom, while the music of *Cavalleria Rusticana* beckoned almost irresistibly from the auditorium, were now forgotten. It had been worth it. As the guests returned to their appointed places she had been able to isolate the one unoccupied box, and the rest was easy.

The footlights blazed upward, taking her breath away. If there had been one last doubt in her mind before that moment, it was gone now. This is my world, she thought. This is the place where even in the depths of winter, in the dead of night, there is always sunshine. The stage was a brilliant oasis, each color intensified under the spotlight, as the fool in his motley took his place for the prologue. She longed to be down there too, to feel the warmth of the lights on her bare arms, sense the stir of anticipation in the audience. The hundred-headed animal, her mother used to call it, hungry to be fed and caressed until it purred and nuzzled into your hand.

Corrie kicked off her shoes and curled her toes with pure delight. She'd never felt so happy and at home in all her life. This was where she belonged. It was all there, everything she'd always wanted. A golden fantasy, a feast of imagination and romance.

She was so intent on the performance that she didn't hear the click of the door opening behind her. But a cold draft on the back of her neck made her turn around in irritation. A man had entered the box and was standing there motionless in the dark.

"Ssh." She held her finger to her lips imperiously. It was doubtless an usher, looking for somewhere to sit down and smoke a quiet cigarette. Well, it wouldn't be here, the Philistine. She was aware that he hadn't closed the door behind him.

"You may stay—but close the door, for heaven's sake!" He smiled faintly and seated himself on a chair at the back of the box. Satisfied, she turned her back on him and plunged back into the performance. The prologue, half warning, half lament, sung with bitter intensity by the crippled fool, was nearing its end. It sent a shiver down her spine. Of course she knew now that *Pagliacci* wasn't a great opera, or even a good one. It was clumsy and coarsely constructed. But it had power inside the clumsy framework, a hurtling, onward rush to its terrible conclusion which was irresistible. It was an opera for people of flesh and blood, direct, earthy and full of shameless Neapolitan emotion. It wouldn't be despised, it wouldn't be dismissed. Critics might reject it, but give it an audience and it came triumphantly alive, conquering time with its combination of passion and pathos and sheer drama. Its message was raw and simple:

"We are men like you, made only of flesh and bone, breathing the same air of the same orphan world . . ."

Love is real, the music said, and tears are real, and this story I am telling you is only for one night, but we will share it before time carries us all away.

The prologue was over. Shouting, laughing, whistling, heedless as children of what was to come, I Pagliacci, the Players, poured onto the stage. Corrie leaned forward over the edge of the box, drinking in the fanfare of sound from an out-of-tune trumpet, the heart-shaking beat of a big old drum. She was filled with a wild exhilaration, she could have danced and whistled with them on the stage. There, pretty as a flower in her traditional costume, was Nedda, the peasant girl who would act out the role of Columbine in the play-within-a-play performed in the village square, and Canio, her bullying husband, in his Pierrot black and white, and her gentle lover Silvio in his Harlequin cloak and mask . . .

A second shiver ran down Corrie's spine. Despite what her Harlequin had said, she knew she wouldn't be here, she'd have missed her chance altogether, if it hadn't been for him. As the familiar music released its fragrance into the auditorium, conjuring up magical warm nights and light-filled days, she felt an enormous rush of gratitude. How odd that those two strangers—Harlequin and long-dead Leoncavallo, the composer of *Pagliacci*—had saved her life.

For there was a difference between living and existing. Existing was what she'd done after her mother's death. There had been only one thought in her mind—to escape. She'd had no plans. She'd simply walked out one winter morning, hitched her way to the nearest seaport and boarded a cargo ship heading south. But she'd been discovered. She remembered with hallucinatory vividness standing in the bursar's cramped untidy office on board, waiting for him to radio the port authorities, like a prisoner awaiting execution. On his desk had been a tall cut-glass bottle, with an inch of green absinthe in the bottom—such a vivid un-English green, the green of grass on the other side of the fence.

And then, out of desperation, was born her great idea. Remorselessly she emptied the bottle down the sluice, snatched up paper and pencil from the bursar's desk. It was her last chance, she knew it with an instinctive wisdom. There had to be someone, somewhere in the whole wide world, who would hear her call for help.

But what to write? Of all the languages she knew, none of them would convey what she was feeling. Words were not enough. Quickly, pressing hard with the pencil in her urgency, she scrawled on the torn paper two lines of music from *Pagliacci*, from Columbine's famous aria:

"Vanno laggiu verso un paese strano
Che sognan forse e che cercano invan."
"Birds journey toward a strange faraway land,
A land they've dreamed of, but will never find."

Beneath, in clear schoolgirl capitals, she printed her name and address. Quickly, as she heard the bursar's steps returning, she sealed the bottle, unfastened a porthole and hurled it far out to sea.

All the way back to her prison, she thought of her bottle, bobbing on the warm tide of the Gulf Stream, carried slowly south. Like the birds flying into the sun, it might never reach its destination. But she had made her small gesture of faith, she had tried. Her belief in magic was restored.

Winter passed into spring, a late cold spring preceding a cool, cloudy summer. Last thing at night, before she went to sleep, Corrie thought of her bottle, glowing like a jewel on the dark night tide.

That autumn, on a wild wet evening, she was summoned to the housemistress's study. There was a parcel waiting for her—an unauthorized parcel, bulky, heavy and covered with French stamps. The older woman's eyes presumed the worst as Corrie sliced through string and brown paper to reveal—an absinthe bottle. The housemistress's disapproval deepened into horror. True, the bottle contained no absinthe, but even so . . .

"What a distasteful joke." The housemistress picked up the bottle between thumb and forefinger, ready to dispose of it.

"No."

Surprising herself, Corrie took the bottle firmly from her hands. Fragments of sand still clung to the cork. There was something inside it, a coil of pale blue paper. Inside that, neatly rolled, two tickets for an evening performance of *Pagliacci* at Covent Garden. Across the face of one, "*From Harlequin.*"

Of course she wasn't allowed to go. The hours, they said, little knowing of her midnight picnics under the cypresses, were much too late, and in any case she couldn't accept a gift from someone she didn't know. Corrie didn't protest. There was no point in trying to explain that Columbine's call for help had been answered so perfectly, so completely, that mere introductions were irrelevant. The tickets were returned to the theater. But with the money, defiantly, Corrie bought a cassette recording of *Pagliacci*. Listening to it that evening was a quiet revelation. Her unknown benefactor had shown her the way out of her prison. She was no longer alone.

Methodically, careful not to arouse suspicion at school, Corrie set about finding Harlequin. With the remainder of her ticket money she placed an advertisement in the personal columns of *France-Soir* and *France-Dimanche:*

"*Cher Harlequin. Votre Columbine anglaise vous remercie de tout son coeur.*" And indeed she did thank Harlequin with all her heart.

Two months later a letter with a Paris postmark arrived for her. No one queried a mere letter, for what danger could a letter be? It was short, guarded. She didn't mind. She wrote back to the box number indicated, luxuriating in the chance to write French, the language of her childhood, to someone who would understand what she had to say. For she never doubted that he would understand. He was Harlequin.

Gradually, over the years, that anonymous Paris box number became as familiar to her as her own name. She forgot that there had ever been a time in her life when she hadn't known Harlequin. Theirs was the perfect relationship. Because they'd never met, there were no barriers between them. He'd never seen her as an awkward ten-year-old child, adrift in a world she didn't understand. The girls at school might find her difficult and aloof and irredeemably foreign, but never Harlequin. With him she could be the person she wanted to be, aspired to be—warm, beautiful, full of music and laughter, someone to be loved. He understood her longing for independence, her secret, overwhelming ambition, because he had felt the same way. The pulse of sympathy beat noiselessly behind every word they wrote to each other. Nothing more tangible than paper would pass her guardians' eagle eye, so she sent him her thoughts, her fears, her poems, and he sent her in return a chain of paper clowns, so delicately cut they floated on the slightest breeze.

And that wasn't all. Out of nowhere he conjured up an ideal world for her to live in, an imaginary Paradise called Uscady, where the sun always shone. Uscady had its own language, its own rules and landscape. Its people never spoke when they could sing, never rode if they could walk. Red was their favorite color, chocolate their favorite food. They always built their houses on the highest possible point, and carved hearts and flowers and mermaids above the door. They were the oldest and wisest people in the world—they sailed to America before Columbus, made friends with the Eskimos, dined off tables made from the backbones of whales. They had no words for heaven or hell, only Paradise—rolling hills covered with golden gorse, oak and chestnut forests, mountains small enough to climb in a day, trout streams and maize fields, vineyards and apple orchards, and always sunshine. A lost world, Arcady and El Dorado and the only place to be.

And this, her very first live opera, was a province of Uscady. She'd known the score by heart ever since she could walk, had played her recording more times than she could remember, but that was nothing compared with a live performance. The music reached out to her across the years, itself a message in a bottle, launched hopefully into the indifferent sea, saying to anyone who could understand, "I am here, I am alive too, you are not alone." It made her one with the other strangers below her in the darkness, united by the same warm Gulf Stream. It told her, inside everyone there is buried treasure. Every stranger's face is a new chance, a new beginning. Some things can only be written, some things can only be sung, some things only a stranger can understand.

"La commedia é finita!" Nedda lay dead in the arms of her dead lover. Above them Canio, his face a contorted mask behind the white Pierrot paint, stood frozen, the dagger still in his hand. For a long, heart-stopping moment the audience on stage and in the darkened auditorium died too, swept by the cynical gaze of the crippled Fool. What did you expect, said that long silent look, a happy ending? You are more fools than I am. This is no world for Harlequin and Columbine . . .

Then abruptly, the music disappeared as if it had never been, the curtain fell. Corrie rested her head on the plush-covered balcony and cried.

As the curtain fell on the last encore and the house lights went on she remembered her uninvited visitor. She turned around, expecting to find he'd gone to do his duty in the rest of the house, but to her surprise he was still there, watching her with amused indulgence.

She drew herself up, conscious of the tears still wet on her face, and rose to her feet. She searched in her narrow bag but of course she hadn't a handkerchief. The man was still watching her from the shadows.

"Here." He stepped forward into the light and with a sickening jolt she recognized him. It was the man from the Maria Callas suite. She recoiled.

"Don't worry, it's perfectly clean."

Now she realized he was holding out a white linen handkerchief, still with that faintly amused expression on his face.

Glad of the opportunity to collect herself, she accepted the handkerchief and blotted her cheeks. The fine linen smelled of pine and expensive cologne. She looked up to find his expression hadn't changed. Clearly he hadn't recognized her as the maid he'd accused of theft that morning.

Some impulse of pure devilment entered her then. So . . . he didn't remember her. For all he knew he had destroyed her life, yet her face hadn't been worth remembering. What did she matter to him, after all? A mere maid, an underling, a cipher. Ciphers don't have faces. She drew herself up to her full height and glanced at him coquettishly under her lashes. He was arrogant, superior, unfeeling—but she'd make sure he remembered her this time . . .

"Thank you." As she handed back his handkerchief she used her best, throatiest, whipped cream voice. It was a strangely intimate moment. He pocketed the handkerchief and moved into the full light. Seeing him clearly for the first time she realized that he was extraordinarily handsome. The severity of evening dress suited him, accentuating his rich man's pallor, the crisp darkness of his hair, those disturbingly light eyes. His good looks confirmed her instinctive dislike. Handsome men were not to be trusted, they were vain, shallow and treacherous. He was eyeing her with a similarly appraising glance. She saw him take in the perfection of the Balenciaga with a glint of appreciation and her contempt deepened. He was so easily misled. A change of dress, a different location, and he was fooled. As if mere packaging mattered. Harlequin would never have been so blind.

"Well, I must say this is a very pleasant surprise."

His voice had none of the clipped coldness he'd used to a servant. It was low and deep, with the unusual clarity of diction peculiar to a foreigner.

More of a surprise than you could imagine, she thought wickedly. She inclined her head. He bowed.

"Guy de Chardonnet, at your service." She ignored the hint of sarcasm in his tone. She could afford to. She had the advantage over him. The very intensity of her dislike gave her a buoyant sensation of security and power.

"Corrie Modena."

He nodded, the merest inclination of the head.

"I'm so glad you decided to take advantage of my box, Miss Modena." Now his tone was silky smooth. Her scorn doubled. Any man so musically insensitive as to arrive at a gala performance of *Pagliacci* halfway through the first act was beneath contempt.

"I have a box of my own." She lied unashamedly, the actress in her rising to the occasion. She was as good as he was, had as much right to be here. "It's just that yours has a better view."

"I see." She could tell that he hadn't believed her. Somehow his disbelief irritated her even more than if she'd been telling the truth. He smiled again, that mocking half-smile. Against her better judgment she tried to convince him.

"It's true . . . why else would I be here?"

One eyebrow lifted.

"To meet me, of course."

It took her breath away. The sheer, unshakable vanity of the man.

"I suppose it happens to you all the time." Her tone was as acid as she could make it, but he was unperturbed. He paused consideringly.

"No, not all the time. But frequently."

He turned gracefully to the door and opened it wide.

"Well, Miss Modena, shall we go?"

She hesitated, then swept through the doorway as haughtily as she could manage. She was uneasily conscious of his eyes on the bare skin of her back as she preceded him down the corridor, forced to walk slowly because of her high heels. She threw up her head, determined to make the best of it, and glad that her flushed cheeks weren't visible.

The entrance foyer was deserted apart from the ushers. One stepped forward with alacrity when he saw her companion, reserving for herself that special brand of indifference accorded to a mere possession.

"Monsieur de Chardonnet . . . Allow me." The usher hastened to open the door, still studiously avoiding meeting Corrie's eyes. Her companion acknowledged his attentions with a brief nod. Corrie's blood began to boil. He was getting the full star treatment, but he didn't deserve it. What did he know or care about opera? Even *Pagliacci* hadn't brought a flicker of emotion to those cold, pale eyes. He was dead from the heart up.

A rush of cold air greeted them as they emerged out onto the pavement opposite Bow Street Magistrates' Court. Corrie felt a pang of doubt. Inside the opera house's private world she'd enjoyed her masquerade, but now, in the amber light of the street lamps, the tall figure beside her seemed only too real and substantial. Something cold touched her bare arm and she looked up in astonishment. Snow . . . in April? It couldn't be. But she'd forgotten the vagaries of an English spring. Unseasonable but unmistakable, icy flakes came drifting singly from the night sky to brush her skin with ghostly kisses. She shivered.

"I will see you to your car." His tone was coolly polite.

"That won't be necessary," she answered superbly. "I haven't got one."

His mouth twitched in the first sign of genuine amusement she'd seen him show. He touched her elbow with a light yet somehow possessive pressure. She shivered again and told herself it was because of the snowflakes melting on her shoulders.

"In that case, I will give you a lift. Where are you staying?"

She hesitated, then her resident devil and the infuriatingly mocking glint in his eyes made up her mind.

"The Savoy, of course." As soon as it was out she regretted it, though the faint flicker of surprise on his face was almost worth it.

"Of course. Come, I will drive you there."

"No, no . . ." With an effort she detached her arm from his. "That won't be necessary." Why hadn't she thought of somewhere else—the Ritz, Claridge's—anywhere except the Savoy. Playing for effect was one thing, but the consequences were quite another. To arrive in the company of Guy de Chardonnet and be publicly exposed as an errant chambermaid would be humiliating beyond words. "I'm . . . I'm expecting someone." She improvised wildly, searching her mind for suitable excuses. "Someone is coming to meet me. I have an appointment."

His eyebrows rose. "I see." She felt an unwanted blush rising to her face. It didn't sound good, not at all. It was nearly midnight, and hardly the area for a respectable young girl to be waiting alone. But what did she care for the opinion of a man like Guy de Chardonnet? Let him think what he liked.

"Well, if you insist . . ."

"I insist," she answered firmly, with as much assurance as she could muster. Frowning, he turned on his heel and walked away. She breathed a sigh of relief and waited till he was around the corner before hurrying away down a sidestreet. The last thing she wanted was to be arrested for loitering outside the opera house. With luck she would find a taxi to take her back to the Savoy before M. de Chardonnet, with his cynical gaze, was there to see through her charade.

But there wasn't a taxi in sight, and the snow was falling thicker all the time. After a few hundred yards of slow progress in her high heels she stopped, looked around quickly and removed them. Carefully she rolled down her silk stockings, pulled them off and stuffed them into her bag. Barefoot she made much better progress.

Within a minute she had forgotten her encounter. The snow was oddly beautiful as it fell against the amber light and silently kissed the ground. She swung her shoes in her hand and gave a small skip of jubilation. Her head was full of music, the cold didn't matter. She turned into the Strand. A passing pedestrian on the other side of the road looked up in astonishment as he saw her.

"You'll catch your death!" he shouted.

"I doubt it," she sang out in reply. Her veins were full of liquid sunlight, she fully expected to live forever.

She was still a few hundred yards from the side road leading to the staff wing when she sensed a car crawling noiselessly along the curb behind her. She tightened her lips and kept on walking. She hadn't far to go, but her innocent pleasure in this midnight adventure was ruined. The car continued to follow her, an irritating shadow on the edges of her vision.

"Go away." It ignored her. How infuriating. She had just as much right as anyone else to walk where she chose, when she chose, but simply because she happened to be a woman it seemed she was fair game for harassment. The snow was coming faster now, in whipping flurries that got in her eyes. She blinked furiously but went on walking. If this obtrusive stranger didn't stop following her soon he'd have the surprise of his life.

"Wait." A man's voice, of course. Her eyes narrowed. He hadn't gotten the message, whoever he was. And now he had the temerity to address her. She stopped and stepped right up to the curb. The car halted, its engine purring noiselessly. She saw that it was a long silver gray Mercedes and felt faintly mollified. At least the Balenciaga continued to attract the right sort of clientele.

"Look." She spoke clearly and loudly. "Stop following me, whoever you are. If you don't, I shall scream for a policeman."

Without waiting for a reply she stalked off. Out of the corner of her eye she saw the car start up again and follow her. Her heart sank. The last thing she wanted was to arrive back at the Savoy with an entourage. She was in enough trouble as it was. She sighed. She should never have taken off her shoes, it obviously gave the wrong impression.

She stopped, took a deep breath, then turned to face her pursuer. She stepped over to the open window, bent down, smiled sweetly and launched into the speech she'd been preparing. She was glad to see that she hadn't forgotten her training. The choice Mediterranean oaths rose to her lips with gratifying fluency. She covered the ground thoroughly, starting with sonorous Greek, adding a dash of Italian and a good measure of richly descriptive French, and finishing off with some engaging English schoolgirl frankness. When she'd finished she was pleased with herself. From the car there was a stunned silence. Then the rear door opened, surprising her because she'd addressed her monologue to the driver. A man stepped out. Her cheeks went scarlet. It was Guy de Chardonnet. And, infuriatingly unmoved after her outburst, he was clapping his hands lightly in an ironic imitation of applause.

Suddenly she felt about six years old, her shoes in her hand, as if she'd been walking on the beach. What must he think of her, coatless and barefoot in the snow? Where, now, was her sophisticated façade?

At last he broke the silence.

"I take it you have, er . . . canceled your appointment?"

Her head went up. So, he was determined to continue the charade. Well, she was game.

"That's no business of yours!"

"Of course." His tone was irritatingly bland, as if he saw nothing unusual in talking to a barefoot girl in the middle of a snow flurry. "I simply thought you might like a lift after all."

"Oh." For a long moment she was at a loss for words. The contrast between his meticulous politeness and her performance of a few minutes ago made her ears burn. What could she do now? To make matters worse the snow was settling in a white down over the pavement and her feet were getting very cold. She was uneasily aware of the impression she must make, barefoot and coatless, dampened hair clinging to the sides of her neck and face.

"No, thank you." She narrowed her eyes against the flakes and lifted her head. She had no choice. "I prefer to walk."

To give him credit, he didn't attempt to dissuade her.

"In that case, I shall accompany you."

Before she could protest he signaled over his shoulder and the car, as if by magic, slid away from the curb. Of course—a chauffeur. She watched in dismay as it disappeared down the turning leading to the Savoy. It was too late now, with a vengeance. The man beside her seemed to sense her dismay and looked at her curiously.

"With your permission, of course."

"I can't stop you, it's a public sidewalk." She knew she sounded rude, but she couldn't help it.

Side by side they walked along the sidewalk in silence, Corrie taking small steps in a desperate attempt to gain time to think. Just before they reached the Savoy entrance she halted.

"Excuse me." She turned against the wall and slipped her bare feet back into her shoes. Her feet were numb, the shoes could hardly hurt her now.

"Tell me . . ." Her companion's tone was conversational. "Purely as a matter of interest, why did you take off your shoes?"

"Because they hurt, that's why." It looked as if she was going to be unmasked very soon, so what did a little frankness matter? To her astonishment he gave a deep spontaneous chuckle.

"What are you laughing at?" she asked him suspiciously.

"I don't know." His tone was faintly surprised. "I suppose because none of the women I know would take off her shoes in the street just because they hurt."

"In that case you must know some very stupid women," she replied tartly.

He smiled at her, unmoved. His eyes rested lazily on

her bare feet, grimy with London dirt and blue with cold. "Stupidity in a woman is not unbecoming."

Indignation left her speechless. Before she could summon up a fitting reply he turned to face her.

"Are you hungry?"

Such a simple question . . . She thought furiously. He could hardly be aware of its ramifications.

"Are you inviting me out to dinner?"

"Hardly. All restaurants worth considering will have closed their kitchens by now. No, I was hoping you would dine with me in my suite."

"In your suite?"

A slow smile broke over Corrie's face. Guy de Chardonnet studied her expression under the lamplight. There was some nuance here that eluded him. He was intrigued, challenged. He usually found women easy to read, but this girl was such an odd mixture of maturity and innocence, alternating like quicksilver between feline poise and childish gaucherie. Was it an act? He couldn't tell. At the opera house, given her appearance, the dress, so indubitably Balenciaga, the unconscious throwaway elegance with which she wore it, he had known at once what kind of girl she was. But now, with her bare feet and the snow in her hair, he wasn't so sure. She was such a baffling combination of practicality and abandon, he almost found himself hoping she would accept his invitation. She wasn't his type, it was true, she was too unfinished for that, but there was something about her that intrigued and provoked him—the way her dark hair grew in a point on the nape of her slender neck, the rich curve of her mouth, the curiously arresting slope of her heavy-lidded eyes.

"Are you making a pass at me?" Her voice had a challenging edge.

He frowned. Perhaps his invitation had been a mistake after all. Such clumsiness, such childish vanity. Passes were for boys, not grown men.

"I doubt it. I am booked on the early flight to Paris. And in any case, I prefer blondes." She returned his gaze with more composure than he'd expected, clearly unaffected by his directness.

"That's good. I prefer gentlemen."

"Indeed." His eyes widened just a fraction, then narrowed again. There was a certain attraction in her outspokenness. He had a few hours to kill, she might be a diversion. "Shall we go in?" He offered her his arm.

Corrie hesitated only a moment. The idea of having dinner in the suite she'd been thrown out of in disgrace only that morning had an almost irresistible appeal. And she had to admit she was hungry, she'd missed lunch and dinner, and music always gave her a raging appetite. But even hunger counted for nothing beside the dazzling, heaven-sent opportunity that now presented itself. She calculated swiftly. He could hardly have had time to report her misdemeanor of this morning before leaving for the opera, since the supervisor never returned before 8 p.m. So if, somehow, using all the wiles at her command and more besides, she could keep him occupied between now and the time his plane left for Paris, she'd be in the clear.

She eyed her escort. Of course, there was a risk involved. A man like Guy de Chardonnet was used to having what he wanted when he wanted it, if not before. He was spoiled and arrogant and unbearably confident about his effect on women. But she could handle him. Armored by dislike, forewarned by their previous meeting, what did she have to fear?

She took his arm. Together they swept up through the arcade, under the Savoy sign, now glowing a luminous green, and through the mahogany doors. She ignored the frantic beating of her heart as they entered, hoping her flushed cheeks would be put down to the cold. At any moment one of the staff might recognize her, but she had to take that chance.

The Front Hall looked different—mellow, dimly lit, a secret cave. She concentrated on an air of bored indifference and on not catching anyone's eye. For an eternity she waited while Guy collected his key, realizing as she did so that the same curious process she'd experienced at the opera house was back in operation. For some reason, because she was his companion, his accessory, she was invisible. People were so dazzled by his money that they barely saw her. Guy returned, escorted her smoothly to the elevator. Wearing the same cloak of invisibility she stepped in. She felt strange, breathless, as if she were being spirited off to some other world. Within minutes they were at the door of his suite.

The curtains were drawn in readiness, a glowing fire lit in the gray marble fireplace. Instinctively she moved closer to it. She wanted to feel real again, not an invisible wraith. Money doesn't talk, she thought. It whispers. Firelight flickered over her face, she felt the dampness of the snow on her arms and shoulders.

"Don't you ever wear a coat?" inquired Guy.

"I haven't got one. I don't like them."

She shrugged off his quizzical look. He was so conventional, so sure that his way was the only way to live. But she and Harlequin knew better. If you had the courage never to wear a coat the whole world was open to you—and everyone knew gatecrashers had more fun.

"What a strange girl you are." The expression in his eyes had changed. He looked like a hunter, considering detachedly how best to approach a new kind of quarry. She refused to acknowledge a pang of nervousness. Instead she walked away to the window, uneasily conscious of the swish of damp silk against her bare legs, the slip of her bare feet inside the lizard-skin heels.

"What are you thinking of?" His voice was close, he was standing by her shoulder. Against her will she was disturbed by his nearness, his tallness, the barely perceptible warmth of his shoulder, one just touching hers. And there was something else that tempted as well as provoked her, a sense of distance, withdrawal, a self-control so deep that it was almost instinctive. It made her want to surprise him, annoy him, do anything to melt the distance between them. Fortunately her mother had taught her well. She knew that men with that particular brand of fatal aloofness were the most dangerous. Everywhere he went people would jump to do his bidding, women would flutter like moths against a shade, simply because in some deep, inaccessible part of him he didn't notice them at all. But she wouldn't fall for his spell. She knew better. She had seen the real Guy de Chardonnet, she'd had the valet's eye view.

"I was thinking . . . it's colder in here, looking out, then it was outside." She shivered. "I'm glad I don't live up here."

He looked surprised. "Why is that?"

"It's too beautiful, too peaceful. Too far away from all the other people." High in the darkness, on the top floors of the Savoy, they were light years away from the ordinary world, isolated in a sort of space capsule. Time didn't exist. If they so chose, they could live there for decades and never see another human face.

"I don't particularly want to be with other people."

Of course. Ordinary people wouldn't interest him, they couldn't be turned to his own advantage. And they might, unwittingly, discover his secret—that he was made of stone.

"Then why are you with me?" She faced him abruptly, challenging him with her eyes. His gaze met hers. A small spark—maybe anger, maybe surprise—glowed momentarily in those ice-gray eyes. He took a half step toward her. Tension crackled in the room. I can handle him, she told herself staunchly. But for some reason her feet wouldn't obey her when she told them to move away. She was rooted to the spot, mesmerized. Behind her she was aware of the snow softly patting the window, the silence. I can handle him, she thought, the words slow as frozen water in her mind. But can I handle myself?

CHAPTER FOUR

"I simply prefer not to eat alone." The sound of his voice, cool, impassive, restored her to reality. The room came back to life again, with the comfortable crackle of coal in the grate, the flicker of light on the paneled walls. She felt her breath leaving her in a long sigh of relief. What had happened to her? She'd felt strange, almost faint. Still, it was over now. It must have been hunger.

"What are we having for dinner?"

"Whatever you like." He'd retreated into himself, polite, remote, faintly bored. She knew his words were no idle boast. The Savoy prided itself on serving guests whatever they wanted, at any hour of the day or night. Beluga caviar for breakfast, champagne for tea, lobster at dawn—she had all the world's delicacies on offer. Here was her golden opportunity to make up for the years of institutional meals, to order something wild and wonderful and outrageously expensive, any one of the exotic dishes she'd seen being ferried up to the private suites, steaming and aromatic under their silver lids.

But strangely, now the time had come, she couldn't make up her mind.

"What are you going to have?" It was a silly woman's ruse, a pathetic evasion, and she felt ashamed of herself immediately.

"Whatever you have." There was a gleam of mischief in his eyes. He was playing with her, testing her, waiting for her to reveal ignorance or weakness. His challenge restored her presence of mind.

"In that case I'll stop trying to impress you and have what I like."

"And what might that be?"

She closed her eyes, remembering the perfumed moonlit nights of her childhood. Yes, that was the menu, the perfect feast for all seasons. Crisply, confidently, like a housewife with a familiar shopping list, she began to recite:

"Two loaves of bread, French. Two bars of bitter chocolate, Swiss, minimum fifty percent cocoa solids. A pound of fresh apricots. A dish of olives." There was a short silence. She opened her eyes. He was trying valiantly to preserve his impassive mask.

"Black?" His voice was elaborately noncommittal.

"What?"

"The olives."

"No. Green." She smiled defiantly.

"And to drink?"

"Oh." She and her mother had drunk Perrier water, pretending it was champagne. This was her opportunity for the real thing at last. "A magnum of Bollinger. '75 will do."

Within minutes the floor waiter had delivered her order on a silver trolley. Two golden-crusted loaves wrapped in a linen napkin, two bars of chocolate, tiny glowing apricots in a silver bowl, a jar of olives and champagne packed in ice.

Her host looked down at the feast, his face a rich study of conflicting emotions.

"I hope you like chocolate? Most people do."

"It's some time since I had any. I'm not entirely sure."

Corrie shook her head pityingly. He was a lost soul, that was for sure. Still this was her feast and she was determined to enjoy it. He owed her that much at least. She took one of the linen napkins and spread it on the carpeted floor.

"M. de Chardonnet . . ." She gestured ceremoniously across the napkin. "Allow me to demonstrate the correct way of consuming bread and chocolate. Here—

you break off a piece of bread, like so, and a piece of chocolate, like so, you place the latter securely on the former, and you eat it." She chewed luxuriously. "Mmm. Nothing could be nicer." The texture of bread and chocolate together was extraordinary, almost sinful. The fur of the apricots was a small, sensual shock. If she closed her eyes, she was almost sure she would hear goats' bells on a scented hillside, smell thyme and marjoram and wild mint. She handed him a portion, challenging him with her eyes. She hid a faint twinge of admiration. He ate well, like a Frenchman, decisively. Perhaps he wasn't such a lost soul after all.

She looked up to see him watching her through narrowed eyes, his expression unreadable.

"You're a strange girl, Miss Modena."

"So you said. It's fortunate for you that I'm not a blonde. You might never recover."

She was pleased to see a flicker of surprise in those expressionless eyes. She had his interest now. Hiding her triumph, she continued serenely to devour the apricots, pausing only to inform him that he had chocolate on his shirt front. He took refuge in uncorking the champagne.

She drained her glass at a gulp. "That's very good."

"I should hope so." His eyes widened as she tossed back another glass. Another element was added to the layers of dizzying taste explosions on her tongue. The sweetness of the chocolate, the tartness of the apricots, the smooth saltiness of the olives.

"Tell me . . ." He was visibly intrigued. "How did you come to compose this meal?"

"It's easy." She gestured expansively with her glass. "You do it like an opera. You simply leave out all the dull bits, take the rest and mix it all together. It can't fail."

"It sounds like a philosophy." His tone was dry. "Don't you ever get indigestion."

"No, I don't believe in it." She continued blithely on her way, alternating olives and apricots and drafts of champagne with riotous abandon. She was beginning to enjoy herself. "What would you have ordered?"

"I don't know. Something light, I expect. An omelette, soup. Vodka."

"I thought so." She nodded sagely. "I could tell you didn't like opera."

His eyebrows went up. Clearly he didn't know whether to be amused or offended. But it didn't matter to her how he felt, as long as she succeeded in holding his attention.

"You were late." She shook her head reprovingly.

"True." He shrugged, the spark of interest fading from his eyes. "I'm a busy man."

"Too busy to live?" Her voice was sweet, but her words went home. His head lifted, his eyes narrowed.

"I didn't say that." He spoke coldly, irritation lending his voice a cutting edge.

"Have another olive." As she'd hoped, the abrupt change of subject threw him off his stride.

"What? No, thank you."

"There you are!" She allowed herself one small, triumphant smile. "That shows you're not really alive. You only ate one olive." She threw him a pitying glance. "You can't stop at one olive and be truly alive."

"Really." His drawl was weighted with sarcasm but she ignored it.

"And there's something else, that proves my point conclusively."

"What might that be?" His question was silky smooth, but she knew she'd touched him on the raw.

"You didn't cry."

"Don't be ridiculous." He gave a short laugh. "Grown men don't cry."

"They should." She spoke with authority. "They used to, all the time. Walter Raleigh did, everyone did." She looked down at the ruins of the feast. She noticed for the first time that her head was swimming, her vision slightly blurred. The champagne. Maybe she'd drunk too much, too quickly . . . "My little impatient friend," that's what Harlequin had called her. She had a feeling he wouldn't exactly approve of what she was doing now, no matter how worthy the cause. She felt suddenly saddened, with a deep, hopeless sadness that had nothing to do with the champagne. "People used to do a lot of things they don't do anymore." She spoke softly, half to herself, barely conscious of the man seated opposite her. "Sing out loud. Dance in the streets. Talk to strangers." She looked up at him again. "That's why you have to like opera. It's all singing and dancing and talking to strangers."

"I take it you are an expert?" His tone was drier than the vintage champagne. It was no use, she couldn't reach him. "My dear young lady, your theory is all very well, but there is opera and opera. If you knew anything at all about the genre, you would realize that tonight's performance was hardly worthy of such passion."

"What do you mean?"

He shrugged. "Simply that, as performances go, it was of indifferent quality. Hardly memorable. If you had seen as many *Pagliacci*s as I have—"

"Maybe you've seen too many!" His words stung her out of her reverie, cleared her head as effectively as a deluge of cold water. She'd almost weakened, almost treated him like another human being, a stranger like herself. Now she was glad she hadn't.

He inclined his head politely.

"Perhaps you have consumed too many olives."

For a moment she was at a loss for words. She looked down, to avoid that insufferable, mocking glance. He'd turned the tables on her very neatly. But she wasn't beaten yet. She looked up, her eyes wide, her mouth curved in a deceptively innocent smile.

"Still, I enjoyed them both . . . *Pagliacci and* the olives. Don't you wish you could say the same?"

"That is your privilege." His voice was clipped. "The privilege, if I may say so, of youth and inexperience."

"I see." She cocked her head to one side, fixed him with an earnest inquiring gaze. "Do you think M. de Chardonnet, that if I try very, very hard, I may learn not to enjoy anything at all?"

She saw by the muscle working in his jaw that her shot had hit home.

"You may at least learn to distinguish between mediocrity and true excellence." He was clearly maintaining his good temper with an effort.

"You are a perfectionist, M. de Chardonnet."

He inclined his head. "Discrimination is not a crime, Miss Modena."

"No? Then perhaps you would share with me the benefits of your experience." Her expression was pure innocence, her eyes limpid. "What exactly do you look for in an opera, M. de Chardonnet?"

He eyed her suspiciously.

"I look for balance, control, judgment. A certain poise between the extremes. Something that transcends life, touches eternity. Something of lasting value."

"There, I knew it." She pounced on his carefully considered words with catlike triumph. "Music doesn't last. You can't hang on to it. One moment it's there, then it's gone forever. And opera isn't about balance and control and judgment. It's about love and death and loyalty and children." She leapt suddenly to her feet, snatched up the vase of white narcissi from the table. "See? Look at these. I expect you think these are beautiful? Well, they're not. They're nothing. They're dead. They only look as if they're alive. Oh, they'll last, much longer than if they'd been left growing wild. They'll be kept in here, at an even temperature of sixty-eight degrees, and they'll have their water changed night and morning, and they'll last. But it's just a pretense, a kind of cheating. They're not what flowers are all about. They've probably never even seen the outside air. Look, they're all the same size, all the same color. They're not beautiful, they're just convenient." She set the vase down with such force that water slopped out onto the table. "They're so goddamned perfect they might as well be made of plastic!" She plucked a bloom out of the vase, snapped it ruthlessly in half, let it fall to the floor. "I bet that's how you like an opera to be. So perfect that it doesn't remind you of real life at all." She kicked the bloom viciously with the toe of her high heel. "Well, I don't. I'd rather feel something, anything, than nothing at all."

The silence stretched. She became aware that she was breathing hard, that her face was flushed. But he seemed unmoved. Only his eyes glittered, resting for a troubling instant on her mouth.

"You are an idealist, Miss Modena. You have no discipline."

"You have no faith." She spoke scornfully, trying to hide the uneven fluttering of her heart.

He smiled, a small, acid smile.

"I wonder how long Covent Garden and opera houses like it would survive on faith alone? You say I don't like opera. It so happens that without the very considerable financial assistance provided by myself and other wealthy patrons there wouldn't be an opera for . . . idealists such as yourself to enjoy."

"Money!" She spat out the word with venom. Now at last they'd touched on what he really cared about, the only currency that interested him. Oh, how she hated money and its insidious power! It was money that had separated her mother from Antonio, money that had imprisoned herself in a cold, alien world when she could have been running barefoot on the sand. Money always knew best. Money belonged to the Underworld, but it sent out its black shadowy tentacles into the sunlight, killing everything it touched. "Money." She put all the scorn of which she was capable into the word. "It's always the same story. People like you think everything boils down to money in the end. But it's not true. Music can't be bought and sold. Even you can't own music!"

"Yes I can. So can you—if you condescend to buy a ticket." His mocking allusion brought a tinge of pink to her cheeks.

"I suppose that includes people too?" Her voice was contemptuous.

"Yes, people can be bought and owned." He was

provoked at last. Bitterness filled his voice with cold fire. "You should know that."

"What do you mean?"

He shrugged. "I am tired of this charade. You have seen fit to speak plainly, now it's my turn. I doubt very much, Miss Modena, if you are as independent as you seem. I suspect that both the dress on your back and your rooms here at the Savoy are supplied and paid for by someone else."

"What?" She felt her face go scarlet. He forestalled her.

"There's no need to protest. I am a man of the world. I have no objections to a woman in your position. In France it is a perfectly respectable career, to be the mistress of a rich man. And perfectly reasonable for such a woman, given the opportunity, to attempt to exchange her position for a better one."

Corrie was speechless. He smiled, clearly enjoying her discomfort.

"I am not a fool, Miss Modena. It was clear to me from the first that you were in the market for a new patron. Why else should you be in my box, why else should you be so reluctant to have me accompany you home?"

With an effort she controlled her simmering indignation.

"Didn't it occur to you, M. de Chardonnet, that I might, just possibly might, be there to listen to the music?"

He sighed, looked her slowly up and down through heavy-lidded eyes. "Frankly, my dear, no." His voice held an infuriating note of condescension. "It's not your fault. You did your best. It's simply that you selected as a quarry someone who has been hunted by women of your type many times before. Now, I'm afraid I must call an end to our . . . musical discussion, much as I have enjoyed it. It is late, and I have many things to attend to before I leave."

There was a long pause. Guy watched the girl's face. Clearly, she was thinking hard. At last she looked up.

"So I take it the answer is no?"

He shook his head tolerantly.

"Difficult though it is to refuse a lady, I'm afraid I must decline." Initially she'd intrigued him, with her protestations, her novel ensemble, but now he was glad that she'd proved so combative. It would be a mistake ever to become involved with such a girl, despite her curious charm. She'd provoked him more than he'd bargained for, but he would soon forget her.

"And there's nothing I can do to change your mind?" She was studying him through narrowed eyes.

"I'm afraid not."

"I see." She rose slowly to her feet, brushed down the skirt of her dress. Her skin was oddly luminous in the golden light. He felt a small spasm of regret, then dismissed it, rose politely to his feet to assist her. She took his arm, stepped carefully over the remains of the feast that separated them. She looked up at him, her head tilted slightly to one side, her eyes unreadable. She swayed gently against him. He became aware that she smelled deliciously of chocolate.

"Miss Modena . . ." He halted a fleeting, wayward impulse to pull her closer. "It's late. And I think you have had too much to drink."

"No, I haven't. You can't have too much of anything." She leaned closer and softly, experimentally, kissed him on the lips.

"Well, M. de Chardonnet . . ." She leaned back. "How much was that worth?"

For the first time he looked at her as if she were an equal.

"Miss Modena, what exactly is it that you want?"

She smiled back, a wide tigerish smile.

"That's simple, M. de Chardonnet. Everything. The world. Paradise. And more."

"Paradise costs money."

"Of course. I intend to be rich."

His smile deepened.

"Do you, Miss Modena?"

Another pause. He watched her like a hawk. She was showing him her real self now, a self he recognized like the reflection in a mirror. Her professions of distaste for money had been merely . . . professional. Veils of illusion which, no longer useful, were now laid aside. Perhaps, after all, something might be possible. The warmth of her lips had stirred him more than he cared to admit.

"Tell me, M. de Chardonnet . . ." Her voice was sweet, with a disturbing shot-silk quality he'd never noticed before. She seemed able to change her voice at will, from light to dark and back again, catching the light and hiding it. How pleasant it would be to hear that voice often, to have it readily available. "Tell me, M. de Chardonnet, how rich are you?"

"Rich enough." Yes, he understood her now. This was familiar territory, the complex interplay between the sexes, as subtle and ultimately fatal as a fencing match.

"Very rich?" Her voice was telling him other things, promising, hinting.

"Yes."

"Very, very rich?" The sweetest, softest voice, as plush as satin, as smooth as velvet.

"Yes."

"With expectations of being even richer?"

He smiled again. "Yes. You are thorough, Miss Modena."

"There is the future to think about, M. de Chardonnet."

"The future. Of course." He drew her toward him. He couldn't tell what exactly had changed his mind. Perhaps his recognition of her as someone like himself, perhaps her shot-silk voice in his ear, perhaps nothing more than a whimsical impulse of his own. "Tell me, Miss Modena, how does this sound to you? A house in Paris, your own car, clothes, the usual arrangements. A generous allowance."

"For how long?" Her voice was dulcet, her eyes acute.

He shrugged. "For as long as we both . . . amuse each other. I'm sure we could come to some understanding."

"I'm sure we could." She gazed up at him limpidly. "As long as it doesn't include marriage. I have too many other things to do."

She had taken the words out of his mouth. Better and better.

"Is it a bargain, then?" He held her at arm's length.

"There's just one more thing." Her eyes narrowed. "Why do you want me to be your mistress? You hardly know me."

"You would scarcely be of interest to me if I did. I know enough. You are spoiled, selfish and sentimental."

"Ideal mistress material, in fact."

"I think so."

"Even though I'm not a blonde?" Her smile provoked him. He smiled. His whimsical impulse might prove to have unexpected rewards.

"Who needs perfection?" He bent his head, one hand in the small of her back pulling her irresistibly toward him.

Corrie felt that tingling pressure and pulled herself back to confront those pale ice-gray eyes, so near her own.

"And your heart won't be broken when I leave you?"

"Of course not. We are both adults." He pulled her to him again, but she stepped neatly out of his arms.

"Speak for yourself." In a flash she had whisked up her bag and reached the door. She turned to face him.

"M. de Chardonnet . . ." She spoke clearly, savoring the words, savoring her revenge, savoring the surprise and growing anger in his face. "Rich as you are, I don't think you'll ever be able to afford me." She turned with a flourish of black silk skirt and slammed the door.

And that's that, Corrie told herself ten minutes later as she burrowed luxuriously deep in her single bed in the staff wing. From the look on Guy de Chardonnet's face as she closed the door on him it seemed hardly likely that reporting an errant maid to her supervisor was the first thing on his mind. . . . Her mission was accomplished, honor avenged. She wasted no more time on thoughts of her routed enemy. Only a few floors separated them, but they were worlds, universes, galaxies apart. By the time she woke he would be gone, taking with him memories of his stay in England which she felt sure he would rather forget. She closed her eyes with enormous satisfaction and slept the sleep of the just.

When she woke she could tell from the light behind the thin curtains that it was full day already. She thought of getting up then decided against it. It was her day off, she would lie back and enjoy it. She snuggled back under the sheets. Her dreams were still with her. She'd been floating on a sea of honey, she could almost smell the sweetness still. She breathed deeply, waiting for it to fade. But it didn't. The fragrance was everywhere, heavy, mysterious, with a moist woodland note to it that was oddly familiar.

Slowly she opened her eyes. In the dim light from the curtained windows she saw that the tiny room was filled, every surface packed and crowded, with bowl after bowl of single white hyacinths. She sat up, slid back the sheets, rubbed her eyes. She wasn't dreaming. There must have been a hundred of them, loading the air with their piercing scent. White on white on white—creamy white, chalk white, rose white, lily white. She was lying in a bank of flowers, like Juliet on a bier. She reached out her hand. They were real.

It was too much. Only the Savoy, so sensitive to accommodating a guest's slightest whim, could have smuggled a flower garden into her room while she slept. Suddenly she felt as if she were suffocating. She ran to the window and flung it open, letting in a welcome draft of sooty London air. In the gray light she saw that there was a white card propped against one of the bowls. "Corrie," it said. And on the reverse, in a firm black script: "No is not an answer. It is merely a delay."

She seethed with fury. What had possessed him to send her flowers? He had no right. Hadn't she made herself amply, even eloquently clear? Was he mocking her, testing her . . . or was he so insensitive, so insufferably vain, that he thought her rejection was merely a ploy? Whatever his motives, his gamesmanship wouldn't work on her. She wanted nothing to do with him, or his flowers.

She spent the rest of the day distributing the hyacinths to the staff. By the evening, thankfully, only a few bowls were left. She returned from her labors to find a message asking her to come to the Head Housekeeper's office at once. Regretfully but firmly the Lady Superintendent informed her that she might serve one month's notice and then she must leave.

It was a shock. Somehow, despite all her efforts, Guy de Chardonnet must have found time to report her after all. But she still had a chance, it was only his word against hers. She steeled herself for battle.

"I didn't take anything, ma'am."

But the Lady Superintendent's answer dashed all her hopes.

"No one has accused you of stealing, Miss Modena. Your . . . misdemeanor is a far more serious one." The Lady Superintendent's face was a study in mingled disappointment and disapproval. "You have broken the Savoy's unwritten rule. You have . . . consorted with a guest."

Corrie was stunned. How on earth could she have found out about last night's escapade? The Lady Superintendent's mouth set in a thin line. "The flower shop, Miss Modena. I'm afraid there's no point denying it. It is there on the records in black and white."

Those damned hyacinths. Furious with herself and Guy de Chardonnet in equal measure Corrie returned to her room. It smelled like a flowershop itself. The scent had permeated everything, her clothes, her hair—even the thoughts inside her head. And she had been so pleased with herself . . . Ruthlessly she snipped off the remaining fragrant heads and threw them down the sluice, remembering with a sting of embarrassment her pompous little speech to Guy de Chardonnet. He'd obviously taken note of what she'd said about cut flowers. Doubtless he thought he'd been very clever. It couldn't have been easy to locate so many bowls of white hyacinths in bloom, at such short notice. But it just proved what a gulf there was between them. These hothouse blooms were as far away from being wild flowers as she was from Paradise.

She stacked the empty bowls in the bottom of the closet. By the end of that terrible day, to her relief, the last of the haunting scent had faded, and she could forget about Guy de Chardonnet forever.

Or so she thought. The next morning, in an atmosphere of glacial disapproval, an elaborately wrapped package was delivered to her room. There was no note this time. Inside the silver tissue was a huge crystal flagon of her mother's favorite scent, *Fuite des Heures*. She held the flagon in her hands, repelled and fascinated at the same time. How had he guessed? How many other thoughts had he spirited clean out of her head? What was even more remarkable, he must have had the scent specially made up, because she knew it hadn't been produced commercially for years. She lifted the glass stopper, cunningly crafted in the shape of a bird in flight, and sniffed critically. Yes, it was indeed *Fuite des Heures*. She put the bottle down as gingerly as if it had been brimful of nitric acid.

Two days later, just as she thought she was going to recover, she received a long flat box covered in black satin. Once opened it revealed a dazzling galaxy of handmade chocolates, bitter chocolates, smooth, black and glistening. Just looking at them she could almost feel the delicate birdlike crunch of their highly glazed shells on her tongue, almost taste their centers—truffles, puréed almonds, brandied cherries, creamy nougat, peach liqueur . . . As with the scent, there was no note, no return address. It wasn't fair. Stern-faced, she passed them out to the other maids, forced herself to watch as, preferring their milder English chocolates, they left them half-eaten. But she couldn't, wouldn't eat any. It would mean, obscurely, that she'd be in his debt. She didn't want any connection with him, even at a distance. But it wasn't fair, it wasn't fair!

The presents continued to arrive with a clockwork precision. She lost count. A tiny, perfect bonsai tree, a white flowering almond, heavily scented. More flowers, always white. More chocolates, always black. A basket of hothouse peaches under silver net. A delicate glass atomizer for her scent, again in the shape of a flying bird. Candied violets on a bed of white velvet. A honeycomb in its own wooden box. White Muscadet grapes with the dust bloom still on them, complete with their own small silver scissors. More chocolates . . .

She wrote in desperation to Harlequin.

"I thought I was doing so well . . . but now I'm afraid it's all gone wrong. I've lost my job—it wasn't my fault. I promise you, at least not entirely. And now I'm being pursued by a man I really dislike. But I can't seem to get rid of him. I don't know—the world seems to be much more complicated than I thought. All I want to do is get on with my own life. I've told him to go away but he won't. What should I do?"

His answer came back as quickly as she could have wished, marked urgent and delivered by special messenger from Mr. Whitaker's office. "*You know what you want, chère Columbine. Don't let anyone, let alone your nameless admirer, waste your time. Your loving Harlequin.*"

It was like a weight taken from her shoulders. He didn't question, condemn or criticize. He was on her side. She changed her shift, working mornings and afternoons, so that she could spend each evening at the opera house. Bearing in mind the consequences of her first visit, she dressed plainly, spoke to no one, sat in the balcony stalls and stared determinedly at her score. It was a strange, indoor existence, alternating between the Savoy and Covent Garden, and she hardly ever glimpsed the daylight sky, but it was deeply satisfying. As for Guy de Chardonnet . . . a word to the floor waiter and the flood of unwanted gifts was diverted into more grateful hands.

Then, two weeks later, another telegram bypassed

her careful defenses. She opened it, thinking it must be from Harlequin. It was short and to the point.

"May 15th. 7 p.m. Belvedere. Balenciaga." It was signed simply, Guy.

She tore it into tiny fragments, then pieced it together again. She was flattered, offended and disturbed all at once. She must really have made an impression. Ironically, May 15th was the last day of her month's notice. After that her lifestyle was going to take an abrupt downturn. This was probably the last chance she'd have for a good meal for some time to come. Angry with herself she fought down the temptation and threw the pieces away.

The next day there was another telegram. It read simply, "Peacocks, oysters, Paradise." It was unsigned.

That night she dreamed about peacocks and oysters and woke unrefreshed. She went about her work in a daze. At the opera that evening she couldn't concentrate. She wrote to Harlequin, waited anxiously for his reply.

"*My dear Columbine . . . I've thought very hard about your problem, and I don't think I'm qualified to advise you. From your letter I think that despite yourself you do want to see this man again, to prove to yourself that he means nothing to you. If that's so, then nothing I say can or should prevent you. I think perhaps you're growing up, my Columbine, and that's not a process that can easily be halted. Have I failed you?*"

She wrote back immediately. "*No, you haven't failed me. It's enough to know you understand.*"

On the morning of May 15th, she finally made up her mind. Harlequin was right. She had to prove to herself that even at her lowest ebb, without a job, with very little money and even fewer prospects of achieving her ambition, even peacocks and oysters couldn't change her mind. It would be pure cowardice to avoid the confrontation.

For a confrontation it would certainly be. She'd taken advantage of the Floor Supervisor's absence from her office to slip in and consult the reference section in which were kept details of all the Savoy's regular guests.

From the white card containing details of Guy de Chardonnet's preferences in food, drink, flowers and décor it was clear that as rich men went, he was very rich indeed. He had business interests all over Europe—property, land, light industry, chemical plants. There was even a de Chardonnet bank, based in Geneva. Corrie felt dizzy at the thought of all that money and power invested in one man. But what did he do with it? He simply frittered it away—on women and expensive hotels and opera performances which he didn't even enjoy . . .

But this time their confrontation would be on her terms. Her preparations were careful. She purchased a pair of shoes with lower heels, persuaded one of the valets to refresh the Balenciaga. She needed her armor burnished . . . As she dressed that evening she noticed the difference in herself. In only a few weeks she and the Balenciaga had grown toward each other, it fitted her like a second skin. Now she could take its beauty and power almost for granted.

As the taxi carried her swiftly through the streets to her rendezvous she realized with a shock that the trees were green and heavy with leaf. She'd been so bound up in her own preoccupations she'd missed the coming of spring to the city. And now it was May, one of those magical late spring days that are more like summer than summer ever can be, warm and light and full of impossible promises.

The taxi swept up a long drive and halted. She looked out in surprise. Tall trees surrounded her, their leaves hardly stirring in the warm still air. Ahead light streamed out through white arched windows to mingle with the summer evening.

"The Belvedere, ma'am." She emerged into what seemed the country estate of an eighteenth-century squire. Through mellowed brick arches she glimpsed an elegant ornamental garden, stone paths threading through formal beds edged with box hedges and banks of lavender. The arches were entwined with wisteria, heavy lilac blooms scenting the air, and the delicate tendrils of passionflower. Beneath a slate-tiled belltower, with its wrought-iron weathervane, were tall arched French windows overlooking deep beds filled with roses.

She entered, feeling instantly at home. It was a stage, a set straight out of her own imagination. Tall mirrors glittered, reflecting graceful white bamboo chairs, terracotta tiles, marble jardinières filled with miniature bay trees, golden yellow linen on octagonal tables, small brass lamps set into the walls, leaded glass fronting a mezzanine gallery.

"Miss Modena?" A black-coated waiter was at her side immediately. "M. de Chardonnet would like you to accept this with his compliments and his apologies."

It was an orchid, exotic and creamy, flecked with the palest possible mauve.

"He isn't here?" For a treacherous instant she was disappointed. He wasn't coming. All her bravado had been wasted.

"He has simply been delayed." The waiter smiled politely. "If you would come this way."

She followed him up the white-railed steps to the mezzanine gallery where a table for two was ready by the window. She pinned the orchid to her dress, noting by the mirror opposite that it was a perfect choice. M. Guy de Chardonnet was a profoundly irritating man. She must remember to tell him so.

The waiter brought her an array of crudités, the little slivers of raw vegetables teased and curled into elaborate shapes. She nibbled restlessly, trying to keep her eyes off the clock on the small tower opposite. It was infuriating of him to be late. There was no one else in the restaurant at this unfashionably early hour, which made her feel even more conspicuous. After five minutes she decided to play his game. She helped herself to some rounds of bread, folded them inside a napkin, then descended the gallery stairs with a blithe smile at the hovering waiter.

"If M. de Chardonnet arrives," she put a subtle emphasis on the "if," "kindly inform him that I am in the garden."

Below there was a circular pool with a classical marble fountain in its center. Water trickled soundlessly down the mossy stone, goldfish circled lazily beneath. Rectangular beds of late-flowering irises, a mist of blue and mauve edged with velvety black, framed the pool. She wandered through them, pleasingly conscious of the picture she must make, in her demure bow-fronted shoes and shimmering dress. She hoped that Guy de Chardonnet would have a few doubtful moments when he saw the empty table. He deserved them. She broke some bread and cast it on the water. It was snapped up by a mallard with plumage almost as iridescent as her own.

She walked slowly around the pool, her reflection a dim shadow against the tender blue of the sky, her skirt rustling like summer grass. The air on her bare neck and shoulders was light as a caress. She felt herself beginning to relax. She'd been indoors too long, she'd forgotten all about summer. Even the poor pale English summer was capable of a certain degree of magic . . .

The hair on the back of her neck prickled. Instinctively she looked back up to the window overlooking the garden. Outlined against the light from the restaurant's upper room was the figure of a man dressed entirely in white. She froze. How long had he been there, watching her? Their gazes tangled. He too was motionless. Silently, interminably, there was a battle of wills. But she stood her ground, refused to move. After what seemed an eternity he turned away. Her heart beating hard she too turned away, suppressing a flare of triumph. She had won a small preliminary skirmish, that was all. She forced herself to stay calm, dusted the last breadcrumbs from her hands into the glassy water, folded the napkin neatly and tucked it into her bag. Elaborately unconcerned, she listened for his footsteps in the grass.

"Corrie." His voice was instantly recognizable, with its casual, arrogant clarity. "Welcome to Paradise."

CHAPTER FIVE

She turned, slowly. He looked different, younger. Against the white of his suit his skin was lightly tanned, with a satiny evenness that disturbed her. His hair, touched by the late sun, had reddish hints. Only his ice-gray eyes were unchanged. She felt suddenly confused. Perhaps in these few short weeks he had grown younger and she had grown older, perhaps they were growing together, like herself and the Balenciaga . . . She halted the thought. It didn't make sense.

"You don't seem surprised." She spoke abruptly to hide her confusion.

"Should I be?" He smiled at her, a lazy, self-assured, mocking smile.

"I might not have come."

His smile deepened, touched his eyes briefly.

"I knew you would come. You wouldn't be able to resist it. The oysters or the peacocks would persuade you, one or the other. And curiosity. All women like the same things."

"Really?" She spoke with some asperity. She was not and would never be like all women. "What might those things be?"

He smiled down at her lazily, shrugged.

"Silk. Paris. Compliments. Surprises." He offered her his arm. "Besides . . ." His tone was gently conversational. "I always get what I want."

"Always?" She was uneasily aware of the warmth of his skin through the soft material of his sleeve.

"Almost always."

Ceremoniously he escorted her back to the table

overlooking the garden. She felt strange, as if she were in a dream. The restaurant was still deserted, they had the whole gallery room to themselves. It made her feel unreal, timeless, as if they were both on a stage, acting out a kind of play for an unseen audience. A waiter materialized out of the wings. She noticed for the first time that there was no menu.

Guy nodded in response to the waiter's inquiring glance. Not a word was spoken. The waiter disappeared as silently as a fish.

"I hope you're hungry." She was conscious of his eyes on her face.

"I'm always hungry."

"I know, I remember." He smiled. She felt a blush coloring her cheeks and refused to acknowledge it. The past meant nothing, she could rise above it.

"And you . . . Are you always late?"

"Touché." He spoke mildly, offering neither explanations nor excuses. She felt a fleeting tinge of admiration. His effrontery rivaled her own, though she had to admit his had a degree more style.

The waiter reappeared with a large tray in his arms. As he set it down carefully Corrie saw to her astonishment that it was filled from edge to edge with small shallow bowls, each containing what seemed like no more than a mouthful of different dishes. Guy dismissed the waiter with a nod of approval. Corrie stared at the table. There was scarcely a spare inch of tablecloth to be seen.

"What is this?" She looked up to find Guy studying her with that annoying hint of irony.

"You told me you wanted everything. Well, here it is. Something from every single dish on the Belvedere's not inextensive menu." Her eyes widened. "There's more to come, but there wasn't enough room on the table." His smile was limpidly ingenuous. "Eat up, or it will get cold." He handed her a small silver dish. "I suggest you begin with the smoked oysters."

The unmistakable challenge in his eyes was irresistible.

Corrie instantly resolved to do justice to the feast or die in the attempt. She'd show him what it meant to be hungry.

Manfully, she set to work. He watched in growing astonishment as she polished off dish after dish, chasing the last drops of sauce with catlike delicacy. Lobster bisque and *consommé madrilène, chateaubriand printanier, suprême* of sole, artichoke hearts, soft carps' roe, lamb cutlets, veal escalopes with apples and cream, flamed in calvados, crab claws dressed in pistachio nut oil. Invisibly the empty dishes were whisked away to be replenished with tiny spring vegetables, duckling in green pepper and brandy sauce, wild strawberries, brandied peaches, chicken stuffed with braised fennel roots, shrimp soufflé . . . Recklessly she mixed sweet with savory, fish with fowl, red meat with white. It was a cornucopia of delights, a Roman orgy. White Burgundy followed red, Nuits St. Georges chasing Pouilly Fuissé, and capped with a rainbow assortment of different ice creams.

"Are you quite sure you've had enough?" His tone was elaborately solicitous as she pushed away the last ice-cream dish and patted her lips with a napkin. She nodded, so full she could barely speak.

"Yes, I think so." She glimpsed a remaining petit four and downed it with relish. "For the moment."

He shook his head in mock astonishment. "You'll be sick."

"I'm never sick. I have the digestion of a camel."

"So I see. How do you manage it?"

"It's quite simple. All you have to do is eat with your spine." She took a deep breath. "And there's something else."

"What's that?" He was regarding her with as much polite interest as he would have shown a real camel in a zoo.

"Motivation."

"Motivation?" He frowned, puzzled.

"Perhaps you've never heard of it." She allowed a

slight trace of sarcasm to enter her tone. "It's called hunger."

"Indeed." He seemed unmoved, just faintly curious. "You interest me, Miss Modena. Why should a woman in your position . . ." his eyes rested lazily on her bare shoulders—"ever have to suffer such an indignity? Surely your patron cannot be such an ogre? Or is it . . ." Here his eyes took on a mocking gleam. "Can it possibly be that he prefers slender women?"

Corrie drew herself to her full height and with an heroic effort choked back her anger at the implied insult.

"M. de Chardonnet." She spoke with dignity, as befitted a widow recently bereaved. "I no longer have a patron."

"Oh." He seemed surprised, even concerned. She gritted her teeth, disguised her fury behind demurely cast down eyes. Doubtless he couldn't imagine how a young woman could survive without the support and protection of a man such as himself. "Are you no longer at the Savoy?"

"From tomorrow, no." She thought about coaxing a tear, decided against it. She was bereaved, but brave.

"Because of me?"

The effrontery of the man! He didn't seem in the least abashed—if anything he sounded pleased, almost gratified. He assumed, of course, that she'd been dismissed by her patron because of one evening spent in another man's company. Such arrogance . . .

"You could say so." She sighed deeply. It was true, after all.

"My deepest sympathy." He was smiling a small, knowing smile, as if now at last he had her in his power.

"I don't want your sympathy, thank you very much!" A trace of tartness entered her tone. His smile broadened.

"Perhaps another petit four?"

"Certainly not." She folded her hands primly in her lap. He was still looking at her with that disturbing, assessing gaze. He gestured at the waiter to clear away the remaining dishes.

"At least you enjoyed your meal."

The touch of irony in his voice brought a blush to her cheeks. A healthy appetite hardly became the grieving widow . . . But it was too late now.

"It was delicious." Belatedly she remembered her manners. "Thank you." A thought struck her suddenly; she frowned in puzzlement. "But why has no one else come to eat here? They don't know what they're missing."

He smiled patiently.

"Because I've engaged the entire restaurant."

"What?"

Now he really had managed to surprise her. "Just for us?" It was an extraordinary extravagance, it almost made her feel ill.

"Of course."

"Do you mean . . . they've cooked all these different dishes . . . just for me?"

"Of course."

"You mean, there's a whole rack of lamb back there, and I've just had one mouthful?"

"I've no idea. I should imagine so. It hadn't occurred to me."

He smiled indulgently. "I could ask for it to be put in a bag for you, if you like. We could take it with us."

She leaned back in her chair, half amused, half appalled. He and she were worlds apart. She couldn't even begin to imagine what it must be like to live as he did, to spend as if money were a mere toy for his own amusement. And yet he himself had barely touched a mouthful of the feast.

"Why didn't you eat anything?"

He shrugged. "As you say, it is a question of . . . motivation. I preferred to watch you."

She blushed again. It hadn't been the sort of performance she'd intended. She stared at him. The light from the gardens outside was deepening infinitesimally into blue, flattering, softening, making outlines unreal.

"Well, Mademoiselle Corrie, you have done ample justice to the oysters. It is now time for peacocks."

In a dream she took his proffered arm. She could no longer remember whether she liked him or not, she was too full of good food for logic. As they emerged into the air she saw there were no other people in sight. A thought struck her.

"You haven't hired the whole of the park as well?"

"No." He laughed, the deep spontaneous laugh which she was beginning to like to try and prize out of him. Slowly they walked up toward the ornamental garden. Around them she felt the faintest stir of breeze, bringing with it the hypnotic scent of newly mown grass. Sunlight glinted off the little clocktower with its turquoise copper roof and golden ball. The old rose bricks of the arcade leading to the orangery were soft in the sunlight, the shadows violet beneath the murmuring trees. He was right. It was as near as man could get to Paradise.

Beneath the trees, in the emerald green shade where the grass bloomed with an underwater intensity, rabbits browsed while on the high old walls peacocks strutted and bowed, saluting the evening with their harsh haunting cries. Everything around them was poised timelessly on the brink of summer, every rabbit soft and fat with plenty, every peacock with its hen.

Against her will, she was drawn into the fairy tale. She couldn't resist the peacocks. Their voices had the authority, the aching, soulful penetration of a prima donna soprano. Those slender necks and tiny heads didn't look capable of producing such a noise. And they moved so slowly, sure of their charisma, milking their audience. The last light was brilliant on their opalescent plumage. How much she wanted to be a peacock.

They halted, mesmerized. A peacock eyed them motionlessly with its malachite gaze. His snakelike neck, insufferably blue, waved, searching, swelling. He emitted a superb, spine-shaking shriek. And then slowly, like a magician, he produced his tail, spreading like a moonscape, a heaven full of dancing planets. He stayed there, quivering for enough time to stun them, then shuffled his feathers back with a businesslike air, squawked once and stalked away.

It was a revelation. They looked at each other with a sort of awe. They had been privileged; it was as if royalty had stopped to speak to them in the street. They had shared something irreplaceable, unrepeatable.

"What was that?" Her voice was a whisper. She hardly dared to break the silence, but she wanted to spread her own plumes for him, tell him her plans and dreams, flaunt her secret inner world.

"Serendipity." He turned to her, his white suit dappled under the shimmering leaves. "I never realized . . ." His voice was soft, like someone woken from a deep sleep. "Your eyes are so blue."

They stared at each other. The image of the peacock's tail still seemed to be imprinted on her retina, a dazzling mist of color. She couldn't see, couldn't think.

"Come with me." His voice was low. "Come with me to Paris. Now, tonight."

Paris, Paris, Paradise . . . It sounded so easy. It would be easy. She could float away and never be heard of again, supported by him and his money, like a swimmer in the Dead Sea. But it wasn't enough, it couldn't be enough for her.

She shook her head. The peacock's plumes were fading, the moment was lost. She couldn't go to Paris with a man who'd only just noticed the color of her eyes.

"I'm sorry. I can't."

"I see." He turned away abruptly. In silence they retraced their steps to the ornamental garden. The flowers were still transparent with the evening light but the magic had faded. She didn't meet her companion's gaze, though she was conscious of his figure beside her with every nerve in her body. He must be angry, he had every right to be angry.

But when he spoke his voice was cool, remote, his question the most detached of inquiries.

"What have you got against Paris?"

"Nothing." If only he knew . . . everything she wanted was there. Harlequin, M. Beyer, the culmination of a lifetime's hopes and dreams . . . "In fact I'd like to be there more than anything in the world."

"But not with me?"

She shook her head.

He smiled, a small, wry smile.

"Are you always so appallingly frank?"

She shrugged. "Politeness wastes time."

"Hmm." He halted, turned to face her. "You make it very difficult to help you."

"Why should you help me?" She eyed him suspiciously. If he was hoping to apply a little pressure he'd better think again.

"Because I feel responsible for you losing your position." She hesitated. He spoke seriously, with an unexpected sincerity. But knowing what she did she could hardly trust him.

"What had you in mind?"

He paused, considering.

"I would like to make you a proposition."

"But I've already told you, I don't want to be your mistress!"

"Oh, that." He dismissed her indignation with a wave of the hand. "I have already abandoned the idea. It was merely a whim on my part and I was intrigued by your so evident dislike for me. It seemed unusual, I wanted to see if it was sincere."

She was silenced. The presents, his dedicated pursuit of her—she'd been completely taken in.

"You seem surprised."

"Yes." She couldn't help a reluctant smile at her own naïveté. "I thought you were desperately in love with me."

"You flatter yourself, Miss Modena. One of the more . . . stable elements in our relationship so far has been a degree of mutual dislike. Which leads me to the proposition I mentioned."

She looked up at him with narrowed eyes. She was at home with him now, she knew where she stood.

"Marriage, M. de Chardonnet? You are old-fashioned."

His eyes showed a momentary gleam of appreciation. "Hardly, Miss Modena. Though I appreciate your judgment that mutual dislike is a sound basis for marriage. No, I had in mind more of a business proposition." His voice took on a mildly sarcastic note. "That is, if I can trust you to be businesslike?"

Something in his expression brought a blush to her cheeks. He was clearly thinking of her brazen behavior in the Callas suite. But before she could think of a suitable riposte he turned the subject abruptly.

"Why do you want to be in Paris?"

"I haven't the faintest intention of telling you."

"Better and better. Yes, I think it will work very well."

"What will?" Against her will she was intrigued.

"Let me explain." His tone was brisk, matter-of-fact. "Let me see . . . I have a house in Paris which I rarely use but would like to have occupied; you want to be in Paris for reasons which, mercifully, you do not see fit to disclose."

"Important reasons!"

"Of course." The tinge of irony in his tone infuriated her.

"Are you suggesting that I stay in your house? I couldn't possibly."

"Why not? Is it so very different an arrangement from your . . . er . . . recently terminated position? I appreciate your concern for the social niceties, but are you sure you have a reputation to lose? Or is your anxiety on my behalf?" His tone was dry. "If so, believe me, I am deeply touched."

She bit back her instinctive retort. She could hardly protest, it was true, after all the effort she'd put into convincing him she was a *femme fatale*. And in one way his assumption was right—she really didn't care what people thought of her, she had more important things on her mind.

And this was such an opportunity—it had risks, but what other options did she have? It would be months before she could afford to go to Paris under her own steam, or stay there for any length of time. She thought furiously. What would Harlequin advise? His words came back to her. "You know what you want." Yes, and as long as she knew that, nothing could touch her . . . But there was one thing she had to get clear.

"You're sure this isn't just a cunning way of persuading me to become your mistress?"

He sighed patiently. "Of course not. Ours would be like any other business relationship, with its own rules. Unless, of course, you intend to be irresistible?"

She bit her lip, then decided to ignore the jibe.

"This house . . ." It was crazy, but it seemed the answer to all her problems. "Does it have a garden?"

"You are exacting, Miss Modena. But yes, it does have a garden. A small but secluded garden."

"And work . . . you'd have to find me something to do." Her tone was pugnacious. "I couldn't accept charity."

He shrugged.

"If you insist. You seem reasonably intelligent. I'm sure there is some way in which you could make yourself useful."

Still she hesitated. Could she really trust him? If only there was some cast-iron way of making sure. An idea occurred to her.

"I want a contract."

"A contract?" A flicker of astonishment showed in his face.

"Yes." She stuck firmly to her guns. "I want everything written down. Exclusion clauses and all." Mr. Whitaker would have been proud of her.

"Very well." The idea seemed to amuse him. She didn't mind. He could laugh himself into a blue fit, as long as he signed on the dotted line. A contract was a contract.

They sat down on a cedar bench, on which someone had inscribed, "And this eternal summer shall not fade." She liked the sentiment, it seemed suitable for the occasion. It should be possible to legislate for summer too. They hadn't any paper between them, but she produced the Belvedere's sunshine yellow napkin and he provided a rolled gold pen. Carefully, printing because writing on linen, even starched linen, was not the easiest thing to do, she inscribed a set of four clauses.

1. No passes.

2. No questions as to how I spend my free time.

3. A room of my own.

4. 250 gms chocolate, to be supplied daily. Best quality only.

She hesitated, still doubtful. She wanted to cover everything, especially her exit. What was the clause the insurance companies always used, the universal get-out? Something about Acts of God . . .

5. Contract to be terminated if circumstances arise which are beyond my control.

She leaned back, pleased with herself, then handed the napkin to him. He glanced at the list in a cursory fashion that would have annoyed her if she'd let it.

"That seems fair enough." He was humoring her, she knew. But she could take it.

"Now it's your turn."

"If you insist."

Within a few minutes, he handed the napkin back. He'd added four more clauses.

6. No "patrons."

7. The pleasure of your company at occasional social events on twenty-four hours' notice.

8. Uniform to be supplied.

9. Discretion.

She studied them carefully. The first was easy, the second tolerable, apart from one detail. She added "in writing" to the end of the line. Harlequin had taught her well. But the third and fourth stipulations confused her.

"What's this about a uniform?"

"Don't worry, you need only wear it when you are with me."

"And discretion?"

He shrugged. "A small matter to you, perhaps, but I thought it advisable to mention it, given your . . . er

. . . penchant for frankness. If you accept my offer, you will find many people curious about the exact nature of our relationship. A man in my position is always newsworthy. The press, servants, social acquaintances—there will be many questions. I suggest you do not answer any of them. How is your French?"

"Well . . ." Instinctively she realized that given his obsessive need for privacy she had better keep her fluency a secret. "I know a lot of swearwords." A small white lie.

"So I gathered." His tone was silken smooth. "They may well prove useful as a deterrent. But it is fortunate that you do not speak French, it will make it easier for you to be discreet. I take it that you know no one in Paris?"

"I've never been there." A rather larger, rather grayer lie. It was true that she'd never been to Paris, but she knew quite well it wasn't in any way a full answer. Still, there was no real need to mention Harlequin. Mr. Whitaker would forward his letters under separate cover, no one need ever know.

Now he held out his hand, suddenly all efficiency.

"Well, Miss Modena. I have a plane to catch in forty minutes. Is it a bargain?"

"Yes." They shook hands solemnly, signed their names with a flourish. He handed the contract back to her.

She folded it and tucked it into her bag.

"My legal adviser will want to look at this." She enjoyed the flicker of surprise on his face. "But perhaps you'd like to make a copy first?"

"No, I trust you." Again that mocking glance. "When can you start?"

"Tomorrow." She saw his eyes widen, smiled at him wickedly. "Or is that too difficult to arrange? Surely nothing is too difficult for Guy de Chardonnet."

He eyed her consideringly. "I think I am a little relieved that you are not to be my mistress after all." He took her hand, lifted it to his lips in a graceful, impersonal gesture, noting her reluctance with a wintry little smile. "Don't worry, Miss Modena. You will be safe with me. Remember, we dislike each other. And now, I must bid you *au revoir*. My chauffeur will see you home. Your tickets will be at your hotel tomorrow morning."

CHAPTER SIX

Guy de Chardonnet proved to be as good as his word. Promptly the next morning her first class air ticket to Paris was delivered by private messenger, along with a slender cardboard box in which she found a cream silk slim-skirted dress of shattering simplicity, a cream linen jacket and matching sandals. Pinned to the jacket lapel was a curt, typed note. "Uniform. Please wear. Guy."

The other maids were impressed and intrigued. Corrie herself was suddenly doubtful. She hadn't realized how much she was going to miss her new friends. And cream silk—she saw from Shevaun's round eyes what she thought. A dress for a mistress if ever she saw one . . .

But she'd signed the contract. As she put it on she noticed that the pale silk matched the cream of her arms exactly, caressed her skin with a light cool touch, made her feel young and alive. Her eyes were a deeper violet, her lips a warmer red.

"I don't know, Corrie . . ." Shevaun had tears in her eyes. "You look like a stranger."

"Don't be sad. I'll be coming back, I promise." Corrie felt her own eyes fill. Shevaun shook her head wisely. "Paris . . . it's a long way from home." And Corrie knew she didn't mean just miles.

When Shevaun had gone Corrie felt suddenly vulnerable and alone. She wiped her eyes, splashed on a reckless quantity of *Fuite des Heures*. She needed all the moral support she could get. As a last, defiant gesture she pinned a small posy of common daisies to her jacket lapel. She might be entering Guy de Chardonnet's employ but she didn't belong to him entirely.

Two hours later, in the space-age magnificence of Orly Airport, her doubts were forgotten almost instantly. She found it enchanting, an exuberant funfair, full of glass and chrome and machines that leapt into action at the slightest footfall. She would have liked to stay and ride its carrousels forever, but time and her cream silk forbade. And there was Paris waiting . . .

Regretfully she made her way to the arrivals area. There would be someone to meet her, she could rely on Guy de Chardonnet for that, but who it would be she didn't know. She stood still, assuming what she hoped was a suitably regal, *grande dame* air, and wishing her scuffed leather suitcase matched her pretensions. Still, she was English. she must be allowed her eccentricities.

"Good morning." She wheeled in surprise at the familiar voice. It was Guy himself, his eyes appraising her from head to toe with a Frenchman's thoroughness.

"Will I do?"

His gaze halted on the defiant daisies at her buttonhole. He sighed.

"This passion for wild flowers. You must permit me to advise you." With surprisingly sure, deft fingers he removed her posy and handed it ceremoniously to the uniformed chauffeur standing respectfully behind him. "For day, you should wear violets only. For the evening, orchids."

"What's wrong with daisies?" She wasn't going to give in to his high-handed ways.

"Nothing. In their place. In grass, usually."

She was about to protest further when he forestalled her.

"The contract, remember?" His tone was gentle, but it had an undertone of steel. "When you are not with me you are welcome to wear anything you like as a corsage. Cabbages, if you must."

She had to suppress a smile. He was infuriating, but he was right. She must be businesslike. She tried without much success to recover her aplomb as the gray limousine drew away from the airport to join the stream of traffic heading toward Paris.

"But why do I have to wear violets? They're so old-fashioned." Guy, startled out of his preoccupation, looked at her in surprise.

"I shouldn't have to tell you that, surely." She was nonplussed. He shook his head. "English girls . . ." He lifted her chin casually with one hand, indicated the vanity mirror set into the pale leather above her seat. "To match your eyes, of course."

"Oh." She couldn't think of a thing to say. She subsided into her seat, feeling like a foolish little girl. Still, she was obscurely flattered that he'd remembered the exact shade of her eyes. It was frivolous of her to care—after all, what did the color of her eyes matter—but she couldn't help glancing a second time into the mirror and imagining the look of a posy of violets in her lapel.

Then, as they moved from the featureless autoroute into the streets of Paris itself she forgot everything in the intensity of her pleasure. It was all there, as familiar to her as if she'd lived in the city all her life. She'd waited so long for this moment. Impulsively she wound down the window, inhaled deeply. She smelled soot and sunshine on tarmac, gasoline fumes, fresh-ground coffee, newly baked bread . . . a magical, altogether enticing smell. She was sure the very dust on the streets was different. There was a sidewalk café, complete with white chairs and striped umbrellas, waiters dipping like gulls among their clients. She could almost hear the rapid birdlike chatter of Parisian French all around her, as intoxicating as a breath of sea air. Cars hooted and spun around corners with an unmistakably French insolence and vigor, women strolled the pavements looking as only Parisiennes could look, each sure of her own distinctive beauty. Down an avenue of ruthlessly pruned trees there was a glimpse of the river, anglers motionless under the massive towers of Notre Dame, the golden spire of the Sainte Chapelle, the slate turrets of the Conciergerie. Silver willow leaves trailed in the water, *clochards* smiled in the warm May sunshine. Now they were sweeping past the Tuileries, fountains and ornamental basins a riot of gods and horses, nymphs and sylphs, and into the vast sunlit plain of the Place de la Concorde.

There, looking down on the panorama that was Paris, the car came to a halt. Guy turned to her, his eyes full of amusement at her excitement.

"What would you like to do today?"

She hesitated, confused by the sudden change of plan.

"But I thought I was to start work."

He shrugged.

"As your employer, I have decided to give you the day off. A whim. Indulge me."

Still she hesitated. It would be better, she knew, if their new relationship started off on a properly official footing.

"Unless, of course . . ."—his tone was solicitous—"you are too fatigued by your journey?"

Too tired? How could she possibly be too tired? It was May, the sun was shining, and down there, glittering in all its glory, was the Eiffel Tower.

"No, it's just . . ."

"Ah." He nodded his head sagely. "I have it. Your palate is jaded. You have seen too much, now you are too sophisticated a traveler for mere tourism."

She sighed inwardly. Maintaining her sophisticated façade was going to be hard work if it meant missing out on all the things she enjoyed. She repressed a longing glance at the Tower.

"I suppose there are things that everyone must see." Perhaps he would take her hint. She waited hopefully.

"Of course. Well, where shall we begin? Doubtless, knowing your appetite, you would like to sample everything. Let me see—there's the Tower, of course, or Notre Dame, the Ile de la Cité, Napoleon's Tomb . . ." The hint of boredom in his voice alerted her just in time. Regretfully she said a mental goodbye to the classics of Paris for today. They would have to wait. She'd visit them later, on her own, without his attendant scornful presence. Then she could peer up the gargoyles' noses to her heart's content, trail her fingers in the water from a *bâteau mouche*, walk in the Ile de la Cité's ancient cobbled streets and imagine that Voltaire and Cézanne and sad-eyed Baudelaire were just around the corner.

But today she wouldn't let him spoil her first taste of Paris. Nothing must come between her and the city of her mother's stories and Harlequin's letters, the city of legend, the city of light. A city for lovers, where they could sit and dream and pretend they were invisible, or parade their public extravagant delight in each other on graceful boulevards, in animated cafés. A city for and about women, dedicated to fashion and conversation and love, where each girl in the street, pretty or plain, looked as if she'd just been kissed.

She knew, from Harlequin's letters, where that Paris, a very different city from the one that belonged to Guy de Chardonnet, could still be found. Harlequin knew the hidden places that caught the sun and the imagination, where you didn't have to pay the earth to watch the cavalcade. That's where she wanted to go today. Who knows, she might even succeed in showing the haughty M. Guy de Chardonnet a side of his city he'd never seen before.

"May I?" She smiled dazzlingly at her companion, indicating the glass partition that separated them from the chauffeur.

"Please do." His answering smile was lazily self-assured. "André is at your disposal."

With an effort she controlled her exhilaration. All Paris was hers for the day. She leaned forward, rapped primly on the window.

"The Rue du Faubourg St-Honoré, please."

In the wildly expensive boulevard she window-hopped, falling in love first with a pair of lilac suede gloves of ridiculous price and no conceivable usefulness, then with a small enamel snuffbox that could have belonged to Marie Antoinette if she'd lived to be a hundred and fifty years old. He observed her passionate absorption with an indulgent eye.

"Shall we go in?"

"Certainly not."

He was clearly nonplussed.

"It is usual in these cases, *n'est-ce pas?*"

She sniffed. "You're so conventional."

Enjoying his surprise—clearly he'd been prepared to buy her some wildly expensive trinket—she led them back to the car. Next she directed André to the Marais, where behind medieval façades green with age lay hidden sleepy courtyards filled with tiny workshops, an Aladdin's cave of ribbons and braid, feather flowers and artificial pearls. She lingered, extolled their beauties, but again bought nothing.

Then she took him to Montmartre—not to the over-popular artists' squares or the Moulin Rouge, but to the miracle vine in the Rue de Saules, twisted and gray, but still producing its annual quota of wine grapes. She stared, fascinated, at the lichenous trunk.

"I wonder what it tastes like, the wine?"

He smiled his small ironic smile.

"Delicious, no doubt—if you appreciate the flavor of exhaust fumes and pigeon droppings . . ."

She ignored his jibe. "Which reminds me . . ." She treated him to a dazzling smile. "I'm hungry."

"That at least comes as no surprise." He waited patiently while she drank *citron pressé* and nibbled on spiced pistachios in a café by the Fountain of the Innocents, and even consented to share with her a lunch of *tarte aux blettes*, strawberry spinach pie, in a backstreet restaurant. Through the window they could see Chinese chefs in the restaurant opposite slicing mangoes paper-thin with razor-sharp cleavers and near suicidal speed.

"I wonder . . ." Her eyes rested thoughtfully on the spectacle.

"Don't tell me." He interrupted hastily. "Doubtless it has happened, once or twice."

"In batter, do you think? Or sweet and sour sauce?"

He pushed aside the rest of his pie.

Hiding a smile, she took him on another pilgrimage, to the oldest tree in Paris, a tumbledown acacia in the Square Viviani, planted in 1601 and still in bloom every spring. A few mimosa blooms still remained on the gray-green branches.

"Just think . . . four hundred summers." She was filled with memories of southern sunshine.

"Four hundred winters too." His voice was caustic. Clearly he hadn't forgiven her for the Chinese interlude. But nostalgia left her in need of more refreshment. In another backstreet she located a dark little bar where she munched roast beef sandwiches washed down with black coffee, soaking up the hot, bitter liquid on sugar blocks the shape of dominoes, and afterwards sampling the delights of a Turkish toilet, placing her feet with an explorer's excitement in the footprints on the floor and crackling the stiff wax paper with a connoisseur's relish. He followed her, half amused, half protesting, into a Citroën Pallas so that she could experience the legendary feather-bed ride of its suspension, though he drew the line at accompanying her into Monoprix, the cheapest, most colorful store in town. In solitary splendor she rode on the escalators and bought a neon-bright shiny plastic belt with a huge, offensive buckle. Outside he was waiting for her with a buckwheat crêpe filled with bananas and flambéed in Cointreau.

"I wouldn't want you to starve," he said, with a splendidly straight face.

That reminded her. Next she simply had to see the street market in the Rue Mouffetard, as vivid as a Braque painting, a feast of glossy green, red and white peppers, melons, mangoes, papaya, wood strawberries, fresh unpeeled almonds, Spanish blood sausages from Auvergne . . . There were Camemberts and Pont l'Évêques from Normandy, goats' cheeses caked in cinders, a Gruyère from Pontarlier as large as the wheel of an ox-drawn cart.

She eyed it longingly. Guy looked at her expression and drew away in mock horror.

"Certainly not. It would never fit in the car."

"We could roll it?" Her tone was wistful.

He shook his head, laughter tugging at the corners of his mouth.

"Here." He spoke rapidly to the vendor, handed her a little gray-wrapped packet. Inside was a morsel of Chaume, the world's mildest, wildest, most sinfully creamy cheese. "A consolation prize."

With a last reluctant look at the array of fancy breads—*viennoise*, butter-glazed—and rainbow *pâtisseries*—éclairs, *madeleines*, babas, *brioches*, *tartelettes*, *millefeuilles*, petits fours, the nunlike *religieuses* with their *choux* pastry coifs overflowing with fresh cream—she allowed herself to be dragged away to a nearby café where she drank a restorative cup of chocolate washed down with a palate-cleansing glass of iced Perrier.

Then there was only one thing left to do. They drove back down the Champs Élysées, through the pink and white chestnut trees, pausing only to listen to a gypsy accordion player. Then, near the Étoile, she made a sudden dash from the car, teetering slightly on her new shoes, and without looking to the left or right, in a cacophony of hooting horns and screeching brakes and shouts of anger turning rapidly to approving whistles, she made it to the other side, waved defiantly, then did it all the way back again.

"Why on earth did you do that?" Guy de Chardonnet's face was a study. She smiled wickedly to herself, thinking of her mother's words. She'd finally made the grade, she was a woman.

"It was a promise I made to myself, years ago." He looked at her curiously, but made no comment except to take her arm and escort her to the Champs Élysées Drugstore, where France met America and fell in love. There he bought her a milk shake with real peaches in it and a bandage for the blister beginning on her heel. In the Jardins du Luxembourg he sat her on a wrought-iron bench and they watched the children chasing each other in the sand, the old men playing *boules* and the old women in black just sitting in the sun.

"You are tired."

"No, I'm not." Reluctant though she was to admit a moment's weakness, there was one thing she had to confess. "But my feet are killing me." Her companion looked at her with amusement.

"A woman is not supposed to say that sort of thing."

"Why not? It's the truth."

He smiled. "This passion for truth and wild flowers . . . Most civilized people have learned to prefer a garden to a wilderness. Let me explain. Instead of saying, 'My feet are killing me,' graphic though that may be, you should say, 'My foot hurts.' It is more pleasing, more feminine. It gives the impression of a delicate little white foot that needs to be kissed."

"I think that's ridiculous. Feet are feet." Corrie spoke staunchly, but she felt an unwelcome blush rising to her cheeks. She looked down at her bare toes, kicked free of the beautiful but bad-tempered shoes, and stuffed them hurriedly back inside.

"I stand corrected." His expression was once again remote, ironic. He glanced at his watch. "But bearing in mind the lateness of the hour and the, er . . . condition of your feet I suggest we return to the house." She was struck by what he said—not "my house," or "home," but simply "the house," referring to it as impersonally as he might a hotel.

They drove in silence. He looked out of the window with a preoccupied air, she nursed her feet and wondered what kind of home he would have. Probably something modern, high-rise, with a jet-age elevator, automatic doors and a lofty view over all Paris. She had to admit she was surprised when the car halted in front of a classic two-story house in the Avenue Pierre I de Serbie. Its cut-stone frontage was immaculate, the tall windows revealing the highly prized height of the rooms within. It was a simple eighteenth-century house, but everything about it spoke of money—not careless, extrovert money but solid, old money, which believed in stone and endured like stone. Immaculately maintained, it was the sort of house that Corrie's Italian blood longed to paint pink and cream and violet, in a riot of Neapolitan colors, to cover with trailing vines and scarlet geraniums, but she wasn't immune to its graceful, discreet charm, the delicate detail of doors and windows, the lightness of the proportions.

Guy led the way up the steps to the door with its beautifully polished brass where a uniformed maid waited.

"Come, I will show you to your room." The maid took her case from the chauffeur and followed them up a graceful curve of marble-floored stairs. Tall windows looked out onto the cool dim well of the courtyard below, light filtering greenly through the branches of a central tree. Her room was austerely furnished, with that ultimate austerity which is the product of unlimited expense. Like the rest of the house it was decorated in neutral colors, beige and gray and cream. The effect was impersonal, restrained, almost somber. The gray silk-lined walls shone like a pearl underwater; more heavy slubbed silk in a darker gray hung at the windows. There was no color or clutter to detract from the room's classical dignity and spaciousness; it was bare, dim and quiet, as impersonally welcoming as a room in a hotel. Adjoining it was a spacious gray marble bathroom and a dressing room with enough closet space to house a family of four. The maid placed her case beside the bed, bobbed a brief curtsy, then left Guy and herself alone together.

The silence after she had left seemed to echo. No traffic noise penetrated through the double-glazed windows, even though they were in the center of Paris. Guy took a step toward her. She retreated, almost tripping over the case.

"The contract!"

He smiled. "I was merely going to relieve you of your package." The garish Monoprix bag contained her neon belt and the beermat she'd purloined as a souvenir from the backstreet bar. He took it gently from her hand and deposited it beside the case. "Toinette will unpack for you. I suggest you change for dinner. You have twenty minutes."

"What?" She couldn't hide her consternation. She was more tired than she'd admitted. "I thought you'd given me the day off?"

He smiled thinly. "The day, yes. But now it is evening." He turned on his heel, pausing only at the door. "The drawing room. Twenty minutes."

Twenty minutes! It was hardly fair. But then she should know better than to expect fairness or consideration from Guy de Chardonnet. After all she was now a mere minion. She had better learn to function like a machine, as he did. He seemed totally unruffled by the day's exertions. He put her on her mettle. She'd boasted of her strong constitution and she wasn't going to be outdone.

She glanced at her watch. A minute gone already in useless speculation. She must act fast. She rang for ice, lots of it. It was a question of priorities. By the time the maid, Toinette, brought the ice she had already skipped in and out of the bath and hung the Balenciaga up to lose its creases in the steam. She filled the bidet with cold water and added the ice. Gritting her teeth she plunged her feet into the freezing cocktail and held them there for a full minute, restoring them to life by a quick dip in tepid water in the basin. She combed out her hair, whisked *Fuite des Heures* through it with her fingers, shook her head violently and then reassembled her chignon. She would be early, if it killed her. She slipped the Balenciaga over her head. The dress felt happy, as if it was glad to be returning to its birthplace after all its travels and its long imprisonment. She smoothed cocoa oil on her brows and lids to add a trace of sheen, reveling briefly in its delectable scent, then touched her lips with color. Her pale skin glistened against the black shot silk. Tonight she was not a matador, an assassin, a cat burglar, but a Parisienne. Less meant infinitely more. She removed her watch and most of the lipstick. She had three minutes to go. She briefly held a block of ice to her temples, breathed deeply, grabbed her shoes and ran down the stairs barefoot. Outside the drawing-room door she paused to collect herself and put on her shoes.

"I'm ready."

She was gratified to note the flicker of surprise on Guy's face. He had already changed into a pale gray evening suit. She saw that the drawing room was decorated in the same muted grays and creams as the rooms upstairs, but was more fully furnished, with a gleaming antique writing desk and luxuriously deep de Sede sofas and chairs covered in cream chamois leather. There was only one glowing note of color, a large oil painting above the desk which she recognized instantly as a Chagall. It showed a clown-faced boy dancing under a brilliant smiling moon, his lady on his arm, birds wheeling crazily in a peppermint sky. It was as unexpected as an icon in the bare, almost soulless surroundings, as lush as the entrance of full strings in a classical plainsong. What on earth was it doing there?

"Come here." Her employer's voice startled her out of her trance. One look at his impassive face supplied her with the answer to her unspoken question. He barely saw the painting's dreamlike beauty; to him it was merely an investment, art on the hoof. He'd moved to the marble fireplace, picked up a black velvet-covered box. Reluctantly she obeyed his impatient gesture.

"Turn around." She complied, heard the snap of the box opening, felt something cool and silky slide around her neck. The brush of his fingers, unexpectedly warm, sent a small shiver down her spine.

"Yes, I think that will do."

She turned to look at herself in the beveled mirror over the mantel. Around her neck was a fortune in matched black pearls—only, as she now discovered, black pearls weren't black at all but green and rose and deepest ultramarine, like the sheen of oil on water. They glowed with an altogether corrupt and sinister luster against the pallor of her skin.

"But why . . ." She turned back to him, astonished. "Why are you giving me these?"

"My dear Miss Modena, you anticipate." His voice was silky, but the mocking expression in his eyes made a blush rise to her cheeks. "I am not giving them to you at all, merely lending them. They belonged to my grandmother. She would not have approved of their use for an informal evening, but there is no alternative. You must look your best tonight. At least the pearls will distract attention from your dress."

"What's wrong with my dress?" Suddenly she was deflated.

"Nothing. It is simply that this is the third time I have seen you wearing it." His tone was brusque. "When you are with me, you must not wear the same dress more than once at any evening function. It is an unwritten rule. The same dress can be worn at most three times—once at an evening party or afternoon reception, once perhaps in July in the Bois de Boulogne, once, if you must, at the Casino in August."

He noticed her stunned expression and shrugged.

"You will learn. In the meantime I will see that you are supplied with enough . . . uniforms to cover most eventualities. In your own time, of course, you may wear what you like."

Corrie gritted her teeth. She didn't know which was worse, his patronage or his insults. She'd had better treatment as a Savoy chambermaid.

"Now, to work." Already he was at the door.

"Wait." Hurriedly, she attempted to recover her self-possession. "You still haven't told me exactly what sort of work I'm supposed to be doing."

"Oh, that." He hesitated, a curious expression on his face. "I suppose it is essential for you to have some sort of label."

"It certainly is." He made her feel foolish, provincial, but she was determined to have some kind of official status. "What am I, a housekeeper, a secretary, a paid companion?"

He was silent for a long moment. "All of those . . .

and none of those. Let me see." He looked up, smiled his small, ironic smile. "Yes, I have it. Please think of yourself as . . . a chaperone."

A chaperone? What on earth did he mean? There was no time for further questions as he hurried her to the waiting car. Had he some young female relative who needed a chaperone? She hardly thought so. His house showed no signs of a female presence, and in any case he'd made it clear he was hardly ever there.

The intriguing possibilities of her new job occupied her so thoroughly that the car had come to a halt before she thought to ask where they were going to dinner. A raised eyebrow greeted her hurried query.

"Maxim's, of course. It's fortunate that it is not a formal night, or you would never have been admitted, even with me."

Her heart sank. Maxim's . . . the buckwheat crêpes were suddenly a solid lump of lead in her stomach. She was glad of her Savoy training as she followed Guy to the entrance. She felt about six inches tall, but none of her nervousness showed in her face.

Maxim's turned out to be exactly as she'd feared, only more so. Very Right Bank, Harlequin would say, a place to be seen, not one to enjoy, filled with beautiful, bored people, inured to the turn of the century décor and the earth-shaking prices. The sort of place where you lost points if you didn't pay the bill without blinking. As she entered on Guy's arm she was conscious of a small hum of inquiry, at which her companion underwent another of his lightning transformations. His gentle touch at her elbow was a model of courtesy as he lowered her into her chair. She might have been a piece of priceless Lalique glass. She resisted the temptation to stamp fiercely on his toe.

The buzz of interest died away to a manageable murmur, but she was conscious of many curious glances from neighboring tables. She stared moodily at the table setting. This was going to be hard work.

"That's good." His expression was approving. "Don't smile, it makes you look more assured."

"Can I take off my shoes?" she begged him in a whisper across the table.

"Certainly not." He smiled to an acquaintance at a nearby table, his face a pleasant mask. "And for heaven's sake don't eat too much."

Worse and worse. How was she going to fill the time? She could feel eyes boring like hot pokers into the back of her neck. Resolutely she kept her face impassive, ignoring the *maître d'hôtel* who greeted Guy with a practiced combination of deference and detachment. Fortunately after her day's gourmandising she wasn't very hungry and was able to toy with her *noisettes d'agneau Édouard*, *mangetout* peas and braised asparagus, though she had to batten down a slight upsurge of enthusiasm at the sight of the *crêpes joyeuses Sophie*. She frowned in a suitably surly English fashion at anyone who dared to catch her eye, while Guy ate little, scanning the crowded room between the pillars with narrowed eyes. She hadn't any idea what he was looking for or what useful purpose this dinner served, but over coffee he relaxed a little. She watched him with misgiving. He was a strange man, alternating at will between charm and icy detachment.

"This seems a suitable moment." He refilled her wine glass. She waited hopefully. Perhaps, at last, he was going to introduce her to her charge, or at least explain her duties. "I have a great deal to tell you, and you must remember everything I say because I will only say it once." There was no disobeying that quiet but commanding tone. He meant what he said. She concentrated.

"Much will be forgiven you in society because you are English, and know no better, but there are some things that even you must know, if you are to pass muster."

She nodded.

"It is not so difficult," he went on. "It is simply a trick, an illusion. No one must know who you are, but everyone must assume they know. Do you understand?"

She nodded again.

"Good." His expression was approving. "You have had some practice in this kind of role, you should fall into it quite easily. Most people will accept you immediately since you are with me. They will assume you are either an heiress or my mistress."

"Or both."

He inclined his head. "*Merci du compliment*. Luckily, neither an heiress nor a mistress has much need of conversation. But all the same there are some things you must know, some questions you must be able to answer without hesitation, when you are unlucky enough to meet someone with sufficient English to ask them. For instance, you will doubtless be asked what your plans are for the rest of the summer. What will you reply?"

She frowned. "I shall be in Paris, of course."

"No, no. That will not do. No one who is anyone stays in Paris in July and August. The season ends in June, and to be seen in the capital after that is social suicide."

"But I want to stay in Paris, you know I do. It was part of our agreement."

He sighed patiently.

"I don't think you understand. Whether you stay in Paris or not this summer is a matter of sublime indifference to me—but you must *say* you are going elsewhere. *Compris?*" She nodded. He was treating her like a child, she was determined to show him she could be as sophisticated as he was. "Now, where is it to be?"

She thought long and deeply.

"Money no object? I can go where I like?"

"Of course. Remember, you are either an heiress or my mistress."

"In that case, I know exactly where I'm going." She paused triumphantly. This at least must be acceptable. "The Riviera."

"Just as I thought." He shook his head disparagingly. "It is fortunate that I have taken this opportunity to prepare you. Let me explain . . ."

"Wait. I think I can guess what you're going to say." She mimicked his own words. "No one who is anyone goes to the Riviera in the summer."

His lips twitched but his face remained serious.

"Exactly so. You may, if you must, go there for Christmas or Mardi Gras—Cap d'Antibes, please, never Saint-Tropez—or possibly in May, for Cannes, for it's such fun, you know? Though I would prefer you to be in Normandy for the apple blossom. But above all never, never the Riviera in July or August, I beg you. That is only for the masses."

From the sound of it, it seemed that the masses had a great deal more fun. But it wouldn't do to say so. She paused, by now completely bewildered and not a little cross.

"Where on earth am I allowed to go in July and August, then?"

"One of the Atlantic coastal resorts, naturally." His voice was smoothness itself. "The Mediterranean is highly overrated as well as overcrowded. Deauville or La Baule is infinitely preferable. In September Biarritz would be suitable."

"I take it you've never been to the Riviera?" Her voice matched his in smoothness, though she had to bite back her instinctive passionate defense of all her childhood memories. She couldn't afford to reveal the fact that she knew it well.

"Once or twice, in winter, when I was a boy. But nowadays it is very passé, *déclassé*. I prefer to winter in Corsica." His tone was purely dismissive. She fumed in silence.

"But then," he continued, "I doubt very much if you have ever visited the Atlantic resorts."

"No, and I don't want to. From the sound of it I'm sure I wouldn't like them."

He smiled that insulting, patronizing smile.

"You are so quick to judge. You might be surprised to discover in yourself a *côté Atlantique*, as well as a *côté Méditerranéen*. With age and experience it is possible to develop a subtler palate." He ignored her furious glance. "Côte d'Azur, Côte d'Or . . . gold and turquoise have an element of the vulgar, have they not? I prefer the Côte d'Argent, the silver coast."

"I like gold, and turquoise!"

"That may be so." His voice brooked no disagreement. "But in my company you will wear only silver."

Again she was silenced. He continued as if nothing had happened.

"Where were we? Ah yes, it is November. From now on you will be winter sporting, in the Alps or in Corsica—again, this is not permissible in the summer, even at high altitude in Val d'Isère or Chamonix, because summer skiing cannot be regarded as truly serious. In spring you intend to return to Paris for the *vernissages*, the racing at Longchamp or Chantilly. You may mention the Prix du Diane." He paused. "Let me see, what else? Ah yes. In the Champs Élysées you must walk only on the north side, the even-numbered side. You may also ride in the Bois de Boulogne, but never on a Sunday, it is too crowded."

"What do I do on Sundays?" she inquired sweetly.

"You may perhaps attend an afternoon auction at the Hôtel des Rameaux in Versailles." He smiled as she sat back, her mind reeling.

"Any questions?"

"Yes." She shook her head in disbelief. "How am I going to remember all this?"

"You will remember." He was inexorable. "It is essential. Otherwise you will be of no use to me." He waited, scanning her face. "Well, what do you think?"

She shrugged. "I'll tell you what I think." Her smile was wry. "I think it would be easier to be your mistress."

He frowned. For an instant his ice-gray eyes bored into hers with an intensity she found unsettling. Then he smiled, his enigmatic, wintry smile.

"Any time, my dear Corrie." His voice was lazy. "Any time." He quite clearly didn't mean a word of it. She'd meant her words lightly too, but now he was mocking her.

"You are trying to make things difficult for me."

"Yes, a little." He shrugged. "That is my privilege. I am your employer."

"In that case," she snapped, "it's about time you gave me some real work to do."

For a second his expression was almost sympathetic. He was about to reply when he caught sight of something or someone behind her left shoulder. Instantly his face returned to its detached mask. She followed his eyes. Threading her way through the crowded tables between the pillars was a tall redhead, her escort tracking respectfully behind.

"*Bon soir, Guy, comment ça va?*" The redhead's eyes rested eagerly on Corrie, with a mingled look of consternation and speculation.

Guy was unperturbed by the redhead's evident curiosity.

"Allow me to present Mlle Corrie Modena, a friend from England." He spoke in English, to the redhead's obvious frustration. "Corrie, this is Agnès, one of my oldest and . . . er . . . closest friends." Corrie shook the redhead's hand, dodging a double kiss with what she hoped was the right haughtiness and lack of interest. Agnès was about to address her eagerly when Guy intervened. "Unfortunately Corrie doesn't speak a word of French." This time he spoke in his own language. "Though I'm sure you would love to interrogate her."

"But what are you up to, Guy?" Agnès' expression was pleasurably shocked. "Are you sure you know what you're doing? What will our little Blanche say?"

Guy smiled, a slow, dangerous smile. "Blanche and I understand each other, my dear. And in any case, I don't think it is necessarily any of your business."

"But who is she? Where did you find her? Where is she staying?"

By this time Corrie was beginning to feel like a prize heifer in a cattle market. It was quite a struggle not to reveal she could understand every word.

"Her name, as I have already informed you, is Corrie, she is English and she is my house guest. That is all you need to know."

Agnès' eyes widened. She looked at Corrie with a new respect, laced with a little envy, a touch of disapproval and a great deal of speculation. She turned back to Guy.

"*Elle n'est pas mal, quand même* . . ." Her expression was reproachful. "*Mais si jeune!*"

She's not bad, I suppose . . . but so young!

Corrie seethed inwardly. Detecting a slight chill in the air, Guy intervened smoothly.

"If you don't mind, *ma chère* Agnès, we would prefer to be alone. I'm sure you understand."

"*Bien sûr*. Yes indeed." The redhead flounced off, towing her escort behind her in her wake. When she reached her table, Corrie saw heads bend eagerly toward her, could almost hear the buzz of interest.

"Who is that woman?" She could hardly conceal her irritation.

Guy shrugged. "She is not important. She is a satellite, a communication center. One can send a message via Agnès faster than by *pneumatique*."

Corrie felt uneasy. "A message? To whom?"

Guy smiled ingenuously. "Why, to all Paris. At least to everyone who counts. The women, particularly."

"I don't understand." Corrie was losing patience. With an effort she returned to her most pressing problem. "And you still haven't explained to me what work I'm supposed to do."

He was smiling that smile again.

"My dear Corrie, you are doing it at this moment. And most efficiently, if I may say so."

"What do you mean?" She looked around crossly. "I thought you said I was supposed to be a chaperone. How can I be a chaperone when there's no one to . . . well, chaperone?"

He smiled again, a devilish gleam in those pale gray eyes.

"But there is." He lifted his glass ceremoniously, clinked it against hers in a mocking toast.

"Who?"

He drained his glass, set it down neatly.

"Me."

She stared at him in stunned silence for a full minute. He was making fun of her again, he must be. He returned her gaze with the utmost seriousness.

"You?"

"Why not?" One eyebrow rose. "Is it so strange?"

"Of course it is. It's ridiculous. Why on earth should you need a chaperone?" Her voice deepened into sarcasm. "Surely you're old enough to defend yourself?"

"Not too old to be susceptible." He toyed lazily with the stem of his empty wineglass. "And women are persistent, as you have amply demonstrated." Steel flickered momentarily underneath the lightness of his manner, then faded. When he continued his voice was blandness itself. "After all, it is not surprising that women are interested in me. I am attractive, I have the entrée to a world that many women enjoy, and I am an excellent lover. More important, as you have taken considerable trouble to point out, is the fact that I am also extremely rich. Women are logical creatures, French women the most logical of all."

His detachment took her breath away. He was talking of love as if it were a business exchange, a matter of routine. She restrained her indignation with an effort.

"If that is the case"—her voice was as cool and matter-of-fact as his—"why not lie back and enjoy it?"

"One very good reason." He paused, frowning slightly. "I am to be married."

CHAPTER SEVEN

"What?" She almost choked on her wine, set the glass down with an unsteady hand. She felt as if the ground had suddenly caved in under her feet.

"You seem shocked." His eyes probed hers. She couldn't think what to say. Why should she care, after all, what he did with his private life? It was no concern of hers . . . and yet there was this strange, hollow feeling, as if she'd been robbed or tricked or somehow deceived into thinking something was hers when it wasn't and never could have been. How could she have been so wrong about Guy de Chardonnet? He'd seemed so detached, so very much the connoisseur of women, the expert hunter of quarry, including, at one point, herself. Indignation filled her. It was as if she'd been lured into taking part in a competition when the winner had already been decided on behind the scenes. It wasn't fair. Even games had rules . . .

"Well, yes. I take it you knew you were going to be married when you asked me to be your mistress?"

"Of course." He inclined his head politely. "But if I may remind you, the suggestion first came from you."

She felt her cheeks redden. "That may be so . . ." She rallied. "But I didn't notice any overwhelming reluctance on your part!"

"It would be churlish to resist such a charming offer." He touched her hand lightly with the base of his chilled glass. A drop of condensation rolled onto her skin, making her shiver. "You—what is the expression? —knocked me off my feet. And anyway, I fully intended to . . . er . . . terminate our arrangement well before the wedding."

"How thoughtful of you." She sat there, fuming. "How . . . chivalrous."

"I think so. And that is where you come in. It is a chivalrous notion, *n'est-ce pas*, a fitting tribute to one's fiancée, to acquire a chaperone for the months preceding the wedding?" She felt his eyes on her face. "Already it is beginning to work. Seeing you, all those lovely women—and Parisiennes are the loveliest, the most *alléchantes*, women in the world—will think twice before attempting to seduce me from the path of virtue. Already it is beginning to work. By tomorrow all Paris will be talking about you."

"And your fiancée? What about her? What will she think when she hears about me?"

He shrugged. "We understand each other. We have been betrothed for many years. It will . . . amuse her."

"I take it that she is a relation of yours?"

A flicker of surprise crossed his face.

"Yes, she is my cousin. How did you know?"

"Just a guess." She knew more than he suspected about the French way of marriage, especially in the upper echelons. His poor fiancée—betrothed since childhood, trapped by class and social pressure, and the need to keep the family fortunes intact, into a marriage of convenience. With an arrogant, cold-blooded womanizer.

"Naturally, you will be faithful to your wife?" No trace of her scorn showed in her face or voice.

"Naturally. For as long as is necessary."

Of course, the son and heir, to secure the succession. It all made perfect, logical, French sense. But where was passion, longing, romance—everything that made life worthwhile?

"And your fiancée . . . will the same license extend to her after you are married?"

"Certainly not." His tone was adamant, even slightly shocked. "For an unmarried woman an *incartade*, a straying off the map, is permissible. After marriage, never."

"I see." Her sympathy for his poor fiancée deepened. "What is natural for you is unthinkable for your wife."

He shrugged. "It is the way of the world."

Not mine, she wanted to say, but he forestalled her. "This discussion leads nowhere. Not every woman has your obsession with independence, or your . . . eccentric notions of how to achieve it." The sarcasm in his tone brought a renewed blush to her cheeks. "But in any case my marriage is not the issue in question. Do you accept the post I'm offering you, or not?"

She stared at him over the snowy whiteness of the table setting. Something in her rose to the challenge in his eyes. He thought he could play with her, use her as part of whatever game he was presently engaged in. But he might find that his chaperone was a little more than he'd bargained for. When she decided to do a job, whether it was cleaning out hotel rooms, memorizing a score, or watchdogging a professional Don Juan, she liked to do it well.

"I accept. It seems like an excellent notion. One of the few ways, given our mutual dislike, in which we could be of use to one another." Her eyes flashed fire, but her smile was serenity itself.

"Good." He showed no sign that her barb had gone home. With impersonal, punctilious courtesy he escorted her from Maxim's and installed her in the waiting car. But he didn't get in himself.

"Where are you going?" She felt a moment's irrational panic.

"I have . . . business to attend to." He smiled his enigmatic smile. "I will not be requiring your services any longer this evening. André will see you back to the house. I suggest an early night, your first appointment is for 10 a.m. tomorrow. Be ready."

Before she could ask him any further questions he signaled to André and the car drifted silently away from the curb. She was momentarily disoriented. Guy de Chardonnet, despite his limitations, was the only person she knew in Paris. Back at the Avenue Pierre I de Serbie she found on the hall table a small package addressed to her. A typed note propped against it read simply: "Clause four." Inside the package was the enamel box that could have belonged to Marie Antoinette, filled to the brim with Dutch chocolate dragées.

She was suddenly tired, too tired even for chocolate. Guy de Chardonnet was such a confusing man. Even his generosity had a cold, impersonal quality.

She sighed. Why did the thought of his approaching marriage rankle so much? She should have been pleased, because it made her own position that much safer. It wasn't as if she'd wanted him for herself.

Wounded vanity, that's all, she told herself, as despite her fatigue she lay awake for hours. Eventually she fell into a restless sleep to dream that she was dressed in mirrors from head to toe.

Promptly at 10 a.m. the next morning André deposited her outside the house of Dior. Inside, in the discreet dimness, scented lightly with lily of the valley, she was greeted by a black-clad *vendeuse* who showed her to the private salon where Guy de Chardonnet awaited her. He suppressed a small sigh at the sight of her simple yellow cotton dress.

"Daisy yellow, I presume?" he inquired gently as he installed her on an excruciatingly uncomfortable white painted chair.

"You should be glad I didn't wear my scarlet shawl," she riposted gamely.

"You have my heartfelt gratitude, believe me." She noticed that despite yesterday's late night he didn't look at all tired, while she herself was feeling distinctly jaded. He ordered coffee and they sat and sipped while models paraded before them, dipping and twirling and spinning like gaily painted horses at a fairground. Soon, despite her fatigue, she was caught up in the magic of the occasion. There was a cocktail dress, in alternating bias-cut bands of jade green velvet and satin, that she longed to wear, and an evening gown of black tulle peppered with golden roses that was frankly irresistible. And a day dress of scarlet foulard with a matching reversible jacket, and a dragonfly blue silk shirt with a ruffled collar, and a rainbow kimono coat, and a full-skirted summer dress in sizzling apricot with a wide striped sash . . . Halfway through the display she recovered herself enough to notice that the models' eyes were fixed on Guy, as if her presence at his side was a pure irrelevance. One, batting her eyelids and swinging her hips outrageously, was openly flirtatious. Guy, she was glad to see, gave her no encouragement, but frowned solidly throughout the performance, then summoned the *vendeuse*.

"This will not do."

"But they are beautiful clothes, monsieur." The *vendeuse* was clearly torn between diplomacy and the honor of the house.

"I agree, but they are not for mademoiselle."

Corrie buried her nose in her coffee, trying hard not to show that she could understand every word.

"Let me explain," Guy went on. "Mademoiselle, as you can see, is not like the other girls I have brought to you."

"No, monsieur?" The *vendeuse* was clearly most interested, though still treading carefully. Corrie felt a warm flush of gratification sweep through her body. No, she certainly wasn't like the other girls. She was glad her employer had seen the light at last. She was herself—different, special, unique. She was Corrie. But Guy's next words took the wind out of her sails with disconcerting abruptness.

"It's a pity, but she is not a classic beauty. She is not tall enough, as you see, and her figure is too full. Still, I have the utmost faith in you. With your help I hope we may be able to disguise, if not remedy, some of these defects. Do you understand?"

"Oh yes, monsieur." The *vendeuse* eyed Corrie with the expression of a housewife assessing the ripeness of a tomato. Corrie, smarting inwardly with indignation, drained the dregs of her coffee and almost choked.

"Well, what do you think? Can something be done? Her coloring at least is passable, *n'est-ce pas*?"

"Yes, it is interesting." The *vendeuse*'s eyes began to sparkle at the challenge. "I will see what I can do."

Out came the models again, but this time, to their own evident chagrin, they weren't wearing the striking styles they'd worn before. Instead, demure and monochrome as doves, they were all in cream and gray and every shade of beige. Corrie watched them, aghast, every cell in her body crying out for color and glitter. There wasn't a fringe or a starched petticoat in sight, not a ruffle of lace or a twinkle of diamanté. Not even a polka dot.

"Yes, that is much better." Guy nodded approvingly. "Simplicity, severity is the key. I think it will do very well."

Corrie stood, fuming, while the *vendeuse*'s assistants measured every nook and cranny of her body. Her heart longed for savage scarlet, singing yellow, and what had she got? A uniform better suited to a governess than a woman of the world. What did it matter that the jersey and tweed were silk, that every stitch was done by hand? It was dull, dull, dull. And Guy's words still smarted in her memory. So, she wasn't a classic beauty . . . well, who wanted to be a classic beauty anyway? That kind of beauty went out with corsets and tight lacing. She, Corrie, was a classic of the future!

Unfortunately for her self-respect, the session at Dior was only the first of a series of similarly humiliating experiences. At Balmain, Givenchy and Madame Grès it was the same story. Guy allowed each couturier to parade his latest, most delectable fashions, then made the same little speech, and walked away with orders for clothes Corrie would have found unremarkable on her grandmother.

To make matters worse, as the car spirited them along the crowded streets, she could see, almost within arm's reach, girls wearing just the sort of clothes she herself would have chosen—youthful, dashing clothes, in vivid colors, unusual shapes. She pointed them out to Guy.

"Totally unsuitable," was his terse reply. "You are a chaperone, not a gypsy."

"But they're so pretty," she protested.

"Maybe." He was inexorable. "But they are also garish, obvious and cheap."

She fulminated in silence, searching her memory in vain for a suitable retort.

He unbent a little. "It is a question of finding what suits you, a question of style. Elimination is the secret. Of course, if you were a classic beauty—"

"Yes?" She began to bristle. He continued unabashed.

"If you were a classic beauty, you would be able to wear whatever you liked. But since you are not, you must be more careful in your choice."

"You mean I need all the help I can get?"

"That's one way of putting it." His smile was equable.

She refused to give up.

"But surely there are other couturiers, respected couturiers, who are a bit more . . . fun?"

"Whom did you have in mind?"

She searched her memory.

"Yves Saint Laurent?"

"Out of the question." He dismissed her suggestion with a shrug. "Altogether too Left Bank."

"Courrèges?"

"*Garçonne.*"

"Lanvin?"

"Passable—but much too *jeune fille.*" He shook his head dismissively.

"Schiaparelli?"

He laughed. "Are you not a little out of touch? The house of Schiaparelli has been closed for years. In any case, she was not a serious designer, her clothes were much too outré. Gloves with fingernails, blouses with cock feathers and gilt épaulettes? *Ce n'est pas de la couture, c'est du costume.*" He smiled at her tolerantly. "Again this Mediterranean obsession . . ."

She was stung. She remembered a shocking pink ball

gown of her mother's, a spun sugar confection of net and spangles. It had been an icon of her childhood, she'd thought it the acme of glamour and sophistication. Could she, possibly, have been wrong? She banished the doubt that suddenly invaded her mind. It was just that he was so sure of himself, so insultingly dismissive. But there was one thing that proved him wrong.

"What about Balenciaga, then?" She paused to relish her triumph. "He was the greatest dress designer the world has ever known, and he was Spanish!" She smiled sweetly. "Or isn't that Mediterranean enough for you?"

"It is true that Balenciaga was a genius, a master. There I agree with you entirely." But even now he didn't seem particularly chastened. "If his salon was still open it would be our first and probably our last port of call. His style suits you. That is not in itself surprising, it suits all women. He could make a Mexican chorus dancer look like a duchess."

She swallowed the insult, it couldn't dampen her glee. At last she'd managed to score a point. One up for the Mediterranean! But he still seemed unaware of her triumph. His expression was blandness itself as he went on.

"What does surprise me, however, is your conviction that his was a talent inspired by the Mediterranean. The essence of his style is surely not mere self-indulgent chicanery à la Schiap, but discipline, elimination, simplicity. I suspect that you have forgotten, in your admirable urgency to prove me wrong, that Spain possesses, besides its Costa Brava and Costa Dorada, an Atlantic coast. It is there that Balenciaga was born and grew up. And one more thing—I doubt if he would be altogether pleased to hear you call him a Spaniard. He was a Basque, which is a very different thing."

She was silenced. He was infuriatingly knowledgeable, and even more infuriating was the half-mocking glance of commiseration he gave her.

"Balenciaga versus Schiaparelli, Atlantic versus Mediterranean . . . a pretty contest, *n'est-ce pas*?" His voice was light, then it deepened into seriousness. "But I suspect that in such a contest the Atlantic will always triumph in the end. After all, how can a mere lake compete with an entire ocean?"

Corrie ignored his question as beneath contempt. She knew very well what he was inferring. She was cast as the common, crowd-pleasing Mediterranean, he was the noble Atlantic. But maybe she had a few surprises up her sleeve. He'd given her dull clothes to wear, but she would wear them with spirit, with dash, with what the Italians called *slancio*. She'd show him.

She made no further protest as he chose severely simple silver necklaces and earrings for her at Torum, handmade shoes at Céline, gloves and scarves at Hermès. She too was capable of a *côté Atlantique*. Her manner as she accepted his casual largesse was a model of wintry grace. She listened attentively to his advice, pulling out notebook and pencil to record it.

"An excellent idea." He nodded approvingly. She cast her eyes down meekly over her inner scorn. "Silver jewelry only," he went on, "gold is for nouveaux riches and kept women." He watched her as she scribbled. "There's an x not an s in nouveaux," he intervened helpfully. She corrected it obediently, pressing so hard with her pencil that the paper nearly tore. "No color stronger than lilac," he continued.

"What about white? Surely that's as uncolorful as you can get?"

He shook his head. "A common misapprehension. White is the most difficult, the least flattering shade of all. It is suitable only for brides, or—"

"Don't tell me," she interrupted. "I think I know. Classic beauties."

"Precisely. That is why you should never wear white."

"Not even when I get married?"

"If I remember correctly your plans for the future, by the time your wedding day comes around you will almost certainly be too old to wear white."

Her pencil point snapped, along with her patience. "In that case, I shall marry in scarlet, like the gypsies!"

Pointedly she wound down the car window and dropped the notebook into the gutter.

Back at the Avenue Pierre I de Serbie he informed her that until her new "uniforms" arrived she was to consider her time her own.

"I suppose it's more than your reputation's worth to be seen with me wearing anything less?" Her tone was caustic.

"I didn't say that." His reply was aggravatingly mild. "Much as I would enjoy spending every waking hour in your delightful company, I do have other . . . affairs to attend to, which necessitate my absence from Paris for a short while."

"I could come too." She didn't like his use of the word "affairs." "You might need a chaperone."

"Your diligence is praiseworthy." The corners of his mouth twitched. "But I am only under your jurisdiction in Paris itself."

The cunning devil. He wasn't even going to keep to the arrangement he himself had initiated. Still, she didn't care. His absence would give her time to perfect a plan of campaign for when he returned.

"When may I expect you back?" she inquired sweetly.

"I will let you know twenty-four hours in advance, as arranged."

"In writing?"

"Of course."

He bent, kissed her lightly on both cheeks.

"Till then the servants have instructions to regard you as the . . . mistress of the house. Please feel free to call upon them for anything you may require. *Au revoir*, Miss Modena."

She didn't waste a moment. As soon as the car had disappeared out of sight she rushed upstairs, splashed her face with cold water and unpinned her hair. She threw on her scarlet shawl, grabbed up her bag and caught the first Métro to the Place de l'Opéra.

* * *

"M. Beyer."

Karl Beyer lifted his head, momentarily disconcerted. He had left express instructions that he was not to be disturbed. All the cast had dispersed for their lunch break and the staff knew better than to interrupt him while he was at work.

"M. Beyer."

He frowned and laid aside his heavily annotated score. He needed these peaceful times alone, to concentrate his thoughts. As musical director the success of the opera finally depended on him. The singers, with their natural God-given talents, which he did not envy them in the least, were as helpless as children; especially the new South American soprano. But he had age and experience behind him. They had made him ruthless; that was his strength.

He turned from his seat in the orchestra pit to search the gray gloom behind him. There was no sadder, emptier place than an empty opera house on a sunlit afternoon. But down the aisle, like a ray of sunlight that had somehow found its way into the auditorium, came the incongruous figure of a girl in a yellow dress with a scarlet shawl around her shoulders.

"M. Beyer?" She arrived at his seat. He eyed her haughtily, noting her flushed cheeks, her tumbled hair. He felt a curious shock of recognition. There was something familiar about her, even though he was sure he'd never seen her face before. He saw that she was observing him with equal interest. He frowned.

"Yes?" The clipped Austrian accent that he'd never tried to lose had been of great assistance to him throughout his long career. Each of its many different inflections was worth its weight in gold. Sarcasm, command, courtesy, grudging approval—he was able to convey all these with a tone of the voice and an inclination of the head. "What do you want?"

"I want to sing." Her eyes, he noticed, were the color of amethysts. "For you." His heart sank. He almost lifted his voice to summon assistance in getting rid of her, but something—not pity, but curiosity, and a certain staleness he felt in himself after a long and unproductive morning session—changed his mind. She looked so young, so vital, with her wayward hair and those piercing eyes. Now he knew why she seemed familiar to him. He'd seen those eyes before, on a Greek statue of a boy charioteer, the lids tugged back at the corners by the onrushing wind.

"What makes you think I should listen to you?" His tone was dangerously quiet, reasonable.

"Because you may regret it for the rest of your life if you don't."

He said nothing, hiding a small smile. At least she wasn't dull, this fledgling Valkyrie. She probably had a voice like a corncrake, but she wasn't dull.

With a jerk of his head he indicated the stage above them.

"So. You have five minutes."

To give her credit, she barely hesitated a second. With a quick, agile movement, disdaining the steps, she scrambled up onto the boards. The steel safety curtain was down; her vivid face stood out against the gray. The outline of her figure had an oddly definite look. He narrowed his eyes meditatively. There was a word for that quality—presence. Yes, she had it in good measure. She was very, very present. He found his heart beginning to beat just a little faster. There was a disturbing, tangential quality about her. She looked the sort of girl who would break rules, go her own way. There was promise there.

But of course she wouldn't have a voice. Perhaps, if he was lucky, she might be able to sing in tune. Her voice might even be a sweet one, but it wouldn't be what he would call a voice. To fill an opera house with sound, to rise above the massed strings of a full orchestra, you needed more than ambition alone. You needed a throat of asbestos, the lungs of a whale, the constitution of a horse. He sighed inwardly. Girls were all the same—dreamers, romantics. They thought that opera was all birdsong and sweetness. But it was not. Far from it. It was all sweat and phlegm and aching muscles, more like humping a field gun over an army obstacle course.

"What are you going to sing for me?" His tone was polite but he made no effort to conceal his impatience.

"Columbine's aria from Act One of *Pagliacci*. Beginning 'Oh, beautiful midsummer sun . . .' " Her voice was quietly confident. He sighed again. It was worse when they tried to sing in Italian, that most musical, most unforgiving of languages. He bowed his head in acknowledgment and hoped she wouldn't make him suffer too much. He planned to interrupt her as soon as humanly possible.

She settled herself on her feet, seeming to draw up some sort of strength from the ground. There was no doubt about it, she was watchable. But that quality was a mere accident of inheritance, it meant nothing. A caged tiger was supremely watchable, but that didn't mean it could sing.

She drew a deep breath and began to sing. He sat up in his seat. She had surprised him. The rendition of the first, recitative phrases was unusual, sung deep in the chest, a tone so dark it sent shivers down his spine. The voice was low and soft, yet each word could be heard crystal clear. And then, with a suddenness that took him aback, she launched into the aria. He blinked. The voice was big, far bigger than he'd expected, so big he couldn't get a grip on it. He rose to his feet, began to retreat back into the theater. Around him the air was filled with her voice, he could hear nothing else. But despite its penetration, it still had that smoky, shot-silk tone, an individual, slightly blurred quality, not strictly, technically permissible, but undeniably attractive. The high notes were achingly pure and strong, with none of the metallic quality which could affect a dramatic soprano, while the chest notes were so deep and dark, so roundly contralto, that they filled him with a sort of pain.

And she was enjoying herself, he could see. He could hear the pulse of pleasure in her voice as she hit the notes with a passionate accuracy.

"Stop, stop!"

Instantly the sound died away. But her voice went on ringing in his head, profoundly troubling. It had a haunting quality. "*L'heure bleue,*" he thought. That strange blue hour between summer twilight and summer night. Dusky, fragrant, elusive, ever changing. That was her voice.

"Who is your teacher?"

There was a long pause. She came to the edge of the stage.

"I haven't got one." Her tone was matter-of-fact.

He was filled with a sudden irrational anger. It explained a great deal. She had taken such a risk. With a voice so full of potential it was a crime to take such a risk. And yet, despite all the odds, the voice had survived.

"I was hoping you would teach me."

"Ach!" He made a grimace of irritation. Deep inside himself, hardly acknowledged, he felt a tremor of pure terror. He was no longer young, he was a busy man, with many commitments. His career was at its apogee, he had no need of such a challenge. He cursed the moment she'd entered the theater.

"Come down here, at once." Obediently she descended from the stage. He looked at her with new eyes. He should have known. Now he could see, from the depth of her chest, the width of her shoulders, the strong column of her neck and her wide mouth, where that voice derived its power.

"How old are you?"

She frowned at him. "Does it matter?"

He glared.

"I am not in the habit of asking unnecessary questions."

She wasn't cowed, she appeared to find his answer eminently reasonable.

"I'm eighteen."

He gave a deep sigh, of pleasure and dread combined. That voice at eighteen—what would it be like at twenty, twenty-five? A voice to shatter hearts, remake lives.

"Your middle voice is not good." He was in no mood for the refinements of politeness. Her face fell.

"I know. It doesn't always feel right." She looked at him fiercely. "But I will make it better!" She seemed to glow with an inner light.

"Yes." It was in any case a trifle, maybe even an asset. *L'heure bleue*—once seen it was impossible to forget. A shimmering blue haze between the darkness of the lower register, the brilliance of the top.

"Will you teach me?" The intensity in her face startled him all over again. Was she beautiful, pretty, plain? He had no idea. He was old enough to find any young face attractive. It was in any case irrelevant. The voice, the voice was all that mattered.

"No." She lifted her chin. He could tell she was already thinking of ways to change his mind. She was a bully. That was good. The way ahead was going to be difficult, very difficult. "I am not a teacher. A teacher is . . . a mechanic, a doctor. I am an artist." He paused. "And in any case, you are not ready, you are too young."

"What do you mean? Is it the middle voice?"

"No, no." He made an impatient gesture. "That is not important. In any case the instability will cure itself as the voice matures. No, it is not the voice that is too young, it is you."

"I don't understand." Her expression was defiant. "Can I sing, or can't I?"

"Oh, you can sing. No doubt about that. But opera is not simply about singing, it is about feeling. That aria from *Pagliacci*—you sang it like a goddess, an immortal. But Columbine is also Nedda, a Sicilian peasant. She is married to one man, in love with another, too weak to decide between them. That weakness will cost her her life. You sang her—too pure, too strong. Too young." She tried to interrupt but he forestalled her. "Don't tell me. I know what it is like to be young. You feel so much, you feel you know everything there is to feel. But when you sing, you are not to relive these feelings, but to communicate them to others. That requires discipline, training, experience. And most of all courage. Now, at this moment, you think you are brave, but really you are frightened, so frightened of failing that you are competing with the part. Nedda is not a great part. If you sing her as a tragic heroine you destroy her charm. You must learn to sing her with the lightness and poignancy of a bird flying. It must seem natural, unforced, simplicity itself. That is the most difficult thing in the world. If you can achieve it, you will sing a truer Nedda at the age of ninety-five than you did at thirty. For by then your heart will have been broken many times." He eyed her vivid, rebellious face. "There is a Basque saying that has always pleased me. It is simple. 'Remember death.' What does it mean? Does it mean, nothing is worthwhile for death is coming, or does it mean, laugh now, for it is wonderful to be alive? Who knows? But that is what you should remember when you sing Nedda. Remember that in the end, like love, she dies."

"But I don't like the end." Her face was flushed.

"Of course not. You are young, you want Nedda and her lover to run away together and live happily ever after. That is natural. But if it was so, no one would still come to see *Pagliacci*. It would be a nothing, a frippery, a charming comedy. A play."

"But why doesn't she go off with her lover? There's nothing to stop her."

"No, nothing . . . Except weakness, and fear, and habit, all those things to which the young are not subject."

"What has she got to be frightened of? He loves her."

He shrugged.

"Happiness. The future. The death of love."

"But she dies in the end anyway!"

"Yes, but for love. She dies trying to save her lover's life."

"But it doesn't work, he gets killed too!"

"Of course. Love either dies or destroys. You either lose part of yourself and go on loving, or keep yourself and lose love."

There was a long pause. She was obviously deep in thought. Then, at last, she spoke, abruptly.

"I would have gone. Run away with her lover, I mean."

"I know." He smiled at her. "That is why you are not old enough to sing Nedda. Columbine, yes—but not Nedda."

Another pause.

"Then what should I sing?"

Ah, she was so practical. He had spoken more frankly to her than he would have dared to an established star, and still she was not cowed.

"Nothing. You will not sing at all." Filled with a sudden vigor, he leapt onto the stage and walked to the piano. "You will simply do this." He played a few notes in the middle voice, singing along with them on a gradually increasing scale of intensity. "You will sing this over and over again, controlling every breath. And when you have done this enough times—it may take months, it may take years—you will come to see me again."

Her face was intent as she memorized the sequence. Her intensity made him feel tired all over again. Perhaps it would be better if she did not succeed. "And you will never use full voice. You will build up gradually, perfecting the smallest, most beautiful sound. Then, we will see."

"Is that all?"

He smiled. "Is that all? It is possibly the most difficult thing you will ever do, as difficult as the first breath you took when you were a baby. You may never be able to manage it. But while you are practicing, perhaps you will also be acquiring that most essential attribute of an artist, a divided heart."

"Hmm." A spark of amusement showed in her amethyst eyes. "I don't suppose you can tell me where I could get one?"

"An opportunity will come along sooner or later. Life is generous with her unpleasant surprises. I wouldn't be in too much of a hurry if I were you. And now . . ."—with a small shock he realized he hadn't found out her name—"I'm afraid I've done quite enough teaching for one day." The thought of the afternoon's rehearsal was oddly soothing. At least then he would be working with finished artists, no matter how flawed. It was raw potential that was the terrifying thing.

"Wait." She fished suddenly in her bag. "I didn't mention it earlier, but I think we have a friend in common." She held out a scrap of paper in her hand, shook it briefly. It fountained out unexpectedly into a chain of dancing clowns.

He stared at her, the pieces falling suddenly into place. So this was his old friend's protégée . . .

"Why didn't you tell me?"

"I didn't want you to be prejudiced in my favor. I wanted to make it on my own."

"My dear girl, I am far too old for prejudice."

"No one is too old for prejudice. Come on, admit it." Her eyes were disconcertingly direct. "It would have made a difference, wouldn't it?"

He had to admit the truth of what she said. It would have made a difference. He would have been more circumspect, less frank.

"I'm sorry. This changes everything. As you are his protégée, I will of course give you all the help you need."

"You mean you'll teach me?"

"Of course."

She smiled, a sudden three-cornered smile so brilliant it was as if a light had suddenly been turned on in the auditorium.

"Thank you, M. Beyer, but no. I have it on the best of authority that I am not yet ready for what you have to offer. And I wouldn't change that for the world."

She extended her hand to him. Her grip was surprisingly strong.

"I'll be back." It sounded almost like a threat. With relief he watched her walk back up the aisle. Her back was extraordinarily expressive. He was both glad and sorry to see her go.

* * *

Regretfully Corrie retraced her steps between the golden caryatids and marble pillars of the huge auditorium. It was the biggest theater in the world, she longed to see it packed to its ornate gilt ceiling with a bejeweled crowd, eager faces in each brocade-curtained box, lining each velvet parapet. She looked back one last time at the great stage. Her imagination colored the scene, discounting the dimness, filling the emptiness with the unmistakable electric hush of anticipation. In her mind's eye she saw herself, a tiny figure, alone, full center stage. She would hold them. Her voice would reach out like light into every dark corner of their souls. She would set them ablaze, show them worlds they'd hardly known existed. That was the ultimate dream, the ultimate magic.

And she could do it, she knew she could. She emerged into the deserted grand foyer, staggeringly beautiful with its white marble and onyx staircase and Chagall ceiling, and made a vow. One day, it would be filled with people who had come to see and hear her. It would happen, because she would make it happen.

Outside in the sunlight she bought a nectarine from a street stall and sank her teeth deep into the sweet flesh until the juice ran down her chin. She accepted what M. Beyer had said about her middle voice. She had to, he was the best, Harlequin said. But as for the rest . . . She refused to believe that you had to have been in love to sing about it. If that was so, then all the Irish maids at the Savoy were better singers than she was.

It was strange, though, and a little disquieting, that he'd made such a point of discipline and restraint. His words came uncomfortably close to some of the things a certain M. Guy de Chardonnet had told her, though in a different context. She meditated, then spat her nectarine stone with profoundly satisfying accuracy into the nearest grating. Discipline, restraint . . . she was tired of the words. What did they know—they'd forgotten what it was like to be young, perhaps they'd never known. She'd show them. When she was famous, she'd wear what she liked, sing how she liked. She'd show them all.

CHAPTER EIGHT

But somehow, after a whole day practicing M. Beyer's infuriatingly simple but unexpectedly taxing exercises to an audience of none, followed by a solitary dinner in the spacious dining room, some of her confidence had ebbed. After dinner she retreated to the privacy of her room and consoled herself with a helping of dragées and a letter to Harlequin.

Dear Harlequin,

I have so much to tell you that I hardly know where to begin.

Here she paused, chewing the end of her pen. How much could she tell him without breaking Guy de Chardonnet's clause nine? He'd kept his side of the bargain, she must try to keep hers. But it would be difficult. She wasn't used to leading a double life with Harlequin.

I am in Paris, and it's everything you said it would be. I feel like someone who's died and gone to Heaven. And yet, if I didn't know that it was your city, if you hadn't told me so much about it in your letters, I think it would be possible to feel very lonely here. If it wasn't for you, I'd feel like a stranger. To think I was going to take Paris by storm! It frightens me a little—it's so beautiful, so stylish . . . a Belle Dame Sans Merci. Why should she be kind to a country girl fresh from the provinces?

But I have been lucky, I mustn't forget that. At the

moment I am working as social secretary to a French businessman, who has been kind enough to find lodgings for me. But please go on writing to me care of Mr. Whitaker. I don't know how long I'll be at my present address. A great deal depends on M. Beyer.

Yes, I went to see him, the very first free moment I had. I like him. You said I would, remember? I was so excited—I thought I wouldn't be able to sing at all, but there was something about him . . . He listens as if it was the most important occupation in the world. I don't know what he thought, he wouldn't tell me, not in so many words. He sent me away, with some exercises to do, and told me not to sing until I saw him again.

Now you know why I'm feeling as I do. It's as if he's told me not to breathe or eat. How am I to improve if I can't sing? How can I tell if I'm making progress? It's so frustrating, to be in Paris at last, and not to sing. Maybe I shouldn't have come at all, maybe I'm not ready. My mind is full of doubts. I wish you were here, I wish I could see you, talk to you. Couldn't we meet, just once? I'd like to drink coffee with you in a little bar, we could talk about music and Paris and people, and pretend that the city belongs to us.

I want to see you. Please.

Your poor, provincial Columbine.

At least, while she waited for his reply, there were other things to occupy her energies. Her new wardrobe arrived, and she discovered to her amusement that Guy de Chardonnet had assigned each outfit a number, ranging from one to twenty-four. It was typical of him; he wasn't even going to trust her to choose which one to wear. Her determination to thwart his high-handed arrangements redoubled. She planned and plotted carefully, with all the meticulous attention to detail she'd otherwise have put into her singing. Her campaign had several fronts. Knowing his preference for women with a sophisticated pallor, she researched the daily progress of the one beam of sunlight that penetrated the inner courtyard. In every spare moment she was out there, exposing every inch of skin she could. The garden held nothing but greenery—sober shrubs and low hedges trimmed within an inch of their lives, so she bought a packet of poppy seeds and planted them in the balcony tubs which caught the most light. In the evenings she spent many hours behind the locked door of her room, testing the possibilities of her wardrobe in front of the mirror. Gradually, inexorably, her plan took shape.

Five days later Harlequin's reply arrived.

"Patience, my dear Columbine. I told you from the beginning that once you were in Paris everything else would begin to fall into place. But I had no idea you would be here so soon. What sorcery have you been practicing? It is extraordinary to think that you may be only a door or a street away, that if I lean out of the window I may hear your voice, practicing scales. I feel I would recognize it instantly.

But no, my Columbine, we must not meet. Not yet. Just now I know I can help you more by remaining in the wings, a sort of deus ex machina. For that I need my mask. Without it, who would I be? Just another face, a man in the crowd.

I don't want to take that risk. What we share matters too much to me. You are my talisman, my hidden treasure, an element in my life that nothing can tarnish. Try to understand. One day, who knows . . . ?

As for your singing, I know it is difficult, but you must believe in your talent. I do, and I have never heard you sing. M. Beyer does too—he might not tell you in so many words, but he listened. You can't expect the encore before the curtain goes up on the first act! And your talent won't disappear from lack of use, not if it's the real thing. Gold doesn't rust. Think of your gift as a seed lying dormant underground. Some seeds need a touch of frost before they can begin to grow. When the time is right you'll find all the waiting has been worthwhile."

Chastened, Corrie returned to her exercises. She stood by the drawing-room piano, singing softly, sweetly, pacing herself as she'd been instructed. They were long, boring hours, enlivened only by the thought of the surprise she was going to give Guy de Chardonnet when he returned.

A week later, another typed note on the hall table announced that Guy de Chardonnet would be requiring her services the next evening. It was curt and to the point. "6.30 p.m. No. 9." Number nine was a demure high-collared lilac jersey tunic and matching skirt, with absolutely no ornamentation and as much personality as a filleted fish. She smiled as she crumpled the note in her fingers. She knew the rules, but rules were made for bending. She would add nothing to the austerity of Guy de Chardonnet's choice, merely . . . rearrange a little.

The next evening, promptly at 5.30 p.m., Toinette brought to her room a small posy of violets. They'd been kept fresh in the fridge since delivery that morning, and drops of icy water clung to the tiny velvet petals.

"How thoughtful," said Corrie, wishing that for once, just once, Guy de Chardonnet might find himself capable of an unpremeditated action.

At 6.10 p.m. André collected her and delivered her to an address in the Faubourg St-Honoré, one of a row of stately classical mansions in the grand manner. In the vestibule, before the astonished gaze of the concierge, she made a few final adjustments to her costume.

"Would you keep this for me, please?" she asked him sweetly as she swept into the lift. He was too stunned to think of a reply. She found her way without difficulty to the right door. From inside a gracious hum of conversation drifted out into the dimly lit, plushly carpeted corridor. She paused, straightened her tunic, then made her entrance.

She would treasure forever the memory of Guy de Chardonnet's expression as he saw what she had done to number nine. It had started life as a demure Chinese-collared tunic, but that was no more than a memory. She was wearing it back to front, leaving the tiny little pearl buttons undone as far as she dared. She'd removed the stiff fabric belt, so that the silk jersey clung to her body as she walked. Her silver necklace, instead of being around her neck, was looped twice around the flesh of her upper arm. And there was one other small detail. She had left off the skirt. Beneath the tunic was nothing but a bare, dizzying length of golden brown leg.

The effect was electrifying. She could feel every man's eyes on her as she entered, pretending a nonchalance she didn't entirely feel. It wasn't altogether surprising. She knew from her mirror that she looked extraordinary, half slave-girl, half sophisticate, with her severe chignon and rich brown tan. She'd painted her toe nails scarlet, accentuated the slanting corners of her eyes with lacquered black wings. She waited long enough for the silence to acquire a thunderous momentum of its own, then called across the room in a clear, loud, ultimately English voice:

"Guy! I'm over here, darling!"

All eyes swiveled as Guy, his face dark with fury, made his way slowly through the guests.

"What is this?" His expression was fierce.

"Number nine." Her eyes widened innocently. "Don't you recognize it?"

"But where are your stockings, your belt . . . your skirt?"

"But M. de Chardonnet . . ." Oh, how she was enjoying herself. "I thought you said elimination was the secret? And look . . ." She lifted one slim ankle. "I didn't forget the violets." There they were, neatly pinned to the strap of her delicate suede sandal.

His face was black. She smiled winningly. "Don't be angry. You wanted me to attract attention. I'm just doing my job. And look around you." She gestured at their fascinated onlookers with considerable pride. "It's working."

With an effort he resumed his pleasant mask. His manner as he kissed her briefly on the cheek and drew her into the gathering was courtesy itself. Only she heard the words he whispered in her ear.

"It's war, then?"

She smiled winningly at the aristocratic elderly couple, evidently their host and hostess, to whom he introduced her, but didn't bother to cloak her reply in a whisper.

"Total war."

His face was grim as they progressed through the gathering. She took pity on him. "Don't worry. At least"—she winked outrageously at a wide-eyed blonde in gray grosgrain and pearls—"you won't be bored. I think I can see to that."

"Your thoughtfulness overwhelms me," he replied through clenched teeth. Then, at last, a reluctant grin spread across his face. He shrugged with true Gallic fatalism. "What does it matter? I am already ruined. Do your worst."

And so she did. The next day, at the famous *déjeuner mondain* at the Ritz she wore not one but two dresses, and divested herself of one after the first course. Crude, but undeniably effective.

And that wasn't the limit of her invention. As she and Guy progressed through the height of the Paris season, in a ceaseless round of cocktail parties, evening receptions, visits to the races, select dinners at the Plaza-Athénée, the Crillon, Prunier's, Fouquet's, Le Doyen, she perfected and refined her technique. He made a few attempts to restrain her, but it was impossible. He couldn't very well rip the clothes from her back. He tried vetting her before she left the house, but then she simply retired to the ladies' room as soon as she arrived and rearranged her clothing to her own satisfaction. At Prunier's, over the exquisite clams for which the restaurant was famous, it took him a full half hour of uneasy scrutiny before he realized she was wearing odd shoes. At the Tour d'Argent, over pressed duck with its own serial number and against the backdrop of Notre Dame, he noticed that something about her appearance was attracting attention from the other diners. It was only when she turned her back to visit the ladies' room that he saw she had fixed a huge paper number three across her shoulder blades. "A little aide-mémoire," she explained. "Just to remind me which dress you wanted me to wear tonight." For dinner in the Eiffel Tower's second floor restaurant, in honor of the view of the illuminated fountains in the Place de la Concorde, she painted her fingernails with luminous paint, while in the echoing pillared magnificence of La Coupole, which, she declared dismissively, reminded her of St. Pancras station, she accepted his compliments on her softly ruched gray velvet cape with demure pleasure. It was only later, somewhere between the Baltic herring and the ice cream sprinkled with rum-soaked raisins, that she added, "I'm surprised you didn't recognize it. It's the skirt I was wearing yesterday."

It was only after three hectic weeks that she realized her campaign, successful as it had been, hadn't achieved its main object. Instead of causing a massive scandal, her escapades had simply provided amusement. She was still welcome everywhere, her eccentricities forgiven, even expected. She had earned herself a nickname, "*la folle anglaise*," the crazy English girl, and after a while the eyebrows stopped going up every time she entered the room. Now, finally, she realized why Guy de Chardonnet hadn't tried harder to control her. He understood the society he moved in, he knew that it had to be treated with blasé indifference, like a pedigree cat, until it crept into your lap and fawned to be petted.

Still, she had a few triumphs. At a formal *thé dansant* a society hostess was scandalized to learn that the dress Corrie was wearing was constructed entirely out of silk scarves held together with silver earrings, while at a literary reception for a Prix Goncourt winner an eminent French writer could hardly be prevented from testing her claim for himself.

And her chaperonage, if unorthodox, was certainly efficient. She noticed the attention which surrounded him wherever he went, the sly glances from the young and elegant Parisiennes, the knowing glances from the older ones, of an intimacy she suspected wasn't based on pure friendship. Whenever a discussion with an unattached woman seemed to reach an interesting stage she would drop one of her more drastic English comments, for his ears only.

"Why her? She walks like a rhinoceros" was effective, especially on the third or fourth occasion, when the mere sight of her approaching with a warlike gleam in her eye was enough to destroy his composure.

The general speculation about their relationship amused them both. She played the scarlet woman with gusto, and once, after a late party in one of the modern ateliers of the old Halles area, Guy whispered to her in the hall, just as they were saying goodbye to their host, a Spanish sculptor, "Let's give them something to think about," and pulled her into a Valentino clinch. She moved instinctively to slap his face but the devilish twinkle in his eye forestalled her.

"Don't forget, we are perfectly safe with one another." It was true, her dislike of everything he represented protected her as surely as his preference for blondes protected him.

But even sworn enemies could learn to respect each other. At the Louvre he listened with an expression of polite interest as she explained to him that the museum's greatest treasures, the Venus de Milo and the Mona Lisa, weren't French at all but Italian. Later that same day, he didn't seem in the least surprised when she turned to him after the first act of an English language performance of Marivaux' champagne comedy, *The Game of Love and Chance*, and announced in ringing tones that she thought the plot was a lot of nonsense and the characters fools to be taken in by a mere change of costume. He simply shrugged.

"Love makes fools of us all, *n'est-ce pas*?"

"Not me," she replied tartly. "I know exactly what I'm looking for."

He inquired, with the same expression of amused curiosity, what she would consider the credentials for the perfect lover. She replied without hesitation, thinking of Harlequin.

"A man who loves me for what I am, not for what he thinks I am."

"Ah . . ." His face darkened momentarily, his voice had an edge of bitterness. "Now who is the perfectionist?"

The only subject that remained taboo was his fiancée. Her sympathy for the poor girl increased when she learned that she lived in the country. How could a country cousin cope with the sophisticated city life of a man like Guy de Chardonnet? It seemed that his fiancée was frail as well, because she couldn't take the heat of Paris even in June, spending the early summer in the family château just outside Paris and retiring for August to the Breton coast.

The days passed, acquiring a curious rhythm of their own. The household rose late after the evening's junketings. In the mornings she would check on her secret poppies, already unfurling their heads; in the afternoon, when the servants were occupied well out of earshot, she would practice her exercises, and late at night she would retire to bed with her day's ration of chocolate, always waiting for her on the hall table when she returned, write letters and study scores. Sometimes Guy stayed the night, but she never saw him after he bade her goodnight in the hall. Sometimes, rarely, they had supper together, and read in the drawing room, in an oddly companionable silence.

"Being with you is almost as good as being alone," he said to her.

"Thank you." It was an odd, backhanded compliment, but she knew what he meant. Both of them were beginning secretly to enjoy their masquerade.

But then something happened that changed everything. One evening they returned late from a function at the Élysée Palace, and the hall was full of a strange, heavy scent. Guy's expression altered instantly. Despite the lateness of the hour he summoned Toinette.

"When?"

"This evening, monsieur."

Looking around her in the gloom Corrie traced the source of the scent: white lilies, huge baskets of them, overflowing on every table, their waxy transparent blooms brimming over with sweetness. She looked from them to Guy and back again. His face was dark, with an expression on it she'd never seen before. Suddenly, he looked like a stranger. She didn't understand what had happened. How could something so innocent as a gift of flowers have such an extraordinary effect?

When his eyes met hers they were curiously blank, as if he hardly registered her presence. There was a long frozen moment in which she felt the draft from the still open door behind them touch her bare shoulders like the first breath of winter. She shivered.

"You are cold, Corrie." His voice was distant, completely lacking in emotion. "Go to bed." His tone was so peremptory, so dismissive, that before she knew it she found herself walking up the stairs. As she entered her room the scene in the hall below seemed still to be printed on her retinas, Guy alone and motionless, surrounded by lilies, the cold outside air stirring his hair.

She went immediately to bed, but somehow, even after piling on all the spare bedding she could find, she couldn't get warm. She thought longingly of her chocolate on the hall table. She'd forgotten to collect it. She lay awake, for some reason frightened even to move. Hours later, it seemed, she heard Guy's door close, but the light in his bedroom stayed burning. Eventually, holding onto the thought of Harlequin, her one certainty in the strange glittering world that Guy de Chardonnet inhabited, she fell asleep.

Then, suddenly, she was awake. She felt disoriented. It was still dark. Moonlight streamed in solid silver from the open window. She shivered and pulled the covers closer around her. It was late, somewhere in the chilly pre-dawn hours. She could have been anywhere, nowhere. A noise sounded from the hall below, the slamming of a car door, raised voices. What was going on? For some reason she was suddenly panic-stricken. Even half-asleep she could sense the atmosphere in the air. It reminded her of things she'd rather forget—the night her mother died, the sudden hushed, urgent commotion in the hotel corridors, lights snapping on and off, the tread of official footsteps at her door . . .

But she was older now, she could look after herself. She didn't have to wait, like a small helpless animal cowering in the dark, for her fate to be decided. She could face her fears and end them.

Bleary-eyed, she tumbled out of bed. The floor was cold, the moonlight made her dizzy. She poked her head around her door. The hall beneath was brilliant with light. Framed in the doorway was the figure of a woman all in white.

Corrie blinked, half-dazzled. For a long moment she couldn't make out in the blaze of light whether the woman was old or young. She was tall and slender, with that unmistakable pure natural fairness that cannot be achieved by any artificial means yet looks artificial. A corona of white-blond hair framed a purely, severely classical face, moon-pale, from the aristocratic narrow nose to the diamond-bright pale gray eyes. Her skin was so pale Corrie could almost see the blue blood flowing underneath. If she had blood at all . . . she hardly looked real.

But this was no dream. The murmur of voices below was only too real. Despite her sleep-fuddled state and the lateness of the hour Corrie could sense that the atmosphere crackled with tension, strange forces that she didn't understand. She felt like a child, stumbling by accident into an adult world far beyond her comprehension.

"*Eh bien, où est elle?*" The woman's voice rang out, clipped and high, each syllable icy clear. "I can hardly wait to see her, this new discovery of yours."

"You will have to be patient, my dear Blanche. It's much too late for . . . social calls." Guy's voice, deep and harsh, held a note of strain she hadn't heard before.

"I don't care." The woman's eyes glittered. "I want to see her, now, this minute. I insist. It's my right."

Guy sighed. When he spoke his voice was muffled, with a sound of infinite weariness.

"She is not my mistress, Blanche."

The woman stared at him curiously through narrowed eyes.

"*Vraiment* . . . Can it be that you are losing your touch, *mon petit* Guy? Then why bring her here?"

"Why not? She had nowhere to stay, no friends. I felt sorry for her."

"Such chivalry . . ." Blanche's voice deepened into sarcasm. "I shall believe that when I see her."

Belatedly, with a shock of outrage, it dawned on Corrie exactly who it was they were discussing. Instantly she was wide awake, pure fury coursing through her veins. How dare they? "I felt sorry for her . . ." Guy's casual, dismissive voice rang in her ears.

"Guy?" With an effort she controlled her voice. The discussion had been entirely in French, she mustn't show that she'd followed every word.

"Corrie?" Guy stepped out from beneath the stairwell and looked up.

Corrie saw with surprise that he had changed from evening dress into the elegant chalk-white suit he'd worn for their dinner together at the Belvedere. But that was all that was familiar about him. As their eyes met his face was blank, a shadowed mask, the face of a stranger.

He turned back to Blanche. The look he gave her was unreadable, but his voice held a note of warning. "Permit me to present to you Corrie, an English friend who is presently staying with me. She speaks no French." Even his voice was barely recognizable. The tone was impersonal, the words had no meaning. It was the voice of an automaton.

There was a profound, electric silence as the woman stared up the flight of steps at Corrie.

"Corrie." Guy reverted to English. "May I introduce my fiancée, Marie-Blanche de Chardonnet?"

Astonishment left Corrie momentarily speechless. Surely this couldn't be his country cousin? But looking closer she could see an eerie family resemblance, centered in those pale gray eyes, colorless as melted snow.

Suddenly, as shocking as the sound of breaking glass, the woman's laugh rang out.

"*Mais qu'est-ce que tu fais là, mon ange?*" Ignoring

Guy's cue she continued to speak in French, as if Corrie didn't even exist. "I am ashamed of you. Where is your judgment, your sense of discrimination? Look at her . . ."

Corrie, meeting that razor-sharp stare, was suddenly acutely conscious of her bleary eyes and tangled hair. She tugged her ancient dressing gown more tightly around her. It was almost as if Blanche could see her naked body beneath the fabric.

"My poor darling." Blanche stepped closer to Guy, looked up at him through lowered lashes. "Were you so lonely without me?"

"Perhaps." Again his voice was harsh. "Or perhaps I felt in need of less . . . demanding company."

Blanche's eyes gleamed. "Don't play games with me, *chéri*. I know them all."

"Maybe not this one." Guy smiled a small, totally mirthless smile.

Blanche shrugged.

"Play on, my darling." Her answering smile held both threat and challenge. "Just so long as you don't forget who makes the rules."

She lifted up one long white languorous arm, touched his mouth with one long white finger. Corrie, frozen on the stairs, burned with embarrassment. It was a supremely personal gesture, yet oddly theatrical, almost as if it were for her benefit. She saw Guy's hand tighten on Blanche's wrist.

"*Assez*." His voice was rough. "We are not alone." Corrie's ears burned. Enough—it certainly was. Blanche smiled, a small triumphant smile, and turned away in a swirl of snow-white drapery. There was a calculated elegance to the movement which Corrie envied. She seemed invincible, cocooned in her shell of light, with the matchless, self-generated radiance of a woman who has always had everything she wanted.

"*Tu viens?*"

Are you coming? It was exquisitely, appallingly rude, the indifference with which Blanche turned her back on

Corrie, her hand resting on Guy's arm with an insolent, predatory, possessive carelessness.

For a moment, as she saw them standing side by side in the doorway, Corrie felt their images blur together. They both wore white, they were almost the same height, their eyes were disturbingly alike, but the resemblance wasn't merely physical. There was something else that bound them together, some invisible link, some strange gravitational pull. They might never touch but they would circle each other forever, like the earth and the moon.

Guy's eyes met Corrie's, briefly, then the door closed and they were gone. Outside there was the roar of a highly charged engine, a spurt of gravel under tires, then silence.

Corrie stood on the stairs shaking, and not just with cold. "I prefer blondes," he'd said. What he hadn't told her was that in Blanche de Chardonnet he already had the ultimate blonde, the master original. All the others were simply pale copies.

And there was something else he hadn't told her, an omission so obvious it was unforgivable. The ultimate betrayal. How his friends must have laughed behind her back as he paraded her before them, like some sort of circus clown. They knew Blanche, they knew that a lantern might as well try and outshine the moon. For Blanche, the poor little country cousin on whose image she'd wasted so much faintly scornful pity, was quite simply the most beautiful woman she'd ever seen.

By morning her rage had simmered down to a cold, quiet resolution. Guy had betrayed her, used her as a pawn in some dark game of his own, but she wouldn't let him get away with it. Given time, she could come up with a suitable revenge.

As she'd expected, she didn't see Guy all day. That evening she didn't collect her chocolate after dinner. It would have choked her. Guy, obviously just on his way out to another assignation with Blanche, caught her halfway up the stairs.

"What's the matter? Are you on a diet?"

"Certainly not." She hated him in that moment, with a total, irrational hatred. She drew herself up with dignity to her full height. "I have simply given up chocolate."

"Why?"

"Oh, I don't know." She shrugged with what she hoped was a suitably world-weary air. "It's a childish habit. I don't think I ever really liked it."

"As you wish. *Bonsoir*." Obviously, he couldn't wait to be gone.

That night, at 4 a.m., she slipped down to the hall and collected the chocolate. There was no light from Guy's bedroom and the door was open, revealing an empty room. The house seemed suddenly very quiet. She went back up the stairs and ate the entire bar under the bed clothes, wishing she'd never set eyes on Guy de Chardonnet.

The next morning, after a few hours' restless sleep, she looked in the mirror and didn't like what she saw. My eyebrows are too black, she thought angrily. Perhaps I should streak my hair. She drew in a cupid's bow mouth with lipstick, grimaced, rubbed it off. It made her look at best like an actress, at worst like a woman of the streets. Why? Maybe it had something to do with her body, the full curve of her breasts, the sturdy line of her throat. She looked earthy and sensual, like a peasant, when what she wanted to look like was a princess in a fairy tale.

No wonder Blanche had dismissed her so utterly, without a moment's hesitation. Suddenly she felt fat and frumpish and hopelessly inelegant. She wanted pallor, an aristocratic profile, hair like platinum . . .

And none of those were to be found in the closet. She ran her finger over the serried ranks of clothes, chose a silver-gray suit, rejected it because it made her feel forty, finally selected a lilac blouse and skirt, adding silk stockings and a trace of rouge.

As she'd suspected Guy was already at the breakfast table. She'd heard him moving about, though she hadn't heard him come in the previous night. He looked disgustingly cheerful and refreshed.

"You look tired. Didn't you sleep well?"

Instantly she regretted choosing the lilac, it only accentuated the violet shadows under her eyes. She felt bitterly offended. Knowing what she did, she resented even his solicitude.

She sat down and regarded the hot croissants, which she normally devoured, with disfavor.

"Just coffee, please, Toinette. Black."

She sipped her coffee and watched as Guy opened the morning's mail with an ivory paper knife. Against her will she found herself fascinated by the swift, dextrous movements of his hands. He was very systematic, dividing the correspondence into invitations, circulars, urgent letters, routine letters that could be answered by his secretary. She waited, trying to disguise her impatience, for him to tell her which was to be their next function. She could barely prevent herself from craning to look over his shoulder.

A respectable pile of engraved cards was mounting on his left. She stared at them with sudden, almost proprietary jealousy. They were her invitations . . . but perhaps now that Blanche was back in Paris she would be taking her place? Somehow, she didn't like the idea.

Still the invitations mounted, still Guy said nothing. One in particular held his attention.

"May I see that?" She was suddenly consumed with curiosity. He hesitated, adding fuel to the flames. With a facility that amazed her, she said, "The crest intrigues me."

He shrugged and handed it to her, with only a trace of reluctance. It was an invitation to a Grand Ball, the Nuit Blanche, at the Château de Corbeville. Replies were to be directed to Marie-Blanche de Chardonnet. Across the top, in an elegant slanting script, was one word. *Chéri*. Darling. Corrie dropped the invitation as if it had been red hot.

"I take it you won't be requiring my services for this one?"

"I don't think you would enjoy it." He made a dismissive gesture. "It is simply our annual ball, a family affair. Very dull." She narrowed her eyes, fuming with inward rage. He was deliberately attempting to mislead her. Only last week she'd seen an old copy of *Paris-Match* describing the Nuit Blanche, only she hadn't made the connection. It was a glittering affair, the event of the season, its triumphant, logical conclusion. All the guests, by unwritten rule, wore black or white—black for the men, white for the women. For the women it was a test, a challenge, an exercise in ingenuity and social one-upmanship. It had been known for couturiers to include a special white number in their collections for this single event. Reputations would be made or lost, friendships cemented or destroyed, images gilded or tarnished, at the Nuit Blanche. It was an elegant, bloodless battlefield. Everyone who was anyone, or ever hoped to be, would be there.

Except her. With a blinding flash of insight she realized that this was the reason he hadn't allowed her one single item of white in her wardrobe. It wasn't anything to do with her not being a classic beauty—how many of the other women guests could aspire to that, after all?—it was simply so that she wouldn't be able to go to the Nuit Blanche. She was to stay meekly at home, while he and Blanche acted out the starring roles at the most important event of the season. She'd done all the hard duty—the endless standing at cocktail parties, the exhausting round of receptions and gala nights, only to prepare the way for Blanche's glory. She, Corrie, had been reliable, prompt, ever entertaining and cheerful—the perfect wife, in fact, with none of a wife's privileges. And now Blanche was going to scoop up all the credit and the cream at once.

Envy, jealousy and pure fury raced through her mind in a scalding stream. She came to herself with a sudden jolt of recognition. She wasn't thinking like a wife, she was thinking more like a mistress. And she was neither. With an effort she regained her equanimity.

"Do you want to come?"

He was watching her closely. Her mind was in turmoil, but not a hint showed.

"White doesn't suit me. I have it on the best authority."

She smiled, feeling her jaw muscles ache with the effort. She laid aside her napkin and rose from the table. She felt as if she'd just been run over. She could barely move. She went slowly upstairs and changed into an outfit of beige silk jacquard. In the same shocked daze she went down to the drawing room. Her heart was beating erratically, and she felt hot flushes running over her body.

"I'm going out."

He was standing by the window reading a letter. He didn't even look up, just nodded. It was as if she didn't exist. She was instantly, instinctively sure that it was a love letter he was reading, nothing else could merit such complete attention. Look at me, she felt like shouting, look at me. Tell me with your eyes whether you think I'm pretty or not. Does my dress suit me, do you like the way I've done my hair? But he didn't look up. She shut the door with a slam. For the first time in years she seemed to have lost control of the most ordinary actions.

She spent the morning in the boutiques of the Left Bank, looking at everything, buying nothing. When she returned to the house in the afternoon, tired and cross, a note on the hall table informed her that Guy would be spending the three days preceding the ball in the country, helping with arrangements, and would not be needing her services until further notice.

Three days. They were the longest days Corrie had ever lived through in her life. She moped about the house, unable to read or study or sing or settle down to do anything. She began a letter to Harlequin, then couldn't think what she wanted to say. She'd become a stranger even to herself. The days were bad, but the nights were worse. Instead of falling into the exhausted sleep she craved, she dreamed, endlessly, of vengeance. In black and white.

She wasn't sure when she first got the idea. It began as a fantasy, a crazy midnight scenario she played out in her head, something to while away the hours. But it grew. It was a last-ditch, burned-bridge sort of idea, yet it had its own destructive appeal. She tried to resist it, told herself Harlequin wouldn't have approved. She hardly approved herself. But it was too late. The seed had taken root and blossomed.

The morning before the ball she knew she was going to do it. Once the decision had been taken the rest was easy. Coolly, efficiently, with only a faint inward tremor to remind her of the enormity of what she was planning, she set about her preparations. She took her gray Dior two-piece to a backstreet clothes dealer and with the money she got from him paid a visit to a theatrical costumier's near the Opéra. She knew exactly what she wanted and was willing to pay the exorbitant charge. She smuggled her packages upstairs without being seen, then waited till the sun had left the inner courtyard before she culled a bunch of the splendid black-hearted crimson poppies from the balcony. They shone like Burmese rubies in her hands.

She canceled dinner and gave the servants the evening off. Alone in the house at last, she unpacked her new acquisition. Hers for an evening only, but hers. She hardly dared look at what she'd selected from the costumier's crowded racks. Was it too much? In the spartan surroundings of her bedroom it certainly seemed so. But she rallied. Nothing could be too much for this occasion. He'd called her taste outré . . . well, she'd show him he didn't even know the meaning of the word. She'd worn daisies and gone barefoot, but that was a mere peccadillo compared to this. Tonight, once and for all, she was going to be noticed.

She slipped the heavy material over her head, struggled with the unfamiliar fastenings. She loosened her hair, threaded it with poppies, slid on the beaded slippers. Finally, her heart thundering in her ears, she looked in the mirror, nodded once. Yes, it was effective. She didn't smile at her reflection, the occasion was too serious for that. Tonight she was no light-hearted, frivolous Parisienne. Tonight she was Italian, dangerous, possessed. She swung the full black cloak around her shoulders and pulled the wide hood over her head. Now her preparations were complete, except for one thing. Noiseless in her beaded slippers she ran down to the drawing room and collected the invitation Guy had left on the mantelpiece. Without hesitation she added a bold black "e" onto Blanche's inscription, so that it read "*Chérie,*" blotted it carefully, and tucked it into her cloak.

A ring sounded at the door. The taxi was waiting. She was ready.

CHAPTER NINE

Silver *feux d'artifice* laced the sky. Guests watched the fireworks from the stone terrace, looking down between the columns of tall cypresses where fountains played, reflecting the glittering light of the fireworks above. Other guests wandered in the green and white classical garden for which the Château de Corbeville was justly famous. Spotlights hidden in the inky depths of the cypresses illumined the tiny stars of jasmine, the translucent bells of convolvulus, twining around trellises and spilling from stone urns. In the center of the maze was an ancient magnolia framed in sea-green rosemary, its trunk a black silhouette between twin Falconet sphinxes.

Back on the terrace, lily-scented candles, tall and white, illumined the cold buffet. But the food was hardly touched. The night was too important, too magnificent for mere hunger. The champagne was iced, the conversation careful. The fireworks ended with a last incandescence, leaving the velvet summer sky blacker than before. The moon swam up palely behind the cypresses. In the momentary silence as the guests began to return from the terrace to the pillared eighteenth-century hall where the twenty-piece orchestra was playing a stately gavotte, Guy de Chardonnet allowed himself a moment's relaxation. His eyes strayed to Marie-Blanche, moving gracefully among their guests. She outshone them all. No one understood the subtle language, the possible intonations of white as she did. Tonight, for the official announcement of their engagement, she had gone one step further, allowing herself the license of both a hostess and a prospective bride. Her ice-white satin, of supreme elegance and simplicity, was interleaved with strips of rippling silver which captured and reflected all the light of the moon. It was a clever piece of sleight-of-hand, almost a cheat, but supremely effective. Citrine diamonds set in platinum glittered in her ears and at her throat, but her fingers, in readiness for the evening's climax, were bare.

"*La belle Blanche* . . ." Guy caught the admiring whisper and nodded in complete agreement. Here in her natural setting Blanche was invincible. No woman could rival that perfect, classic beauty. Every time he looked at her he was reminded of the first time he'd seen her. He'd been a gauche boy of sixteen, she a year younger. But even at that early age her beauty had been fully mature, fixed in its imprint.

She'd seemed untouchable, unreachable, accepting as her natural right everything he lacked—security, admiration, a sense of belonging. Even now, years after he had left that gauche boy behind, he sometimes dreamed he touched her and her flesh melted in his hands . . .

In the great hall dancing had begun again, a slow waltz. He saw Blanche excuse herself from her guests and come toward him. Her scent, lily-based, the one he had devised for her himself, filled his nostrils as he encircled her in his arms and led her out onto the marble floor for the first waltz of the evening. He was conscious of the whispers as they circled the floor gravely, conscious of her smooth cool skin under his hand. Her eyes, pale gray, unreadable, the mirror of his own, gazed into his. They understood each other, he and Blanche, they were made for each other. She was his, he was Guy de Chardonnet, everything was as it must be in his chosen world, the only world that could be allowed to matter.

Suddenly something interrupted the music's even flow. There was a moment's discordant confusion in the orchestra. The musicians pulled themselves together and continued, but it was too late. Blanche frowned. Now there was a commotion, mild but unmistakable, among the guests nearest to the entrance, a ripple of interest and curiosity and mild shock as perceptible as a change in temperature. The orchestra played louder, losing some of its harmony in the process. Blanche pressed lightly on his sleeve in a secret signal.

He turned. Standing in a pool of light was the strange, oddly dramatic figure of a woman in a black cloak. She was wearing a jeweled mask. The other guests, almost as if they sensed danger, had shrunk away from her in a circle. He felt his senses prickle. There was a long moment of immobility as the orchestra, aware that the principals had surrendered the floor, faded into silence. They were all frozen, silent, like courtiers in a tableau. Slowly, almost as if she were enjoying her audience, the masked woman loosed her hood and let the cloak slip from her shoulders.

A muffled gasp rose from the assembled guests, a little shock wave ran around. It was as if the sun had suddenly come out from behind a cloud, as if before their very eyes, from a dusty black chrysalis, an enameled butterfly had emerged. She was dazzling, her dress of gold cloth starred and studded with a riot of jewels, amethysts and sapphires, rubies and emeralds, ringing the hem of her heavy skirt, edging the deep neckline of her close-fitting bodice, out of which rose her golden neck and shoulders, glowing with a pagan radiance.

You could have heard a clock tick, a pin drop, a heart beat. There was something so undeniably theatrical, so unashamedly exotic about her that Guy half expected music to strike up in the background. He wouldn't have been surprised to see a dancing bear, a blackamoor page, a gypsy with his accordion. She was summer incarnate, an icon, an Aztec queen, a Medici princess. And she was definitely not, but not, wearing white.

"How did she get in?" Blanche's face was even more pale, her lips tight. Guy tore his eyes away from the golden idol with difficulty.

"I have no idea. I don't even know who she is." Laced in the woman's hair, bound in with gold thread, were scarlet flowers, outrageous against the glossy blue-black mane.

"What does she want?" Blanche eyed the woman with the first trace of nervousness he'd ever seen in her.

Guy advanced. The woman watched him, her eyes dark and unfathomable behind her jeweled mask. Her lips curved in an oddly familiar smile. Blanche signaled to the orchestra. Uneasily, it began again to play.

"*Bonsoir, madame* . . ." He didn't know quite how to begin. She seemed so poised, so sure of herself, rather like a leopard. Then, suddenly, she began to laugh, a full, creamy laugh that he'd never heard before but which was instantly recognizable. She spun in front of him, her crazy panoply of jewels striking fire.

"Corrie." He was torn between anger and a curious, ridiculous uplifting of the heart. He maintained his composure with an effort.

"What on earth are you doing here?"

She dimpled at him outrageously beneath her silken mask.

"I've come to ruin your party, of course."

As always, her frankness was unanswerable.

"You could at least have worn white!"

"But I am." She had the audacity to look hurt. "Apart from my jewels, and they don't count." She gestured at her golden gown. "White gold . . . haven't you heard of it?"

"And these?" He indicated the poppies in her hair.

"Oh." She reached up one smooth golden arm, disengaged a single scarlet blossom, leaned forward and tucked it into his lapel. "These are for you. I'm your scarlet woman, had you forgotten?"

He glanced around. Astounded faces surrounded them. Her words were clearly not going unnoticed. He gripped her arm, almost dragged her from the dance floor to the slightly less compromising shelter of a pillar.

"You are not my scarlet woman." Forced to whisper, he was uneasily aware of the buzz of speculation from the onlookers.

"Only for lack of opportunity!" She smiled up at him sweetly.

He stared at her, trying to read her face.

"Take off that ridiculous mask."

"No." She retreated out of his reach. "Not unless you take off yours."

"What do you mean?" He smiled through clenched teeth as he caught up with her. "I'm not wearing one."

"Aren't you? Are you sure?"

Nimbly she scooped up a glass of champagne from a waiter's tray, her eyes bright as diamonds over the rim of the glass. He saw that Blanche was making furious signals at him from the dance floor. As unobtrusively as he could he edged Corrie again into the protective shadow of the pillar. But even in the relative darkness her jewels shimmered and glowed. He couldn't take his eyes off the golden skin of her throat, the nubs of her shoulders, paling imperceptibly into cream where the neckline skimmed her breasts.

"Are those jewels real?" It was inconsequential, but his head was spinning.

"Would you love me if they were?" Her eyes taunted him. From deep inside him anger flared.

"What do you know about love?" He gripped her arm so hard that the pressure of his fingers left white marks on the golden skin. "Don't forget, I know what kind of woman you are!"

She stared back at him reflectively, slowly rubbing her upper arm. He could still feel the treacherous warmth of her skin.

"I may not know much about love, as you say . . ." She paused, lifted one hand to her mask. "But I'm willing to learn. How about you?" With a swift, startling movement she took off the mask.

He was suddenly speechless. The orchestra struck up a new piece, Glück's "Invitation to the Dance," but he hardly heard them. He was seeing her face as if for the first time, as if it were a stranger's face. How had he never noticed before? She was beautiful. Her skin was golden as summer corn against the mysterious scented blue-blackness of her hair, her large violet eyes under their smoky lids were the exact color of moonlight on running water. Her mouth, with its disturbing cleft in the full lower lip, was made for singing and laughter. She was like a bright newly minted coin, as perfect and magical as a cloudless day. She reminded him of things he thought he'd forgotten, things it was safer to forget, childish pleasures—the smell of new-mown hay, the taste of spring water, apples straight from the tree . . . What was she, a witch, a corn goddess, a courtesan? These feelings were out of place; he of all people, at this of all times, could not afford them.

"Dance with me." She had taken advantage of his silence and now swayed toward him, lifted her arms. He caught her wrists.

"Certainly not. You will not dance with me or anyone else."

"Why not?" She smiled. "Are you jealous?"

Before he could stop her she'd slipped away, as smoothly as a shining snake, into the mêlée of guests on the dance floor. He caught sight of her a moment later in the arms of a black-clad guest, smiling, her head thrown back.

"Corrie . . ." He was suddenly furious, with a blazing white heat he could scarcely control.

"Try and stop me," she called back, laughing.

He was helpless. The dance was a fast, free-flying polka, a dizzying whirl in which he could scarcely follow her progress. He saw her first in one man's arms, then another's—there seemed to be no shortage of partners. He fumed in silence.

The movement of the dance swung her close to him, tantalizingly close.

"Dance with me." He could barely hear her above the music, but the message was clear.

"No." She shrugged, bobbed away before he could reach her, dancing out of his grasp like a piece of flotsam on the current of the music. He was waiting for her when she swung around again.

"I've ruined your party, haven't I?"

"Yes."

"Good." Her partner's face was a study in mild incomprehension as she whirled away, but she clearly had him dazzled. Guy waited grimly for the music to deliver her back to him.

"You'll never forgive me, will you?"

"No."

"Good." Her face was brilliantly flushed, her eyes sparkling.

Corrie whirled away again, aware that though she was dancing with another man, she barely saw him. It was Guy's face she saw, Guy she danced for. Out of the corners of her eyes she searched the crowd constantly till she glimpsed his dark, unsmiling profile. At last, at last she'd made him notice her. What would happen when the music had ended she didn't know. She was riding a tiger, it was going to be difficult to dismount gracefully. But she didn't care. Her head was spinning with the wild rhythm of the dance and the champagne she'd consumed, but her heart was filled with triumph. Revenge tasted sweeter than any wine . . . She passed from one man's arms to another's in a headlong spiral, conscious always of Guy's motionless figure on the sidelines. His face was a polite mask but his eyes burned, setting the air between them on fire. And that burning gaze was fixed, not on his guests, not on his fiancée, but on herself. For once, just once, she had his complete attention.

Suddenly, the music ended. She swayed on her feet as her partner pressed her for another dance. She hardly heard him. She was aware only of Guy, his arm half imprisoning, half supporting her, his voice in her ear.

"That's enough. You've had your dance. Now it's time for you to leave."

"But I don't want to."

"You don't?" His eyes might burn but his voice was icy.

"No. I want to dance some more. With you."

"Very well." Smoothly, without any apparent effort, he bent and swept her bodily into his arms. "If you won't leave of your own accord, I shall have to take you." She was so surprised by his action that for a moment she was completely motionless. Then she began to kick and struggle.

"Put me down!"

"My dear Corrie . . . I have been trying to put you down since the day we met. It doesn't work." She beat ineffectually on his chest. His arms were like iron. A ripple of amusement passed through the crowd. Suddenly conscious of her dignity she stopped struggling. Guy looked at her with suspicion.

"Don't worry. I'll go quietly." She tossed her head. "The best part of the party is over, anyway."

He set her down unceremoniously. "And what might that be, oh connoisseur?" She was delighted to see how difficult he was finding it to keep his usual irony on an even keel.

She smiled at him blithely. "Me, of course."

His lips tightened. "Wait here." She watched him as he threaded his way through the crowd to make his excuses to Blanche. She saw Blanche's lips tighten into a thin white line, saw her throw a glance of pure Arctic poison in her own direction, and took a wicked delight in her hostess's predicament. For what could Blanche do? She was trapped, by her own good breeding, her vanity, her guests . . . She tossed her lovely white-blonde head and turned her back on Corrie as if she were too unimportant to acknowledge. But Corrie wasn't taken in. Nothing could subdue her exultation, a reckless crazy tide which surged in her like the sea.

Guy escorted her in silence to a white convertible Corniche parked in the graveled courtyard. He clicked his fingers once and a servant came running with the keys. He gunned the powerful engine and drove the car at breakneck speed down the drive between the cypresses as if he couldn't bear to have her sitting beside him a moment longer than necessary. The silence between them deepened as they drove through the warm June darkness. The highway lights flashed by hypnotically, turning everything to gold. Guy's face was a golden mask, her gems had turned from green and crimson to topaz. She closed her eyes, reveling in the wind whipping through her hair. Nothing could be more invigorating than the sure and certain knowledge that she was in disgrace. She could feel the poppies detaching themselves one by one. By morning their fading petals, scattered over the Boulevard Périphérique, would be all that remained of tonight's adventure. Unless . . . for one crazy moment she would have given up everything, her dreams, her ambitions, her soul itself, to be able to drive on beside him to the ends of the earth, and beyond.

But it wasn't to be. It was strange, his determination to get rid of her as fast as possible was his own undoing. On the outskirts of Paris, just after they'd left the Périphérique, the big heavy car suddenly spun out of control. There wasn't time to think or wonder what had happened. Around her there was only the high-pitched squeal of stressed tires, the even tenor of the road ahead suddenly transformed into a dazzling kaleidoscope. The car bucked and lurched, buffeting her from side to side. She was dimly aware of Guy beside her, wrestling with the wheel, and then, as suddenly as it had begun, the nightmare ended. The car came to rest against the guard rail, its hood jacked up at an unnerving angle.

The silence following the impact seemed deafening. Slowly, as her senses returned and the drumming in her ears receded, she became aware of Guy's hand on her bare shoulder.

"Are you all right?"

If she hadn't known better, she might have mistaken the look in his eyes for one of concern.

"What happened?" The muscles of her face and mouth seemed stiff, her voice would hardly obey her.

"A brick on the road." Now his voice was calm, unemotional. He reached forward and switched off the ignition with a deliberateness that annoyed her. "There was nothing I could do."

Suddenly the shock hit her. She was instantly furious with him and with herself.

"You were driving too fast!"

He shrugged. "I always drive too fast. Be grateful you're still alive." His door was jammed against the barrier. Unceremoniously he reached across her to open the side door and clambered out. Her fury deepened. He hadn't even said "excuse me." He was a boor, a selfish, unfeeling boor. And to think she'd wanted to go with him to the ends of the earth. She must have been mad. He strode around to the front of the car and bent to check underneath the hood. Without speaking he came around to her side and opened the door.

"Out."

"Out?" She couldn't understand what was going on. "What about the car?"

He made an expressive gesture. "*Foutue*."

She clambered out, a little unsteady with shock, champagne and the weight of her jeweled skirt. What he said was all too true. Both wheels were badly buckled, not to mention the hood, which looked like a badly folded paper dart. It was an impressive sight. They were indeed lucky to be alive.

"What are we going to do?"

"It's no problem. I will simply telephone André and have him pick us up."

"That's a very good idea." Then why did she have this curious sinking feeling? "Except for one thing."

"What's that?"

"I gave him the night off."

He looked at her in silence. At last he spoke.

"What admirable forethought. Whatever would I do without you?"

She winced inwardly, then rallied.

"It doesn't matter. We can phone for a taxi."

"That's a very good idea." His voice echoed hers uncomfortably. "Except for one thing."

"What's that?"

"The average taxi driver, whatever his other virtues, has one unfortunate eccentricity."

"What's that?"

"He likes to get paid."

"So?" She didn't know what he was getting at, but suspected there was more to come.

"So have you any money?"

"Me?" She gestured crossly at her elaborate costume. "Just where do you think I'd have room to keep a purse?" Naturally, her purse was in the pocket of her cloak, which she'd left behind.

"Just as I thought." His tone was infuriatingly smug.

"Surely you've got some money?" An awful doubt was beginning to creep into her mind.

"If I had, we would not be having this conversation." His tone was caustic.

"What?" She was thunderstruck. "You mean you've got no money . . . none at all?"

He shook his head. "When we left I was somewhat distracted. Money was the last thing on my mind." He looked at her with grim satisfaction, almost as if he blamed her for everything that had happened.

"Well, Miss Modena, what do you suggest we do now?"

She thought furiously.

"Wouldn't a taxi driver take us once he knew who you were?"

He smiled coldly. "Without any form of identification? Hardly." He paused. "Unless, of course, you've brought your passport?"

She shot him a fulminating look, but had to admit she was baffled.

"Have you any better ideas?"

He leaned back in an irritatingly casual manner against the crippled car.

"There seem to me to be two possible alternatives. We can either stay here all night . . ."

"No, thank you!"

". . . or one of us can go for help."

She glanced around the deserted, dimly lit streets, then steeled herself.

"I'll go."

He shook his head.

"Just how far do you think you'd get, dressed like

that, and with no identification?" He gestured at her tangled hair and dizzying cleavage. "You'd be picked up by the police in no time. No, it's best if you stay and I go."

"No!" Suddenly the deserted streets around her began to seem not only empty but faintly sinister. The clang of a garbage pail lid hitting the ground rang out eerily from a nearby sidestreet. She jumped. "I'm not staying here by myself."

He glanced at her with evident amusement, clearly enjoying her moment of weakness. "What's happened to all that fiery independence you were so proud of? You're not scared, are you?"

"Certainly not." She drew herself up with dignity. "It's just that you could be hours . . . it might begin to rain . . . or something."

He shrugged.

"Then there's only one thing for it."

"What's that?"

"Walk."

He turned and strode rapidly away. She caught up with him just as he rounded the corner. They walked, through the featureless suburban streets, for half an hour, an hour. He didn't speak, and she had to concentrate all her energies on keeping up with him. He made no concessions for the length of her stride or her beaded slippers, hardly the ideal footwear for prolonged hiking along concrete sidewalks. He didn't even stop when she bent down and removed them. She tied the laces hurriedly together and slung them around her waist. When she caught up with him, he glanced at her in surprise, as if he'd hardly noticed she'd been gone. As he saw her bare feet a reluctant smile touched his lips.

"It seems you are fated to be barefoot in my company."

"At least it's not snowing." But, she thought, nothing could be colder than the atmosphere between them. It was a lovely summer night, warm and soft with every star present in its place, she was young and full of feelings she hardly recognized, and he . . . well, he wasn't even thirty, though he might as well have been a middle-aged father of four for all the attention he was showing her. It couldn't be allowed to go on, it was bad for her morale—and there were miles yet to go.

"Is she a virgin?"

"What?" He almost stumbled, recovered himself in time.

"Blanche. Is she a virgin?"

"Really, Corrie . . . what a question!"

She smiled to herself. At least she'd managed to startle him out of his preoccupation.

"Well? Is she?"

"For heaven's sake, Corrie, what do you expect me to say? Why do you want to know, anyway?"

"I was trying to think of a good reason for you wanting to marry her. I know she's a bit old to be a virgin, but—"

"Enough!" He raised his voice suddenly, silencing her, but failing to extinguish completely the small spark of glee in her heart. She waited a few minutes, then glanced up at him sidelong. He was shaking his head. She waited a minute longer, then was rewarded. He turned to her abruptly.

"Is it so surprising?" She kept her eyes demurely fixed on the endless sidewalk ahead.

"Is what so surprising?"

He made an impatient gesture.

"That I should want to marry Blanche. No one else finds it at all strange."

She shrugged.

"Getting married is always strange. I think so, anyway. It's like—committing suicide. You can't be sure what's going to happen afterwards, but the prospects don't look good."

He shook his head again.

"So young . . . and so cynical. Have you never been in love?"

She considered long and deeply.

"Falling in love has nothing to do with marriage, you should know that."

He stared at her.

"Don't tell me you're in love with Blanche?" Corrie was beginning to enjoy herself. "If you are, you really shouldn't marry her. It will spoil everything."

"How kind of you to be so concerned for my happiness." He paused, frowning. "But what makes you so sure I'm not in love with Blanche?"

She smiled. "I don't think you're capable of falling in love with anyone. I think you're spoiled and selfish and unreasonable. Like me. That's why I wondered if she was a virgin. You can't be marrying her for her money, because you've already got plenty."

He shook his head in amazement. "Why am I listening to this?"

"Because you know I'm right." Her glance was innocence itself. He drew a deep breath, clearly finding some difficulty in restraining his temper. She pretended not to notice.

"I can see that I am going to have to explain in words of one syllable." He paused, wearing an expression of weary patience. "I don't know whether you are capable of understanding this—but Blanche is . . . a lady. If you are a lady, the question of virginity, as you so bluntly put it, is supremely irrelevant."

"How do you get to be a lady?" Corrie's expression was one of suitably scholarly interest. He sighed.

"Ladies are born, not made. It's a matter of natural fastidiousness, a certain reserve. No matter what her life has been a lady will always be different, rare, perpetually fascinating." He paused again. "The reverse is also true, of course. There are some women, like yourself . . ."

"What?" There was a sharp edge to his smile that she distrusted.

"Don't be offended. I'm not referring to your misspent past. It's simply that in the terms of this . . . er . . . purely academic discussion you and Blanche represent opposite ends of the spectrum.

"Some women lose their virginity as soon as they learn to talk, and you're one. It's something a man can sense immediately."

"Really." She was furious. "So Blanche is the Snow Queen and I'm the grubby kitchen maid!"

"That's not what I said. Why must you always be so literal? It's just that your . . . eagerness, your willingness to sample everything, give the game away. When a man looks at Blanche he thinks of one thing, when he looks at you he thinks of quite another."

She was slightly mollified, and wildly curious.

"What sort of thing? What does a man think of when he looks at me?"

He gave her a wry sidelong look. "I thought we were discussing Blanche?"

"Oh, all right then, what do you think of when you look at Blanche?"

"I think of . . . the future. Blanche is a woman I can depend on, to say the right thing, to be perfectly groomed, to be an asset. Take this evening for instance. What would you have done if another woman had gatecrashed your engagement ball and insisted on dancing with your fiancé?"

Corrie considered for a moment. "I'd have scratched her eyes out."

"Exactly. Blanche, by contrast, behaved perfectly. And there's one more thing. I can trust her. She would never break a promise."

Corrie kicked moodily at a stone, stubbing her bare toe painfully in the process. "I suppose you think I would?"

He looked at her consideringly. "Yes, I think you would. If you felt like it."

She smiled unwillingly. "You're right. Life isn't worth living if you can't change your mind."

"And there's another thing. When I look at Blanche I know that she will be as beautiful when she is eighty as she is now."

"How dull." His praise of the faultless Blanche was beginning to get on her nerves. Perhaps she should never have begun this line of conversation.

"What about me? What does a man think when he looks at me?"

He paused, studied her face. "I can only tell you what I think. I think—that your eyes are a strange shape, that your lips are too red, that your hair is too black. I think how much you irritate me. I don't know. I wonder what you're going to do next."

"Oh." She didn't quite know how to reply. Had he complimented her or insulted her? "What about when I'm eighty? What will I look like then?"

"I can't tell. It depends what life you choose to lead. Knowing you, you'll probably pack as much in as you can. You may end up with five chins and a bosom on your knees."

"You bastard!" She swung out at him but he caught her wrist before she made contact.

"Don't waste your energies. We have a long way to go."

She gritted her teeth. She was tired, yes, but she'd rather die than admit it to Guy de Chardonnet. He and his precious Blanche, they deserved each other. Her fury stood her in good stead. Inside an hour they were in sight of Montmartre. The narrow winding cobbled streets led up to the lovely chalk-white cupola of the Sacré Coeur, the chapel of the Sacred Heart. A faint light was tinging the horizon, but here, in Paris's private heart, there was still warmth and life. The broad steps beneath the Sacré Coeur were scattered with people, late-night revelers, lovers, the homeless or sleepless or those simply too much in love with the midsummer night to say goodbye.

Instantly she forgot her sore feet and bruised ego. Barefoot she flew up the steps, skipping between the moon-bathers. Beneath, Paris stretched out in a blue, sparkling panorama, a soft breeze bringing the scent of newly washed streets. He caught up with her on the lower flight, where the steps spread out into a broad stone floor. She felt dizzy. It was so beautiful, so perfect, Harlequin's city. She was glad she wasn't alone, the moment was too marvelous not to be shared.

"Look," she whispered, unwilling to break the magical predawn silence. He followed her gaze out over the sleeping city, so tenderly cradled in the shining arms of the Seine.

"I have been here before, you know." She closed her heart to his insensitivity. She wouldn't let him spoil this moment for her, she could make him see what she saw.

"But you've never seen it like this. You can't have. Not just as it is now." The blue was paling, brightening, infinite gauzy layers lifting one by one in a vast, hushed theater. The prologue was over, the first act yet to begin. The scene was changing before their eyes. The light beckoned, promising them another world for a minute, an hour, a day, for as long as their minds could keep the memory intact. There is only one now, the light said. Remember this, the exact line of one pearly plume of smoke against the silver slates, the flight of one bird, wings trembling like a compass needle over the deserted streets. Remember this. This light, this moment will never come again.

She turned to him. She was so full she was spilling over. It was so strange . . . the glitter and tension of the ball, and now this. The shadowy streets edged with blue and lilac, the fragile arch of the sky, so simple, so everyday, but as miraculous as a stranger's smile. The world was full of treasures, would she ever have time to discover them all?

She would have sung, if she'd been allowed to. The feeling inside her had to have an outlet, the moment had to have its celebration. There was only one thing left to do. The wrong person, the wrong time, but there was no other. She turned to him, held out her arms.

"Dance with me. Please."

Someone on the steps beneath them began to pluck a guitar, a sad, dissonant sound that was somehow beautiful. Nothing is perfect, it said, nothing is forever. Catch the moment as it flies.

"Just one dance. It doesn't matter now. No one is watching, no one will know."

The half-light made his face a stranger's face. He was

motionless, a tall, frozen courtier with empty eyes. She waited, feeling herself suspended, between past and future, darkness and dawn. He didn't move. She closed her eyes, felt herself sway with the movement of the earth around the sun. The next thing she knew she was in his arms.

Slowly, tentatively, bound by the music's one fragile thread, they began to revolve on the ancient stones. His chin just touched the top of her head, his arms were unexpectedly warm. He held her so lightly, so firmly, that she was weightless. She heard the golden fabric of her dress rustle against her skin, felt the movement of the muscles in his arms, as if their bodies were engaged in a private dialogue of their own. Something was happening, something over which she had no control. They were dancing over a precipice, blindfolded . . .

She opened her eyes. Who was he, after all, this man who held her so tenderly and expertly? Did she know him, had she ever known him? Now, it was too late. She couldn't see his face, it was too near, or too far away. She felt his breath ruffle her hair, felt the sensation continue down the whole length of her spine, as if she were being charged with an electric current. She was helpless. Her eyelids felt heavy, as if she'd been drugged. Dimly she was aware that other people had got up from the steps and were dancing too. A boy and a girl in jeans, laughing softly, revolved in each other's arms, an elderly couple smiled and whispered. The moment was right, the magic was right. Every Harlequin had his Columbine . . . As the darkness drained from the air she felt as if she too were being emptied, drop by drop of her old self, to be filled with—what?

She lifted her head. His face was a shadow, but she could feel the warmth of his skin. His head bent, she felt his mouth brush lightly against her cheek. Her eyes closed, irresistibly. The world narrowed down to the touch of his lips, the current of his warm breath in her ear. She could feel her heart beating so loudly that it shook her whole body. She couldn't think, couldn't breathe. She was blind, deaf and dumb, her ears filled with a soundless rushing. She was poised on the brink of the precipice, longing to launch herself but dreading collision with the ground. What was happening to her? She was dissolving, all the familiar boundaries melting away under the touch of his lips. She was being destroyed, inch by inch. She was going to die.

His lips found hers. She felt her heart race, then stop beating entirely. She was falling now, plummeting endlessly to the center of the earth. His arms held her remorselessly. She was his prisoner, small and very helpless. She couldn't have spoken if she'd wanted to. She was in a dark place, his mouth the only reality, all the blood in her body answering its insistent pressure. She was extinguished, swallowed up. The darkness invaded her absolutely. She ceased to exist.

How long he kissed her she didn't know. When at last he drew back his head her mouth felt swollen and hot. She could barely open her eyes. She felt strange and heavy, almost ill. She couldn't move. If he hadn't been holding her, she would have fallen.

With an enormous effort she lifted her head to face him. Their gazes locked. His pupils were so dilated that his eyes were black. She couldn't look away. She was rooted to the spot. She felt, like the tug of an irresistible tide, the warmth of his body. She found herself searching his dark face as if she'd never seen it before. The line of his eyebrows, the angle of his jaw, the crisp thickness of his hair where it waved at his temples . . . She wanted to touch him, devour him, absorb every bone and sinew. How had she never noticed before the perfect triangle of his cheekbone, the dark point where his hair grew down in the center of his forehead, the particular scent of his skin, pine, snow, almonds . . . She could spend every minute of every day just looking at him, watching every flicker of his astonishing eyes, every movement of his mouth. She found herself staring at his lips as if they were her own.

"Is this another of your tricks, Miss Modena?" His

voice was harsh, almost ragged. His eyes burned. "I thought the English believed in fair play."

She flinched as his grip on her arms tightened painfully. His eyes bored into hers. She felt suddenly lost, disoriented. What had she done? She'd crossed an invisible barrier into a country she hadn't dreamed existed, whose language she didn't understand. How could she get back home? With a superhuman effort she pulled herself away from the landscape of his face.

"What's one kiss between friends?" She tried to speak lightly, but her voice didn't seem to belong to her, she had to feel for the words.

"We are not friends." His eyes were cold, the pupils shrunk again to hard points. "We have never been friends, never will be."

"Do you dislike me so much?" To her horrified amazement she felt treacherous tears fill her eyes. She blinked them away furiously. She was tired and confused, that was all.

"What am I supposed to feel?" She felt the current of anger run down his arms into hers. "I don't know whether I like you or hate you. Ever since the day we met you've been nothing but trouble. You set out from the beginning to hurt me in every way you could think of—you've done your best to alienate my friends, ruin my engagement ball, and now you want to destroy my marriage. What have I done, what crime could I possibly have committed, to deserve you? Oh, I've made excuses for you . . . your youth, your . . . unfortunate background, but this time you've gone too far. I've had enough. I'm going to put a stop to it once and for all."

"I'm sorry. I won't be any more trouble. I promise." For some reason she couldn't respond to his anger with fire of her own. She felt small and guilty and helpless, like a little girl.

"It's too late for promises. Anyway, we both know you're totally untrustworthy. Maybe, once, I would have believed you. I did believe you. I believed you when you said you had good, important reasons for wanting to be in Paris. I was a fool. What use have you made of your time here? None. You've done nothing. You say you're different from other women, but you're not. You're just the same—lazy, worthless, trivial. All you think about is yourself. You are vain, Miss Modena. Vain and empty-headed and shallow." He paused. "I'm glad." His voice dripped scorn. "It makes it easier to deal with you."

"What are you going to do?" She was trembling, whether from fear or cold or outrage she didn't know.

"I'm going to call your bluff, Miss Modena." Without releasing her arm he turned and began to descend the steps. She had no choice but to follow him. His grip was like iron.

"What do you mean?" Her teeth were chattering, her bare feet slipping on the cold stones. "Am I fired?"

He laughed out loud, a cold hard sound. "No, Miss Modena. Far from it. That would be too easy." He halted so suddenly that she stumbled. "Don't you understand? Or are you blind as well as foolish?" His face was dark, his lips a thin line. "I want you." His grip tightened. She felt a tremor pass through her body. She couldn't tell if he was shaking her or if it came from within herself. "Don't look so surprised. There's no need to play the innocent with me. What did you expect? I am a man after all, and you have done your best to provoke me at every opportunity." His mouth twisted wryly.

"You should be pleased, Miss Modena. You've won. I want you. So badly that I am prepared to jeopardize my entire future to have you."

"Are you asking me to be your mistress?" She challenged him, ready with her refusal, but he forestalled her.

"Hardly. The time for such . . . gallantry is long gone. In any case, that is a position of honor for which you are entirely unsuited. Your total lack of tact, your absence of savoir faire, your general abrasiveness disqualify you completely. No . . ." His voice became silky. "I merely said that I was going to have you."

"Just like that?" She heard her voice fade, felt her knees go weak.

"Just like that." His voice was uncompromising. "It is time."

He was right. It was for just this moment that she'd planned and plotted, striven and schemed. Then why didn't she feel triumph, elation? Why did she feel so . . . empty, sad, as if instead of winning the game she'd lost it entirely?

"Wait . . ." She struggled to draw breath as he half led, half dragged her across the cobbles. She was uncomfortably aware of the startled glances of passersby, but he seemed unmoved. "The contract, what about the contract . . . you agreed?"

"The contract? I have kept my part of the bargain. You broke it first. Clause one, remember? No passes."

Remorselessly he dragged her on. The streets were becoming familiar now, she had a terrible sense of time running out. The lovely half-light, which had made things look insubstantial as a dream or a play, had gone. In its place was ordinary daylight, uncomfortably clear, revealing only too well the real world. She searched her mind desperately. There had to be something he'd left out, some loophole . . .

"But you don't love me!"

A wry smile flickered over his dark averted profile, but his grip on her arm didn't slacken. "Isn't that a trifle inconsistent of you, Miss Modena? What has love to do with us? As you so rightly pointed out, I am incapable of loving anyone."

Toinette was waiting in her neat starched uniform in the doorway of the house. Not a flicker of expression crossed her well-trained face as she saw them coming. Corrie winced inwardly at the picture she must present, flushed and disheveled, her feet stained and dusty. Unceremoniously Guy half pushed, half pulled her up the stairs. Gone was his old mocking courtesy. The charade was over.

"Monsieur Guy." Toinette's voice was hesitant, her expression doubtful. "Your cousin telephoned—"

"Of course." Guy cut short the awkward moment, ignoring Corrie completely. "Ring her for me and tell her I have been delayed. I have . . ."—for a moment his eyes locked with Corrie's—"urgent business to attend to."

His grip on her arm was like iron as they ascended the stairs. She felt limp, nerveless, like a rag doll. He led her not to his own room, but hers. One-handed he drew her in and closed the door behind them.

Soft sunlight spilled onto the wide white bed, the cover stretched smooth as the pages of a book. For a brief moment, as his grip relaxed, she thought he might have changed his mind. Then he reached behind her and with swift, sure finality locked the door and pocketed the key.

"Now, Miss Modena . . ." His voice was silky, his breath warm in her ear. Her own breath fluttered. She shivered. Her head was spinning. Against her will she remembered the touch of his lips. A treacherous weakness invaded her body.

Slowly, luxuriously, his hand traced the curve of her cheek, buried itself in the heavy hair at the nape of her neck. She felt every hair on her scalp stir and lift at his touch. He took her hands and placed them inside his jacket. Through the thin silk of his shirt she could feel the heat of his skin, the pulse of his heart. It seemed like the most intimate, outrageous thing she'd ever done. She felt herself begin to tremble uncontrollably, like a trapped bird. His breath was coming faster, she had ceased to breathe at all.

"Guy . . ."

If she'd hoped to sway him, one look at his dark face was enough to show her that it was no use.

"No more words." His voice was low and hard. "*C'est décidé.*"

He laced his own hands at her waist. With a remorseless pressure he propelled her to the bed. His eyes, the lids half lowered, never left her face as he raised his hands to her back and with one sure, sudden movement ripped the tiny fastenings of her dress. It slid from her shoulders with a rustle.

"Yes, I thought so." His hands traced her spine. She felt tears prick at the back of her eyes, it was as if no one had ever touched her before, as if she were losing a skin she'd worn all her life. "You are beautiful."

She watched as he slipped off his jacket and shirt. His chest and shoulders had a silky sheen. Why didn't anyone tell me, she thought. She felt an aching longing to trace the curve of his collarbone with her finger, but he was so far away, like a figure in a dream. She closed her eyes, felt the smooth coolness of linen sheets against her skin, felt the bed sway and curve around her as he extended himself full length beside her. All down her side she could feel the heat of his body. One warm, strong hand traced the curve of her body from her neck to her hipbone.

"Corrie . . ." Some deep warmth in her flowered instinctively at the sound of his voice, like a spell breaking. I didn't know it, she thought, but I've been only half alive till this moment. She reached forward tentatively and touched his shoulder. Like a deep sea current his body drew her, like the Gulf Stream. Their bodies touched full length, and she shuddered, little bubbles of pure joy rising in her from her toes to the crown of her head.

"Skin . . ." He smelled so good, like newly baked bread, like sun-warmed sand . . . Her voice was a hum, a deep throaty purr. An answering chuckle stirred deep in his chest. Hairs tickled her nose. How could she ever have thought he was cold, and distant? He was warm, warm all over, so close now she could barely see him, like part of herself.

They lay like that, motionless, until she could hardly bear it. She felt her mind racing, wheeling, far above her body, caught in a trance of mindless delight. Then, slowly, he began to make love to her. It was a feast he placed before her, a banquet of little dishes, presented with the utmost delicacy, for a connoisseur's palate. She ate, at first with astonishment, then with delight, then with greed, as if she'd been starving all her life. She discovered appetites she hadn't known she possessed. He molded and shaped her, redrew her body's boundaries then sewed her up in a web of silk only to unfold her yet again. It was nothing like anything she could have imagined. It was another world. When he entered her finally she felt her heart move. She was full of him, full of herself, the richest woman in the world.

Afterwards she lay still, sightless, boneless, feeling the lapping of his body against her own as if the movement inside her would never stop.

"Guy . . ."

"Ssh . . . sleep now."

The command in his voice was irresistible. She closed her eyes, wondering deep in herself how she could ever have thought anything was important, compared to this, the pressure of his chin against her cheek, the muscles of his arm under her neck, and slept.

When she awoke she knew instantly she'd made a terrible mistake. She sat up, the sudden movement making her head spin and ache. How could she have done it? Turning with aching carefulness on her elbow she looked down at his sleeping dark head, the close-cropped hair rumpled on the pillow. With his eyes shut he looked boyish, almost innocent, the long lashes barely flickering on his tanned cheeks.

I've done it, she thought with sudden, desperate hilarity. I've eaten the pomegranate seeds. If only they'd been labeled.

He stirred in his sleep, sighed, flung out a casual, possessive hand. Oh God, she thought, as her insides turned to molten liquid. What shall I do now?

Her face burned as she thought of all her plotting and scheming. She thought she'd been so clever, with her cheeky backchat, her veneer of sophistication. She'd flirted and provoked and ensnared her quarry just as she'd planned. But she hadn't realized that the trap she'd prepared so carefully was big enough for two.

Somewhere, between the grand ballroom and the steps of the Sacré Coeur, between darkness and dawn, she'd fallen helplessly, hopelessly in love with Guy de Chardonnet.

She didn't know how long she sat there. She was as still as a stone, but she could feel the whole world wheeling and spinning around her. How had she been so blind? She knew what falling in love was like, you couldn't be half Italian, familiar with the operatic repertory, and not know. But she wasn't prepared for it. Nothing in the world could have prepared her for this moment. It was so sudden, so violent, this desire to follow him to the ends of the earth, to tread in his footsteps, live in his dreams. She wanted to hold his hand. She wanted to run away. She wanted to climb into his pocket and stay there. She wanted to watch him shave. She wanted to know all the people he had ever loved.

But it wasn't possible. She knew that, with a frightened animal's instinctive knowledge. He would destroy her. No, loving him would destroy her. Because he was incapable of loving her in return. She'd fallen in love with a shadow, a dream, a man who didn't exist. The real man, as she knew only too well, was cold and calculating and heartless. He would take her and use her, and soon, because she loved him, she would bore him, and then he would throw her away. And that would be the end. All her proud dreams and plans canceled by one night in a man's arms.

And her body had betrayed her, deceived him more thoroughly than he would ever know. It had been her first time, but there had been no blood, no pain. Her mother had told her it was sometimes like that, with the right man . . . It had seemed so easy, so natural. He could have had no suspicion that he'd taken a virgin. She'd melted into him like a river finding the shore. It was just as he'd said that very evening—some women lost their virginity as soon as they learned to talk, and it appeared that she was one of them.

So no blood, no pain, nothing to show for a night's

careless passion. Only this aching, this slow loss from a wound that would never heal . . .

But she wouldn't let it happen, she wouldn't let her own inexperience make her his victim. She was a survivor, she had no intention of spending her life longing for the impossible. There was a chance, one chance, if she was strong enough to take it.

Slowly, she moved about the room, gathering up her possessions. There was no time to lose. She had to act now, with a surgeon's calculated brutality. There was no one to comfort or advise her, she must perform the operation alone. She shivered as she slipped on the yellow cotton dress. She was cold, colder than she'd ever been.

It will pass, she told herself. But it didn't help. Every movement was an effort. Her head ached, her throat felt dry. She was conscious of his silent sleeping form on the bed with every nerve in her body. She hesitated. The smooth, strong curve of his shoulder was disturbingly tempting. Perhaps if she woke him, just to say goodbye, it would resolve this terrible emptiness, ease the aching in her heart?

It was then, with an agonizing clarity she could have done without, that she realized the worst was still to come. Why, why hadn't anyone told her it was so easy to let the tiger out of its cage, but so hard to get it back in again? She was numb now, but soon, all too soon, sensation would return and the real struggle would begin. Not with Guy de Chardonnet. He wasn't really her enemy, he didn't care enough about her for that. No, she had another, far more serious adversary to contend with, one from whom it would be impossible to escape.

Herself.

"Toinette!"

The maid, startled by the harsh note in her master's voice, nearly dropped the flagon of water she was taking to refresh the bouquets of lilies in the front hall.

"Yes, monsieur?"

"Where is Mademoiselle Corrie?"

"Mademoiselle Corrie?" Toinette hesitated. Her master looked pale and tired, his face set in a frown. "I'm afraid she isn't here, monsieur."

"What do you mean?" His frown deepened. "Has she gone out?" Toinette shook her head. Silently she handed him an envelope.

"She's gone, monsieur. She left this for you."

He scanned her face. "When?" His voice was abrupt, though now his face was expressionless.

"I don't know, monsieur. I didn't see her leave. I could ask André . . ."

"No, there is no need." His manner was curt but the maid saw his fingers tremble slightly as he ripped open the envelope. Inside was a thin square of yellow linen, unstarched but carefully folded. Barely perceptible on the newly washed fabric were faint lines of writing. Attached was a scrap of paper. It read "Contract terminated. Clause five. Circumstances beyond my control."

Guy cursed, crumpled the paper savagely and hurled it away. Toinette, watching anxiously, saw that his expression was thunderous.

He turned to her.

"This is impossible. Completely out of character. She has no money, she knows no one in Paris. Where can she have gone?"

Toinette hesitated. She'd never seen her master in such a fury. And she thought she understood his concern. Paris, of all cities, was no place for a young girl alone. She hesitated a moment more, then made up her mind.

"I think perhaps, sir, that she does know someone . . . at least, she was getting letters regularly."

"Letters?" He searched her face with narrowed eyes. "From England, surely?"

"Yes, sir. But there were others." Toinette was disturbed by the expression on his face, but she'd begun now and must go on. "I couldn't help seeing the envelopes, sir, when I emptied the wastebasket in her room. They were postmarked Paris."

She kept her eyes down, uneasily aware of the explosive quality of the silence that followed.

"I see." Her master's voice was icy cold. There was an odd sort of finality in his tone as he said, "That will be all, Toinette. Thank you," walked into the drawing room, and closed the door quietly behind him.

CHAPTER TEN

"No, no, no!" Karl Beyer narrowed his eyes and glared, running a hand through his shock of white hair so that it stood on end. The soprano's chin quivered. He ignored it. The chorus shifted restlessly, sensing trouble.

"Madame . . ." His tone made of the respectful title a profound insult. "May I ask you to remember something? This is a French opera, you are playing a French courtesan. Passion, yes, by all means—but let us not forego a certain lightness, a certain delicacy? *Du tempérament, je vous en prie!*"

The soprano bridled. Beyer winced. He hated dress rehearsals. He hated the way the principals altered their costumes without permission, to make them more comfortable, or more flattering, so that the costume designer whimpered at his side all the way through. He hated the inevitable confusion in the wings as the leading lady's crinoline eddied and trapped the baritone's legs. He hated the graceless, fumbling mess, the fits and starts, the petulant half-finished chaos of it all—the delay between lighting cues, the mournful cries from backstage of "Wait," and "Stop!", his own voice repeating inexorably "*Encore!* Again!" Most of all he hated the fact that the orchestra, well acquainted with union rules, would leave in ten minutes time, whether or not he was satisfied with the performance.

"Once again, Madame. Look at Sergio. As if he were your lover, not the man who has come to investigate the drains. Is this too much to ask?" He sighed inwardly. She was a beautiful voice, that was all. She had the soul, not of an artist, but of a pig. And a girth to match.

"But maestro . . ." The soprano had coaxed two tears. He unbent. It was time for sweetness.

"Listen, *chérie* . . ." Oh, how he hated this charade too. He left his position beneath the footlights, ascended the stage, took her moist, plump hand, preparing honeyed words. And then he noticed something. All the chorus suddenly went silent, halting their whispers and surreptitious adjustments of costume. The soprano too looked away, her tears forgotten, her eyes swiveling to the back of the auditorium. Against his will his eyes followed hers.

"*Bonsoir, M. Beyer.*" A rich, clear voice that he recognized instantly floated down the aisle.

"You." She reached the footlights, gazed up at him limpidly. She was wearing the same sunshine yellow dress and scarlet knotted shawl. The light thrown up from beneath illumined the hollows of her face, those strange tilted eyes with their heavy lids. She looked older, thinner, more mature. But still implacable.

"It is indeed me."

The chorus behind him took a deep breath in unison, aghast at her temerity.

"My dear young lady, do you perceive that I am presently conducting a dress rehearsal?" His tone was dangerously quiet. The soprano permitted herself a smirk of satisfaction at the opportune arrival of a distraction.

"I do." The young woman's gaze didn't falter. In her eyes was commiseration, respect and a lurking twinkle of amusement. "I also perceive that it isn't going very well. I thought you might like to be relieved of it."

He stared at her, rendered speechless by her audacity. She returned his gaze with equanimity. He recognized that gaze, the gaze of someone who has nothing to lose.

Abruptly he signaled dismissal to the singers. Slowly, in a clanking of swords and a rustle of starched fabric they filed into the wings. The soprano, head held high, flounced off, her stays creaking. The orchestra melted away with the faintest metallic rattle, like cockroaches disturbed by a sudden light.

Silently he returned to his seat and gathered up his

score. Irritation was mingled with relief as he turned to his uninvited guest.

"Since you are such an observant young lady, perhaps you can advise me . . ." His tone was silky. "What is wrong with my soprano? Yesterday she sang like an angel, today she is a crow. Tell me, why should that be?"

"It's simple, M. Beyer. Something a man would not notice." That limpid gaze again. "She is wearing the wrong shoes. One cannot sing in a crinoline without the right shoes."

He stared at her. She was full of surprises. She was maybe even right. Large as she was, his leading lady was inordinately proud of her tiny feet. It would be just like her to wear stiletto heels under her hooped skirt.

"I take it you have come to sing for me again?" She nodded. He sighed. There was no doubt about it, she was going to be a problem. He almost regretted having invited her back, Harlequin or no Harlequin. A man in his position could barely afford the time to eat and sleep, let alone do favors for a friend.

"You must understand . . . this is the end of a long day, not a good day. I have been persecuted by the costume designer, the orchestra resents me, and the baritone insists on singing in Swedish."

"I don't care." His eyes widened. Such disastrous frankness. One could take it or leave it. He decided to take it.

"Sing away."

He watched her as she ascended the stage, noting with approval that this time she didn't scramble up but went up by the steps. She moved slowly, deliberately. He wondered if his previous impression had been wrong. Perhaps, in the hard glare of the footlights, her appeal would prove a mirage. What he saw as she reached center stage both satisfied and disturbed him. Without lights she had been striking, with lights she was extraordinary. Since he had last seen her her face had changed, achieved a strength and definition it hadn't had before. Somehow, standing quite still, she managed to give the impression of movement. Her silence had the quality of a pulse beat. What had happened to her? Her vitality that he remembered so clearly wasn't dimmed but somehow held in check. She was like a hovering seabird. One flap of her wings and she would soar away effortlessly out of sight.

He shook his head, forcing himself to think in practical terms. She had a face that read, enough of a rarity in itself. Even without make-up it would be easy for an audience to follow each expression, each nuance of emotion. But that was merely a question of design, an accident of fate. More unusual was the quality of projection. It was rare to find someone of the right stature—not in physical terms alone—for the really big roles, the tragic heroines, the women of legend, the goddesses. Someone who could fill a theater with her presence before she even opened her mouth. As a man of the theater he knew that it wasn't enough simply to have talent. One must first of all be noticed.

"Nedda's lament, I take it?"

"No. Mozart. 'Porgi Amor,' from *Figaro.*"

He was filled with dread. A dangerous choice, a totally unsuitable choice. Mozart's music, so superficially simple, was a deadly trap for the unwary and inexperienced singer. It was the high wire, unforgiving of the slightest lapse. Sung without feeling it was dead, sung with too much it could be physically painful to hear. Bizet, for one, had found it could make him retch.

He prepared himself for the worst. Mozart was not for the young, not for a big voice. She had made an offensive, possibly fatal error. Mozart required lightness, delicacy—the quality and technique of the famous Schwarzkopf at the least. Only a lyric soprano, an experienced soubrette, could be expected to do it justice.

But when she opened her mouth every thought, every comparison, left his mind instantly. She sang softly, hardly using the enormous volume of her voice, yet with a perfect purity, each note carrying precisely. No cold, passionless perfection here. Serenity, yes, but a fragile, human serenity, hard won, the calm after the storm. The voice no longer overpowered, it beckoned, like the sound of a faraway flute in a glade. It neither boasted of its mysteries nor explained them, it simply contained them, in a delicate golden bubble of sound. To be human, her voice said, is a very simple thing.

But he knew better. He knew what it cost to surrender technique, to let the music speak. She sang with delicacy, flexibility, serenity, but these would have meant nothing without humility. The transformation astonished him. Where had she learned this control, this perfect submission to the music? What had persuaded her down off her pedestal, to become the music's servant, not its mistress? He would not have thought it possible for such a change to take place in the few short months since he'd last heard her. But perhaps he'd forgotten the flexibility and enthusiasm of youth. Her voice told him how much he'd forgotten. Unforced, supremely natural, it defied criticism, drove every thought from his head, made him forget every other interpretation he'd ever heard. The future was in her voice. Now, too late, he wished she hadn't sung Mozart. The melody would be in his head for days, interfering with his current production, making every note he heard seem overrich and decorated.

When she had finished she stood completely silent. He contemplated her.

"You are clever. Very clever." She bowed her head.

"Thank you, M. Beyer."

He paused, at a loss for words.

"The middle voice?"

"Ah." He had forgotten. What did the middle voice matter? You might as well worry about Paganini breaking a string in midconcerto. "The middle voice is still not good, but it is better, better." She had woven the break into her performance, using its color to set her voice apart from any other.

"You must not sing Mozart again, not until you are at least thirty." His tone was dogmatic.

"Why is that, M. Beyer?"

"To spare me." He allowed himself a small smile. "I hope I shall be dead by then."

"Was it so terrible?"

"Yes." He glared at her in mock anger. "It made me wish I was young."

She eyed him consideringly.

"I shall sing Mozart if I like, M. Beyer." Their eyes met. He recognized an obstinacy as great if not greater than his own.

"Yes. You have that right." Looking at her face now, he could see that she had earned it. There was a shadow in her eyes, a new severity to the line of her wide mouth. Somewhere, somehow, she had learned that it takes more courage to be weak than to be brave.

"Where have you been . . . what have you been doing?" He shot the question at her suddenly, his eyes fierce under the thick white brows. She shrugged.

"I have been doing as you told me, M. Beyer. Practicing my exercises."

Not only the ones I set you, he thought, looking into those shadowed eyes. But if she had a secret recipe she clearly wasn't going to give it to him.

"And now?" He frowned at her interrogatively.

"And now . . ." She took a deep breath, her mouth curved in a wry smile. "Now I'm ready to learn. I've found out I need music more than it needs me. Will you teach me?"

He looked at her thoughtfully. She met his gaze without flinching. "No." He picked up his score. "I will not teach you. We will learn together."

It was the worst and best time of his life. He'd never met anyone like her. August wore on into September, she didn't falter. She devoured scores and exercises with a hunger that he found almost frightening, as if she were under sentence of death. Her appetite for work was astonishing; she lived, breathed and ate work. He worried about her. September faded into October and the evenings began to grow darker and cooler, he saw how thin and pale she was becoming.

"You will have to buy a coat soon," he admonished, gesturing at the rain rolling down the window panes.

"Not until you give me a role, M. Beyer." Her face was unsmiling. It was some sort of wager she'd made with herself, as unshakable as her determination to pay him the going rate for each hour's lesson. Where she was getting the money from he didn't dare ask. She was capable of anything, and her pride made her as unapproachable on the subject of money as a porcupine. When he offered her free lessons she was furious.

"No favors!" Her mouth was a grim line, her eyes snapped blue fire. Realizing that he was trespassing in foreign territory he wisely decided to hold his tongue. Instead he adopted an oblique approach. He took to preparing *cassoulet*, or onion soup, or one of his native Austrian layer cakes, in readiness for her lessons. She suspected charity at first, but a lifetime of coaxing skittish prima donnas stood him in good stead. He managed to convince her there was far too much food for one poor old man living alone.

"You must protect the voice," he added, casually, as one should always play a trump card. "Callas was finished at forty because she was too thin, too quickly. You must be as strong as an Olympic athlete, for the voice." She fell on the food like a famished dog, eating with the same relentless determination she applied to her work. The next time she came to his cool, dim little house off the Boulevard Saint Michel, as the air filled with the entrancing aroma of freshly baked strudel, he returned to his task. Against his will he found he was getting fond of her, worrying like a father. Surely life for a young girl alone in Paris must have its difficulties?

"I can manage." She was still defensive, but the delicious smell was clearly undermining her resistance. "In any case. I'm not alone, I have Harlequin."

And then, to his relief, because he was beginning to think that though she could sing with heartfelt sweetness about human frailty, she was immune to it herself, a faint blush rose to her cheeks. As they folded up their scores and embarked on the strudel she let her defenses drop, just once.

"Tell me, maestro . . ." She was hesitant, almost diffident. "Have you known him long?"

"Who, Miss Modena?" He helped himself with meticulous care to a glossy brown slice.

"Harlequin." The blush was marked now, but he ignored it studiously.

"Ah, Harlequin." He shot her a swift glance. "I'm not sure if he would want me to tell you. If he wanted you to know, he would tell you himself."

"Not necessarily." She rallied staunchly. "He might not think I would be interested. You see . . ." She frowned. "I never was, before."

"Before what?"

She gave him one of her quelling looks.

"Before now, M. Beyer." She always called him by his surname when she was annoyed. She was capable of such quaintly Victorian dignity that he was put to shame.

"Very well. What little I can tell you will do no harm." He poured himself a cup of the thick black coffee that always stood warming in its pewter pot above the piano. "I first met him many years ago, more years than I care to remember. He arrived backstage one night, after a particularly poor performance of *I Puritani*, and proceeded to tell me, in comprehensive detail, exactly what was wrong with it." He smiled reminiscently. "Of course I would have thrown him out, if I had not agreed with him in every detail."

"What was he like?" Her face was eager.

"Why this sudden curiosity? You have known him through your letters almost as long as I have."

"I know. It's just that . . . it never occurred to me to wonder what he was like. I felt I knew. Like one of those dreams, when everything makes sense, only you forget when you wake up. He was like—one of the family. I never needed to know what he was like, because . . ."—she tapped her chest lightly—"he was in here." She paused anxiously. "Does that sound stupid?"

"No." For a moment he felt the stir of an ancient pain. He had had a family once, many years ago. "Sometimes it is only when you lose someone that you realize how much they meant to you." He blinked away the film of years. The young face in front of him, vital and eager, was the best antidote. She and young talents like her were his family now.

"That's what I mean." She drew a deep breath. "I'm frightened. I wasn't before. I took it all for granted. You know what it's like when you're young. You think things will go on the same forever. But now . . . I'm frightened that I may lose him."

"And you think, by asking me about him, that you will keep him?" He smiled at her. "Sometimes it's best not to know too much. Remember Pandora's Box."

"But why? Why doesn't he want to meet me? It didn't matter to me before, the letters were enough. But now . . ."

"Now you've suddenly realized he's a real person, like yourself."

"Yes. He's my friend. I want to know what he's like."

He shrugged. "What can one man tell you about another? You probably know him as well if not better than I do. When I first met him he was very young, very intense. Proud, ferociously independent, ambitious, poor. He wanted to study music, but he had not the means."

"I never knew that." Her eyes were wide. "Did he have talent?"

"Oh yes."

"Then why . . ."

"Not everyone has your single-mindedness or your good fortune. I told him what I told you, to come back and see me again."

"Did he?"

"Yes. But by that time things had changed. He was no longer able to pursue his studies."

"Why?" Clearly she couldn't imagine any reason good enough to stand in the way of talent.

"I am not at liberty to say. But for him it was no

longer possible. He never told me the whole story. There were . . . family problems. Let us say simply, circumstances beyond his control."

"That's terrible!"

"I suppose it is, in its way. But think of it like this. If it had not been for that, if he had not been driven to make his bargain with circumstances, you might not be standing here today."

"I know. I owe him everything. That's why I want to meet him, I want to tell him . . . there are so many things you can't say in a letter. Do you think you could persuade him?"

He shook his head. "I doubt it. Just this once I think you had better be content with only half the cake. Sometimes the whole is simply . . . not available."

"You think I'm being greedy?"

"A little." He smiled to take the sting out of the words. "Don't you see? If you met him, you would both lose one very rare, very precious freedom, almost unheard of between a man and a woman. The freedom to tell each other everything."

There was a long pause. Then she looked up.

"Tell me just one more thing." Her face was intent. "Do you like him?"

Again she'd surprised him. He'd expected her to ask what Harlequin looked like, or some other triviality.

"I don't know." Such a simple question, but it had been so long since liking or loving had played a major part in his life that he'd almost forgotten what it felt like. "He is . . . reserved, difficult to know. I think perhaps you are the only one who has ever come close to knowing him at all. And that . . ." He stood up, glared at her over the coffee cups and all that remained of the strudel. "That is the last word I am going to say on the subject."

He expected that womanlike, she wouldn't take no for an answer, but again she surprised him. She never mentioned Harlequin to him again.

October passed, the gutters were filled with dead leaves, the wind developed a cutting edge. But inside his house it was perpetual summer. She filled the air with gold. It was a joy to work with someone who dipped in and out of French and Italian with the ease of a swallow, who understood instinctively that a language is a finely tuned instrument, a music in its own right. But he feared for her still. Hers was a natural gift, and her technique was growing day by day like a miracle, but the life she wanted and the speed with which she wanted it would place unnatural strains on both. Had she the determination, the spirit to survive?

"You are so young." He shook his head as he watched her sink small white teeth into a succulent slice of Black Forest gâteau, liberally laced with kirsch and popping with cherries the size of plums.

"Not so young as I was." She smiled that new, small smile with the edge of bitterness to it. If he hadn't known she had no time for lovers, he would have suspected a man in her life. Not that she made any effort to be pretty. She wore no makeup, dressed simply, tied her hair back in that severe knot at the back of the neck. Perhaps her heart had already been broken. If so, it was all to the good. The voice was whole, really whole for the first time. Some canaries sang all the sweeter for being blinded.

She shook off his scrutiny. Enough of this small talk, she seemed to say, as she licked the last coal-black crumb from her fingers.

"When can I start to sing?"

"But you are singing, every day."

"You know what I mean. I want a role. When can I have one?"

"I am not God," he replied tartly. "You can have one when you are given one."

"But I'm ready now."

"My dear Corrie . . . that isn't the way of the world. The world doesn't say, 'Now,' it says, 'One day . . . perhaps.' "

And then it was November. One dark, wet evening she arrived at 6 p.m., punctual as always, but she didn't look well. He could tell from her pallor and the touch of her hand that she was cold. It was hardly surprising. She was still wearing the thin cotton dress. The sight of her, the knowledge that she wouldn't let him help her, filled him with fury. He stoked the fire—central heating was anathema to voices and pianos alike—and sat her as close to it as he could.

But the lesson didn't go well. She seemed, for once, absentminded, unable to concentrate. He noticed that her hand trembled slightly as she held the score. All his concern, so carefully hidden, surfaced once more.

"Corrie, how are you managing to live?"

She blinked at him, but for once she wasn't angry. She seemed suddenly lost, young, infinitely vulnerable.

"Maestro . . . outside this room I do not live at all."

He tried to persuade her to stay for *carbonnade flamande* and *haricots verts*, but she refused. She was late already, she said. Distrait, flushed, she hurried away, leaving behind her cherished score of Massenet's *Manon*. It was so unlike her to be careless that he was filled with foreboding.

CHAPTER ELEVEN

It was past 8 p.m. by the time Corrie reached the Métro. She hurried down the long dimly lit platform, eager to reach the comparative warmth of the train. Her carriage was almost deserted. All Paris was dining, or soon would be. She closed her eyes. Despite the warmth there were small shivers running through her body, she felt alternately flushed with heat and icy cold. She concentrated hard, running the afternoon's music through her mind like a string of warm pearls.

"How do I live?" she thought wryly. "Does it matter? I live." Off canapés, and stolen snatches of music, off charity and hope. But how much longer could she go on?

Soon, all too soon, she reached her station. She hurried through the garishly lit streets, tugging her shawl close against the biting wind, and slipped through a green-painted door in a side street.

"*Salut, Philippe.*" The barman, lining up his glasses under the canopy of plastic greenery that passed as a Hawaiian bar, smiled and winked. She sighed inwardly as she threaded her way through the network of cramped corridors that backed onto the tiny basement theater. Her minute white-painted cubicle, windowless, unheated, with only a small iron-barred grille leading up to the street for ventilation, managed to be stuffy and cold at the same time. In the fluorescent light above the spotted mirror her face looked pale and drawn, the only color the greenish shadows beneath her eyes. She stuck out her tongue at her reflection then slipped out of the yellow dress.

Her routine was automatic by now. She flung her scarlet shawl around her bare shoulders, then sat down before the mirror. Systematically she spread white pancake base over the entire skin of her face and neck. She smiled, beginning to enjoy herself as her familiar features disappeared little by little behind the stark mask. Slowly she outlined her eyes with a smooth, thick black line, canceling their upward slant with a melancholy downward tilt at the corners, completing the effect with a single black teardrop beneath the left eye. She redrew her obliterated eyebrows in a mannered, plaintive arch above their natural line, then redesigned her lips into a tiny cupid's bow of dark scarlet.

She leaned back, studied her reflection. It never ceased to amaze her, not just the transformation in her appearance, but the effect it had on how she felt. Suddenly the cold gray streets were a hundred miles away. Here and now she was Columbine, the moon-faced girl on the poster outside, the heroine and object of a million bittersweet masquerades, ready to dance under midsummer stars . . .

She stood up, slid the skimpy, clinging black shift over her head, added the trailing red feather boa. She braided her hair and twisted the plaits into precise little cartwheels on either side of her head. It gave her head a doll-like shape, accentuated the huge black-lined eyes. She looked like a puppet, a moon girl, a night creature. What would Guy de Chardonnet think of her now? She banished the thought. It was easy to forget, when she was Columbine, less easy when she went back to her room at the Louisiane, the hotel on the Rue de Seine that she'd chosen for three very good reasons: it was Left Bank to its fingertips, Jean-Paul Sartre and Juliette Greco had once stayed there, and most important of all, it was cheap.

It had taken her exactly a week to prove finally and conclusively to herself that Paris was no place for a woman to be poor on her own. For such a person, especially in August, the city of light was a very fair approximation of hell. The streets were hot and dusty, and crammed with tourists, bent on pleasures only two could enjoy. The few native Parisians who remained in August were bad-tempered and resentful of the invasion, clearly wishing they too were by the sea, or on the moon, or anywhere that wasn't Paris in August.

Yes, it was a very different city. Without a chauffeur, without the comforts of a quiet house on the Avenue Pierre I de Serbie and the guidance of someone who knew Paris intimately, it was a city of dusty Métro rides and hard pavements, where the grass, what was left of it in the scorching heat, was never to be walked on, and shopkeepers threw a fit if she dared to touch a peach. And yet, it would almost have been better if she'd been a newcomer to the city. It felt strange, to pass places she'd visited with Guy, and know that they were closed to her, to look up at the Closerie des Lilas' moonlit terrace and know that she couldn't even afford the price of an apéritif.

She discovered something else, too—she didn't like going hungry, and she liked even less the ever present alternative, clearly available in the eyes of the well-dressed men patroling the streets in the poor quarter where she was staying, or brushing her shoulders in the Métro. But what could she do? Paris was flooded with casual laborers, students, foreigners, for everyone knew it was the *grandes vacances*. She tried, but every position, even the most menial, was filled.

On the seventh day she went to the cheapest booth in the local market, and bought herself a skinny red dress. She outlined her eyes with kohl, painted her fingernails magenta, spent her last five francs on a pound of cherries and went to Montmartre. At the first club she reached that seemed remotely respectable she asked for the manager, a glass of water, and a job. She got everything but the glass of water.

"Can you dance?" asked the manager, standing a little too close and taking a little too much interest in the cut of her red dress. She looked him straight in the eyes and lied outright. But strangely, that first night, as she waited in the cramped space by the stairs that served as wings, she wasn't even nervous. The smell of dust on the lights, the clatter of eating, the smoke filling the air, the hubbub of different languages, reminded her of the happy years with her mother. As for the dancing . . . well, she'd soon swing them around to her way of thinking. The management might have different ideas, but out there was an audience, unsuspecting, but available if she could reach them.

As she made her entrance that first night there was a gasp of surprise. Only the pianist, blind to everything but the prospect of his fifty franc fee and the free drinks the management would provide before the club closed, ambled on unperturbed. Corrie smiled. The reaction to her costume and make-up had been all she'd hoped for. Now she had their entire attention.

She pirouetted, executed a few steps, placated the manager, a hostile shadow on the edge of her vision, with a token flash of leg. She knew very well that her clown makeup above the provocative dress was arresting enough to cover any inadequacies. As for the rest . . . She took a deep breath as the pianist, obedient as a circus horse, launched into the simple twelve-bar blues number she'd selected to introduce her act. Only she had no act—except one. Without hesitation she spun to a full stop, center stage. There was no microphone, but when had she ever needed one?

"Well, I'm going, going away, baby,
And I won't be back till fall . . ."

She posed, prettily, finger under her chin, her mouth curved in a cheeky grin. Her voice was deep, dark, throaty as a southern dusk.

"If I find me a good guy,
I won't be back at all . . ."

She closed one black-ringed eye in an outrageous wink. She held the note, milking it of its last sensual appeal. She saw by their faces that she had them. She had chosen well. American blues slipped down continental throats as smoothly as American ice cream. It was foreign enough to intrigue, familiar enough to be digestible. Fortunately too there was a scattering of

Americans in the audience. She moved on swiftly from the lonesome blues to a quick uptempo number, a real crowd pleaser. Three numbers later she exited, triumphant, to find the manager waiting for her in the wings.

"It won't do." His face was agitated as he followed her down to the cubbyhole she was to share with Annie, a genuine cabaret dancer. "You will bankrupt me. Did you see them? Not a bottle of wine ordered during the whole performance!"

"M. Grasset . . ." Corrie whisked off the red circles on her cheekbones with an expert hand that trembled only slightly. "Don't worry. What is the mark-up on that cleaning fluid you serve as house wine? Ten francs, fifteen at most? You need a better clientele, more Americans. I will get them for you. Inside a week, I guarantee it, you will be serving champagne." She sent him a sidelong glance. "And you know the mark-up on champagne."

She'd touched the right chord. He was an Algerian, a *pied noir*, one of the thousands who had flooded into Paris after independence, and therefore a practical man.

"Very well. You have a week. But please, you must find something more cheerful to sing. My clients come to the Chat d'Or for a little amusement, a little pleasure, not a . . . bloodletting!"

She laughed. She had no intention of changing her material. The popping of champagne corks would be sufficient music for his ears. He looked at her appraisingly, then laid a proprietary hand on her bare arm.

"You have talent, *ma petite*. A man in my position could be of great assistance to you in your career." She gazed at him expressionlessly through the remains of her clown's mask. The effect was oddly offputting. He shrugged and removed his hand.

"Thank you, M. Grasset. I'm glad we have reached an understanding." She opened the door politely. "A week. I guarantee it."

Within a week, as she'd predicted, there was a perceptible hush of anticipation as she left the wings, and a sprinkling of evening dress in the audience. Alert to the main chance and to the popping of champagne corks, M. Grasset flyposted the door and walls of the club with her photograph. She had no hesitation when he asked her, belatedly, for her stage name. "Columbine." It was her one small revenge, her one rebellion against the seedy straitjacket in which she found herself. For it was a straitjacket, despite her growing band of faithful followers, who hushed any late entrants to her performance and called out the titles of her songs. She knew what was required of her, knew what they'd come to see—an act, a routine—and she stuck to it with grim determination, even though at times she longed for something more substantial to sing, something which would rock them in their seats, bring them tears and terror, as once the blues must have done.

But she was a professional, doing a professional's job, for one reason only, to survive.

And survive she did. It was hard. There were many things she didn't know and had to learn, fast. How to fend off the unwelcome masculine hands that reached for her, with a well-placed word and a vitriolic stare. How to walk past *pâtisserie* shops with her eyes averted and her wallet firmly closed. How to stretch a *baguette* for two days, and hold a top note on stage when she felt faint with hunger and dizzy with cigarette fumes. How to avert her eyes from the grimy floor and peeling walls of her dressing room and pretend she was somewhere else entirely, a sunlit beach, a green mountainside . . .

As soon as she had enough money to pay for lessons she went to see M. Beyer. Knowing he wouldn't approve of her singing in the club she didn't tell him. She wanted it that way. She wanted her days completely filled with work, so she wouldn't have time to think about anything else.

But at night, when she returned to her small top floor room at the Louisiane she lay sleepless in the stifling heat, staring out at the rooftops and the city's many twinkling lights and thinking of something her mother had told her about Maria Callas . . . How once, in an Italian country town, she'd been singing a love duet at her window, when from far away in the darkness came a man's voice answering, the most beautiful, impassioned voice she'd ever heard. The duet continued night after night, but Maria never found out the identity of her Mario, he remained just a voice in the darkness, something out of a dream.

And maybe that was the better way. Try as she might, she couldn't make herself forget Guy. She was like a sleepwalker, nothing else seemed real. Sometimes she wondered whether she was in fact ill. She alternated between feverish activity and bone-deep lethargy. Hypersensitive to every noise, she began to think she heard his step on the stair, his voice in the hall below. Half the time she couldn't eat, the rest she was consumed with cravings for wild strawberries, oysters and caviar. She wasted money she couldn't spare on crêpes filled with Chantilly cream, only to find they tasted like leather and shaving soap when she eventually got them.

Dear Harlequin,

What's happening to me? Why can't I stop thinking about him? He's nothing special, just a collection of cells and corpuscles like me, and yet I think if I saw him in the street I'd throw away everything, all the future we've planned, just to hear his voice again . . . Does that sound crazy? I wish I knew how long this was going to last. Some days I think I'm cured, I hardly think about him at all, and then at night he comes alive again as soon as I fall asleep, and I wake up crying.

I was such a fool. I don't know how I came to fall in love with him of all people. He's the worst kind of man you could possibly imagine—cold, ruthless, egotistical—a real King Pluto. All he cares about is possessions. I never even liked him, I swear. You know how I feel about rich men—surely I should have been immune?

Please, tell me I've done the right thing.

Columbine

Dear Columbine,

First love . . . there's always a first time, but that doesn't make it any easier, I know. I remember when I first came to Paris, a naïve country boy sure that the world was going to be my oyster, I too fell in love with someone unsuitable, impossible, out of reach . . . But you are braver than I was. You have cut him out of your life entirely. Believe me, that is the better way. Love is most dangerous when it turns sour, poisons itself with regret and bitterness and disappointment. Love becomes more difficult, after the first time—it becomes harder to take the risk, to go on believing. When you fall in love again you will understand.

Does that sound cynical? If it does, forgive me. I'm afraid I am more than a little jealous.

Your Harlequin

Dear Harlequin,

What do you mean, again? Do people go through this over and over? How can they? I don't think I could bear it. Surely lightning never strikes twice in the same place?

Wait a minute . . . an awful thought has just occurred to me. Maybe you're speaking from experience, maybe you're in love with someone right now?

Yes, that's it. I've been blind and foolish, ranting on about my doomed love affair as if I were the first one to discover the emotion. It explains so much . . . why you want us never to meet, why you never mention other women in your letters. I'm sorry, I should have known before, it's just that, selfishly, I assumed you belonged to me. I never thought of you—I know this sounds bad—but I never thought of you as a man, one of those dangerous creatures who destroy women's lives with a word, or the lack of one. You were my friend, you were always there when I needed you, I felt safe. . . .

And now—I'm not sure what to think. I'm trying very hard to be grown-up, I hope you've noticed. But it's very difficult. Why didn't you tell me? I'm not a child anymore, I would have understood. Who is she, what is she like? Is she beautiful? Does she love you?

I'm sorry, but I think I hate her already. She's able to talk to you, laugh with you, see you whenever she likes . . . it's not fair, I knew you first.

And yet, I'm beginning to realize how little I really know about you, my man in the moon. Maybe it's time you came down?

Your Columbine

Dear Columbine,

You know me too well already. Yes, I am in love. Why didn't I tell you? Because I was ashamed. All my life I've dreamed of the perfect love—I think all men do in some secret corner of their souls, though they may not admit it. I've never stopped searching for that perfect union of passion and loyalty, beauty and strength . . .

Fine words. If only I had been able to keep to that ideal! But no. Instead I have fallen in love with the worst possible kind of woman. Unsuitable, impossible, out-of-reach. Beautiful, mercenary, sophisticated. A grown man should be able to resist such folly, but somehow she managed to catch me off my guard, to cross all my carefully constructed barriers like . . . a dove flying home. La Colombe, that was my name for her. A play on words perhaps, a piece of wishful thinking. I see that now. She is utterly unlike you, my Columbine, and yet I hoped . . . there was something about her, some softness behind the hard veneer . . . I was taken in, I went further than I should have done.

She had a strange effect on me. With her I felt like a young boy again, gauche, unsure, clumsy. I made mistakes, I know. If I hadn't, perhaps I could have made her love me. For she isn't cold or indifferent to me. I think she is even attracted, a little. But not only to me.

And there is one other thing. She wants money, a great deal of it. I am not rich enough for her, she tells me. I admire her honesty. If it weren't for that, if I could give her everything she needs, I think I could hold her.

If it weren't for you, my Columbine, my talisman, my ace-in-the-hole, I think I might give up my search for the perfect love. It is so painful, n'est-ce pas? *I have been in love before, but this time, I admit it, I am badly afflicted. Every time I see her she takes my breath away. Of course I will recover sooner or later, I know that—but I'm afraid I lied to you when I said that experience lessens the pain. When you fall in love, it seems as if each time is the first time. I'm not sure whether that is a reason for hope or despair.*

So you see, we're two of a kind, my Columbine. Two cripples trying to help each other over a stile.

Your loving Harlequin

Dear Harlequin,

I knew I would hate her. What's wrong with her, how dare she not love you? And how could you allow yourself to fall in love with a woman like that? I know the type, all sweetness on the outside but hard as nails underneath! Aren't there other women in the world? She's not worth it, she doesn't deserve you!

Yes, I know what you're thinking. I'm no better. It's not that easy to choose who to love. King Pluto is hardly a suitable citizen for Uscady. Did you know, in Greek "pluto" means the wealth of precious stones and metals that lies underground? Whatever treasure my King Pluto is concealing is very well buried indeed . . .

But that doesn't mean I'm going to take back what I said about your Colombe. I still hate her—but for your sake I'll try to be charitable. There must be some good in her, I suppose, for you to have loved her in the first place.

I'm not sure, but I think I feel a little better. It's nice to know I'm not the only one with feet of clay.

Your foolish Columbine

In the months that followed they discussed their plans and symptoms like two invalids, using their shared code. She could write to him, after a sleepless night, "*King Pluto is bothering me today,*" and he would understand without further explanation, and she could inquire after La Colombe, presently in one of her periodic absences in the arms of another, richer man, and he would say that he was feeling a little better today, thank you, and they could laugh a little at each other's foolishness.

One evening she cut out a wide red satin heart and pinned it to the brief sleeve of her costume. She was a fool in love and didn't care who knew it. She wasn't hiding anymore, she was no longer an automaton. She was an artist, she wouldn't bury her pain away in the dark cold earth, she'd cut it and polish it till it shone with all the light and beauty of the sun.

Full of a new enthusiasm she began to plot and plan. She'd made her peace with love, and now maybe some of all this misdirected emotion could be turned in Harlequin's direction. Their new closeness couldn't be allowed to fade. She wrote, winningly, persuasively, stressing how much her suggestion would help her in her work.

"*I know we've agreed never to meet, but it would mean so much to me, just the thought that one day—years from now, maybe decades—on my first night in a major role, you would be there in the audience to listen. I have no one else. It would make all the difference to me, give me something to work for. Would you? Would you, please?*"

At last, he was persuaded. "*Yes, I will come to your first night. Whenever it is, wherever I am, I will come. More than that I cannot promise. But I will be there.*"

She hugged the thought to her like a secret talisman. It was the one sure bright spot on her horizon. One day, she would sing for Harlequin.

A sharp rap on the door startled Corrie out of her reverie. She shivered. That day was still far off, if it would ever come. Now, as always, there was only one reality, the evening's performance, the waiting audience. She hurried out of the tiny cubicle and almost collided with Jean-Louis, the fancy juggler, who'd just come off stage. They skirted each other as cautiously as major powers, she careful not to alarm the pigeons secreted in his padded jacket, he not to snag the beading on her dress.

"How is the audience today?"

He shook his head, spat, muttered succinctly, "*Cochons*. Pigs."

She made a sympathetic grimace. As it got colder the warmup acts found their task more difficult. She suppressed another shiver. What was wrong with her? Usually the pre-performance flood of adrenaline was warmth enough for her. It must be the drafts in the narrow corridor. Once she was on stage the lights would do the trick.

"Trouble, eh?"

"The manager shouldn't have put those tables so near to the stage—they swore they could see my secret pockets. One even tried to trip me."

"The rewards of success, Jean-Louis."

He snarled at her, barely appeased.

"I will believe that when he doubles my salary."

Forewarned, she peeped through the wings. Her heart sank. Jean-Louis was right. In his determination to cash in on the club's unexpected popularity M. Grasset had edged three tables right up to the footlights. They were occupied by a particularly well-dressed party, and by the look of the champagne corks on the table it seemed they were having a very good time. Some of it at the expense of the performers . . .

But she would deal with them. Corrie looked at the well-coiffed, exquisitely gowned women, enjoying their evening's slumming as an opportunity to flaunt their expensive winter tans, and took an instant dislike to them. Any one of them could be La Colombe, who was presently engaged in breaking her Harlequin's heart, and at any moment they might be joined by Blanche de Chardonnet, who was presently engaged in breaking hers . . .

But she would show them. She would make them laugh, make them cry, make them realize that life still held a few surprises.

If only she didn't feel so cold . . . The footlights had a hazy blue ring around them, as if they were moons on a frosty night. She blinked to clear her vision. The pianist struck up the opening bars of her music, but she waited in the wings, milking the pause, making the silence sing. Well-trained, the pianist played the introduction again. The hubbub died down to a mere murmur, with a ripple of curiosity in it. She entered, walking lightly, almost insouciantly, silent in her small black slippers. When she reached center stage, not before, she turned to face the audience. She took one step forward, looked once to left, once to right, giving them the benefit of her strange clown's eyes in the white mask of her face. She waited a few moments for the warmth of the lights to touch her skin, permeate her chilled body.

But it didn't happen. She stared out into the tiny packed theater, saw the intent lifted faces as if they were faces in a dream. Suddenly she felt strange, out of place. What was she doing here, singing about love to a room full of strangers? What did they care about who she was or what she felt? What did anyone care about anything? She looked down at the party just beneath the stage. They had expectant, half-patronizing smiles on their faces. They'd come for the blues, to hear songs of loneliness and loss sung in an idiom they could afford to despise.

Suddenly, with a choking feeling in her throat, she knew that she'd had enough. She was tired of playing a role, fitting herself into a convenient capsule so as to slip easily down their throats. She wanted to be taxing, indigestible, she wanted to be remembered. She wanted, just once, to sing for herself as well as for her supper.

"Winter Moon." The pianist raised his eyes in surprise. She never introduced her numbers, it was part of her act. He glanced at her doubtfully. She nodded, a small, definite nod. A faint smile touched his face. He was a Hoagy Carmichael fanatic, she'd heard him playing in the bar.

She began to sing, using full voice for the first time. The plaintive, haunting deceptively simple melody filled the air. She rode it, carving the notes out of the silence with a craftsman's pleasure. How she'd longed for something to get her teeth into, something with class and style, which dipped from major to minor, used all the singular power of the human voice. She played with the melody like a cat, putting everything she had into a single thread of sound, then taking it back again. She flattened one note, rebuilt it, stretched the melody savagely to let it spring back again, only to be transformed once more. Notes came alive as she touched them, caressed them, replaced them upside down and sideways. The pianist played like a man possessed, the audience was as silent as the grave. They didn't know whether they were witnessing a birth or a funeral. Her voice was at times a flute, at times a clarinet. Winter always comes, her voice said. Darkness always comes. You are not immune. There is always someone left alone.

It was a performance she knew she was going to regret. As she laid the last note reluctantly in its grave she was aware that a whole roomful of people had stopped eating and drinking. On the white faces below there was an expression of shock, outrage, loss—the expression of a man who's just discovered someone has pinched his wallet. The manager would not be pleased. Not a single order had gone to the bar since the performance began.

But she didn't care, not at that moment. It was

enough to have broken out of the mold, done what she wanted to do. She was warm again, with a nervous febrile warmth that started in the pit of her stomach and crackled out to the ends of her fingers. Cold sweat trickled down her forehead, mingling with the white greasepaint. She stepped forward again. More Hoagy Carmichael, it had to be.

"I Can Get Along Without You Very Well." Oh, the lies people told each other—none greater than the lies you told yourself. She breathed deep, all the suppressed knowledge and feeling mounting inside her like a tide. The things she had to say . . . they wouldn't forget them.

Nor could they. She could see that from their faces as she finished. No one moved, no one smiled. The pianist surreptitiously wiped his forehead. She could see from M. Grasset's face that he was having serious second thoughts. In the shocked silence her eyes were drawn to a new arrival, a man dressed in white, threading his way steadily through the narrow aisles between the close-set tables. His face was a dim mask in the glare from the footlights. Her head swam as she tried to make it out. Phrases from the song she'd sung echoed in her mind, she wondered whether she was still singing. She felt herself sway, saw the lights merge and blur into one huge phosphorescence. The man was now right at the foot of the stage, motionless, staring upward. His friends at the table under the footlights called to him. He was frowning. He looked a little, just a little, like Guy de Chardonnet. Illogically, she felt a momentary spasm of regret that the stranger had come too late to hear her sing. Then she fainted.

"She's sick. Feel her forehead, she's burning up."

"Send for a doctor."

"Get some water."

"What's wrong with her?"

"She's ill, can't you see? Get a doctor."

"Here's some water, what shall I do with it?"

"Give it to me. Where's that doctor, for God's sake?"

Corrie lay motionless, dimly aware of the hubbub of voices above her head. They disturbed her peace. It was so pleasant, so comfortable to be lying down. Someone pulled at her arm.

"It's no good, she's unconscious."

"Give that to me."

She felt cold water on her face, jerking her back to reality. She struggled up to a sitting position.

"Mind my boa!" If water got on it, it would be ruined.

Someone patted her arm soothingly.

"Don't worry, the doctor's on his way."

"No." She struggled up farther. She couldn't possibly afford a doctor, they charged a fortune for emergency calls. Her head reeled. She sank back again to the friendly boards.

"Bring the curtain down, for the love of God." It was M. Grasset's voice, with an undertone of panic in it. Yes, I'm fired, thought Corrie. She opened her eyes again. She'd never seen how interesting people's feet were from this angle. She hoped no one would tread on her.

"Out of my way."

A commanding voice. It must be the doctor. She tried to protest, but couldn't summon the strength even to open her eyes. Her head began to spin even though she was lying still. Her cheek was pressed against some smooth material that smelled good. Overhead lights flashed behind her closed lids. Her head felt strange, enormously large, but without enough room for a single coherent thought. She half opened her eyes, realized that the material against which her cheek was resting was white, knew in the same second that it was black where her stage makeup had smeared it.

With difficulty she lifted her head away. Another thing she couldn't afford was cleaning bills. "Put me down. I'm all right now."

"Shut up." It was a pleasant voice, heard from this close, and strangely familiar. How rude, she thought, but for the life of her she couldn't find the energy to resent it. It was only when she felt cold November air on her face that she realized she was outside the theater.

"Where are you taking me?" She felt it only polite to inquire.

"Where would you like to go?" The same voice, with that oddly reassuring note of command in it. A car door opened, she found herself ensconced in the front seat, swathed in a fluffy mohair blanket, the colors as soft and bright as a magic carpet. She was warm at last. Above her, through the tinted glass of the car roof, she could see a hoarfrost scattering of stars. She took a deep breath. There was a moon, high and pale. A Winter Moon . . .

"Where would I like to go?" Her voice sounded muffled even to her own ears, but she couldn't help it. She was full of a warm contented drowsiness. She had the utmost faith in her rescuer, he was clearly a magician.

"Somewhere . . ." She sighed, snuggled deeper into the soft wool. "Somewhere *warm*."

She heard the engine start. Through heavy lids she looked at the driver, trying to make out his face. What did a magician look like? It was dark, but he still looked a little like Guy de Chardonnet. But then she couldn't remember what other men, who weren't Guy de Chardonnet, looked like. Ever since that night in his house she'd been suffering from a kind of blindness. She closed her eyes. It felt strange, and yet wholly natural and right, to be traveling through the winter darkness with a man who looked like Guy de Chardonnet. Trying to remember why this should be so she fell asleep.

She woke only once, to see through half-closed eyes that they were rushing at what seemed enormous speed down a dead-straight road. Pine trees, black and impenetrable on either side, framed the night sky. But the moon was still there, floating weightlessly like herself. She had no idea what time it was, where she was, who she was. She fell asleep again, to dream of riding a huge black horse through fields of daffodils.

CHAPTER TWELVE

She opened her eyes on a totally strange room. She blinked, trying to remember how she'd gotten there. Soft light bloomed behind louvered shutters, a faint breeze stirred thin white curtains. She'd slept, for the first time since she'd left the Avenue Pierre I de Serbie, as sweetly and soundly as a baby.

But somewhere along the line she'd also acquired a baby's weakness. It was all she could do just to raise her head from the smooth linen pillow. She felt curiously boneless and soft, as if some long, taut string inside her had suddenly snapped.

A knock sounded at the door.

"*Entrez.*"

Light flooded into the semi-darkened room, dazzling her, outlining the figure of a man in white. She struggled upright on her pillows. Blood rushed to her head as she remembered the man who looked like Guy de Chardonnet. He did. He was.

The sight of him, so exactly like the image she'd been carrying around in her heart and yet so different—living, breathing, moving, so real he took her breath away—made her feel suddenly giddy. She sank back on the pillows, convinced she was seriously ill. How many times she'd dreamed of this moment, rehearsing endlessly in her mind how it would be if they chanced to meet again. Of course he must never know she loved him, but perhaps he would sense a difference in her, a new depth, a softness, a maturity, and be touched by them. Now she was a woman, fully fledged, mysterious, alluring, even a little tragic.

Only she didn't feel like that, not at all. However many times she'd played the scenario over in her head, she'd never dreamed it would be like this. She'd been proud of the way she'd rebuilt herself after the first shock of realizing she was in love with him. She'd worked at her recovery, set her love for him apart in a little hidden shrine so that she could get on with her life. But the mere sight of him knocked down all her carefully constructed walls as if they were made of paper. Her heart, which she'd disciplined so well, was racing out of control, blood drummed in her ears, she felt faint and breathless and very scared. It was like going onstage at the Chat d'Or, only infinitely worse. She had no act to offer, and this time the heart on her sleeve wasn't shiny red satin but living flesh and blood. Raw, aching, vulnerable, every sensitive nerve exposed.

So much for her naïve resolutions. She winced inwardly. She'd been so sure she'd made her peace with love, she'd even boasted that fact to Harlequin.

If only doing it was as easy as saying it. Just the turn of his dark head, so familiar and so mysterious, melted her heart, twisted a hook in the pit of her stomach. She was tied to him, like a fish on a line, like a puppet on a string.

"What have you done to me?" she whispered in a voice she hardly recognized as her own.

"I?" The sound of his voice, as cool and self-assured as she'd remembered, restored a little of her poise. "Surely you can't blame me for this, at least! You have been ill."

He advanced into the room, closed the door behind him. She shrank back against the pillows in a sort of panic. Her head was buzzing, she wanted to hide or scream or vanish in a puff of blue smoke. Don't come any nearer, she begged inwardly. It's not fair. I've been ill. I can't fight anymore.

Fortunately he didn't look at her, giving her time to disguise her panic. He set the big white bowl he was carrying carefully beside the bed.

"Where am I?"

"The Château des Basques."

"Another of your houses?" Nervousness made her speak more scornfully than she'd intended, but he was unmoved.

"I'm afraid so. This one, however, happens to be my favorite." He turned unexpectedly, caught her looking at him. The expression in his eyes was quizzical.

"What is it?"

She looked down, uneasily conscious of the blush that stained her cheeks. She'd been staring at him as if she'd never seen him before.

"I was just thinking what a luxury it must be, to have a favorite house. Some people don't have any at all."

He frowned. She couldn't meet his eyes. The silence stretched unbearably.

"How did you find me?"

He raised one eyebrow. "So many questions. What makes you so sure I was looking for you?"

"I didn't mean that . . ." Her flush deepened. She didn't know what she meant, didn't even know what she was saying.

"I'm glad to see a little color in your cheeks. You must be feeling better." He laid a hand gently on her forehead. She flinched at his touch, tossed her head uneasily, aware that her braids had come uncoiled while she was asleep and now straggled across the pillow. She must look like a schoolgirl.

"Hmmm." He nodded noncommittally, then sat down on the bed and held out the white bowl. "Here. Drink this."

She looked at him suspiciously. "What is it?"

He shook his head. "You still don't trust me, do you? You forget . . . I am your gallant rescuer. I'm hardly likely to go to all this trouble merely to poison you."

She'd forgotten how impossible they'd always found it to understand each other. Meekly she took the bowl, irritated to find that her hand was unsteady. A delicious, rich aroma floated upwards. She took a tentative sip. It was chocolate, warm and rich and sinfully sweet.

"Thank you." She drank deeply, surprised to find how hungry she was. "Believe me, I'm very grateful."

"Good." He watched her, unsmiling, until she'd drained the last drop. "Now . . . I must decide what to do with you."

She smiled. Whether it was the chocolate or the oddly comfortable warmth of him sitting there on the bed, she didn't know, but she felt much better. Perhaps she was going to survive after all.

"I'm sorry. I'm always a bit of a problem to you, I'm afraid." She leaned back against the pillow. It was nice to be someone's problem. She hadn't realized it, but she'd grown tired, bone-achingly tired, of coping on her own. If it hadn't been for Harlequin . . .

He was watching her, his face unreadable.

"You should have chosen me." His voice was level.

"What do you mean?"

He shrugged, rose to his feet. She noticed again the curious elegance of his movements, never studied, but as much a part of him as his hair or his skin.

"You should have chosen me as your protector. I would have taken better care of you. At least, you would not have gone hungry."

She sat bolt upright, suddenly outraged. She might have known it—he thought she'd gone straight off to the arms of another man.

"What makes you think I can't take care of myself?"

"You've given me no indication to the contrary." He paused, clearly amused at her fury. "But please . . . I did not mean to be critical. I was merely pointing out that you would have been more sensible to choose me. I can at least afford to support you in the style to which you have become accustomed."

It was no good. He was the same Guy de Chardonnet, blinkered and cynical and soulless to his fingertips.

"There is an English saying with which you may be familiar." Her tone was acid, but she managed to lean back on her pillows with the dignity befitting an invalid. "Man cannot live by bread alone."

"Indeed not." He paused in the doorway. "But I would have given you chocolate."

He was smiling, that cool, provoking, gray-eyed smile. She couldn't think of a thing to say, and he knew it. "You are not to get up." His voice had that familiar note of command. She was instantly furious.

"So you're going to keep me prisoner?"

He sighed. "Why must you always be so theatrical? I am simply informing you of the doctor's orders."

"But I'm not ill." She refused to acknowledge her own weakness. "I'm never ill. I'm just . . . tired, that's all."

"Perhaps." He inclined his head politely. "How long have you been here?"

"What do you mean?" She was caught off balance by the suddenness of his question. "You brought me here yourself, last night."

His smile broadened. "I thought so. You may be interested to know that you have slept for almost three days."

The door closed behind him. She stared at it, open-mouthed. Three whole days! She felt robbed. That explained the gnawing ache in the pit of her stomach, her feeling of weakness when she woke up, her faintness when she'd first seen him. Not so much love, as hunger! No wonder she'd felt so much at a disadvantage.

But he wouldn't get another chance to outmaneuver her. He didn't know how strong she was. With determination she threw back the covers and swung her feet to the floor. Her legs nearly buckled but she grabbed the headboard just in time. She noticed for the first time that she was wearing a long white flannelette nightgown, ankle-length, with a high neck and long sleeves. Not exactly her taste, but in keeping with her role, she supposed. She smiled to herself. Given a chance, she could enjoy playing the invalid. Holding onto the furniture, rather impressed with the cottonwool feeling in her knees, she propelled herself to the dressing table mirror and peered in. Angelic pallor, hollow cheeks, heavy lids—that was the least she hoped for. But as she saw her reflection she gave a small scream. Confronting her was a ghost, cheeks blotched with chalky white, under great smudged shadows of eyes. She'd forgotten her stage makeup. That, and the spiky mess of her partly unraveled plaits, made her look more like a Raggedy Ann doll than a romantic heroine.

Her ears burned with embarrassment as she scrubbed her face with lavender scented soap and unplaited her braids. No wonder he'd given her that patronizing look. She showered in brutally cold water till her skin glowed, washed her hair till it squeaked clean, then looked for her clothes. She was weak and dizzy, but she forced herself to go on. In the old-fashioned walnut armoire she found a pile of white woolly blankets, a spare bolster and a pair of blue-and-white striped pajamas, obviously the husband of the nightdress she'd just discarded. The dress she'd been wearing when she arrived was nowhere to be seen. All that was left was her black slippers, neatly ranged on the closet floor, and the red boa, hanging rather forlornly over a hanger. As raw material, hardly promising.

But by the time she'd toweled her hair dry she had the germ of an idea. She tried on the pajamas. They were overlarge but nevertheless well-tailored, and the size was easily adjusted by rolling up the sleeves and hitching up the trousers. Only one more detail was needed . . . She took the red boa and twisted it around her waist, draping the excess elegantly down one side. Her reflection in the mirror pleased her. The blue stripe on the fabric exactly matched her eyes, and her still damp hair rioted in tendrils around her head. She looked dashing, eccentric, a diminutive buccaneer. She left the room with more enthusiasm than she'd felt for months.

The narrow stone stairway led down to a dim alcove of a hall. From a door on the right came the clatter of cutlery and a murmur of voices. She waited one moment for her head to stop swimming and her legs to steady, then pushed it boldly open. Guy was sitting at a long white-covered table reading a newspaper. Behind him a maid was busy clearing dishes from a sideboard. Corrie waited impatiently in the doorway for him to notice her. He didn't stir.

"Good morning."

At last he looked up, and she was gratified to see a flicker of surprise cross his face.

"Well, what do you think?" She turned sideways in the doorway to give him the full benefit of her ensemble.

There was a long pause as he eyed her up and down.

"I think that if I had realized your pallor was artificial I would have decided against rescuing you. You look, if I may say so, grotesquely healthy."

"Thank you." She didn't know whether to be pleased or offended. He was smiling at her in a way she recognized of old. A sudden suspicion crossed her mind. Why wasn't he ordering her back to bed immediately?

"You meant me to come downstairs, didn't you?"

His smile broadened. "Of course. I knew that if I ordered you back to bed you would, er . . . rise to the challenge." He laid aside his newspaper. "But I didn't realize you would do it in such style."

"I surprised you then, a little bit?"

"My dear Corrie, you are a constant source of surprises. I think you may consider honor well and truly satisfied."

Ignoring the irony in his tone she leaned against the doorway, with what she hoped was convincing casualness. In reality she was trying very hard to disguise the shakiness of her knees.

"Are you all right?" He frowned at her as he rose to his feet.

"Perfectly." She felt a little breathless as she made her way carefully to the table and sat down rather more suddenly than she'd intended. She concentrated hard until the pounding in her ears subsided, then looked up.

What she saw drove every other thought from her head. She could hardly believe her eyes. Around her, on three sides, like medieval stained glass set deep in the gray stone walls, was the shimmering blue panorama of the sea. They were high above it, but surrounded, almost in it, like sailors perched in the rigging of a tall ship. Sunlight glinted off the hammered pewter waves, dazzling. She looked around in perplexity. She'd stepped from a gray room straight into summer.

"What have you done with it?"

"Your dress? I gave it to Sylvie to have it cleaned. She must have forgotten to replace it."

She shook her head impatiently. "I didn't mean that." Suddenly nothing could have been less important.

"What then?"

She gestured at the windows, the whole glowing sunlit mass of the sea.

"Winter. Where is it?"

"Oh, that." He smiled disarmingly, rose to his feet. "Come, I will show you."

She was glad of the light support of his arm as he escorted her out of the dining room and on to a narrow stone terrace. Below, the drop plunged dizzyingly to the sparkling water, white-crested where it drove against the rocks. They were halfway up a stone tower. Above rose miniature battlements, a fairy palace crowned with a slender pointed slate roof, flanked with smaller towers and little terraces—all rising improbably, impossibly, out of a rocky stone outcrop, projecting so far into the sea that it was almost an island. Below, in the crevices of the rocks, even more improbably, was a garden, studded with small palms, dwarf tamarinds and tiny eucalyptus trees.

As if that wasn't miracle enough, the sky that stretched away into infinity was tender blue, the air that touched her bare throat and neck had a playful, springlike freshness.

It was almost too much to bear. In that moment she would have believed anything—that she'd slept for a hundred years, that she'd sold her soul to the devil, that she was asleep and dreaming still. It was so sudden, so magical, the transition from gray city streets to Paradise.

"Well?"

She shook her head. Words couldn't express what

she was feeling, but she must say something. She leaned back, half closed her eyes.

"It's like . . . it's like being an angel!"

He laughed. "An unfamiliar feeling, I take it. But not inappropriate in the circumstances." He pointed to a rocky promontory in the distance, where a tall blue-cloaked figure stood outlined against the pearly horizon. "That's the Rocher de la Vierge, where Mary guards the passage of sailors into safe harbor."

"I don't understand." She was suddenly disoriented. Whether it was the height or her own weakness she didn't know, but her head was spinning. "You mean we're still in France? How can that be? How can it be November in Paris and spring here?" She swayed, leaning in to him for support. "What are you, a specialist in time travel?"

For a long, suffocating moment he looked straight into her eyes. His face was so close against the dazzling blue of the sky that she felt mesmerized. But when he spoke his voice was harsh.

"Didn't they tell you, time and money are interchangeable?" His tone was icy, sending a shiver down her spine. "Everything out here, from the sunshine to the westerly wind, has been hired expressly for your benefit."

It was as if he'd turned and cut her. It hurt, more than she could possibly have imagined, because her defenses were down. And after the hurt came anger, at herself for being hurt, at him, for making the air grow cold and the sky grow dark.

"If that's so, then I don't want any part of it!" She would never understand him, no matter how hard she tried. To her distress and astonishment she felt two huge hot tears well up and course down her cheeks before she could stop them. His arm tightened around her almost roughly.

"I'm sorry. That was a foolish thing to say."

"I'm sorry too." She couldn't look at him. "I don't know what's wrong with me. I'm not usually like this."

She brushed her cheek surreptitiously. "I'm afraid you're right. I'm not quite better yet."

"You're crying."

She shook her head valiantly, smiled a watery smile. "I never cry."

"And you're never ill?"

She laughed, an unsteady laugh that threatened to dislodge more tears.

"Touché. All right, I'm an invalid. That means you'll have to humor me. Just till I get my strength back."

He looked at her consideringly.

"Truce?"

She took a deep breath. Yes, she was tired—of fighting and struggling and defending beliefs she'd never known she'd had till she met Guy de Chardonnet.

"Please. Just till I'm better."

He smiled at her, that disturbing smile that threatened and promised at the same time.

"You will be better soon. Biarritz will cure you."

"Biarritz? You mean . . ."

"I'm afraid so." Now his eyes danced with suppressed amusement. "*Côte Atlantique.*" He paused, averted his eyes, mock-serious. "Of course, it's not a patch on the Mediterranean . . . but all the same, it has its merits, don't you think?"

She shook her head, speechless. She'd been trapped, again. Biarritz of all places—snobbish, fashionable, a playground for the rich and well-connected. If she'd known, she'd never have allowed herself to like it.

She shrugged, belatedly offhand. "I . . . reserve judgment."

"As you wish." That irritating sparkle of amusement was still in his eyes. "I will not try to persuade you. Biarritz will do that for me. They say it is something in the air. No one knows why, but in Biarritz everything—judgment, winter, even death itself—can be postponed almost indefinitely. The scientists have a word for it, they call it a "micro-climate," a geographical accident caused by the configuration of the bay, the tide of the

Gulf Stream and the mountains behind. You will be able to see its effects for yourself. A week, two weeks, and you will forget winter ever existed."

In the days that followed she began to understand what he meant. None of the usual rules seemed to apply in Biarritz. She tried very hard to dislike it, but she couldn't. As he'd predicted, Biarritz forced her to suspend judgment. Sunshine was trapped in the narrow winding streets, with their glimpses of the sea set like lapis lazuli among the gold and cream and pink of the little houses. There was always the smell of bread baking, of fresh ground coffee and newly printed papers. It seemed to be always breakfast time, the day only just beginning. It was timeless, with the shuttered calm of a resort out of season, and something else—the charm of a society beauty on a Sunday morning, relaxed and off her guard. Under its influence she couldn't help relaxing too.

Corrie had to admit it, Guy took very good care of her. It took her longer than she'd expected to regain her strength, she was filled with a sort of dreamy lassitude she'd never felt before, but he never lost his patience. As she'd asked, he humored her, smiling indulgently when she hurtled downstairs one day full of excitement because she'd found a fly, a sure proof of perpetual summer, buzzing in her tower room. He even allowed himself to be dragged away to witness the miracle at first hand.

Later, he insisted on a régime of sea air and gentle exercise. He took her first to the Port Vieux, a tiny sheltered cove where every grain of sand was a different color. It was like walking on jewels. One, pure white quartz, was the exact shape of a tiny heart. She gave it to him. It seemed the natural thing to do. As she grew stronger he introduced her to the perfect crescent bay of the Chambre d'Amour, pointing out on the way the gold-encrusted Hôtel du Palais, where Empress Eugénie once entertained half the crowned heads of Europe. A dog racing along the beach adopted them, tearing through the shallow crystalline waves with delirious delight. Each afternoon, as she returned for the nap he insisted on, she was weighed down with shells and stones and sunshine and a relief she felt right down to the marrow of her bones. She could feel her vitality returning like a green tide.

And for the first time in her life, she was content with just that. Eating and sleeping and wandering aimlessly in the miraculous silver light. Her new wardrobe, striped shirts and loose-fitting trousers tucked down into soft leather ankle boots, matched how she felt. It was comfortable and ordinary and didn't merit a second glance.

Of course, she knew, deep in her heart, that it couldn't go on forever. Her real self, with its prickly hungers and ambitions, was only on holiday, not gone for good. And she doubted very much if Guy de Chardonnet's solicitude would last forever. He was one of those cold, impatient men who were capable of unexpected short-term tenderness, provided it could be lavished on someone inferior to themselves. But somehow, that knowledge didn't trouble her. For once, she was willing to accept things as they came. She'd been so sure about everything all her life, so quick to jump to conclusions, so impatient for summer . . . In the endless Biarritz autumn, a long period of grace deepening infinitesimally into winter, she began to see that half-measures, even a certain degree of compromise, could have a charm of their own. Her prejudices were drawn from her little by little, like the bitter sap from the pines, leaving nothing but the pastel light, the soft cool air, the silver sea.

As she grew stronger he began to take her farther afield, tempting her with delights just around the corner. They went to the Landes, the strange severe forest, all gray sand and thorn bushes and tall black pines, which stretched for hundreds of miles along the Atlantic coast above Biarritz. At first, in the perpetual twilight under the trees, where each footfall was muffled in the matt brown carpet of dead needles, she felt it was a sinister, colorless landscape. But Guy transformed it for her, pointing out the mauve and gold and lemon yellow fungi, velvety as sea fruit against the dry bark, the luminous green and ghostly gray of lichen, the silhouette of a raven, watching them with shining coal black eyes. They lunched in a small seaside township, silent and deserted behind its salt-bleached pastel shutters. He plied her with tiny oysters, which slipped down her throat as soft and salty as tears. At sunset they went back to the forest, to see hunters in their sage green waders stalking duck through the pink mist underneath the trees.

The next day, for contrast, he took her to Bayonne, up the sunburst cobbles of the Rue de la Monnaie to the twin spires of the cathedral. It seemed as if every other shop were a *chocolatier*, the air was thick with the dark sweet scent of it.

"Bayonne is the chocolate capital of the world," he informed her, dragging her away from yet another window packed with truffles and liqueurs. His words reminded her of something, but she was too relaxed and happy, too dazed with sun and sea air, to identify it.

It was only later, after they'd lunched on *pipérade*, eggs scrambled with Bayonne ham and pimento, *tioro*, the local fish soup, spiced sausage and almond cake laced with hazelnut paste and candied fruits, that the memory crystalized.

"This," he said, pointing to a dish on the menu, "this should appeal to you especially."

"What is it?" The name meant nothing to her.

"It's a Basque dish, of isard, Pyrenean antelope, in a rich bitter chocolate sauce."

She pushed away her last slice of almond cake, her appetite forgotten. The coincidence was too remarkable to ignore. Chocolate stew, just as it was served in Harlequin's imaginary Uscady.

"Basque, you say?" Her heart began to beat faster, with an irregular rhythm that was almost painful. She felt as if she were on the brink of a tremendous revelation, something that might change her life entirely.

"So this is the Basque region." She tried to keep her voice calm. If he knew what she was thinking, he'd never tell her what she wanted to know, had to know. "I didn't realize. You should have told me."

He looked at her curiously. "I had no idea you would be interested. Biarritz and Bayonne are hardly Basque, they are more French in atmosphere. To find the real Basques you have to go much farther afield." He studied her for a long moment.

"Why this sudden interest?"

She smiled, shrugged.

"Balenciaga was a Basque. You told me that yourself. Isn't that enough of a recommendation? I'd like to know more, will you tell me?"

"I'll do better than that. Come." He rose abruptly to his feet. "I'll show you."

They drove inland, along narrow twisting roads, through steeply sloping green valleys covered with gorse and oak trees. She could hardly believe her eyes. It was as if she'd opened a book of fairy tales and the pictures had come to life under her hands. So many times, on chilly winter nights, she'd warmed herself in Uscady's imaginary world. It had seemed real to her then, but she'd never dreamed it might actually exist. Yet here it was, unfurling before her eyes on either side, every perfect detail just as it had been described to her all those years ago. Here were the whitewashed houses with their steep-pitched roofs, decorated with birds and flowers and mermaids, their chocolate colored beams hung with sweet red peppers and garlands of onions drying in the sun. Here were the shining streams and patchwork fields, the vineyards and apple orchards. The roadsides, every patch of available land, every square inch was a garden, lovingly planted with corn, potatoes, turnips, hayfields the size of handkerchiefs.

For some reason the sight of those brave green plots, coated with dust and roadside grime but neatly weeded, bursting with peasant pride, made her want to cry. There was something so human, so determined, so crazily optimistic about all that effort, as doomed and hopeful as any message in a bottle.

She leaned out of the window, searching each face they passed, convinced that she might see Harlequin. They passed a man walking slowly, with an insolent, easy grace, behind his small solid-wheeled cart drawn by a fawn colored ox. The road was narrow and precipitous, trucks roared and thundered past, but he didn't glance to left or right. It was as if, for him, they didn't exist. He was timeless, they were mere interlopers.

As they passed him she wanted to call out to him. His eyes, under the black beret pulled low, were hidden, but she caught a glimpse of his face. Now at last she had an image of Harlequin. He would have that upright, easy carriage, that stern long face, those strong square shoulders, like an Egyptian hieroglyph, that air of belonging solidly and entirely to himself. He would be tanned and coatless, a stick swinging in his hand, a scarlet handkerchief tucked into his wide leather belt.

It was like waking up out of a dream. Mile by mile, as village succeeded village, each place-name canceled out with typical Gallic neatness by a diagonal red stripe, her certainty grew. Uscady wasn't a story made up to entertain a lonely child, it was a real place, in the real world.

"Well, what do you think?" Guy glanced at her curiously. She shook her head. She couldn't have explained how she felt even if she'd wanted to. It was like seeing a long-lost friend, or opening a Christmas present and finding for once that it was what you'd always wanted.

"It's . . . different. Different from anywhere else."

"Yes, the Basques are a remarkable people. No one knows who they really are or where they came from. One thing's for certain, they were here first. In medieval times they used to hunt whales in the Bay of Biscay. Even today all their houses, like the Château des Basques, are built like watchtowers facing out to sea. It's a leftover from the glorious past, when they used to sail as far as Newfoundland. Some say they discovered America before Columbus."

"But they always came back?"

"Yes, until now." His smile faded. "But I doubt if they can survive much longer."

She felt a chill come over her. There was such certainty, such finality in his tone.

"Why is that?"

He shrugged.

"It's a question of character. They are proud, insular, intransigent people. Fiercely, foolishly independent."

"Why foolishly?"

He shrugged again.

"That kind of complete independence is an anachronism in the modern world. It's as rare as the Great White Whale, and it comes as expensive. It's cost the Basques their lives, their liberty and, in the end, their land."

"I don't understand."

"It's simple. Modern governments, or governments that would like to be modern, find a desire for independence very inconvenient, especially when it crosses borders, like the Basques'. There are various ways of dealing with it. You can either, like Spain, choose outright oppression, or like France, more subtle means. Here the government has simply abandoned the area, encouraged tourism on the coast but made no economic investment elsewhere. The region's lifeblood has quietly drained away. A less dramatic but I think more effective method. One by one, the Basques have been driven away—the Spanish Basques to South America, the French Basques to the industrial towns. Of course they have to sacrifice their language and culture, but at least they live. And they are often very successful." He gestured at the laboriously cultivated verges. "As you can see, they are a determined and industrious people."

"But it's so beautiful here . . . how could they bear to leave?" She was thinking of Harlequin. She knew, from the way he'd described Uscady to her, that he must have loved it here. But Harlequin too had been driven out, sucked into the impersonal life of the great city.

What that had meant to him she could only guess. He must have felt as if he'd been driven out of Paradise.

"Even a Basque has to eat." His voice was suddenly harsh. "In Spain, it's a little different, but no better. I won't take you there, you wouldn't like it. Industry thrives, but that's about all. You should see Bilbao, it's an eyesore. The estuary is polluted, the sky is black with factory chimneys, the air hardly fit to breathe. The streets are patrolled by the Guardia Civil, the military police, the Basques themselves are packed into filthy, decaying tenements." He shook his head. "But even then, they don't give up. Even among all that grime and dirt, on each tenement balcony there's a line of snow-white washing . . . No one is prouder than a Basque." He turned to her, his expression grim. "But I think they know the end is coming. There's a poster you see everywhere across the border, in Basque and Spanish. '*Nuestra gente, nuestra ilusion*.' 'Our nation, our illusion.' "

She sat in silence. It wasn't right, it couldn't be. She stared out at the patchwork fields. A man was scything hay on a forty-five degree slope, where even the most sophisticated tractor couldn't have operated. So much effort, so much love, had been ploughed into this landscape, she could feel it. She couldn't believe all that effort could be wasted. She might be a cock-eyed optimist, but she wouldn't believe this people, who could feed their families off roadside verges and wear white in a slum, could be defeated.

"Couldn't it mean, 'Our people, our dream'?"

He frowned. "I suppose so, but what difference would that make?"

"All the difference in the world." She spoke with total certainty. "Dreams can come true."

He smiled reluctantly.

"Always this touching faith in miracles . . ."

"Not miracles. People." She paused, thinking hard. "Couldn't you do something?"

He raised his eyebrows.

"What had you in mind? One man can't reverse history."

"Maybe not, but you could try. You know lots of people, important people. They'd listen to you. You could campaign, arouse sympathy for the Basque cause . . ."

"It's work they need, not sympathy."

"Get them work, then. Persuade people to invest money here, bring the place back to life."

"It's not quite as easy as that."

Something in his calm superior tone angered her.

"You haven't tried. It's all very well to come here and enjoy everything the region has to offer when it suits you, but how about giving something back?" She warmed to her task. "You're rich, you can afford a gamble for once. Someone in your position could do a great deal, and you know it."

There was a long pause. He looked at her flushed face and combative expression, then nodded. "Yes, I think you're almost better."

"Don't change the subject." She wouldn't let him escape so easily. He frowned.

"Let me give you a little advice. I don't think you should get involved, there's nothing you can do. It would be better if you forgot everything I've just told you and stayed a simple tourist."

"It's too late, I am involved!" she retorted hotly. "You can't be a tourist all your life!" She made no attempt to hide the accusation in her tone.

"Very well." His lips tightened as he reached forward to restart the engine.

"What are you doing?"

He shot her a wry look as he maneuvered the car back in the direction they'd come. "Something I shall very probably live to regret."

He drove, fast and in silence, for what seemed miles, then turned down a newly built road. After a couple of hundred yards it petered out into a rocky, bumpy track. Stones flew up around them, hitting the windshield and rattling against the bodywork, but he ignored them. The track plunged deep into pine forest, then finally emerged into a broad clearing.

The scene that met her eyes was one of total chaos. Great craters yawned in the raw earth, huge excavators and bulldozers were tearing at the edges of the clearing. The air was full of sand and the noise was ear-splitting. Through the dust she could see a construction gang hard at work, vast stacks of concrete blocks, iron girders, scaffolding . . .

"Wait here." He left her, stunned and deafened, then returned with two bright yellow helmets. "Put this on."

Numbly she followed him into the heart of the chaos. He showed her around, pointing out the facilities for the workmen, the gaping crevasses where the foundations would be laid, the seemingly random movements of the great machines. Obviously there was some logic behind all the activity, but it escaped her. Men were hard at work everywhere, determined, dark men with the same long stern faces and upright carriage she'd seen in her ox-driver, only here they were dressed in neat dark blue overalls. They tipped their hard hats to Guy as he approached, but didn't let up for an instant.

She took advantage of a momentary lull in the din to ask the question uppermost in her mind.

"What on earth is going on?"

"That depends on your point of view." Guy hesitated. "To you, probably a piece of ruthless commercial exploitation. To them,"—he gestured at the workmen, "to them and their families it's a miracle."

"And to you?"

He smiled, a small, wintry smile.

"To me . . . let's call it an investment."

"Profitable, I expect." He ignored her sarcasm.

"It will be. When it's completed it will be one of the most modern factory installations in the country, employing over two hundred people."

"A factory?" She couldn't hide her shock and distaste. He gave a grim smile.

"Not quite the miracle you had in mind, I take it?"

She shook her head.

"I thought as much. But don't be too quick to judge. Perhaps you might like to know what it is we'll be manufacturing here."

She suppressed a shudder.

"Concrete? Iron bolts?"

He shook his head.

"It's something you're very fond of."

"Chocolate?"

"No . . . though that's a good idea for the future."

"What then?"

He paused, maddeningly. "You should be able to guess. It's a luxury, like beauty and freedom. Something people, especially women, are willing to pay a great deal of money for."

She racked her brains.

"You can't eat it or wear it?"

"No. Like beauty and freedom it's . . . intangible."

"I give up. You'll have to tell me."

He smiled.

"Perfume."

"Perfume?" She couldn't hide her surprise. "Here? In a factory?"

He nodded. "Where did you think it came from, bees?"

"I hadn't thought . . ." She began to look around her with new eyes. Suddenly the great gaping holes didn't look so sinister after all. "But are you sure you've got the right climate here? Wouldn't the Mediterranean be better?" She was thinking of the great perfume centers of Nice and Grasse, the fields of lavender she remembered from her childhood.

He smiled at her naïveté.

"Times have changed. Most essences—bergamot, musk, benjoin—are imported nowadays, and the rest are available in distillation. The synthetics, of course, can be produced anywhere. All you need is a pure rainwater supply and a willing workforce. Curiously enough the most important ingredient of a perfume is not its essential oils but the fixative, ambergris, a strange waxy substance, very rare, secreted by dying whales. Since this was once a great whaling area, in a way it's apt that perfume should be made here."

"Oh." Against her will she was impressed by his evident expertise. Perhaps he wasn't quite the dilettante she'd thought him.

"Will you produce your own brands?"

"Certainly. We already have one in production at another factory in the Auvergne."

"What's it called? Would I have heard of it?"

He hesitated, his expression suddenly hard to read.

"Probably not." His tone was suspiciously dismissive. "It's a sophisticated scent, lily-based, with a touch of jasmine. I doubt if it would suit you."

Her curiosity was aroused.

"But what's it called?"

He shrugged.

"Well, if you must know . . . *Nuit Blanche*."

"Oh."

She felt oddly defeated. It was only the name of a perfume, but no one had ever named one after her. There was a short, uncomfortable silence.

"I have plans for others, of course." He paused. When he spoke again it seemed to be at a tangent. "Do you know, the perfume of violets is so elusive that it has never been distilled in its natural form? Not yet, that is, but our research workers have come up with a process that may be successful."

"How interesting." She tried to summon up polite enthusiasm but all her interest in the discussion had evaporated. Suddenly she felt tired and bad-tempered and childishly disappointed. "Will you be making that here?"

"Yes, I think so. Not in its pure form, but as a blend. I had in mind a light, elusive fragrance, one that seduces when it is least expected. Fresh, springlike, yet hauntingly sweet. You know that irresistible smell of a wild wood after rain? That's what I'm aiming for, something reminiscent of dew and twilight and country nights."

She sniffed. How like him to wax romantic over a perfume, something that could make him money.

"What are you going to call this concoction, Leaf Mold?"

He seemed unruffled by her disagreeable tone.

"I'm not sure . . . something charming, romantic, even a little old-fashioned. Names are very important. There's a flower you used to see in cottage gardens everywhere, a graceful thing, lilac and cream and silver, with long white spurs, like a little ballerina. It's called columbine. The bottle, I thought, could have the shape of one windblown blossom, with a violet tinge to the glass."

She stared at him, suddenly breathless. But his expression was matter-of-fact, his eyes unreadable.

"It's a lovely name. When did you . . . er . . . think of it?" She had difficulty getting the words out. Suddenly it was very important to know. "Was it before you came to the Chat d'Or or after?"

"Oh, long before." He made a dismissive gesture. "That's one of the reasons I came to the club in the first place, I was intrigued by the coincidence. A lucky chance, *n'est-ce pas*?"

"Oh yes." But at that moment she didn't feel at all lucky. Her heart, so suddenly buoyed up, was now leaden. She hadn't realized how much she'd been hoping against hope that he had in fact been looking for her. As for his choice of perfume being inspired by her stage name, nothing could be further from the truth.

She looked around the site with a jaundiced eye.

"Have you seen enough?"

"More than enough." She was overtaken by a sudden upsurge of bitterness. "I realize now why you took so much trouble to find out about the Basques. It's important to understand your workforce."

His face went white.

"You mean, if I am to screw the last ounce of work out of them, no?" As always his French accent was more marked when she'd angered him.

They stared at each other for a long, speechless moment.

"Why did you bring me here, anyway?"

"I can't imagine." His voice cut like ice. "I should have known better. I should have left you lying on the stage at the Chat d'Or. That's where you belong."

Seeing the expression on his face she felt sourly, obscurely satisfied. She'd been living in a dream, a fool's paradise. Now at least she knew where she stood.

"I'll go back to Paris tomorrow." She'd rather resign than be dismissed, any day.

"Very well."

He drove her back in silence, very fast, the highly tuned engine noiseless but the wind rushing past the windows indicating the speed of their progress down the violet-stained middle of the road.

CHAPTER THIRTEEN

It was dark by the time they reached Biarritz. In stony silence Guy parked the car on the Promenade des Anglais, helped her politely out and escorted her to the flight of stone steps leading down to the Château des Basques. This is the end, she thought numbly. It's over, and I've destroyed it. It hadn't taken much. Their fragile truce, unlike the Basque watchtowers, had hardly been built on stone. A few words, one breath of reality, and it had simply crumbled away . . .

And for her, the end couldn't come soon enough. If this was love, this explosive mixture of hatred and jealousy and pure terror, she didn't want any part of it. She wanted to be herself again, not this violent, unpredictable stranger, who swung from ecstasy to despair in the same tick of the clock, who said terrible things she'd never meant to say . . . Oh, how she wished he'd never taken her to see that factory. Why was he always turning her ideas upside down, why couldn't he leave her alone? A few hours ago she'd have been quite happy to dismiss him as a profiteer, but now, knowing that he was helping Harlequin's people, whatever his motives might be, she didn't know what to think. She wasn't used to shades of gray. One thing she was sure of—he was easier to resist as a villain.

She steeled herself not to look at him. She was herself again now, a free agent, he couldn't touch her anymore. She gazed out over the glittering sea that stretched beneath the Promenade des Anglais and told herself that it was a pretty view, no more, no less, one that she might remember with affection in years to come, but without the slightest increase in the beating of her heart.

And then, down on the shoreline, where the perfect crescent of the Chambre d'Amour curved beneath the Promenade, she saw something so beautiful that it took her breath away. The beach was covered with a multitude of lights, revolving, flashing, coruscating as if with some ocean phosphorescence.

She tugged at Guy's sleeve. "What's that, down there?"

"The November fair." His face was cold, his voice hard. "I had forgotten. It comes every year."

Corrie gazed longingly down at the beach. Fragile temporary light, with no lasting warmth to it, no sure defense against the darkness, but it drew her like a magnet. Without a backward glance she began to run down the rocky steps, her hair flying behind her. Her feet slipped on the wet stone, but she didn't care. It was as if the devil himself were after her. She plunged into the noise and light and color like a fish into water. The music eddied and whirled, behind it, luscious as a full orchestra, the soft inward sigh of the waves. She closed her eyes. She wanted to forget, just for a moment, who she was, where she was, remember long ago carefree days . . .

"Corrie!" She heard him calling, opened her eyes to see his tall figure as if from a lifetime away. The colored lights from the brightly painted merry-go-round played over his pale suit, transforming him into a traveling player, a Harlequin. She heard, with the plaintiveness of a music played near water, the beginning of an old song, so old she couldn't remember its name. Once, centuries ago, she would have kicked off her shoes and danced in the sand, but she was older and wiser now, those days were gone forever . . .

Suddenly, as if a giant gloved hand had descended, the lights were extinguished, the music ceased to play.

"It's over." He was beside her now, so near she could have reached out a hand and touched him, so near she might have seen herself reflected in his eyes. In the darkness and silence his words seemed to echo her own sadness.

"I know. We were too late."

Behind them in the shadows the attendants were beginning to pack their equipment away. With one accord, like mourners at a funeral, they turned away.

Too late . . . For the first time, walking across the sand with his silent presence beside her, she realized what it meant. It hardly seemed possible, but after tonight she would never see him again. No more arguments, no more kisses, no more surprises. No more anything. Slowly, as she paced the wet sand, her footprints filling with water that seeped away almost invisibly, she felt the bitterness drain away. Behind them were the distant lights of the township, ahead the limitless whispering expanse of the sea.

"Corrie . . ." His voice was low. There was no need to speak any louder, they were the only two people alive in the whole world. "There's one thing I must know before you go."

"Ask away." What did it matter now, after all?

He hesitated, but when he spoke his voice was calm, almost matter-of-fact. "Why do you find it so difficult to commit yourself to one man?"

"I . . . I . . ." To her dismay she found herself stammering like a schoolgirl. Once, she would have handed him a glib rejoinder, but something, the tender warmth of the night, the clarity of the light on the waves, made all her charades and disguises and masquerades seem trivial and out of place. There was a grain of truth in what he said, she knew it. Deep down, she was terrified of committing herself, losing her independence. She wanted to be mistress of her own fate. And maybe that, in its way, was the worst sort of cowardice.

"I don't know . . . There are things I want to do, have to do, ambitions I can only achieve if I'm by myself. I need time, and that's what you lose if you get deeply involved with someone else's life."

"And you're willing to give up everything else—love,

marriage, children—for these ambitions of yours? Are you sure that's what you want?"

She hesitated. "I know. It's difficult. But why can't I have both? Not all at once, but one after the other. Fame followed by family. Why not?"

"But fame first?"

She nodded. "It has to be." She paused, thinking hard. How could she explain? He'd probably think it vanity, foolishness, but she had to try.

"It's like this. I . . . I have something to offer. I know that about myself, I've always known it. It's like—like lying on a hillside at night looking up at the stars. There's so much darkness, so little light. But what there is is very, very bright." She drew a deep breath. "I can go a long way, maybe right to the top. I was given something, and I've got to give it back. It's . . . a debt of honor. I owe it to the world to shine before I die."

There, she'd said it. She'd told him as much as she could, more than she'd ever told anyone, apart from Harlequin. Let him laugh, let him dismiss it as childish vanity—it was as much a part of her as the air she breathed.

But he didn't laugh. For once, as he turned to her, his expression was purely serious.

"The right kind of man would help you to do that. If you would let him."

"Maybe." She looked at him. "But I can't afford to make mistakes."

"No one can." His voice was grave. "But that explains a great deal."

"Really?" She was oddly flattered by his interest.

"Of course." He paused didactically. "Your need for a patron, for instance. Given your particular requirements, it's the only possible arrangement. You couldn't afford anything more . . . engrossing, you have to keep the upper hand. As it stands, you have the perfect solution. Safe, limited, the ultimate in convenience. With an added plus—built-in disposability."

She was stung by the sudden touch of scorn in his voice.

"No more 'convenient' or 'disposable' than your relationships with safely married women! Don't think I hadn't noticed!"

"Touché." He smiled his lazy, familiar smile. "But then, I never claimed to love them."

"That word again." She shook her head in mock reproach. "We seem to have done a lot of talking about love, for people who don't even like each other."

"Maybe that's why." His voice was unexpectedly serious. "The Eskimos have seventeen different words for snow—it's what they fear most, so they talk about it all the time, study it as patiently as any lover. Perhaps that's why the French have so many words for love. It goes against all they hold dear—logic, efficiency, style . . ."

She felt a strange, bittersweet warmth. She couldn't let him know she loved him, but talking about love was the next best thing. "Do you think it exists at all, in real life?"

He looked away. "Yes, I think so. But it's rare, and you never know when you'll find it. It's like the ambergris I told you about. You can't go and hunt it down on the high seas, you can only wait. One day, when you're least expecting it, the sea may wash it up at your feet."

"So there's hope for us all."

"I'd like to think so." He halted in his tracks, turned to face her. They stared at each other for a long, aching moment. Around them everything seemed to be moving, the tide drawing in, the stars wheeling in their courses. They were the only still and separate things in the world.

"I wonder . . ." His voice was very low. He was frowning, as if he were trying to work out some theorem. "Perhaps it's possible after all . . ."

"What is?" For some reason she could hardly breathe.

"To start again. Re-read the book and write our own ending."

"It wouldn't work." She kept her tone light with an

effort. "We'd still be totally unsuited. I could never trust a man who's never known what it's like to be poor."

"Of course." His voice was mildly regretful. "And I could never trust a girl who doesn't know how it feels to be rich." He paused, eyed her interrogatively. "I don't suppose you're secretly rich?"

She shook her head. "I'm afraid not. I will be rich one day, of course. When I'm famous."

"One day . . ." Again that faint note of regret. "But then it'll be too late."

Another long, echoing pause. The incoming sea fawned and sighed at their feet like a huge gentle animal.

He took her hand, raised it almost absentmindedly to his lips, blew gently on her fingers. Against her will she remembered that night in the Avenue Pierre I de Serbie and her whole body stirred and melted at his touch.

"Don't." Her head was swimming, reality slipping further and further away. "It won't work. Not for us, not now."

"Why not?" His voice was calm, eminently reasonable. So why did she feel this tremor running through her, as if the earth were going to part under her feet? "It's like that riddle someone once asked me, 'How do you spell eternity?' There's no answer, you have to make up your own. We could do that. We could forget about everything, the past, the future—just be ourselves. You and me."

"It's not that easy." Oh, if only it were. "There isn't a 'you and me,' there never has been. Half the time with you I don't know who I am." She fumbled for words, struggling to be honest. "I find myself—playing roles, as if there weren't enough of the real me to go around."

"But not here." He stated his case as clearly and convincingly as if it were a law of nature. "Not in Biarritz."

Their eyes met. "You're right." She laughed, a small, shaky laugh. "But that's no good. I can't stay here forever."

He paused to consider. "Well, if Biarritz begins to bore you, we could move on. There's a food fair next week in Burgundy that might appeal to you. Think of it, you, me and all that pâté de foie gras . . ."

"Pâté de foie?" Suddenly, as unexpected as a winter daffodil, she felt an upsurge of pure, ridiculous joy. A day, a week—one more postponement of winter, what could it matter? "What is this, a proposal or a proposition?"

"Neither." He regarded her gravely, then bowed with a strangely elegant, old-world courtesy. "It's simply . . . an invitation."

Oh, if only it were possible . . .

"What about Blanche?"

His face hardened.

"I can promise nothing. No plans, no contracts, no explanations. You and me. Nothing else."

She stared at him, remembering with sudden pain the love she'd always wanted, all laughter and music and happy endings. What had she got instead? This painful mixture of doubts and contradictions, this dizzying, terrifying, weightless spiral, like falling endlessly through space. No wonder they called it falling in love.

"Well?" His voice was harsh.

She couldn't speak. She felt as if she were suffocating. All those long sleepless nights at the Louisiane she'd dreamed and longed for this moment, but now it was as alarming as if the moon itself had sailed down into her hands. It weighed heavier than she'd thought.

"How do I know I can trust you?" The words spilled out before she could prevent them.

"You don't." His dark face was inscrutable. The expression in his eyes as he looked down at her sent a shiver down her spine. "But what have you got to lose?"

My heart, my soul, my life, that's all.

He must have read how sorely she was tempted from her eyes, for without a word, without even so much as a backward glance, he turned and began to walk back to the car. She stared after him, half furious, half admiring.

Her big moment, and he'd upstaged her! Breathless, she caught up with him twenty yards farther down the beach.

"But I haven't said yes yet!"

He smiled down at her. "You will. And I don't see why I should starve to death while you're trying to decide exactly how to phrase it. You can make up your mind over dinner at the Hôtel du Palais."

"You're trying to bribe me!"

"Of course." His tone was silky. "I have no scruples. You of all people should know that."

The Hôtel du Palais, that wide, white Atlantic smile . . . how could she resist?

"But I can't go like this!"

He studied her fisherman's jersey and sand-stained boots with a straight face.

"Why this sudden concern for the conventions? I seem to remember they never cramped your style before."

"I know." She found herself blushing. "But that was before." Before I fell in love. Now I want to outshine every other woman in the room.

"Very well." He sighed. "Change if you must. You have twenty minutes."

She drew herself up with dignity.

"Kindly remember, M. de Chardonnet, that I am no longer in your employ."

He threw back his head and laughed out loud. "You learn fast, Miss Modena. Half an hour, then, and no more. I'll be waiting, here." His eyes met hers for a brief instant. What she saw in them made her feel cold and warm at once, turned her bones to liquid. "And I'm an impatient man."

She raced up the rocky steps to the château as if her feet had wings. Just outside the door she paused to look back over her shoulder. Guy was standing motionless, his dark head outlined against the silver sea. He looked up, and her heart stirred. It was a strange, terrifying feeling, as if an invisible string tethered her body to his.

She shivered despite herself. Would she be able to bring it off at last, this crazy balancing act called love? It was such a gamble . . . she'd need the agility of an acrobat, the daring of a trapeze artist, the poise of a walker on the high wire. There was still so much she didn't know about him, so much she didn't understand.

But how much could anyone ever really know about anyone else? Maybe this was all there was, the reaching out of two strangers in the dark. And she would learn. She loved him, that much was certain. Surely there had to be a way to make him love her in return? At least, now, there was hope. All she needed was time.

She swung into the hall, slammed the door behind her with an exuberant crash. There would be dinners, and dinners, and adventures, and nights that made her senses sing . . . surely that was enough for anyone, to begin with?

"*C'est toi, Guy?*" A high, clear, autocratic voice floated into the hall. Corrie froze in disbelief. The door to the dining room was ajar. There was the sound of rapid steps on the flagged stones, then the door swung wide. And there, outlined against the light, a superbly simple white alpaca coat slung casually from one shoulder, as commanding and complete as a vision in a dream, was the last person in the world she'd wanted or expected to see. Blanche de Chardonnet.

"Well, well, well . . ." Blanche spoke softly, almost to herself. "*La folle anglaise*." Her pale, heavy-lidded eyes, so unnervingly like Guy's, scanned Corrie from head to toe with appraising thoroughness. Salty, sandy and out of breath, Corrie felt a chill run over her body. Time stopped. It was as if the air were being slowly emptied out of the room, to be replaced by a vapor only Blanche could breathe.

"Guy's not here." Her voice came out cracked and small.

"So I gather." Blanche raised one perfect arched eyebrow in faint surprise. "But I think, just maybe, it was you I came to see."

Corrie stared at her blankly, trying to hide an irrational surge of pure panic. "I'm sorry, I'm in a hurry." It came out rushed and awkward. Blanche regarded her curiously through narrowed eyes.

"You have an appointment? In that case my chauffeur can drive you."

"No, thank you." Corrie felt herself begin to flounder under that expressionless Arctic gaze, then pulled herself together with an effort. "It's all right, I think I can spare a few minutes." With as much dignity as she could muster she allowed herself to be ushered into the dining room.

Achingly conscious of the passing minutes, she was forced to wait as Blanche extracted a long black Turkish cigarette from a platinum case, inserted it in an ivory holder, lit it, inhaled once, then extinguished the rest of the cigarette unsmoked. As an exhibition of self-indulgence mixed with self-control it was enormously convincing.

"I see congratulations are in order." Blanche spoke slowly, almost meditatively, grinding out the last spark from the ash with a delicate movement of her long pearl-tipped fingers. Instinctively Corrie's eyes flew to the windows overlooking the sea-front. How long had Blanche been here, how much had she seen?

"What do you mean?"

Blanche shrugged. "Your recently acquired command of French. Most impressive, for a girl who three months ago spoke not a word . . . I must remember to mention it to Guy."

"Thank you." Corrie felt a blush rise to her cheeks. Without realizing it, in the stress of the moment, she'd given herself away. What mileage Blanche would make out of her discovery she didn't dare contemplate.

"I wondered, you know . . ." Blanche brushed lightly at the fabric of her skirt, where the tiniest flake of ash had lodged in the weave. For a crazy moment Corrie was reminded of a snake's shimmering coils. "I wondered what Guy could be doing closeted away down here, out of reach of the telephone. It's not like him at all." She shook her head reprovingly. "Don't you realize what trouble you've caused? My cousin is a busy man, he's spent far too much time with you already, more than he can afford. I'm afraid it can't go on."

"I don't see why not." Corrie stood her ground, trying not to forget the fact that again Blanche had hit home. Guy's business commitments had been the last thing on her mind. "As long as Guy wants it that way."

"Such idealism . . ." Blanche's voice held a hint of sarcasm. "I suppose you think you're in love with him? Yes, of course you do. The young are so predictable, so totally without imagination. But I'm afraid you've made a mistake this time. Guy will never marry you."

"I don't care." Something—Blanche's insufferable poise, her assumption that she was in complete control of the situation—fired Corrie into anger. "I'm not looking for a husband."

"Really?" For a moment a spark of genuine interest flickered in Blanche's eyes. Then she shrugged. "But that is merely a variation on a familiar theme." She smiled. "Oh, yes, you aren't the first and I doubt if you'll be the last. There have been many women, but Guy always comes back to me."

"What if he's in love this time?"

Blanche's eyes narrowed. "Has he told you so?"

"That's none of your business!"

Blanche's lips curved in a faint, satisfied smile.

"I thought not. He never does. He's not a fool."

She drew one hand through her hair, giving Corrie the benefit of her perfect profile. Corrie noticed with envy how each pale gleaming strand fell obediently back into place. "And even if he loved you, it wouldn't make any difference. There's something that matters more to him than any woman. Ambition." She turned to face Corrie, her eyes glittering. "And for that, he needs me. My friends, my connections—they're indispensable to a man like Guy. I understand that and I accept it. Guy and I, we are alike in so many ways. I too enjoy power. But you . . ." She shook her head disparagingly. "You can be no more than an interlude in his life. Would you be satisfied with that?"

"Yes." Corrie spoke with a confidence she didn't entirely feel. Guy had wakened in her a demanding hunger that might no longer be satisfied with only half a loaf. "If it's what he wants. I think I could make him happy."

"Happy?" Blanche threw back her long white throat and laughed silently. "Such vanity . . . even I wouldn't dare promise him so much." She shook her head, almost pityingly. "But what would you live on, play-acting and dreams? Guy needs challenge, would you confine him to some backwater?"

Corrie stared at her, suddenly doubtful. There was something here she didn't fully understand. Blanche seemed so carelessly confident, so sure of her rights of possession, it hardly seemed natural.

"I would never try to hold him back. I may not approve of everything he does, but I respect his right to do it."

Blanche smiled, her eyes glittering with amusement.

"How modern you are, my dear. And how quaint." She sighed. "But I'm afraid it's time you entered the real world." She shook her head. "It's hardly fair, he should have told you. I can see why he didn't, but even so . . ."

"Told me what?" With an effort Corrie kept her voice level. She felt as if she were struggling in an invisible mist that threatened to choke her. Once she could see her adversary she could defend herself.

Blanche paused, clearly savoring her moment. Corrie bit back her irritation. It didn't matter, nothing Blanche could say would change the way she felt. She loved Guy, and that was all she needed to know.

Blanche leaned back, settled herself more comfortably.

"It's quite simple, really. Under the terms of my father's will, Guy inherits nothing, unless . . ."

"Unless what?"

"Can't you guess? It's obvious, surely . . ." Blanche stretched luxuriously in her chair. "Unless he marries me."

"I don't understand."

"You don't?" Blanche's tone was patient, almost solicitous. She might have been speaking to a particularly backward child. "Let me see, how best can I explain it to you?" Slowly, gracefully, her metallic dress shimmering like delicate chain mail, she rose to her feet, picked up a little Dresden figurine, a plump pink-cheeked milkmaid, from the mantelpiece. She turned the figure lazily in her hand, then, with a carelessness so studied that it was almost brutal, dropped it into the stone hearth.

"How could you?" Corrie's voice, as she stared numbly at the shattered porcelain pieces, was a whisper.

"Very easily." Blanche smiled. "You see, everything—this house and all it contains—belongs to me."

Corrie stared at her. Slowly, surely, like ice closing over a pool, the pieces of the picture began to resolve themselves into place. How had she never guessed? Now she knew, it seemed so simple, so obvious. It was just as Blanche had said before. Guy could play any game he wanted—just so long as he remembered who made the rules. What it could have meant to him, to live his life on those terms, perpetually on approval, she couldn't bear to imagine.

"And you'd marry him on that basis, whether he loved you or not?" Her own voice sounded strange, hardly recognizable.

Blanche shrugged. "What does it matter how you get something you want, as long as it's yours to keep? Possession is nine tenths of the law. I want Guy, and I shall have him. He will love me, in the end. I am . . . necessary to his survival."

"But that's corrupt!"

Blanche laughed, a light, humorless sound.

"No. Merely—practical. But I can understand your sense of grievance. To be the mistress of a man with no prospects is hardly so romantic, *n'est-ce pas*?"

"I don't care. I'm happy with him as he is. I love him."

Blanche's lips tightened into a thin line.

"You call that love? Is it love to want to deprive him

of everything he's worked for, everything that matters to him? If you know him at all, you must realize how much this house alone means to him. Why do you think he didn't tell you about the terms of the will? Because he knew, deep down, that nothing is going to change his mind. Ask him yourself if you don't believe me."

Corrie looked away. Even as denials rose to her lips realization washed over her in a cold gray wave. Blanche was right. Only a few moments ago Guy himself had said to her, lightly but with an undercurrent of sadness she only now understood, "You're not secretly rich, I suppose?" If only, if only . . . If only her rival had been merely another woman, even one so lovely as Blanche, she would have fought for him tooth and nail. But not now. Because she loved him, she was helpless. She couldn't take away from him all the things he cared about. He needed money, power—they were his tools. To part him from Blanche and her inheritance would be to sentence him to prison. That was his bargain with fate, his contract with circumstances, made so long ago she was powerless to break it. She, of all people, knew how much ambition mattered. She couldn't destroy him and everything he'd worked for. She couldn't bear to be a mourner at her own funeral, a helpless witness at the slow, interminable death of love.

"No, I believe you." The room seemed suddenly very dark, very cold.

"Perhaps now you'll be so kind as to tell me where I can find my cousin?"

"Of course." Slowly, each movement dragging as if she were walking through water, Corrie crossed to the window. She felt curiously calm, almost numb. "He's down there, on the beach." So near, yet so far away . . . already, as she looked, he seemed like a stranger. She knew, without needing to be told, as if she were acting out a scene in a play, that it would be Blanche who accompanied him to the Hôtel du Palais. Guy might be disappointed, but Blanche would console him. That was as it should be. She was his future.

"Aren't you going to say goodbye?" She became aware

of Blanche's curious eyes on her, and was glad her face was turned away.

"I don't think so." Looking out of the window she saw that the moon was hidden behind a cloud, the waves, white-capped. The weather had turned. She rubbed her eyes. They felt scratchy and sore, as if they were full of sand. The shrill shrieking of the gulls flying inland seemed like the loneliest sound she'd ever heard. Already, with a pain she knew was going to grow with every passing day, she missed him, missed all the things they'd never done, quarrels they hadn't had, breakfasts they hadn't eaten, dawns they hadn't seen. Moonshine and sunset, starlight and firelight . . . without him, there was no light in the world.

From somewhere, as she turned, she managed to summon a wry, lopsided smile. "Just tell him . . . tell him it does snow, sometimes, in Biarritz."

CHAPTER FOURTEEN

Oh, my Columbine,

I would not have had this happen to you for the world. I feel your pain as if it were my own. I am bitterly angry, but how can I help you? I know only too well that there is nothing anyone can do or say, when love is not enough.

Except one thing. There's something I want to tell you, something I should perhaps have told you long ago. At first you were too young to understand, I was afraid you'd be frightened. And now you're old enough, I have another fear—that after you hear what I have to say our friendship may be ended. But I have no choice. For friendship's sake, I must take that risk.

Still, it's difficult to find the right words. I've never told anyone else what I'm about to tell you, and after so many years of silence and secrecy I hardly know how to begin. I wish this was just a story, like the ones I used to tell you about Uscady, to while away your winter nights . . .

How did you guess? Sometimes I think you know me better than I do myself, my Columbine. Yes, Uscady, or Euskadi, as the Basques call it, is a real place, in the real world. I grew up there. My father was born a Frenchman, but left home as a young man to fight for the Republicans in the Spanish Civil War. There he met and married a Basque woman, and became involved in the Basques' desperate struggle for independence. He was arrested and imprisoned many times, but never brought to trial or executed. He became something of a hero, thought by his fellow rebels to possess a charmed life. They called him Harlequin.

But even a charmed life can't go on forever. He died in jail in San Sebastian, only a few miles from the French border, where three days later his wife gave birth to a baby boy.

And yet, mine was the best kind of childhood. I was neither poor nor rich, simply content, secure in the knowledge that my father had fought and died for what he believed in, that he and my mother had loved each other, that I could be proud of who and what I was. Our house, which my father had built with his own hands, was isolated, my life solitary, and yet I had everything I wanted. The certainty I was loved, the sea for company, music in the air . . . and a goat of my own. What more could any boy ask? I was often alone, but never lonely.

Except when my mother died. I was sixteen, though I thought myself a grown man, and refused to cry at her funeral. I made up for that misplaced pride later, standing in the doorway of the house we'd shared, which had never before seemed empty. And yet even then, at the worst moment of my life so far, I knew I was safe there, as firmly and solidly fixed as a young oak. For it was where I belonged.

Why, if I was so happy in Uscady, did I ever leave it? I've asked myself that question many times over the years, but there's no one answer. Three weeks after my mother's death I had a letter from a Paris based firm of solicitors, asking me to contact my father's brother.

Perhaps I should have left that letter unanswered. But I was young, and confident, and curious . . . I wanted to know more about my father's family, these new relations whose existence I had never suspected. And then there was Paris—it beckoned and challenged as irresistibly as a Basque fisherman's first glimpse of the Great White Whale . . . the fountain in the air, promising fulfillment of every dream—adventure, excitement, untold riches. I was full of plans and ambitions. I had talent, I knew. I was going to conquer the world. And I was young enough to think that Paradise would still be waiting for me when I returned.

So I went to Paris, to my uncle's house. It was a difficult time. My uncle was a circumspect man. Since my grandfather's death he'd taken over the family business, in dire straits after two world wars, and rebuilt it with the aid of a judicious marriage to a Swiss banker's daughter. His wife, a semi-invalid much older than her husband, kept to her bed, but the marriage had produced one child, a daughter. If it hadn't been for her I think I would have caught the next train back to Uscady. From the beginning she sought me out, seeming to take a special pleasure in my company, curious to know everything about me. I was pleased, and flattered, and relieved, for despite my confidence I was more than a little lonely.

First love . . . She was beautiful, I was young—add proximity and Paris and the conclusion is foregone. It didn't occur to me to wonder why such a lovely girl, besieged by admirers, should prefer a gauche country boy. I might be inarticulate in French, but my head was full of marvelous music. And I was a hero's son. Nothing and no one could take that strength away.

I asked her once why she loved me, more to hear her voice than to listen to what she said. She told me it was because I was different from all the rest. For an instant she looked at me as if I were some exotic animal she'd just captured, rare and unpredictable. I was foolish enough to be flattered. "You belong to me," she said. "I saw you first. You're mine."

It wasn't until my twenty-first birthday that I discovered a country boy's idea of love and that of a young Parisienne are very different. That morning my uncle summoned me to his study and offered me a permanent position in the family business. I must admit I was surprised. I had been working part-time for the firm in repayment for my bed and board, but my heart certainly wasn't in it, and every spare hour had been filled with music. I refused, as tactfully as I could. I told him I had to be free, to follow the music in my head.

For some reason my answer seemed to please him. For a moment there was a spark of emotion in those indifferent, lizardlike eyes. He went on to explain that now I was twenty-one, and had declined a position in the firm, he as head of the family could see no good reason why he should continue to support me. I told him that I would not accept such support even if it was offered. I intended to make it on my own. The atmosphere as I left the room was cold.

I went straight to his daughter, told her I was leaving. I asked her to come away with me. At first she was angry with me for turning down the position offered by her father. It had taken her months, she said, to persuade him. He felt I was reckless and irresponsible, he was sure I would turn out badly, like my father. "If I come with you," she went on, "what will we live on? How will you support a wife?"

Oh, the practicality of women. I felt a strange cold chill. She didn't know about my father's house, the house where I was born, which passed to me on my twenty-first birthday. I'd had a vision of us living together, a snow white goat in the yard, myself at the piano, her with a baby in her arms . . . I told her.

I shall never forget the expression on her face. Her beauty seemed to dissolve before my eyes. She laughed out loud, called me a romantic fool. "What, leave Paris, all my friends, to live with you in some godforsaken cottage at the ends of the earth? You must be mad. Go back to my father, now, and tell him you've changed your mind."

There was something in the way she said it. I lost my head. It was my private dream, she'd rubbed me on the raw. I gripped her by the shoulders—I was very strong—and shook her. I'll always remember her eyes as she looked up at me—half shocked, half fascinated, wholly satisfied. She wrenched herself out of my arms and stood there, her eyes glowing with a sort of triumph.

"Go then . . ." She smiled. Her voice challenged and mocked me at the same time. "But you'll be back."

That night, as I caught the Aquitaine express back to Uscady to claim my inheritance, I was consumed with bitterness. Everything was clear to me now. It had been her idea all along to summon me to Paris. She'd been intrigued by the idea of a long-lost country cousin, a naïve boy whom she could mold to her own design. All my dreams and plans—they'd meant less than nothing to her. I was her plaything, her possession. She was to be Queen, I her consort. And my reward? To be pampered and petted and paraded among my betters, and occasionally stirred into blind savagery with a word . . .

And that wasn't all. As I looked out at the familiar landscape of my childhood, everything seemed changed. I seemed to see it through her eyes, the cold eyes of a stranger. Her words rang endlessly in my brain, haunting me. "You'll be back."

The next morning I collected the title deeds to my father's house, but couldn't bring myself to go there. What if her voice followed me? Already I could feel the past, all the solid convictions of my childhood, shifting like sand under my feet. I was filled with rage and shame, and yet . . . I still loved her. That was worst of all.

By the end of that afternoon I knew what I must do. I would go back—but this time, when I entered my uncle's house, it would be on my own terms.

I had the title deeds to my father's house and land, the guarantee of my future, in my pocket. I went to the Casino, that same evening. I won, and won again. After an hour I was a rich man.

I don't know what entered me then. A sort of madness, a black passion of self-destruction. I was rich, richer than I had ever been or wanted to be, but it wasn't enough. I needed more, to wipe out the memory of her voice, her smile, to erase the consciousness of what love had made me. I went on, playing for higher and higher stakes. I was possessed. By the end of the evening I had lost everything, and more. I was in debt, for a sum so huge it staggered me. Ironically, I had only been allowed to continue at the tables on the strength of my uncle's name . . .

I went back to the beach. I remember looking for my footprints and realizing they had been washed away. The tide had risen, high and full and black. I felt strangely light. I had reached the end, there was nowhere to turn. In its way that was a sort of relief. Where there had been rage and passion there was now emptiness. I, the self I thought I knew, no longer existed. With the utmost clarity I saw what I had done. I had gambled away the birthright my father had fought and died for, lost forever any chance to remain in Uscady. And I couldn't blame fate, or disappointed love, or the world for that. Only myself.

As I stepped into the water I knew exactly what I was doing. Love had been burned out of me, but something—some small spark of goodness or idealism, some vestige of honor, remained. I wouldn't go back to beg for charity, but neither would I be a coward. I understood the convention. One may not die for love, but a debtor's suicide, at least, is honorable.

It was then, my Columbine, that I found your message. A fragment of music, on a scrap of paper, washed to me on a random wave. But it said more to me than words could ever say. It was a voice in the silence, a warm hand in the dark. It said—you are not the only one. There is hope. Even the birds, through storm and darkness, fly on. There is a choice. There is always another way.

And one more thing. As I sat there on the deserted beach, your message in my hand, I was stirred by a sense of obligation. I had been sunk so deep in my selfish despair that I had forgotten anyone else even existed. But now, here in my hand was a wordless cry, seeking—what? Help, recognition, reassurance, company—a sign that someone, somewhere, knew what it felt like to be alone. And it was up to me to answer that soundless cry. For if I did not, who would?

The rest, as they say, is history. I went back. My

uncle, under pressure from his daughter, pledged to pay my debts in return for a promise of good behavior. I accepted the position in the company he offered me, and surrendered all thoughts of a musical career. I made the best of it. I had no choice. It was a trap I had built with my own hands. But I tell you, it's a terrible thing, the burden of gratitude. That is why I told you never to become anyone's pensioner. I couldn't let you make the same mistakes that I have done.

As for his daughter, she sensed immediately the change in me. I was no longer the malleable country boy, full of dreams and naïve ambitions. The balance of power had changed. I simply smiled and shrugged in answer to her questions. I never told her what had happened to me on the beach in Uscady. There was no point, now, in explanations. When I looked at her I saw her for what she was, no more, no less. But all that I deserved.

So I set out to prove to myself and to the world that I didn't care, that the past was behind me. I would bend the future to my will. And I did. I never wrote that one perfect phrase of music, the one that haunted me, but I discovered that indifference has a power of its own. You need never lose at love or life if you play it as a game. Women flocked to me. In return I was good to them, in every way but the one that counts.

That is something about myself I have learned to accept. Since that day on the beach I know that the darkness is in me, not in the world. I have learned to distrust passion—only possession is left.

It wasn't until I met my Colombe that I realized I had been living the life of an automaton, the world of women divided into two camps—you, whom I loved and trusted, and the rest, who must never be allowed to come too close. I didn't recognize my feeling, but you helped me see it for what it was. Love.

Let me tell you, if first love is painful, last is more so. The end, when it comes, seems so much more final. But I think I always knew she would never be mine. I could never tell her what I have just told you. Some-

thing—some childish faith in happy endings, some natural unthinking confidence, was destroyed in me that night in Uscady. Since then I have never trusted anyone, least of all myself.

Except you, my Columbine. To you, alone of all the women I have ever known, I have kept every promise, to you I have been completely faithful. You have seen the best of me. My bitterness, my ungovernable tempers, my coldness, you have been spared all these. In my letters to you I have tried to be the man you wanted me to be—your gay, loving Harlequin, your lighthearted companion, your window on a better world. Re-creating my lost Paradise for you has been the redeeming pleasure of my life, the one enterprise that hasn't soured. You have been—my reality, my stranger in the darkness, my constant friend. The one link between myself and the boy I once was, who wanted the moon.

And now . . . now this may be the end of the world we have shared, you and I. I dreamed of meeting you one day, as some dream of America. A new world, a fresh start . . . but now you know what kind of man I am—a fool, a gambler, a failed suicide . . . our friendship may be ended. And yet . . . if I have helped you, if knowing my weakness will make you strong, then telling you will have been worthwhile. You have a voice, and you must use it—for all the voiceless ones, the lost souls, the lonely strangers who cannot speak for themselves. They are out there in the darkness, waiting for you to release them. You must reach them if you can. Who knows, you might save a life. As you did mine.

So . . . adieu, my Columbine. This may be my last letter, but I shall still be writing to you. In my heart.

Harlequin.

CHAPTER FIFTEEN

"M. Beyer."

For the third time Corrie tried to stop the flow of mingled French, Austrian, Italian and Russian from her teacher. "M. Beyer. You know I would have let you know if I was able. I simply was not able."

He glared at her with a fulminating gaze.

"But you have been back in Paris for two whole weeks, you have admitted it! Two weeks, yet you didn't contact me. Why? Were you ill?"

She hesitated, then shook her head. "I was . . . thinking. There was something I had to get clear in my mind."

"Is it clear now?"

"I think so." A shadow crossed her face. Harlequin's letter had reached her when she was at her lowest ebb, and turned her, slowly but surely, like the moon turns the tide. Only he would ever know what she had been through in those terrible weeks. Her secret was safe with him, just as his was with her. She wrote to him.

Dear friend,

Can you love a stranger? Can you love someone you've never met? I don't know . . . All I know is that there are as many different kinds of love as leaves on a tree, and maybe our kind is the best of all.

Your Columbine

M. Beyer looked at his protégée. No, she would never understand, share his fear that this of all opportunities might have escaped her. He suspected that all her life other people would rant and rage at her, for her and on her behalf, while she would remain in the center of the storm, watchful, unmoved, with that level black-browed gaze of hers, saving her energies for the time her role must begin. It was in its way an excellent attribute, in an opera singer as in a racehorse, that quiet eagerness in the stalls. It would stand her in good stead—provided her fellows could survive the strain.

And she had changed again. There was about her an odd impression of fullness, a sort of controlled recklessness, a kind of self-knowledge. As if she'd been down to the depths and come up stronger than before, traveled to the edge of the world and lived to tell the tale, walked on the moon. A Columbus look. The air of someone who has found gold and thrown it all away.

"M. Beyer." Her tone was faintly reproachful. "I'm here now."

"Yes." He knew the finality of what he was saying. "You are here now." She was here, at last, all her power held lightly in check. She had that aura, unmistakable to a trained eye, that the less discerning only discover later in early photographs of the famous—a stained-glass quality, a sort of inner glow. She was almost an icon now.

"What was it you wanted to tell me?"

He drew a deep breath. "I am not going to teach you any more."

She inclined her head, that insufferable self-possession even stronger than before. "As you wish, M. Beyer." A glint of the old mischief showed in her slight smile. "And what do you suggest I do with my time?"

"I suggest . . ." He slapped a score in front of her. She picked it up. It was *Pagliacci*. Inside the flyleaf was a mimeographed sheet of paper. She read it—the names flashed before her eyes like Christmas lights. Padua, Verona, Genoa, Turin, Florence, Naples . . .

"I am taking the current production on tour. The train leaves tomorrow, at 7 a.m. You will be on it."

She looked up at him.

"I am to sing? Which role?"

He sighed in exasperation.

"How many times have I told you life is not a fairy tale composed expressly for your benefit? You are to understudy Camilla Bergsen. Who knows, you may sing—if you are very lucky."

"But which role?" Oh, that single-minded intensity . . . He had no doubt that if the opportunity didn't please her she would reject it out of hand. He paused, savoring the moment.

"Nedda." He frowned at her fiercely. He could see her mind was already racing ahead, planning, preparing. She was a professional, he had trained her well. She nodded, once, then gathered up her things.

He called after her. "Remember—7 a.m. I know how you sleep—Armageddon wouldn't wake you."

"I've changed." She paused at the door. For an instant he saw a trace of the essential hunger that was Corrie in her wide blue eyes. "I'll be there. There's nowhere else to be."

"Curtain up in five minutes!" Corrie's blood filled with adrenaline as she heard the callboy's most theatrical of whispers. She couldn't help it. Even though she wasn't to sing, every fiber of her being responded to the tension, the faint mutter and rustle of the audience as they settled beyond the curtain, the dimming of the house lights, sensed only through the thick fabric, the thronging of bright costumes through the corridors behind the stage.

She bit her lip savagely. At this moment Camilla would be putting the finishing touches to her appearance, arranging the last curls of the glossy black wig that covered her own blondish hair, maybe launching into a few practice trills . . . There was no doubt about it, she could sing. Her reputation as a musician was well-deserved. But was she a peasant? No, she was too precise, too controlled, too melodious for that. Corrie burned with her own instinctive knowledge of how

Nedda's role should be played. But at this rate she'd never be able to show anyone that knowledge. She would spend the rest of the tour backstage, waiting in the wings for an opportunity that wouldn't come until the flame inside her had burned itself out.

She rose to her feet. She couldn't be idle, not at this moment. She peered through the wings at the familiar set, the Sicilian village square blazing in tones of umber and gold, so much a contrast to the gray January skies outside the theater. Even her mother's sun-drenched Naples wasn't immune to winter. At the moment it was raining, though it was not as cold as it had been in Venice, the previous week, when a choking wet mist had risen off the canals and Camilla had refused to go out, to protect her voice.

Corrie sighed. If only Camilla hadn't been so cautious, so very, very sensible. She might have fallen into a canal, caught a cold—something, anything. It wasn't as if she was enjoying the tour. Corrie knew she felt touring was beneath her, that she found the Italian audiences, with their instant response to every breath taken on the stage, interrupted her concentration, that she disliked pizzas and pasta and ice cream. By this time, there wasn't much that any member of the troupe *didn't* know about Camilla's likes and dislikes. But she was the diva, the established star, even if her reputation had been made in Northern Europe, and even if this, her Italian début, wasn't turning out quite as hoped . . . So Camilla missed Venice, and Corrie drank innumerable cups of hot thick chocolate in unheated cafés, and hoped savagely for pneumonia or rabies or stage fright, and returned to the troupe's hotel feeling so guilty that she offered to take the diva's slippers (for she complained they were too tight) to the cobblers to be stretched. So they were stretched, and the diva was placated for a while.

"Curtain up!"

Instantly Corrie forgot all her preoccupations. Tonio, the ugly hunchback (a perfectly handsome young French baritone with an unexpected sense of the grotesque) entered the stage for the prologue. The house orchestra was taking the music faster than usual, for this was Naples, where hearts beat faster, tempers rose quicker, storms brewed more sulphurously. Players and villagers flooded the stage, the heightened tempo generating a sudden tension. She saw that even Edmundo, the Italian-born singer who played Canio, Nedda's jealous husband, was struggling to keep up, but rising to the challenge with a willingness that stirred the mercurial audience. His busking in the role of Pagliaccio, half sinister, half clownish in his white costume, won a few scattered bravoes.

"I say the stage is one thing and life another . . . If I caught Nedda with another man in real life, my story would have a different ending. It's better not to play such games, believe me . . ."

Corrie closed her eyes, Nedda's response so familiar to her that she didn't have to wait for it. But when it came it was a surprise, even to her. She knew that Camilla found this part difficult and unrewarding, preferring the more heroic dramatic roles, where a broad effect (a grand gesture, one of the sustained high notes which were her forte) could always rouse a cheer, to the more complicated verismo roles. But this was an aberration, even for her. The aside was half-hearted, muffled, almost thrown away. A mutter of dissatisfaction ran around the audience. Corrie saw from the wings that Camilla looked sulky, tugging pettishly at her wig. Now she remembered that from the first moment of their arrival in Naples the diva had altered the nature, if not the quantity, of her complaints. They had become specific—the quality of the house orchestra, the heating in the dressing room, the drafts in the hotel—it was almost as if she'd been working up to something.

Corrie gritted her teeth. Suddenly she wanted Camilla to excel herself, not to let the troupe down after all their hard work. For this was Leoncavallo's town, the place where the composer had been born, and the audience knew it. *Pagliacci* was their property, and it wasn't to be taken lightly . . .

But there was time. Perhaps, in the pause before her first big aria, Camilla would relax, her voice would settle, the audience would warm to her. It was essential, for then she must hold the stage single-handed, her voice a wild bird's cry of mingled longing, hope and despair.

Church bells rang, summoning the rest of the cast offstage. The auditorium stilled. Camilla glanced around, swept her skirts about her in a half-hearted attempt to generate some of the tension that characterized her role. Corrie's heart sank as the audience began to hiss and whistle. She began to realize why so many singers, including Camilla, preferred recording in the studio to the rigors of live performance.

The orchestra struck up the famous aria. Corrie's heart sank further. Camilla's voice was leaden. She was glaring at the orchestra, which had suddenly decided to play slower than normal. She missed a high note, committed the atrocity of breathing in the middle of a phrase. A storm of protest rose in the gods, a furious outpouring of whistles and hisses and shouts.

Camilla drew herself up to her full height. From her ringside seat in the wings, Corrie could see that the diva had worked herself up into a grand, ice-cold Scandinavian temper. Her light blue eyes were snapping. The orchestra died away, leaving a breathless hush. With one hand Camilla ripped the wig from her head, hurled it to the ground and emitted a long Swedish phrase which no one understood but all could interpret. After the first stunned seconds cameras began to flash from the orchestra pit. Camilla, roused suddenly to a sense of her own dignity, glanced hurriedly around her then raised one hand to her brow and collapsed gracefully to the boards. There was an electric silence. Hurriedly the orchestra began to play, covering the stage manager's desperate hiss of "Curtain, curtain for God's sake!"

Slowly, oh so slowly, the curtain descended. Camilla

remained manfully still, though Corrie saw her hand inch toward the despised wig. Behind the lowered curtain there was an outcry, a baying for blood as the audience realized how cunningly their prey had escaped. M. Beyer, seemingly unmoved, stepped onto the stage and helped Camilla to her feet. She wilted becomingly on his arm.

"I cannot . . ."—she drew a deep breath—"I simply cannot continue, maestro. My head . . ."

"Of course, my dear." M. Beyer was sympathy itself, only his preoccupied eyes betraying the rapidity of his thought processes. "Come, I will escort you to your dressing room. First of all, as a matter of utmost urgency, we must relieve you of your costume."

"Yes, thank you . . ." The soprano tugged petulantly at her close-fitting bodice. "I can hardly breathe."

"Corrie!" M. Beyer's voice was hardly raised, his eyes didn't stray from Camilla's face, but his words carried with astonishing clarity. "Perhaps you would accompany me to assist Miss Bergsen."

Corrie followed him, observing with admiration his lightning glance at his watch, his muffled instructions to the stage manager, which hardly interrupted the smooth flow of reassurance to his soprano.

Camilla's dresser was waiting, bristling with concern. M. Beyer whispered in her ear and she jumped to her task with alacrity. Unceremoniously the costume—black velvet bodice with tight lacing, wide crimson skirt, white lace blouse, black slippers—was heaped in Corrie's arms. M. Beyer shot her one piercing glance.

"This is your chance. You know what to do." He thrust a tray of makeup into her hands and bundled her out of the door.

Corrie found herself standing in the corridor. Around her there was chaos, the cast from the first scene milling in confusion, unsure whether to change their costumes or go back on stage. Dimly she could hear the orchestra playing an intermezzo from its repertoire, barely drowning out the uproar from the audience. Someone, somewhere, was trying to make an announcement.

Suddenly her mind was ice-cold. She darted into the cramped lavatory and ripped off her own clothes. The bodice was too large around the waist, but she did up the stays as tight as they would go, overlapped the edges and covered the join with her scarlet shawl. The heavy full skirt and its stiffened petticoats was a little long, but would have to do. The shoes were impossible—no matter. She kicked off her own. She would go barefoot. Hurriedly she daubed brown makeup over her bare feet. She was a peasant, it must seem as if she'd gone barefoot all her life.

Expertly, blessing all the times she'd made up at the Chat d'Or, she outlined her eyes with black, her mouth with crimson, deepened her complexion to sunny southern gold. But her hair? The wig would never cover it and there was no time to bundle it into a net. She loosened it on her shoulders, dragging her hands through it till it was a tumbled mass.

A machine-gun rattle of knocks sounded at the door. She opened it; someone grabbed her hand and dragged her down the corridor, petticoats flying. From a hundred miles away she heard Tonio, battling to make his prologue heard again against a hail of catcalls. Breathless, her heart beating so fast she thought she would choke, she was thrust into the center of the players' group in the wings. She smelled greasepaint and human sweat, saw how pale the others' faces were behind their garish makeup, saw how their eyes darted and flared in fear. They had good reason to be frightened, all of them—they were flirting with disaster. Suddenly she was calm. She smiled straight into the face of Canio, her stage husband.

"*In bocca di lupo!*" Into the wolf's mouth . . . It was what she'd always said to her mother before she went on stage. Canio's eyes crinkled in surprise and pleasure behind the white mask. Stage enemies or no, they were part of the same troupe, they sank or swam together.

And then they were on. Nothing could have prepared

her for the onslaught of light. She fought to remember her lessons, transform herself from one heartbeat to the next into a creature big enough to fill a stage and a thousand eyes and ears. At least there was a pause before Nedda's first vocal, to give her time to adjust. The boards were rough and warm under her bare feet. She felt them, and yet she didn't feel them. She was Nedda, veteran of a hundred small village squares like this one, filled with her husband's repetitive busking. It was peace and love she yearned for, with her quiet gentle Silvio. He was out there somewhere in the darkness, her ticket to escape . . . oh, if it were only possible. She shot a nervous glance at her husband. With another part of her mind she was aware of the audience, waiting for her to make it or break. She tossed her hair. They were intrigued, she could sense it, by her loose hair, her bare feet—circumstance transformed into showmanship. The magic begins, Harlequin, she said to herself, letting it take her but riding her own exhilaration like a wave. This moment is not for me, it is for them, out there, hungry for passion and laughter and disaster, waiting for my voice to become their own . . .

"Ring, bells . . . The sun is kissing the western heights. Ring, bells . . . The world is gleaming with light and love. Ring, bells."

Canio nodded a smiling farewell to her as he left the stage with the rest of the cast. From the wings she caught his last desperate wink of good luck.

And then she was alone. She listened carefully as the orchestra struck up her aria. She waited. She must begin slowly, stifle her greed for the lovely music. She stood rigid at center stage, only her eyes moving in a doubtful sidelong glance at the wings.

"What a fire in his eyes. I could hardly look at him for fear he could read my secret thoughts." She shivered. "Oh, if he ever caught me, brute that he is." Slowly, measuring out the silence, she allowed herself an awareness of her solitude. Unfolding inside her was not only Nedda's role, but the realization that she was here at last, where she'd wanted to be. She closed her eyes, lifted her bare shoulders in a wriggle of pure delight. The spotlight beat down on her with tropical warmth. Gone was winter and all its disappointments, for a minute, an hour.

"Oh, beautiful midsummer sun . . ."

All the dreams she had ever dreamed were in her voice. She felt rather than heard the murmur that ran around the audience, a deep wordless sigh, half hunger, half appreciation. She had roused them, but she wouldn't satisfy their hunger, not yet.

She whirled, the sudden motion sending her skirts flying.

"Oh, the birds . . . how wildly they call up there!" Her hands fluttered, hesitant, searching. Her eyes reached out to the audience beyond the footlights. She was drawn now, tempted, fearful but driven. Somewhere, somewhere out there is love, all the things men dream of.

"A strange land yonder, which they seek in vain . . ."

In vain. Her voice was a dark sob. A vast empty echo returned to her from the darkness, a simultaneous indrawing of breath. They knew, she knew, what was to come.

But she would deny them. She dropped into her quietest voice, with its edge of blue steel.

"Vagabonds of the sky, who obey only
The secret force that drives them on and on . . ."

The audience, surprised in its own secret, stabbed to the heart, shivered. We will dream together, her voice said. We will dream, with the violence of the doomed. For that is what it means to be human. To dream, to suffer, to die.

Suddenly, like a dam breaking, the air was filled with a rush of noise, a voiceless wordless roar. It drowned the orchestra, drowned everything but the beating of her heart. It went on and on, like the sea, like a lost child's cry of rage and longing and loneliness. It was a storm, an avalanche . . . and yet in the midst of the uproar she heard as clearly as a trumpet call a single voice. "*Ecco tutto*," it was saying, over and over again. That's all. That's all. That's all.

In that moment, as she looked into the faceless darkness, she knew her life would never be the same. She was their voice, their mirror, she belonged to them entirely. She spread her hands, bowed her head. No more words were needed. "*Ecco tutto*." There is no more than this, not for you, not for me. We are not strangers after all, there is no distance between us. For look . . . my heart too goes barefoot under all my finery.

In the wings, as the first act closed, M. Beyer was waiting. His face was stern, totally concentrated. He said nothing to her about her performance, he had no need. They both knew that tonight would be a miracle, a marvel. One of those nights to be recalled with nostalgia, and pride, and amazement. It was a privilege simply to be there.

In the dressing room she became aware that she was trembling. He sat her down, sent the rest of the cast out of the room.

"You." He handed her a small glass of water. "You will drink this, and no more. And you . . ." He gestured to Camilla's dresser, standing by open-mouthed. "You will help Madame to dress for the second act." He stayed only a moment more, to cup Corrie's face, damp under the makeup, in his hands, and deposit a resounding kiss on her disordered curls. "My Columbine."

CHAPTER SIXTEEN

"*Écoute, chérie.*"

"*J'écoute.*" There was an edge of frost in Blanche's tone. Guy smiled to himself. The day before the wedding he would not see her alone, it was the tradition. A touch of remoteness became the blushing bride. As would the lavish displays of South African lilies flown to Chamonix by air express for this whitest of white weddings.

For what could be whiter than Chamonix at the height of the winter season? Blanche, with her customary efficiency, had even arranged for fresh snowfalls to be delivered overnight—or at least they were promised, according to the weather forecast. They would come. Blanche, as he knew only too well, always got what she wanted.

He held the telephone a moment, staring once more at the slip of paper in his hand. At last . . . He made up his mind.

"I have some apologies to make." His tone was smooth, betraying nothing of his inner feelings. "I shall not be able to escort you to the Saint-Evrémonds' this evening."

There was an instant's silence at the other end of the line.

"I see." The edge of frost sharpened. "But we have already accepted the invitation. You can't cancel at such short notice." Her tone was quietly confident.

"Can't I?" His tone was light. There was another pause.

"It's hardly the action of a gentleman."

Guy's eyes narrowed, but his voice didn't change.

"You must forgive me, my dear Blanche." He allowed himself the faintest tinge of irony. "You of all people must have realized that I am not, and have never claimed to be, a gentleman."

"You have made up your mind, then."

"Yes." Strangely, as he said it, he seemed to feel a great weight, a weight he'd hardly known he was carrying, lifting from his shoulders.

"But what shall I say to the Saint-Evrémonds?" She had accepted the inevitable, he knew, with that cool pragmatism which was her greatest strength. Now more than ever he needed her coolness, that sense of solitude, of privacy, that she gave him—to banish forever the memory of silver light filling the air with radiance, warmth that defied time and loneliness and despair. She was gone, that other girl, if she had ever existed anywhere but in his mind.

"Tell them . . ." He smiled again to himself, looking down the vista of years which had led him to this moment. How could she, how could anyone ever understand what this meant to him, this rendezvous with the young man he'd once been, a young man whom he would hardly recognize today if he met him in the street?

"Tell them . . . tell them I have a prior engagement."

He laid the phone down, slipped the piece of paper he had in his hand into his wallet. Swiftly he gathered up the heavy coat beside him, checked his passport. He needed nothing else. This was no business trip, it was for himself alone.

"The Porsche is ready, sir."

"Thank you." Without a backward glance he left the room and descended the ice-clad steps, his mind already on the road ahead. There was barely time. He glanced at the sky. It was gray, a thick reflective gray that threatened the promised snow. The icy air snapped at his face and hands like a wolf. He settled himself into the deep leather front seat.

"You won't be requiring me, sir?"

Gaston's puzzled face inquired at the window.

"Not this time." Guy gunned the motor, feeling the

powerful pulse under his feet, like the pulse of life itself. "It will be a long drive. And I'm late already."

But he'd make up for that. The roads to the frontier, across the bleak white wastes of the Mer de Glace, were good. Providing the mountain passes were clear he'd reach the frontier ahead of the next snowfall. A little late, perhaps—but what did that matter? For this moment, he'd waited ten long years . . .

"One moment, Madame . . . there!" The dresser inserted one more pin skillfully into the net that retained Corrie's hair and stepped back with a sigh of pride.

Slowly, carefully, Corrie rose from the stool to study her reflection full-length. The costume was new, designed especially for this performance. M. Beyer had insisted. This was no ordinary presentation but a gala night, with an added edge of interest—the new young singer, so suddenly thrown into prominence, whom the correspondent from *Corriere della Sera*, abruptly dispatched to see and hear her for himself, had called "disturbing, dangerous, audacious." He'd ended his piece with a challenge to opera-goers and to Corrie herself. "On the horizon there is a new phosphorescence. Tonight, at Naples' Teatro san Carlo, I heard the future sing."

Corrie shivered. She could hardly believe all that had happened in the few short days since her Naples début. The next morning she'd heard that Camilla had left for another engagement in Oslo which she'd suddenly decided merited her attention. That at least was no surprise. The entire troupe had noticed her noisy departure in the small hours, generating all the drama that had been notably lacking in her performance. But the rest—the newspaper reports, the flowers from strangers, the rain of bookings, calls from agents, requests for interviews—it was so sudden, so soon, it all seemed like a dream.

But tonight, maybe, she would be rudely awakened from that dream. For this was La Scala, the most feared and hated and coveted of opera houses, the ultimate testing ground. Here careers could be made or broken. Legend had it that if a singer failed on so much as one top note the entire gallery would chant the whole aria correctly or whistle her offstage.

But what would they think of the new Columbine? Her costume was deceptively simple, silk velvet of a deep violet blue that exactly matched her eyes, cobwebbed over with a delicate tracery of silver lace. Originally the designer had suggested gold, not silver, but she had insisted.

"But why? Gold has so much more impact."

"Agreed. But silver has more . . . style." It was her secret, small gesture to what she had learned from Guy de Chardonnet, about loving and living and losing. But had she chosen right? Now, looking at herself, she saw a fragile, windblown flower, mauve anemones under silver gray olive trees, moonlight on a wine-dark sea, and knew that he would have been pleased.

"You are beautiful, Madame." Her dresser's voice lifted her out of her reverie.

"I hope so." She lifted one tentative hand to touch her hair. Under its covering of silver net it stirred and shifted like a live thing. She looked like a stranger, her eyes long pools of violet light in the pallor of her face. Her hands were icy cold.

Only one thing would warm them. She hurried out of the dressing room to peer through the wings at the crowded auditorium. The houselights were dimmed, but the glitter of diamonds seemed to fill the theater with a phosphorescence of its own. Out there were ministers and foreign dignitaries, socialites and celebrities, millionaires and their bejeweled wives, the entire Italian establishment including, in the carnation-bedecked Presidential box, the President of the Republic himself. Her eyes searched, probed the line of winter-pale, expectant faces in the front row. Every seat was filled . . . apart from one.

It came as suddenly and swiftly as a blow. Whatever she'd feared, it hadn't been this. She'd been so sure. She drew back. There was barely ten minutes to go before the curtain went up. Enough time, but only just. She closed her eyes, willing the seat to be filled when she opened them. It was still empty, except for a fur wrap thrown negligently across it. On the fur, glittering cold as diamonds, were traces of melting snow.

She didn't know how long she stood there, waiting, hoping against all the growing certainty that chilled her body. Only the first strains of the overture, and a hand frantically tugging on her arm, roused her.

"What's the matter? What on earth are you doing here?"

"Nothing." With a supreme effort she forced her limbs to obey her. There seemed to be a heavy weight dragging her down with every step. Everything around her, even the glittering auditorium, seemed suddenly dim and lifeless. What *was* she doing here? It had seemed so important to her, a few moments ago, but now she couldn't remember why. What was the point, after all? Out in the audience there wasn't one person who knew her, one friend who cared. Oh, Harlequin . . .

Like an automaton she followed the corridor to her allotted entrance. She stood there, listening to Tonio's prologue, with a terrible sense of unreality. It was all so different from Naples. Of the original cast only Edmundo had been retained to play Canio, and he was too preoccupied with his own "prima" nerves even to catch her eye. She felt empty, frozen. What if her overnight success had been just a fluke? In Naples they had been her people, violent, partisan, easily swayed by her Neapolitan accent and the drama of the occasion. But the audience tonight, rich, privileged, hypercritical Milanese, ready to condemn the slightest error—they had seen so many brilliant performances and remained unmoved, so how could she, an inexperienced newcomer, hope to stir them? She was crazy to be here.

As she waited in the wings she felt as if she'd been turned to stone. The music of the orchestra, fuller and more assured than it had been in Naples, filled the auditorium. How could she rise above it? In rehearsals she'd managed easily, but everyone knew the deceptive acoustics of an empty house. And worse . . . she'd forgotten every note of the score.

But what did that matter? Success or failure—it would all be the same in a few hours' time. The audience only wanted distraction, an evening's amusement. She could walk through the performance, sink back into obscurity, and no one would miss her.

She moved like a sleepwalker through the wings and into the blazing light of the stage. The audience was blotted out, though she could feel them there, feel the mocking blank stare from that one empty seat in the center of the front row. There's nothing you can tell me about love, it said. I know it all. Love is just an illusion, a pretense—convincingly lit and brightly costumed, but nonetheless a lie. It doesn't last. A little music, a little dancing, then the theater goes dark.

Except . . . the music lapped at the edge of her awareness, lifted her imperceptibly. She felt herself melt a little. The music had always been her friend, her first love. And it was still there. She owed that long-dead Neapolitan composer something, for all the gaiety he'd given her, those chocolate picnics, her mother's laughter. She clung to that thought tenaciously. Damn it, she thought, I won't be defeated. My mother always put on lipstick when she went out, just in case she might meet Aristotle Onassis. Call it a lie, call it an illusion—she called it making the best of yourself. Lost love, broken promises—that's nothing. I can sing. No one can take that away from me.

And you out there, with your diamonds and furs. You may not be my people—yet. But I'll reach you. It'll be the hardest work I've ever done, but I won't let you go before you've heard what I have to say. I'll stir you and shake you, make you laugh and cry, change your lives or save them. That's my job, that's what I was born for. Listen.

The big gray Porsche flew through the winter darkness like a giant bird. At the wheel, Guy noted only the relentless passage of time, the steady worsening of the weather conditions. He reached for the radio. Heavy snowfalls over the high peaks had blocked some roads. They were now clear, but more was expected.

Guy's eyes narrowed. Bad news—but it made no difference to him. If there was a way through, he would find it. His goal now seemed to fill the whole of his mind, as if all his life had simply been leading to this moment, this ultimate conflict with circumstance. No more bargains, he thought to himself savagely, with a sort of wild exhilaration. Nothing, not the worst that fate can throw at me, will stop me this time.

As the altitude rose, visibility decreased dramatically. Driving snow flung itself against the windshield as he ascended the long winding circuit, skirting an inky abyss on the right, broken only by the few faraway lights of a ski-lodge or resting place. He continued, pausing only to clear the accumulated snow from the wiper blades and check his snow chains. Fortunately the snow was fresh, as yet unchanged to perilous black ice under the wheels. Fortunately too most other traffic, deterred by the conditions, had left the road. He ascended slowly but surely, the Porsche's powerful headlights revealing a white, wind-whipped hell. At the highest point visibility was nil, the world reduced to a black pit bisected by the narrow line down the middle of the road which led him interminably on.

At the Italian border a greatcoated customs official, bent almost double against the onslaught of snow, waved him through unchallenged. Just past the border he halted at a rest-stop. The huge brightly lit building was deserted, though it was barely eight o'clock. The barman looked relieved to see a customer. He was ensconced behind his bar like someone under siege, his back resolutely turned to the vast plate-glass windows outside which the storm raged, and the radio full on to hide the howling wind. Guy downed a cup of scalding coffee, and was about to go when an Italian voice on the radio caught his attention.

"What's that?"

The barman answered him in the heavily accented French of an Italian Swiss.

"The broadcast from La Scala, monsieur. It's due to begin in just a few minutes. This is an interview recorded last week with one of the singers.

"But which one?"

"Ah." The barman warmed to what he sensed was another opera aficionado. "You like opera, monsieur? I too." He gestured at the howling black wilderness outside, speaking simply but with fervor. "It reminds me, out here, that I am human. On a night like this, it's like a warm fire."

"But the singer . . ." Guy could hardly control his impatience.

The barman shrugged. "I've never heard of her. She is a new young discovery, they are all talking about her." He pursed his lips. "Whether she can sing, that is another matter."

"What is she saying?" Guy cursed his inability to speak Italian. The barman turned up the volume with proprietary pride.

"She is saying . . . oh, what they all say. That she has always wanted to sing. That a very good friend was the first to encourage her, that when she sings she feels she is singing to him."

"And tonight's production? No, don't tell me, I think I know." Guy drew out the slip of paper from his wallet. A date, a time, a place. "*Pagliacci*."

The barman leaned over, curious to see why his only customer was suddenly grinning like a boy.

"Ah, monsieur . . ." He smiled benignly as he deciphered the mystery. "You are the lucky one."

"Yes." Guy looked up. "I am the lucky one."

The barman glanced up at the large chrome clock above the bar.

"But monsieur, you had better hurry or you will miss the best."

Quickly Guy belted his coat and drained the last bitter dregs of his coffee. It was the sweetest taste he'd ever had in his life. I will not miss the best, he thought. Not this time.

The warmth stayed with him as he drove. With sure fingers he tuned the radio into the Milan station. Music filled the interior of the car, blotting out the darkness, the rush of the engine, the whine of the storm outside. It was like a lifeline joining him to her. He might not be there in time, but she would wait for him, he knew it. She was his friend, his constant star, his Columbine.

The descent of a mountain is always more dangerous than the ascent. That is when tired minds forget the essentials of survival, when climbers, giddy with relief, plunge to their deaths.

Guy didn't have a chance. He saw the headlights ahead of him, and like the experienced driver he was, without a moment's hesitation, he swung his wheel away, sensing only by the sudden silence that the car had left the road. Outside he saw whirling blackness, knew deep in himself that he had lost his gamble after all.

And yet, in those last few moments before the car hit the unforgiving rocks, he hugged to himself the small triumphant fact of his knowledge. He had not been wrong. It had been worth all the long years of waiting, to hear that voice. For around him, filling the air with the haunting fullness of her voice, Columbine began to sing, like a mother singing to her child, like a lover to a lover, with a soft intensity that peeled back all the layers of time and maturity and sophistication to touch his heart itself.

"The birds fly on, through stormclouds or burning sun,
Reaching out for the light, thirsty for blue sky and splendor,
They must fly on, for they too follow a dream . . ."

His last conscious thought, as he descended into the cold and darkness, was that in her at least he had left behind something that would survive. No one will ever know, he thought, with an odd sort of pride—but she is singing for me.

"Was it like Naples?"

Corrie fell into M. Beyer's arms. Beyond the curtain a storm was raging, of fury or acclaim she couldn't tell.

"No." M. Beyer's face was pale and drawn. "It was worse, much worse. And better—better than you could imagine. I have never seen such a Nedda. You have destroyed the role. No one will ever be able to play it again but you."

Corrie heard his words from a long distance away. Is that what she had done? She didn't know. She felt exhausted, half-destroyed herself.

"I don't believe you." She could remember nothing, feel nothing except that she was drained to the core. "You're just saying that."

He shook his head as he opened her dressing room door. Inside, bent over the radio, was her dresser, her face beaming with proprietary pride. The small space was filled by the high excited voice of the announcer, almost strident against the muted background roar which eerily echoed the commotion in the auditorium.

"Remarkable, remarkable . . . everything they said about her in Naples is true, and more. I cannot remember when I have been so moved, so lifted out of myself by a performance. From this moment, I tell you, Modena *is* Nedda. I can see from my box that some reviewers are already rushing out to file their reports before the papers go to press. I can understand their sense of urgency. This is an event, a celebration. Something is happening here tonight which it is a rare privilege to witness—unmistakable, brilliant, the birth of a new star . . ."

Corrie closed her eyes. It was strange, she still felt nothing, remembered nothing. She was in limbo, still deep in the role, still subconsciously waiting for the next bar of music to bring her back to life. It wasn't like

Naples—M. Beyer was right. It was worse, and yet better, because this time she'd sung because she had to, dredged up the energy when she had none left to spare.

Suddenly another voice, crisp and curt, with an undercurrent of urgency, interrupted the presenter's flow.

"We apologize for interrupting this broadcast from La Scala to warn motorists using the main road between the French frontier and Turin that there has been a serious accident involving a truck and a car. The driver of the truck is unhurt, but the driver of the car, Signor Guy de Chardonnet, a noted French industrialist, has been transferred to a hospital in Geneva. The extent of his injuries is not known . . ."

Corrie froze. It seemed an eternity before she could force her brain to register what the man had said. Perhaps, in the announcer's Italian, she could have mistaken the name? No . . . the coincidence was too great. It was him. She sat, stunned, while the previous announcer, still high-voiced and almost incoherent in his excitement, returned. "In only a few minutes the curtain will rise again—what is awaiting us in the next and final act? The audience can hardly wait . . ."

His voice babbled on, but in Corrie's mind there was room for only one thought. She stood up, ignoring her dresser's surprise.

"Listen, Martina. Find M. Beyer for me. Quickly."

The dresser's face was horrified. "But, Madame, your costume, your hair—it is only five minutes before . . ."

"I know." Corrie kept her voice and manner calm with an enormous effort. "Hurry."

CHAPTER SEVENTEEN

Outside in the auditorium there was an expectant hum as the audience settled into their seats for the second act. Cheeks were flushed, eyes bright, there was an almost electric air of anticipation and excitement. The house lights dimmed, but the orchestra remained silent. Instead the heavy curtains parted, just a little. The white-haired figure in evening dress that appeared before them was familiar to those in the know as the impresario who had discovered the new star, M. Beyer.

"*Signori*." His lightly accented Italian, his quiet, level voice, silenced them with instant authority. He waited, letting the silence spread to the outer reaches of the auditorium. "You have heard Nedda, and Columbine. Now I give you . . . Modena."

There was a gasp, a sudden communal intake of breath. The audience craned forward in their seats. Some, at the back, rose to their feet. What was going on? What other radical departures from tradition was this extraordinary young woman going to perpetrate?

From behind the curtain stepped the singer—or was it Columbine herself, in her age-old finery, graceful and elusive, yet familar as a figure in an old print? She glimmered like spring twilight in her silver and mauve, but her costume couldn't detract from the magnetism of her eyes. Her hand fluttered once to still the beginnings of applause as M. Beyer retired.

Audience and singer looked at each other for a long moment.

"I wish I could see you all." Corrie's voice called in the silence to the edges of the auditorium. As if on cue, the house lights began to go up. The figure alone at center stage smiled. The audience held its breath. "That's better." She held out her hands in an oddly endearing gesture. "I have something very important to tell you. I am not going to sing."

There was a stunned silence, then a roar went up, of frustration, disappointment, fury, betrayal, confusion. She waited, a poised little figure in her sparkling dress, only the toss of her head and the lifting of her chin betraying her nervousness. She held out one hand. The audience, surprised at itself, hungry for reassurance, quieted instantly.

"Now I will tell you why." She took a deep breath, smiled, shrugged. "Singing is easier, let me tell you! It is difficult to find the right words. But we have shared something together, you and I, so I feel that you will understand." She paused, looking straight up into the spotlight. "You see . . . *Jo amo*." It was her richest, most colloquial Neapolitan. Simple, uncompromising. I love. And yet her tone said more than that, much more. It said, "I love, I live, I breathe, I am in love. That explains everything, why you are here, why I am here. It is the stuff of life itself."

The audience began a small murmur, a sort of indulgent croon. Women began to sway in their seats, turning misty-eyed to their escorts. We have all been young once, they seemed to say—had you forgotten, *caro*? There was a time . . .

Corrie drew herself up to her full height. Her face was severe.

"But the one I love . . ." Her voice faltered once, then strengthened. "He needs me. Now. And that is more important to me than anything else." Her voice contained the slightest note of surprise. "So I must go to him." Now her voice carried strongly, filled the air with its urgency. "I could have gone without telling you, but I felt you should know, because you would understand."

There was a moment's silence, then the audience, as one man, rose to its feet, clapping and cheering and whistling. Flowers—roses, carnations, orchids—began to rain down from the balcony and stalls. Corrie stared at them, astonished—then bent to pick one up and place it in her corsage.

"I don't know when we will see each other again, my friends." Her smile had a brilliance that outdid the spotlight, though her cheeks were wet. "But one thing I can promise you." She stepped forward, opened her arms wide. "Nedda will not die tonight!"

"Dr. Ubermeyer!"

The note of panic in the desk clerk's voice halted the surgeon in his tracks. He turned, frowning, every scrupulous Swiss nerve outraged at this breach of regulations.

"What are you doing here? Why have you left the desk unattended?" The clerk sent a flustered glance over his shoulder.

"I wouldn't have, sir . . . only there's a visitor."

"A visitor?" With an effort the doctor restrained his own surprise. It seemed hardly possible, this winter midnight, when all the passes on both sides of the Alps were blocked by the worst conditions in living memory and all air traffic had been grounded. Even the access roads to the hospital, despite constant efforts by the orderlies and groundsmen, were buried under six foot drifts.

"Yes, sir. Come to see the patient in fifty-one."

Dr. Ubermeyer's frown deepened.

"M. de Chardonnet? But my instructions were absolutely clear. No visitors allowed."

"That's what I told her, sir, but she wouldn't take any notice. She said if I didn't let her through, she'd come and find him for herself. It was all I could do to persuade her to stay in reception while I came to find you."

"Very well." Dr. Ubermeyer sighed. "Tell her I'm on my way." The clerk glanced once more over his shoulder and his eyes widened.

"Too late, sir. Here she comes."

As the surgeon followed his glance he began to understand something of the man's panic. For walking purposefully along the corridor was no ordinary visitor but the most extraordinary looking girl he'd ever seen. She was wearing a long black opera cloak, and if it hadn't been for the snow glistening on her shoulders and frosting the edges of her hood he might have taken her for an apparition. Beneath the cloak, outrageous in the stark white light of the corridor, was the shimmer of velvet, the sparkle of silver.

"Are you the consultant?"

"I am." The surgeon's frown deepened. "And who might you be?"

For a moment, seeing his expression, Corrie almost faltered. She was exhausted from the performance followed by the long, nightmare drive through snow and darkness from Milan to the foothills of the Alps. But she mustn't give up now. Nothing must prevent her from seeing Guy. She had to be with him. She felt his presence with every fiber of her body. Nothing they could tell her, in this cold, dead place, with its bare walls and miles of icy smooth floor, its rubber-wheeled trolleys and white-uniformed faces, could deter her.

"I?" Her tone held the true aristocrat's note of surprise and impatience. She put all the conviction she could muster into her voice. Her nerves might be at breaking-point, but she mustn't show it. This was the most important performance of her life. "I am Blanche de Chardonnet."

"Ah . . ." The doctor's face cleared miraculously. "You should have said so before. With a man of M. de Chardonnet's importance one cannot be too cautious." He hesitated, his frown beginning to return. "But I understood from our telephone conversation that owing to the airport closure you wouldn't be able to get here till tomorrow?"

"I came by private plane." She lied quickly, instinctively, superbly. The doctor glanced doubtfully at her costume.

"I was at a masked ball. Of course I came at once.

And now . . ."—before he could protest she fixed him with the intensity of her gaze—"may I see my fiancé?"

"Of course." The doctor unbent a little as he escorted her along the corridor, through darkened passages eerily lit with the greenish glow of fluorescent light. "My commiserations. I heard that you were to be married tomorrow."

Tomorrow? Corrie was glad that he couldn't see her face as she followed him. She hadn't known, hadn't realized . . . perhaps she was too late. As the doctor paused before a white-painted door with a square glass pane set into its upper half her heart gave a suffocating lurch.

"Tell me." Her throat was so dry she could hardly speak. "How is he?"

"Basically his condition has not changed since I last spoke to you." He paused—only a few seconds, but to Corrie they seemed like an eternity. "Physically, as I said, he escaped unscathed. A few bruises, some lacerations, nothing serious. It is fortunate that he was found before he suffered unduly from exposure. It so happened his car's radio was playing and was undamaged by the crash. A lucky chance. Half an hour longer and he would have been dead."

Corrie drew a deep, shuddering breath. "Then he's going to be all right?"

The doctor hesitated again. "One hopes so. But as I told you earlier, there are elements in his case which are . . . disquieting. There is no sign of any head injury but when he was admitted he was showing signs of great mental agitation. He seemed confused about his own identity, claiming that he was not and never had been Guy de Chardonnet. When it was suggested to him that he should remain in hospital overnight for observation he became very disturbed. He seemed determined to continue his journey at all costs. In the end, we had to sedate him." He sighed. "*La montagne*—when the sun shines, people think it is a playground. But in the snow . . ."

"Yes, doctor."

At last, at last, the door swung open. There, on the bed, silent and immobile, was Guy. He was breathing so lightly that his chest hardly lifted at all. One hand lay on the smooth sheet.

Without hesitating she pulled up a hard, rigid chair, sat down and picked up his hand.

"Mlle de Chardonnet . . ." The doctor's expression was mildly reproving. "The risk of infection, grazes . . ."

"Dr. Ubermeyer." Corrie's face was dangerous as she turned to him. "Go away."

The doctor blinked once, then to his surprise found himself on the other side of the door.

As the door closed silently on its rubberized hinges Corrie dropped her head and buried it in Guy's open palm. Now she saw him she couldn't understand why she'd ever left him. She didn't care if he didn't love her, didn't care about anything except the reality of his dark head on the pillow, the feel of his warm skin against hers.

And yet he was so quiet and still, the sheets stretched smooth as if he were lying in a coffin.

"Wake up, *chéri*, I'm here." She tugged on his hand, but he was drugged too deeply to respond. What was it that had driven him here, at the risk of his own life? There were so many things she didn't know about him, and so little time . . .

For in a few hours, as soon as the airports were clear, Blanche would arrive. She would nurse him tenderly, bind him with invisible chains of gratitude and guilt, and this chance would never come again.

Unless . . . the outlines of a plan so daring, so impossible, so ultimately unforgivable that it made her feel weak even to contemplate it, began to take shape in her mind.

Could she, should she? She looked at him, lying there, and knew there was only one answer to that question. This time she was going to consult no one but her own heart. She'd never stolen anything in her life, but there was a first time for everything.

And more ways than one of getting out alive.

CHAPTER EIGHTEEN

One day, that's all I want. One day of borrowed, stolen time. Corrie drew the warm folds of her cloak around her as she listened to the rattle of the train wheels over the rails. Opposite her, in the narrow bunk, Guy slept deeply in the darkness, stained a dim luminous blue by the nightlight. She hugged the knowledge of his sleeping presence to her with a fierce, possessive joy. This was the one place in the cold snowbound world where no one could ever find them, where for a moment out of time they could be alone.

Dr. Ubermeyer had tried to dissuade her, but he couldn't. After all, she was Guy's cousin as well as his fiancée, and therefore his closest relative. She'd signed Blanche de Chardonnet's name on the hospital release forms with a brazen flourish, even commandeered an ambulance to take them to the station. What did that make her? A liar, an impostor, and now a kidnapper. She didn't care. She loved him. This day was hers, and with every rattle of the well-sprung wheels they were leaving the past behind.

She dipped into the deep pocket inside her cloak, drew out a meticulously labeled envelope. That had been the worst moment of their escape. She'd been at the door, watching the orderlies lifting Guy into the ambulance, when behind her she'd heard an urgent cry of "Mlle de Chardonnet . . . wait!" Her mind had raced with possibilities—another phone call from Blanche, some last-minute request for identification—she'd almost run for it. It had taken all her self-control to turn, eyebrows raised, and confront the desk clerk, who thrust an envelope into her hand. "M. de Chardonnet's effects, mademoiselle." She'd signed "her" name once again, her hand trembling with relief—and seconds later they were away, racing to freedom under an icy sky full of stars.

Now, very gently she slid the contents of the envelope into her palm. She felt like an archaeologist. Who was he really, Guy de Chardonnet? There wasn't much inside the envelope. His watch, humbly ticking away till its master chose to return, his passport and wallet, some keys. She stroked the cover of his passport. What was it about the passport of someone you loved? It felt different, unique. The pages were covered with stamps, European, Middle Eastern, South American—a whole world he knew and she did not. She felt a pang of loss. One day—they couldn't travel the whole world together in one day. His photograph showed a stern, unsmiling Guy, as befitted his official image. He photographed well.

His wallet she didn't open, but she took pleasure in lifting his keys, testing the weight of each against her palm. They were part of his life, all the doors he could open. This one, she knew, was the key to the house in the Avenue Pierre I de Serbie, this one to the Porsche . . . and this one, with its old-fashioned hollow barrel, the key to the tower room.

"How dare you?" A hand closed on her arm, startling her so much that she dropped everything. "Those are my private possessions, give them back to me immediately!" It was Guy, his voice distorted with anger, his eyes burning in the pallor of his face.

Hurriedly, fumbling in the semi-darkness, she gathered them up. She felt herself shaking as she did so. Why did he always catch her at a disadvantage? In silence she held out his belongings. Close up she could see that his eyes were still clouded with the sedative, but there was no mistaking their look of startled recognition.

"You." For a long, timeless moment they stared at each other. She saw doubt in his face, then anger, and finally, most wounding of all, scorn. "Of course. I might have known." His voice was icily detached. He took back his possessions and checked them over with a swift, expert thoroughness that hurt more than any blow. Against her will her mind flashed back to their first meeting, when he'd seemed to her the coldest, most callous and uncaring man she'd ever met. And now . . . it was clear that nothing had changed. Despite everything that had passed between them, he still didn't trust her, and he never would.

Suddenly all her fatigue, all the accumulated tensions of the past few days, overwhelmed her. This was hardly what she'd planned for their reunion. It was worse, far worse than anything she could have imagined. She didn't know what to say. She'd risked everything to rescue him and now it was very clear he hadn't wanted to be rescued at all. Sitting there, his keys in her hand, she'd been wondering how to tell him she loved him. Now, her eyes filling with tears of confusion and disappointment and pure frustration, she burst out, "Guy de Chardonnet, I hate you!"

He didn't look up. "That is your privilege." His voice was level. It was as if she didn't exist. He was checking through his belongings again, as if he were missing something important.

"Is this what you're looking for?" She picked up a scrap of paper that had fallen out of his wallet. In the dim light she saw a single line of writing, hardly a message, more like some sort of code. 31 20.30 A7. It made no sense to her, but then nothing made sense anymore. She handed it to him politely, as if he were a stranger. Their fingers didn't touch.

"Thank you." He took the paper from her more as if it were a love letter than a jumble of meaningless figures and letters, and tucked it carefully into his wallet. Then he looked at his watch. When he saw the time he gave a savage, muffled curse.

"Where are my clothes?"

Silently she indicated the hanger on the back of the

door. Without another word, as if he'd forgotten she even existed, he turned away and began to dress.

"What are you doing?"

She watched him in alarm as he swayed slightly on his feet. It was obvious he'd barely recovered from the sedative.

"What do you think? I'm leaving." The determination on his face was only too evident. It was clear he didn't want to spend a moment longer in her company. Her heart sank. What had she done? Dr. Ubermeyer's words came back to her. What kind of urgent appointment could drive a man through storm and darkness at the risk of his own life? Only one kind . . .

"I'm afraid you can't. Not for another five hours."

"Why not?"

She took a deep breath. Something in the fixity of his expression warned her that she was playing with fire. Her heart felt like lead.

"Because you're on a train. A through train. The next stop is in five hours' time."

"What?" He caught at the upper bunk for support. Anger, confusion, disbelief crossed his face in lightning succession. He looked around him, seeming to take in his surroundings for the first time. Then, suddenly, he sat down on the lower bunk and dropped his head in his hands.

"I'm sorry." Her voice sounded small and foolish in the silence. He didn't reply. They sat, facing each other, for what seemed like an eternity. At last, out of the depths of her despair, she said quietly, "Is she very beautiful?"

He looked up. He looked very pale, very tired. His eyes rested on her face with a strange expression.

"She is more than beautiful. She is . . . kind, wise, loving." Everything that you are not. The words echoed in the air as clearly as if he'd spoken them.

"Your ideal woman, in fact." Her body felt hollow, as if all the blood had drained away from it. "You've found her at last. I'm glad."

"Maybe." His mouth twisted, he looked away. There

was a short, aching pause. When he turned back to her his expression was savage. "Five hours, you say?" She nodded. He said nothing, simply flung himself back on the bunk and turned his face emphatically to the wall.

She sat there, listening numbly to the rhythm of the train wheels. Five hours . . . not long, but he could hardly wait for them to be gone. This oasis of time, which she'd planned so carefully, was for him merely a prison. The wheels rattled on inexorably, eating up the miles, mocking her. She is kind, wise, loving. Everything that you are not. Everything that you are not. Everything that you are not. But I could be, she thought blindly. If only you gave me a chance.

But there were no chances left. She knew that, as she huddled herself in her long black cloak, feeling she'd never be warm again. He was so near—she could hear his breathing in the silence, if she reached out a hand she could touch him—and yet farther away than he'd ever been. As soon as the train reached its destination he'd be gone. And she'd never see him again.

For he was in love, that much was clear. This other woman, his ideal woman—what was she, some kind of witch? How had she managed to steal his heart when she, Corrie, who loved him so much it hurt, had failed? The strange message . . . maybe that was the essence of her secret. Some magical charm, some chemical formula for love. The letters and figures danced and swam before her tired eyes. What did they mean? A message in code, a secret password into a world from which she herself was excluded. She thought with a sudden aching longing of Harlequin. She'd had her own world, once, but it had fallen apart. Where was he now, her faithful friend? If only the seat she'd reserved for him had been filled, if only he'd kept his promise, there wouldn't be this emptiness. She could see the seat now, in her mind's eye—a seat in the front row, the A row, number seven . . .

A current of white-hot light seemed to run through her body. She sat bolt upright. A7. The last element in the formula. A coincidence perhaps? She frowned, straining to make her exhausted mind function. A wild chance—but what about the rest? 31—yesterday's date. It could be . . . And 20.30? Some kind of measurement, perhaps? Hope began to fade. It meant nothing.

Then, suddenly, she had it. The twenty-four hour clock. After all the years in England she'd almost forgotten. 20.30, continental time. 8.30 p.m.—the start of the performance.

So simple . . . she rose to her feet, swaying giddily, and not just with the rhythm of the train. She felt as if her mind was exploding. Around her everything seemed to be dissolving, re-forming itself into different shapes. As if without realizing it, she'd been looking at the world through splintered glass, and now, suddenly, with one blow, the glass was cleared away, letting in air and sunlight and the smell of fresh-cut grass, and she could see straight for the first time.

A7. A reserved seat. Reserved all her life, if she'd only known it. For the one man who could know her as she really was, see through all her shams and disguises. She saw him now, that young man, on a deserted Atlantic beach. He was looking out to sea. She called to him in her mind and he turned, looked over his shoulder. Colored pieces of a kaleidoscope scattered, whirled, settled finally into place. Now, at last, she saw his face.

She reached out, touched Guy lightly on the arm. I can't hide from you anymore, she thought. You are the other side of myself.

Slowly, Guy turned his head on the pillow. His eyes flickered open. He must have seen something in her face, because when he spoke his voice was unsteady.

"What is it?"

"I just thought of something." She took a deep breath. Words . . . so fragile and tenuous the chain that had bound them, yet strong enough to span the world. "Remember that riddle you once asked me, how do you spell eternity? I think I've got the answer. It goes like this." She closed her eyes, concentrating hard. The secret formula, the magic password, maybe once spoken it might lose its power . . . "31 20.30 A7."

He stared at her for a long, long moment. Then he reached up and gripped her arm. His eyes were blazing. She felt her own fill with unshed tears.

"Who are you?"

She lifted one hand, unfastened her cloak and cast it aside. With it fell all the masks, all the lies and bitterness and concealments, melting away like winter snow. Her shimmering dress filled the small cabin with its own unmistakable radiance, as bold and breathtaking as a summer night full of stars. She stood before him, hesitant yet proud.

"I am Columbine."

"Was I so difficult?" She nestled in the curve of his arm, her dress spilling prodigal silver over the edge of the narrow bunk.

"You were impossible." He traced the outline of her cheek very gently with his fingers, as if he were afraid she might disappear at any moment. "So distant, so self-possessed . . . I could never tell what you really felt. How was I to know that inside that beautiful, bored sophisticate was another girl entirely, who liked resorts out of season, dogs with curly tails, old ladies in shocking pink, odd china, open windows."

"How was I to know that inside that desk at the Savoy were my letters to you?"

"What else did I have that was worth defending?"

"And that Colombe . . . I was so jealous. I thought—no one will ever feel like that about me, ever?"

"How do you think I felt when you left Biarritz?"

"But I had to! I knew you wouldn't like being poor."

"And now?"

"Oh, now everything's different." She smiled up at him confidently. "I'm nearly famous. Soon I'll be able to earn enough for both of us. Don't worry, you'll be able to keep your factories. I understand how much it means to you, now."

He framed her face in both hands, bent his head and kissed her.

"Corrie . . . Columbine . . . you're adorable."

She pulled herself out of his embrace and regarded him suspiciously. There was a quizzical expression on his face which she couldn't quite interpret.

"Hmm." She sniffed. "Cupboard love, I know. Just because I've got my hand on the purse strings . . ."

He leaned back his head and laughed out loud. She gazed at him, totally mystified, until at last his laughter subsided. His next words surprised her even more. "Poor Blanche." He sat there, wiping his eyes. "She may be a classic beauty, but she's still living in the past. She doesn't realize that owning things outright has gone out of fashion. Nowadays even money has to work for its living. That's why over the years I've invested, not in possessions, but in people. Now I've got my own consulting company. It's done well. So I'm afraid, my little entrepreneur, I'm not going to be poor after all. Blanche may have a lot of money, but I have access to infinitely more."

"Your own company?" Corrie was half fascinated, half appalled. What had happened to her country boy, her sweet innocent Harlequin? It was bad enough discovering that you loved one man instead of two, but now the whole world was turning upside down. "What's it called?"

"What do you think?" He returned her accusing gaze with equanimity, obviously enjoying her confusion. "It lives by its wits, it's small and flexible but something of an acrobat . . . Harlequin."

"What?" Corrie's voice rose to an indignant squeal. "Do you mean to say that all this time I've been writing to a corporation? I suppose you dictated all your letters to your secretary! I know what businessmen are like, they delegate everything."

"Not quite everything." He bent to kiss her again. She felt her head swim. "Marry me?"

She struggled out of the warm net of his arms with an effort.

"I couldn't possibly. You're too rich."

"Only on paper." His tone was eminently reasonable. The touch of his lips just beneath her ear was disturbingly persuasive.

"It wouldn't work." She was finding it hard to think straight. "Your factories, my career . . ."

"We could take turns." Now he was blowing lightly against the nape of her neck. "Flexitime—it's the latest thing. Very modern, very efficient. Maximum turnover, minimum capital inertia. Six months for you, six months for me. Just like King Pluto and his captive bride."

"Very funny." Her tone was petulant. "But hardly romantic. I think I preferred it when you wrote about me in the third person. What was it you said? 'Every time I see her she takes my breath away.' Was that true?"

He looked away. When he turned back to her his face was hard, set, almost angry. "Oh, if you only knew . . ." His voice was harsh. In the semi-darkness his eyes seemed to burn with a cold light of their own. "Remember Biarritz?" His gaze met hers for a long, timeless moment. She nodded, unable to speak. He looked away again. When he spoke again his voice was very low.

"Every time I looked into your eyes I saw . . . endless summer, a dream so tantalizing that it hurt. They're the exact color of that deep blue line where the sea meets the sky. If forever has a color, that's the color of your eyes. I wanted to keep on looking. I thought if I looked long enough I'd forget everything, even myself, the self I have grown to despise.

"Then I lost you. But I couldn't stop looking for you. I was like a cabin boy on his first ocean voyage, lost and dazzled and very much afraid, but once I'd seen the horizon I knew I could never go back to shore. I dreamed of you, so often, so long . . ."

He turned back to her. The expression on his face took her breath away. For a moment, as the train swayed and rattled on in the darkness, she lost all sense of where she was and who she was. The only reality was his face, his voice, his eyes, suddenly full of a tenderness that made her want to cry.

"But now . . . now I know the dream is real. There *is* an America, there *is* a Newfoundland. It was there all the time, a whole new continent, just below the horizon, and I never knew. Paradise, the promised land. And I can get there, with you, my little Columbus. For the first time in my life, I'm free. I loved you before I met you, I fell in love with you the moment I saw you, and I will love you till the day I die. Because you've got the horizon in your eyes."

He reached for her, clumsily, like a blind man. She melted into his arms. They clung together, her head nestled against his shoulders, his face buried in her hair.

"Here." His voice was muffled. "I have something for you." She felt his hands tremble as his fingers touched her bare neck, then she felt a tiny weight against her skin. She lifted it. There, mounted on a simple gold pin and suspended on a slender golden chain, was the small white stone in the shape of a heart.

"You kept it, all this time?"

"Yes." His voice caught. "You had my heart . . . I wanted something that belonged to you."

She touched it very gently with one finger. Of all the presents he had given her, this was the one she would keep forever. She looked up.

"I've got something to give you, too."

He smiled down at her in the semi-darkness.

"No need. I've got everything I'll ever want right here."

"But this is special." She slipped out of his arms and went to the window. Faint light glowed around the edge of the canvas blind. "It's my inheritance . . . my bridal gift to you. My dowry." I would have lost it long ago if it hadn't been for you. You kept it safe for me through all the dark years, like a jewel in the earth, a pearl at the bottom of the sea, until I was strong enough to claim it for my own. And now I can share it with you, multiplied a hundredfold, with love. My secret hoard of hopes and memories, gold and turquoise and mother-of-pearl . . . mimosa and lavender and the scent of thyme, fireflies dancing beneath an apricot moon, a nightingale in the olive tree . . . my Riviera dream.

"Well?" She gestured impatiently at the blind. "Aren't you going to open it?" As he stepped forward she fought down a sudden pang of doubt. Would he like it? Would it even be the same? Perhaps it might have faded, that turquoise sky, the fireflies forgotten how to dance . . .

"Now?" His voice was a whisper, but all the future was in his eyes. In that moment she knew that happiness was real, as warm and solid and sweet as an orange straight from the tree. It was there before her eyes, glowing like a golden lantern beneath the dark leaves. All she had to do was reach out a hand and it would be hers.

"Now." Their hands met and her last doubt vanished. No, it wouldn't be the same, her Riviera. It would be better and brighter and clearer than her wildest dreams, because, now, it was hers to share.

He drew her close, raised one hand to release the blind. And slowly, unforgettably, the curtain went up on a dazzling new world.